P9-CJZ-591

STARLING HOUSE

STARLING HOUSE

ALIX E. HARROW

TOR PUBLISHING GROUP

NEW YORK

This is a work of fiction. All of the characters, organizations, and events portrayed
in this novel are either products of the author's imagination
or are used fictitiously.

STARLING HOUSE

Interior illustrations by Rovina Cai

A Tor Book
Published by Tom Doherty Associates / Tor Publishing Group
120 Broadway
New York, NY 10271

www.tor-forge.com

Tor® is a registered trademark of Macmillan Publishing Group, LLC.

Library of Congress Cataloging-in-Publication Data

Names: Harrow, Alix E., author.
Title: Starling house / Alix E. Harrow.
Description: First edition. | New York : Tor Publishing Group, 2023.
Identifiers: LCCN 2023026718 (print) | LCCN 2023026719 (ebook) |
ISBN 9781250799050 (hardcover) | ISBN 9781250338440 (trade paperback) |
ISBN 9781250799074 (ebook)
Subjects: LCGFT: Gothic fiction. | Novels.
Classification: LCC PS3608.A783854 S73 2023 (print) |
LCC PS3608.A783854 (ebook) | DDC 813/.6—dc23/eng/20230609
LC record available at https://lccn.loc.gov/2023026718
LC ebook record available at https://lccn.loc.gov/2023026719

Our books may be purchased in bulk for promotional, educational, or business use.
Please contact your local bookseller or the Macmillan Corporate and Premium
Sales Department at 1-800-221-7945, extension 5442, or by email at
MacmillanSpecialMarkets@macmillan.com.

First Edition: 2023

Printed in the United States of America

0 9 8 7 6 5 4 3 2 1

for my brothers

STARLING HOUSE

ONE

I dream sometimes about a house I've never seen.

I mean, pretty much nobody has. Logan Caldwell claims he ding-dong-ditched the place last summer break, but he's an even bigger liar than me. The truth is you can't really see the house from the road. Just the iron teeth of the front gate and the long red lick of the drive, maybe a glimpse of limestone walls crosshatched by honeysuckle and greenbriers. Even the historical plaque out front is half-swallowed by ivy, the letters so slurred with moss and neglect that only the title is still legible:

STARLING HOUSE

But sometimes in the early dark of winter you can see a single lit window shining through the sycamores.

It's a funny kind of light: a rich amber that shudders with the wind, nothing like the drone of a streetlight or the sickly blue of a fluorescent.[1] I figure that window is the only light I've ever seen that doesn't come from the coal plant on the riverbank.

In my dream, the light is for me.

I follow it through the gates, up the drive, across the threshold. I should be scared—there are stories about Starling House, the kind people only tell at night, half-whispered under the hum of the porch light—but in the dream I don't hesitate.

In the dream, I'm home.

Apparently that's too far-fetched even for my subconscious, because that's usually when I wake up. I surface in the half-dark of the motel room with a hungry, empty ache in my chest that I think must be homesickness, although I guess I wouldn't know.

I stare at the ceiling until the parking lot lights flick off at dawn.

I used to think they meant something, those dreams. They started abruptly when I was twelve or thirteen, just when all the characters in my books started manifesting magic powers or receiving coded messages or whatever; of course I was obsessed with them.

I asked everybody in town about the Starling place, but received only narrow, slantwise looks and sucked teeth. People in this town had never liked me much—their eyes slide right off me like I'm a street-corner panhandler or a piece of roadkill, a problem they would be obliged to address if they looked straight at it—but they liked the Starlings even less.

They're considered eccentrics and misanthropes, a family of dubious origin that has refused for generations to participate in the most basic elements of Eden's civil society (church, public school, bake sales for the volunteer fire department), choosing instead to stay holed up in that grand house that nobody except the coroner has ever seen in person. They have money—which generally excuses everything short of homicide—but it doesn't come from either coal or tobacco, and nobody seems able to marry into it. The Starling

---

1. According to Lyle Reynolds, the Gravely Power meter man from 1987–2017, Starling House was never connected to the electric grid or the municipal water system. The telephone company sued for the right to place poles on Starling land in 1947, but the project was abandoned after a series of ugly accidents that left three employees hospitalized.

family tree is a maddening sprawl of grafted limbs and new shoots, full of out-of-towners and strangers who turned up at the front gates and claimed the Starling name without ever setting foot in Eden itself.

It's generally hoped that both they and their house will fall into a sinkhole and rot at the bottom, neither mourned nor remembered, and—perhaps— release the town from its century-long curse.

(I don't believe in curses, but if there were such a thing as an accursed town it would look an awful lot like Eden, Kentucky. It used to be the number one coal county in the nation, but now it's just a strip-mined stretch of riverbank containing a power plant, a fly ash pond, and two Dollar Generals. It's the kind of place where the only people who stay are the ones who can't afford to leave, where the water tastes like rust and the mist rises cold off the river even in summertime, lingering in the low places well past noon.)

Since nobody would tell me the story of Starling House, I made up my own. There isn't a lot to do in a town like Eden, and I didn't have many friends my own age. You're never going to be very popular when you wear clothes from the First Christian donation box and shoplift your school supplies, no matter how slick your smile is; the other kids sensed the hunger behind the smile and avoided me out of an animal certainty that, if we were all shipwrecked together, I'd be found six weeks later picking my teeth with their bones.

So I spent a lot of weekends sitting cross-legged on the motel mattress with my little brother, making up haunted house stories until both of us were so thoroughly spooked we'd scream at the sound of a doorknob turning three rooms down. I used to type up the best ones, in the secret hours after midnight, when Jasper was asleep and Mom was out, but I never sent them anywhere.[2] I quit all that years ago, anyway.

I told Mom about the dreams once. She laughed. "If I'd read that damn book as many times as you, I'd have nightmares, too."

For my fourth or fifth birthday Mom got me a copy of *The Underland*— one of the old nineteenth-century editions, the cover bound in cloth the color of cobwebs, the title sewn in silver. It was secondhand, probably stolen,

---

2. This is false. Between 2006 and 2009, Opal used the staff printer at the public library to print several pieces of short fiction. In '08, she received a personal rejection from a literary magazine which said that, regrettably, they did not publish fantasy, horror, or "whatever this is supposed to be."

and somebody else's initials were written on the inside cover, but I'd read it so many times the pages were coming unsewn.

The story is pretty paint-by-numbers: a little girl (Nora Lee) discovers another world (Underland) and hallucinatory adventures ensue. The illustrations aren't great, either—they're a series of stark lithographs that fall somewhere between eerie and nightmarish. But I remember staring at them until their afterimages lingered on the insides of my eyelids: black landscapes stalked by spectral Beasts, pale figures lost among the tangled trees, little girls falling down into the secret places under the earth. Looking at them felt like stepping into someone else's skull, someone who knew the same things I knew: that there were sharp teeth behind every smile, and bare bones waiting beneath the pretty skin of the world.

I used to trace the author's name with my fingertip, draw it idly in the margins of my C+ schoolwork: E. Starling.

She never published another book. She never gave a single interview. The only thing she left behind other than *The Underland* was that house, hidden in the trees. Maybe that's the real reason I was so obsessed with it. I wanted to see where she came from, prove to myself that she was real. I wanted to walk through her secret architecture, run my fingers over her wallpaper, see her curtains flutter in the breeze and believe, for a moment, that it was her ghost.

It's been eleven years and forty-four days since I last opened that book. I came straight home from Mom's funeral, dumped it into a doubled-up grocery bag along with half a pack of Newports, a moldy dream catcher, and a tube of lipstick, and shoved it all deep under my bed.

I bet the pages are all swollen and mildewed by now; everything in Eden goes to rot, given time.

I still dream about the Starling place sometimes, but I no longer think it means anything. And even if it did—I'm a high-school dropout with a part-time job at Tractor Supply, bad teeth, and a brother who deserves better than this dead-end bad-luck bullshit town.

Dreams aren't for people like me.

People like me have to make two lists: what they need and what they want. You keep the first list short, if you're smart, and you burn the second one. Mom never got the trick of it—she was always wanting and striving, longing and lusting and craving right up until she wasn't—but I'm a quick learner. I have one list, with one thing on it, and it keeps me plenty busy.

There are double shifts to work and pockets to pick; social workers to mislead and frozen pizzas to snap in half so they fit in the microwave; cheap inhalers to buy from sketchy websites and long nights to lie listening to the rattle and hiss of Jasper's breathing.

Then, too, there's the cream-colored envelope that came from a fancy school up north after Jasper took the PSAT, and the savings account I opened the day after it arrived, which I've managed to grow using the many and considerable skills my mother left me—wiles, theft, fraud, charm, a defiant and wholly misplaced optimism—but which still isn't enough to get him out of this place.

I figure dreams are like stray cats, which will go away if I quit feeding them.

So I don't make up stories about Starling House or ask anyone else for theirs. I don't linger when I pass by the iron front gates, or look up with my heart riding high in my chest, hoping to catch a glimpse of that lonely amber light that seems to shine from some grander, stranger world, just for me. I never pull the grocery bag out from under the bed.

But sometimes, right before I fall asleep, I see the black shadows of trees rising up the motel walls, though there's nothing but asphalt and weeds out the window. I feel the hot breath of Beasts around me, and I follow them down, and down, to Underland.

TWO

I t's a gray Tuesday evening in February and I'm on my way back to the motel after a pretty shitty day.

I don't know what made it so shitty; it was more or less exactly the same as the days that preceded it and the days likely to follow it, a featureless expanse of hours interrupted by two long walks in the cold, from the motel to work and back. It's just that I had to work eight entire hours with Lacey Matthews, the human equivalent of unsalted butter, and when the drawer came up short at the end of our shift the manager gave me an I've-got-my-eye-on-you glare, as if he thought the discrepancy was my fault, which it was. It's just that it snowed yesterday and the dismal remains are rotting in the gutters, soaking through the holes in my tennis shoes, and I made Jasper take the good coat this morning. It's just that I'm twenty-six years old and I can't afford a goddamn car.

I could've gotten a ride from Lacey or her cousin Lance, who works nights at the call center. But Lacey would proselytize at me and Lance would pull over on Cemetery Road and reach for the top button of my jeans, and I would probably let him, because it would feel pretty good and the motel was pretty far out of his way, but later I would catch the scent of him on my hoodie—a generic, acidic smell, like the yellow cakes of soap in gas station bathrooms—and feel an apathy so profound, so perfectly flat, that I would be tempted to pull out that grocery bag beneath the bed just to make sure I could still feel anything at all.

So: I'm walking.

It's four miles from Tractor Supply to the motel—three and a half if I cut behind the public library and cross the river on the old railroad bridge, which always puts me in a strange, sour mood.

I pass the flea market and the RV park, the second Dollar General and the Mexican place that took over the old Hardee's building, before I cut off the road and follow the railroad tracks onto Gravely land. At night the power plant is almost pretty, a great golden city lit up so bright it turns the sky yellow and throws a long shadow behind you.

The streetlights are humming. The starlings are murmuring. The river is singing to itself.

They paved the old railroad bridge years ago, but I like to walk on the very edge, where the ties stick out. If you look down you can see the Mud River rushing in the gaps, a black oblivion, so I look up instead. In summer the banks are so knotted with honeysuckle and kudzu you can't see anything but green, but now you can see the rise and fall of the land, the indentation of an old mine shaft.

I remember it as a wide-open mouth, black and gaping, but the city boarded it up after some kids dared each other past the DANGER signs. People had done it plenty of times before, but the mist rose high that night—the mist in Eden comes dense and fast, so heavy you can almost hear it padding along beside you—and one of them must have gotten lost. They never did find the body.[3]

The river sings loud now, siren sweet, and I find myself humming along with it. I'm not truly tempted by the cold black of the water below—suicide is a folded hand and I'm no quitter—but I can remember how it felt down

---

3. Willy Floyd, 13, went missing on April 13, 1989; the old mine shaft was boarded up four years before Opal was born. Perhaps she merely dreamed of it, and mistook the dream for a memory.

there among the bones and bottom-feeders: so quiet, so far beyond the scrabbling, striving, grinding work of survival.

It's just that I'm tired.

I'm pretty sure this is what Mr. Cole, the high school guidance counselor, might call a "crisis point" when I ought to "reach out to my support network," but I don't have a support network. I have Bev, owner and manager of the Garden of Eden Motel, who is obligated to let us live in room 12 rent-free because of some shady deal she cut with Mom, but isn't obligated to like it. I have Charlotte, local librarian and founder of the Muhlenberg County Historical Society, who was nice enough not to ban me after I faked a street address to get a library card and sold a stack of DVDs online. Instead she merely asked me to please not do it again and gave me a cup of coffee so sweet it made my cavities ache. Other than them it's just the hellcat—a vicious calico who lives under the motel dumpster—and my brother.

I wish I could talk to Mom. She gave terrible advice, but I'm almost as old now as she was when she died; I imagine it would be like talking to a friend.

I could tell her about Stonewood Academy. How I transferred Jasper's transcripts and filled out all the forms, and then sweet-talked them into saving him a spot next term so long as I pay the tuition by the end of May. How I assured them it wouldn't be a problem, talking bright and easy like she taught me. How I have to quadruple my life savings in the next three months, on the kind of minimum-wage job that carefully keeps you under thirty hours a week so they don't have to give you health insurance.

But I'll find a way, because I need to, and I'll walk barefoot through hell for what I need.

My hands are cold and blue in the light of my phone. hey punk how's the book report going

great, Jasper writes back, followed by a frankly suspicious number of exclamation points.

oh yeah? what's your thesis statement? I'm not really worried—my little brother has an earnest, determined brilliance that's won over every teacher in the public school system, despite their expectations about boys with brown skin and curls—but hassling him makes me feel better. Already the river sings softer in my skull.

my thesis is that I can fit fourteen marshmallows in my mouth at once

and everyone in this book needs a long sitdown with mr cole

I picture Heathcliff hunched in one of the counselor's undersized plastic chairs, an anger-management brochure crumpled in his hands, and feel a weird twist of sympathy. Mr. Cole is a nice man, but he doesn't know what to do with people raised on the underside of the rules, where the world turns dark and lawless, where only the canny and cruel survive.

Jasper isn't canny or cruel, which is only one of the several hundred reasons I have to get him out of here. It ranks right below the air quality and the Confederate flags and the bad luck that slinks behind us like a mean dog, nipping at our heels. (I don't believe in curses, but if there was such a thing as a cursed family, it would look a lot like us.)

that's not a thesis. My fingers snag on the cracks that spiderweb across my screen.

i'm sorry what did you get in 10th grade english again??

My laugh hangs in the air, ghostly white. i graduated with a 4.0 from the School of Fuck You

A tiny pause. chill. it's job fair tomorrow, nobody's collecting essays

I despised the job fair when I was at school. There aren't really any jobs around here except breathing particulates at the power plant, so it's just an AmeriCorps booth and somebody from the Baptist mission group handing out flyers. The main excitement comes at the end, when Don Gravely, CEO of Gravely Power, takes the stage and gives an excruciating speech about hard work and the American spirit, as if he didn't inherit every cent of his money from his big brother. We all had to shake his hand as we filed out of the gym, and when he got to me he flinched, as if he thought poverty might be contagious. His palm had felt like a fresh-peeled boiled egg.

Imagining Jasper shaking that clammy-ass hand makes my skin feel hot and prickly. Jasper doesn't need to listen to any bullshit speeches or take home any applications, because Jasper isn't getting stuck in Eden.

i'll call miss hudson and say you have a fever, screw the job fair

But he replies: nah I'm good

There's a lull in our conversation while I leave the river behind and wind uphill. The electric lines swoop overhead and the trees crowd close, blotting out the stars. There are no streetlights in this part of town.

where are you now? im hungry

A wall runs beside the road now, the bricks pocked and sagging with age, the mortar crumbling beneath the wheedling fingers of Virginia creeper and poison ivy. just passing the starling place

Jasper replies with a smiley face shedding a single tear and the letters RIP.

I send him the middle-finger emoji and slide my phone back in my hoodie pocket.

I should hurry back. I should keep my eyes on the painted white stripe of the county road and my mind on Jasper's savings account.

But I'm tired and cold and weary in some way that's deeper than muscle and bone. My feet are slowing down. My eyes are drifting up, searching through the twilit woods for a gleam of amber.

There it is: a single high window glowing gold through the dusk, like a lighthouse that wandered too far from the coast.

Except lighthouses are supposed to warn you away, rather than draw you closer. I hop the gully at the side of the road and run my hand along the wall until the brick gives way to cold iron.

The gates of Starling House don't look like much from a distance—just a dense tangle of metal half-eaten by rust and ivy, held shut by a padlock so large it almost feels rude—but up close you can make out individual shapes: clawed feet and legs with too many joints, scaled backs and mouths full of teeth, heads with empty holes for eyes. I've heard people call them devils or, more damningly, *modern art,* but they remind me of the Beasts in *The Underland,* which is a nice way of saying they're unsettling as all hell.

I can still see the shine of the window through the gate. I step closer, weaving my fingers between the open jaws and curling tails, staring up at that light and wishing, childishly, that it was shining for me. Like a porch light left on to welcome me home after a long day.

I have no home, no porch light. But I have what I need, and it's enough.

It's just that, sometimes, God help me, I want more.

I'm so close to the gate now that my breath pearls against the cold metal. I know I should let go—the dark is deepening and Jasper needs dinner and my feet are numb with cold—but I keep standing, staring, haunted by a hunger I can't even properly name.

It occurs to me that I was right: dreams are just like stray cats. If you don't feed them they get lean and clever and sharp-clawed, and come for the jugular when you least expect it.

I don't realize how tight I'm gripping the gate until I feel the bite of iron and the wet heat of blood. I'm swearing and wadding the sleeve of my hoodie against the gash, wondering how much the health clinic charges for tetanus shots and why the air smells suddenly rich and sweet—when I realize two things simultaneously.

First, that the light in the window has gone out.

And second, that there is someone standing on the other side of the gates of Starling House.

There are never any guests at Starling House. There are no private parties or visiting relatives, no HVAC repair vans or delivery trucks. Sometimes in a fit of hormonal frustration a pack of high schoolers will talk about climbing the wall and sneaking up to the house itself, but then the mist rises or the wind blows sideways and the dare is never quite made. Groceries are piled outside the gate once a week, the milk sweating through brown paper sacks, and every now and then a sleek black car parks across the road and idles for an hour or two without anyone getting in or out. I doubt whether any outsider has set foot on Starling land in the last decade.

Which means there's exactly one person who could be standing on the other side of the gate.

The latest Starling lives entirely alone, a Boo Radley–ish creature who was damned first by his pretentious name (Alistair or Alfred, no one can ever agree which), second by his haircut (unkempt enough to imply unfortunate politics, when last seen), and third by the dark rumor that his parents died strangely, and strangely young.[4]

But the heir to Starling House doesn't look like a rich recluse or a murderer; he looks like an underfed crow wearing a button-up that doesn't quite fit, his shoulders hunched against the seams. His face is all hard angles and sullen bones split by a beak of a nose, and his hair is a tattered wing an inch shy of becoming a mullet. His eyes are clawing into mine.

I become aware that I'm staring back at him from a feral crouch, like a possum caught raiding the motel dumpsters. I wasn't doing anything illegal, but I don't have a fantastic explanation for why I'm standing at the end of his driveway just after dusk, and there's a fifty-fifty chance he actually is a murderer, so I do what Mom did whenever she got herself in a tight spot, which was every day: I smile.

"Oh, I didn't see you there!" I clutch my chest and give a girly little laugh.

---

4. Lynn and Oscar Starling died sometime in October of 2007. The coroner was not able to determine a more precise date of death; his autopsy report cites the unfortunate delay, and the "goddamned state of them."

"I was just passing by and thought I'd take a closer look at these gates. They're so fancy. Anyway, I didn't mean to bother you, so I'll head on my way."

The heir to Starling House doesn't smile back. He doesn't look like he's ever smiled at anything, actually, or ever will, as if he were carved from bitter stone rather than born in the usual way. His eyes move to my left hand, where the blood has soaked through the wadded sleeve to drip dramatically from my fingertips. "Oh, shit." I make an abortive effort to shove the hand into my pocket, which hurts. "I mean, that's nothing. I tripped earlier, see, and—"

He moves so quickly I barely have time to gasp. His hand darts through the gate and catches mine, and I know I should snatch it back—when you grow up on your own from the age of fifteen you learn not to let strange men grab ahold of any part of you—but there's an enormous padlock between us and his skin is so warm and mine is so damn cold. He turns my hand palm up in his and I hear a low hiss of breath.

I lift one shoulder. "It's fine." It's not fine: my hand is gummy mess of red, the flesh gaping in a way that makes me think superglue and peroxide might be insufficient. "My brother will patch me up. He's waiting for me, by the way, so I really should get going."

He doesn't let go. I don't pull away. His thumb hovers over the jagged line of the cut, not-quite-touching it, and I realize abruptly that his fingers are trembling, shaking around mine. Maybe he's one of those people who faint at the sight of blood, or maybe eccentric recluses aren't accustomed to young women bleeding all over their front gates.

"It's no big deal." I don't generally do sincerity, except for Jasper, but I feel a certain sympathy for him. Or it might be symmetry: he's about my age, underdressed and shivering, hated by half the town. "I'm really fine."

He looks up, and as I meet his eyes I know with sudden and terrible clarity that I was mistaken. His hands aren't shaking with nerves or cold: they're shaking with rage.

His skin is bloodless, stretched tight over the bleak bones of his face, and his lips are peeled away from his teeth in an animal snarl. His eyes are the starless black of caves.

I reel back as if shoved, my smile abandoned, my good hand fumbling for the motel key in my pocket. He might be taller but I'd bet money I fight dirtier.

But he doesn't open the gate. He leans closer, forehead pressing hard against the iron, fingers wrapping whitely around the bars. My blood is slick and shining across his knuckles.

"Run," he grates.

I run.

Hard and fast, with my left hand curled tight to my chest, still throbbing, but not quite as cold as it was before.

The heir to Starling House watches her run from him, and does not regret it.

He doesn't regret the way she ripped her hand from his, or the way her eyes flashed at him before she ran, hard and flat as beaten nails. He especially does not regret the sudden departure of that bright, bold smile, which had never been real in the first place.

He wrestles with a brief, absurd urge to shout after her—*wait,* he might say, or maybe even *come back*—before he reminds himself that he doesn't want her to come back at all. He wants her to run and keep running, as fast and far as she can. He wants her to pack her things and buy a Greyhound ticket at the Waffle House and ride out of Eden without looking back once.

She won't do it, of course. The House wants her, and the House is stubborn. Already her blood has vanished from the gate as if an invisible tongue licked it clean.

He doesn't know why it would want her, of all people: a freckled scarecrow of a girl with crooked teeth and holes in the knees of her jeans, entirely unremarkable except for the steel in her eyes. And perhaps for the way she stood her ground against him. He is a ghost, a rumor, a story whispered after the children have gone to bed, and she was cold and hurt, all alone in the rising dark—and yet she hadn't run from him until he told her to. The House has always had a taste for the brave ones.

But Arthur Starling swore on his parents' graves that he would be the last Warden of Starling House. He is many things—a coward, a fool, a terrible failure—but he is not a man to break his word. No one else will lie awake every night listening for the scrape of claws and the pant of breath. No one else will spend their lives fighting an invisible war, rewarded either with the silence of victory or the too-high cost of failure. No one else will bear the Starling sword after him.

Certainly not a scrawny girl with hard eyes and a liar's smile.

Arthur unpeels his forehead from the gate and turns away, his shoulders hunched in a manner that would have made his mother narrow her eyes, if she still had eyes to narrow.

The walk back to the House takes longer than it ought to, the drive twisting and coiling more than it should, the ground rougher and the night darker. His legs are aching by the time he steps across the threshold of the House.

He pauses to rest a hand on the doorframe. Her blood cracks and flakes from his skin. "Leave her be," he says softly. They haven't addressed one another in civil terms for years, but for some reason he's compelled to add a single, stiff "Please."

The floorboards creak and wail. A petulant door slams down some distant hall.

Arthur slouches upstairs and falls into bed fully clothed but still shivering, half expecting a pipe to spring a spiteful leak above his pillow, or a loose shutter to slap arrhythmically against a sill.

Instead, there are only the dreams. Always, the damn dreams.

He is five, and the House is whole and hale. There are no cracks in the plaster, no broken balusters or dripping faucets. To Arthur, it is not a house so much as a country, an endless map made up of secret rooms and creaking stairs, leaf-shadowed floorboards and sun-faded armchairs. Every day he goes exploring, fortified by the peanut-butter-and-jellies his father packs him, and every night the starlings sing him to sleep. He does not even know how lonely he is.

He is eight, and his mother is shaping his fingers around the hilt, straightening his thin wrists when they want to bend. *You love our home, don't you?* Her face is grave and tired. She was always tired. *You have to fight for what you love.*

Arthur wakes then, sweating, and does not sleep again. He stares out the round window of his attic room, watching the silver sway of the trees, thinking of his mother, of all the Wardens before her—of the girl.

His last, hopeful thought before dawn is that there was a cleverness to her, a canniness, and surely only the very worst of fools would ever return to Starling House.

THREE

I will never, ever—no matter how lonesome or tired I get, no matter how pretty the light looks through the trees—return to Starling House. His voice chases me all the way back to the motel, echoing in my ears like a second pulse: *run, run, run.*

It fades only when I step into the soft lamplight of room 12, panting and shaking, my shoes splattering slush across the carpet.

Jasper greets me without taking off his headphones, his attention on the grayscale frames of whatever video he's been editing. "You took forever so I went ahead and ate the last picante chicken ramen. If you snooze you lo—" He glances up. He slides the headphones around his neck, smug expression falling off his face. "What happened to you?"

I lean against the door, hoping I look nonchalant rather than very close to passing out. "Did you really think I would leave the last picante chicken in plain sight? I have my own supply."

"Opal—"

"I'll never tell you where. Death first."

"What happened?"

"Nothing! I just jogged home."

"You . . . *jogged* . . . home." He stretches the word "jogged" into three skeptical syllables. I shrug. He gives me a long, pursed-lip stare, then looks pointedly at the floor beside me. "And I guess that's ketchup you're dripping all over the carpet?"

"Nah." I shove my treacherous left hand in my hoodie pocket and dive for the bathroom. "Sriracha."

Jasper thumps and hollers and issues vague threats against my person, but I turn on the overhead fan and the shower until he gives up. I sag onto the toilet seat and let the shakes move from my legs to my shoulders to my fingertips. I should probably feel panicky or pissed or at least confused, but all I can summon is the dull, aggrieved sense of having been fucked with and not liking it much.

The effort of actually undressing and getting into the shower overwhelms me, so I skin out of my hoodie and hold my hand under the spray until the water runs mostly clear down the drain. It isn't as deep as I'd thought, actually: just a ragged line slicing ominously across my life and love lines. (I don't go in for palmistry, but Mom ate all that shit with a spoon. She couldn't remember court dates or parent-teacher meetings, but she knew our star charts by heart.)

I dump half a bottle of peroxide over the cut and fish around for a Band-Aid that could conceivably cover it. I wind up tearing strips off an old sheet and wrapping them around my hand, like I did the year Jasper went as a mummy for Halloween.

By the time I open the door the room is dark, the walls tiger-striped by the shine of parking lot lights through the blinds. Jasper is in bed but not actually asleep—his asthma makes him snore—but I creep into my twin as if he were.

I lie listening to him listening to me, trying not to notice the throb of my own pulse in my hand or remember the black of those eyes boring into mine.

"Are you okay?" Jasper's voice has a wobble to it that makes me want to crawl into his bed and sleep spine-to-spine, the way we used to back when there were still three of us and only two beds. And later, after the dreams started.

I shrug at the ceiling instead. "I'm always okay."

The polyester sighs as he rolls to face the wall. "You're a pretty good liar"—I'm a *fantastic* liar—"but that's for everybody else. Not family."

The innocence of it makes me want to laugh, or maybe cry. The biggest lies are always for the ones you love the most. *I'll take care of you. It'll be fine. Everything's okay.*

I swallow hard. "Everything's okay." His disbelief is palpable, a chill emanating from the other side of the room. "Anyway, it's over." I don't know if he believes it, but I do.

Until the dream.

It isn't like the others. The others had a soft, sepia light to them, like old home movies or fond memories you've half forgotten. This one is like diving into cold water on a hot day, crossing from one world to another.

I'm back at the gates of Starling House, but this time the padlock falls open and the gates swing wide before me. I walk down the dark throat of the drive, thorns tugging at my sleeves, trees tangling their fingers in my hair. Starling House emerges from the dark like a vast animal from its den: a gabled spine, wings of pale stone, a tower with a single amber eye. Steep steps curl like a tail around its feet.

The front door is unlocked, too. I sweep across the threshold into a maze of mirrors and windows, halls that branch and split and switchback, staircases that end in empty walls or closed doors. I walk faster and faster, shoving through each door and rushing to the next as if there is something I want desperately to find.

The air grows colder and wetter as I go deeper. A pale mist seeps up from the floorboards, coiling around my ankles. At some point, I realize I am running.

I stumble through a trapdoor, down the stone stairs, down and down. Roots crawl like veins across the floor, and I have the confused thought that they must belong to the house itself, as if dead lumber and nails could come alive given enough time.

I shouldn't be able to see anything in the darkness, but I see the stairs end abruptly in a door. A crude stone door crisscrossed with silver chains. Another padlock dangles from the chains. The lock is open. The door is cracked.

Cold fog pours through the gap and I know with the strange fatalism of dreams that I am too late, that something terrible has already happened.

I reach for the door, choked with a grief I don't understand, shouting a name I don't know—

And then I'm awake, and my mouth tastes like tears. I must have clenched my fists in my sleep, because blood has soaked through the bandaging and pooled around my left hand.

It's still dark, but I pull on yesterday's jeans—the cuffs still wet with slush, the pockets full of stolen cash—and slip outside with a spare sleeping bag draped over my shoulders. I sit with my back against the concrete block and let the hellcat climb into my lap, alternately purring and growling, while I wait for the sun to rise and the dream to fade like the others.

Except it doesn't. It lingers like a bad cold, settling deep in my chest. All that day I feel the press of invisible walls against my shoulders, the weight of rafters overhead. The scattered leaves make wallpaper patterns against the pavement, and the scuffed linoleum of Tractor Supply seems to creak beneath my feet, like old wood.

That night I stay up too late reading a Regency romance by the parking lot lights, trying to drive the house out of my head, or at least get rid of that aching, senseless grief. But the dream takes me as soon as I close my eyes, pulling me through the same tangled halls and twisting stairs, ending with the same unlocked door.

Six and a half days after I ran away from it, I return to Starling House.

Look: I didn't plan on it. I was going to walk the extra half mile to and from work for the rest of my natural life specifically so that I never had to come within a hundred yards of Starling land again. I was going to bum rides from Lacey, or maybe steal a bike. I'm no coward, but Jasper's made me watch enough horror movies to recognize a red flag when it holds my hand and tells me to run.

But after six nights of wrecked sleep—followed by six and a half days of dodging worried looks from Jasper and taking the long way to work, of mistaking the bathroom mirrors for rows of windows and looking over my shoulder for doorways that don't exist—I fold. I'm tired, and I'm moderately freaked out, and I'm running out of old sheets to rip up into bandages because the cut on my hand won't seem to close.

So here I am, using my Monday lunch break to glare at the gates of Starling House.

The gates glare back at me, the beastly shapes nothing but iron by the cold light of day. I run my tongue over my lips, half scared and half something else. "Open sesame. Or whatever."

Nothing happens, because of course nothing happens, because I'm not in one of my silly childhood stories and there's no such thing as magic words or haunted houses, and even if there were they wouldn't have anything to do with someone like me.

I look down at my left hand, fresh-wrapped this morning, then up and down the road, the way a person does when they're about to do something ridiculous and don't want to be seen.

A pickup chugs past me. I give it a cheery, nothing-to-see-here wave and catch a pair of averted eyes in the rearview mirror. This town is good at looking away.

The truck disappears around the bend and I unwind the white cotton bandaging—the cut is still exactly as wide and tattered as it was six days before, still oozing watery blood—and press my palm to the front gates. I feel a thrill of recognition, like when you spot a face you know in a crowded room, and the gates swing open.

My heart does a double-thud. "Okay." I'm not sure if I'm talking to myself or the gates. "Okay. Sure."

It's probably just motion sensors or cameras or rigged pulleys or some other totally rational explanation. But it doesn't feel totally rational. It feels like the beginning of a mystery novel, when you're screaming at the plucky protagonist to run but sort of hoping she doesn't, because you want the story to start.

I take a little breath and step through the gates onto Starling land.

The driveway doesn't look like it's ever been paved, or even graveled. It's just a pair of tire ruts dug into red clay, divided by a scraggled line of dead grass. Pools of rainwater gather in the low places, reflecting the winter-white sky like the scattered shards of a broken mirror. Trees crowd close overhead, as if they're trying to catch glimpses of themselves. Birds' eyes glitter at me from the woods, black and wet.

In my dreams the drive is dark and twisting, but in reality I turn a single curve and there it is.[5]

---

5. Satellite images of the property are notoriously unreliable. If you were to type the address into your phone you would see nothing but slate rooftops and blurry, recalcitrant green, which would never quite come into focus.

Starling House.

The windows are filmy eyes above rotten sills. Empty nests sag from the eaves. The foundation is cracked and slanted, as if the entire thing is sliding into the open mouth of the earth. The stone walls are covered with the bare, twisting tendons of some creeping vine—honeysuckle, I figure, which is only ever a show tune away from gaining sentience and demanding to be fed. The only sign that anyone lives inside is the slow bleed of woodsmoke from a leaning chimney.

The rational half of my brain recognizes that this place is a wreck and an eyesore that should be condemned by the health department and shoved into the nearest sinkhole; the less rational part of me thinks about every haunted house movie I've ever seen, every pulpy book cover with a hot white woman running away from a silhouetted mansion.

An even less rational part of me is curious.

I don't know why—maybe the shape of it reminds me of an E. Starling illustration, all strange angles and deep shadows, like a poorly kept secret. Maybe I just have a soft spot for the neglected and abandoned.

The front steps are slick with matted black leaves. The door is an imperious arch that might once have been red or brown but is now the nothing-color of afternoon rain. The surface is scarred and stained; it's only up close that I see there are tiny shapes carved roughly into the wood. Hundreds of them—horseshoes and crooked crosses and open eyes, spirals and circles and malformed hands that run in long rows like hieroglyphs, or lines of code. Some of them I almost recognize from Mom's tarot decks and astrology charts, but most of them are unfamiliar, like letters from an alphabet I don't know. There's a derangement to them, a desperation that tells me I should leave before I wind up ritually beheaded or sacrificed on a stone altar in the basement.

I step closer instead.

I lift my hand and knock three times at the door to Starling House. I give him a couple of minutes—I figure it'll take a second to finish up his brooding or lurking or whatever it is he does in there—before knocking again. I shuffle through the dead leaves, wondering if he's gone out for a drive, and then if he even has a license. I try and fail to picture him practicing his parallel parking with Mr. Cole in the passenger seat.

I'm about to knock a third time when the door whips open in a rush of heat, and there he is.

The heir to Starling House is even uglier by daylight: his brows flat and heavy over a twisted nose, his eyes like a pair of mine shafts burrowed into a chalk cliff. The eyes widen.

I wait for him to say something normal, like *Hello?* or *Can I help you?*, but he merely stares down at me in mute horror, like a human gargoyle.

I go for a breezy smile. "Morning! Or afternoon, I guess. We met the other night, but I thought I'd come introduce myself properly. My name's Opal."

He blinks several times at my outstretched hand. He crosses his arms without shaking it. "I believe," he grates, "I advised you to run."

I smile a little harder. "I did."

"I thought 'and never come back' was implied."

His voice is so dry, so thoroughly harassed, that my smile goes briefly crooked. I iron it straight. "Well, I'm sorry to bother you, but I'm here because"—*your goddamn house is haunting me*—"because I'm taking an architecture class on-line, and I was hoping to take some pictures for my project?" I don't even know if the community college offers online classes in architecture, but I figure it's a good excuse to go poking around, driving the dream-house out of my head and replacing it with the dull facts of dirty wallpaper and creaking stairs.

"You want to take . . . pictures. For your"—his scowl deepens by several degrees—"architecture class."

"Yep. Can we talk inside?"

"No."

I give the slightly theatrical shiver that generally compels men to drape their sweaters around my shoulders. "It's pretty chilly out here." It's freezing, actually, one of those mean February days when the sun never quite rises and the wind has white teeth.

"Then," he says, biting into each word, "you should have worn a coat."

It's an effort to keep my voice sweet and stupid. "Look, I just need a couple of pictures. Please?" I gesture at the house, the hall vanishing into cobwebs and shadows behind the line of his shoulders. His eyes follow the arc of my hand and linger on the fresh gleam of blood. I tuck it beneath my apron.

His gaze returns to my face. "No," he says again, but this time his tone is almost apologetic.

"I'll come back tomorrow," I threaten. "And the day after, and the day after that, until you let me in."

The heir to Starling House gives me another long, ugly stare, as if he thinks I'll go scampering back down the drive if he's sufficiently unpleasant, as if eight years of retail hasn't given me a spine of sugar and steel.

I count slowly to ten. A loose shutter slaps above us.

He appears to struggle with himself, lips twisting before he says carefully, "It wouldn't . . . help." I wonder if he somehow knows about the dreams, about the way I wake in the night with tears sliding down my temples and someone else's name on my lips. I wonder if this has happened before, to other people.

The hair on my arms stands up. I keep my voice very reasonable. "What *would* help?"

"I don't know." From the sour shape of his mouth I get the impression he dislikes not knowing things. "Perhaps if you gave it time . . ."

I check my phone, a lock of hair sliding out from under my hood. "Well, I have to be back in twenty minutes and I have a double shift tomorrow."

He blinks at me as if he's not sure what a shift is or why one would double it. Then his eyes move somewhere to the left of mine and land on that wayward curl of hair.

The rims of his nostrils go white. Suddenly he's made of still water instead of stone, and I can see a series of emotions rippling across his surface: terrible suspicion, shock, grief, abyssal guilt.

I have the feeling he's about to scream or hiss or tear his hair in a fit of madness, and I don't know whether to run toward him or away—but he merely swallows hard and closes his eyes.

When he opens them his face is perfectly opaque once more. "Or perhaps, Miss . . . ?"

Mom picked her last name according to her mood (Jewell Star, Jewell Calamity, Jewell Lucky). I generally stick with unremarkable Scots-Irish names (McCoy, Boyd, Campbell), to match my hair, but for some reason I say, "Just Opal."

He doesn't seem to like that much. His mouth ripples, reaches a compromise: "Miss Opal." He pauses here for a very long sigh, as if me and my Tractor Supply apron are a burden of unfathomable proportions. "Perhaps I could offer you a job."

FOUR

Arthur regrets the words as soon as they
leave his lips. He bites down on his tongue,
very hard, to prevent himself from saying
anything worse.

"A job?" The girl's—Opal's—voice is bright,
but her eyes on him are cold silver. "Doing what?"

"Ah." Arthur considers and rejects several terrible
ideas before saying, coolly, ". . . Housekeeping." He
wonders briefly about the etymology of the word—
has there ever been a house that required such rigorous
keeping as this one?—and shivers. "Cleaning, I mean."
He makes a disdainful gesture at the floor, nearly
invisible beneath geological layers of grit and dust.

The filth doesn't particularly bother him—
it's one of his many weapons in the long and
petty war between himself and the House—but
removing it might serve several purposes: the House
might be soothed by the attention, lulled by the
false promise of a more satisfactory Warden;

the girl might be driven away by the drudgery; and he might pay some small part of the hideous debt he has incurred against her.

Arthur hadn't recognized her the night before, with her hair tucked under the hood of her sweatshirt, but now he remembers that hair straggling down her neck, clinging to her pale cheeks, soaking the front of his shirt. He couldn't tell the color of it until the first ambulance rounded the corner. In the sudden glare of the headlights her hair became a bed of coals in his arms, or a field of poppies blooming out of season.

It occurs to him that her presence on his doorstep this morning might be part of some long and involved revenge plot, that inviting her into his home might have been a grave miscalculation, but her expression is still cool, mistrustful. "That's nice," she says carefully, "but I already have a job?"

Arthur flicks his fingers at her. "I'll pay you, of course."

A cold flash in her eyes, like light on a fresh-minted dime. "How much?"

"However much you want." The Starling fortune has diminished substantially over the years, but Arthur won't need it for much longer, and the debt he owes her has no dollar value. She would be within her rights if she asked him to leap into the Mud River with stones in his pockets, whether she knows it or not.

Opal says a number and tilts her chin up in some obscure challenge. "That's per *week*."

"Fine."

He expects another smile, maybe even a real one—judging by the state of her shoes and the sharp bones of her wrists she could use the money—but she takes an almost-imperceptible step away from him instead. Her voice goes low and edged in a way that makes him wish she'd taken several more steps back. "Is this a joke?"

"No?"

Opal doesn't seem relieved. Her eyes roam across his face as if looking for the lie. "Just cleaning. Nothing else."

Arthur feels like an actor whose partner has departed from the script. "Well, it might need some extra work here and there. The House has been somewhat neglected." The wind whistles forlornly through a missing windowpane. He grinds his heel into the floor. The wind dies.

She wants to say yes. He can see it in the tilt of her body and the hunger in her face, but she says very clearly, "I mean nothing *else*." He stares. She licks her lower lip. "Nothing for you."

"I'm afraid I don't know what you mean."

She looks away from him, squinting instead into the empty space above his left ear. "See, when a rich man offers a young woman a lot of money out of the blue, and doesn't ask for her housekeeping résumé—I've been cleaning rooms at the motel for years, not that you care—that young woman might have cause to wonder if he expects her to do more than clean. If maybe he has a weird thing for redheads." She tucks her hair self-consciously back under her hood. "If, in fact, he expects her to f—"

"*Oh God, no.*" Arthur wishes very much that his voice hadn't cracked on the last syllable. "This isn't—I'm not—" He closes his eyes in brief, mortal humiliation.

When he opens them Opal is smiling. He thinks it's probably the only genuine smile he's seen from her: a sly twist of her lips, wry and sharp. "Then sure. I accept." A wave of warmth rolls down the hall and sighs out the door, smelling of woodsmoke and wisteria. Her smile widens, revealing three crooked teeth. "When do I start?"

Arthur exhales. "Tomorrow. If you like."

"You got cleaning supplies?"

"Yes." He's pretty sure there are some bluish spray bottles beneath a sink somewhere, and a mop in the third-floor bathtub, although he's never used either. He isn't sure his parents did either; the House simply had a shine to it, back then.

"What are my hours?"

"You may arrive any time after dawn and leave before sunset."

Wariness slides like a fox across her face, there and gone again. "What a super normal way of putting it. See you tomorrow, then."

She's turning away when he says, "Wait."

Arthur draws a jangling metal ring from his pocket. There are three keys on the ring, although there should be four, each fashioned with long black teeth and a stylized, snakelike S. He removes a single key and extends his hand to Opal. She flinches, and he thinks sourly that she is much more frightened by him than she's pretending to be, and much less than she should be.

He dangles the key. "For the front gate. Don't lose it."

She takes it from him without touching his skin; he wonders if her hands are still cold, and why she can't be bothered to wear a proper coat.

Opal runs her thumb over the shaft of the key with the corner of her mouth hooked in an expression slightly too sad to be a smile. "Just like the book, huh?"

Arthur feels himself stiffen. "No."

He tries to shut the door in her face, but it won't latch. It jams for no reason at all, as if the frame has swollen or the floor has warped in the few minutes since he opened it.

Opal's face slides into the gap. The House casts blue shadows across her skin, swallowing her freckles. "What's your name?"

He glowers. She slouches one shoulder insolently against the frame, as if prepared to wait, and it occurs to him that this entire absurd scheme relies on Opal being the sort of person who learns lessons, who lets things lie; he wonders, too late, if he made a mistake.

"Arthur," he says, and the syllables sound foreign in his mouth. He can't recall the last time he said it out loud.

He gets a final glimpse of her face, the wary shape of her eyes and the quick pulse at her throat, that single damned curl escaping again from her ratty hood—red as clay, red as rust—before the door comes abruptly unstuck.

The latch gives a contented click and Arthur is alone in Starling House once more. He doesn't mind it—after a certain number of years the loneliness becomes so dense and rancid it's almost a companion in itself, which creeps and oozes at your heels—but now the hall seems hollow. There's a forlorn slant to the walls, and dust hangs like ash in the air.

"Tomorrow," he says, quietly. The dust motes dance.

W alking away from Starling House feels like climbing back through the wardrobe or up the rabbit hole, waking up from some heady dream. It seems impossible it could exist in the same world as abandoned Burger Kings and cigarette butts and the candy-red logo of Tractor Supply. But there's the key in my hand, heavy and cold and very real, like something plucked from the pages of *The Underland*.

I wonder if Arthur's read it as many times as I have. If he ever dreams in black-and-white, if he ever feels a watchful weight on the nape of his neck, the imaginary pressure of animal eyes.

I slip the key in my apron pocket before I clock in.

"You're late." Lacey says it just loud enough for the manager to hear, but not loud enough to be accused of snitching.

"Yeah, I just swung by the Starling place on the way back. Thought I'd see if they were hiring." Once you've established a reputation for dishonesty, it becomes possible to lie simply by stating the flat truth.

Lacey's mouth bends in a glossy bow. "That's not funny. My meemaw says there were two Starlings living there back in her day, a pair of women." Her voice lowers, bowing beneath the weight of implication. "Neither of them ever married." I would like to ask Lacey's meemaw if she'd considered the quality of potential husbands available in Muhlenberg County, but I suppose, given the existence of Lacey, that she must have made certain compromises. "And one day, they just disappeared. Gone. And that was the *very same day* that little Willy Floyd went missing."[6] This correlation is presented with all the gravity of a lawyer revealing damning evidence to the jury.

"Didn't Willy's friends say he went down the old mines on a dare?"

Lacey has to pause to ring up two bags of dog food and a clearance bird-house. "My meemaw says they were *Satanists,* who needed Floyd for a *blood ritual.*"

Arthur hadn't struck me as a cultist, but neither had he seemed like an upstanding Baptist. I don't think they're allowed to grow their hair past their chins. "What are the signs that someone's a Satanist, Lace?"

"Well, nobody ever saw them inside a church." I remain silent until Lacey recalls that I don't go to church, either. Mom went before I was born, she said, but once you're on the outside, the only way back in is on your knees; neither of us ever liked crawling.

Lacey rushes to add, "And they were always wandering around at night. And they kept strange animals, likely for *sacrifices.*"

"Sounds messy. Bet they could use a housekeeper."

Lacey gives me a disapproving look that would have made her meemaw proud, and I spend the rest of my shift restocking and mopping. I clock out without even bothering to dip a hand in the drawer because maybe—assuming this isn't an elaborate prank or a Satanist ritual or a weird sex thing—I don't have to anymore.

By the time I get back to room 12, Jasper is passed out in a gangly diag-

---

6. Odessa and Madge Starling, who lived in the house between 1971 and 1989, were last seen alive behind the old middle school. The school janitor told the sheriff they were chasing something. A dog, he originally stated, but in a later deposition he claimed it was Willy and his friends. Neither Willy nor the Starlings were ever seen again, although there have been reports of whimpering sounds echoing from the mouth of the old mine shaft.

onal across his bed, headphones mashed sideways, the nape of his neck soft and exposed. He must have finished his homework, because his favorite off-brand editing app is up on his screen.

He's always taking little videos—tree limbs crisscrossing in the wind, tadpoles wriggling in a drying puddle, his own feet running on cracked pavement. Standard moody-teen art, basically, but the angles are odd and unsettling, and he layers so many filters over the images that they acquire a spectral unreality. Lately he's been stitching them together, weaving them into tiny, strange narratives.

In one of them, a giggling white girl is carving a heart into the trunk of a tree. Dark liquid wells up from the wood, but she ignores it, carving until her hands are slicked red to the wrist. The final shot is her turning to the camera, mouthing *I love you.*

In the latest one, you see a pair of brown hands lowering a dead bird into the river. The footage does a funny little skip, and then a hand reaches back out of the water, covered in wet black feathers. The hands clasp tight; with passion or violence, it's impossible to say.

Jasper had red welts all over the backs of his hands for days, where the superglue had taken off bits of skin.

He won't show me this new one yet. The frames on his screen now are just a series of empty white squares, like fogged-up windows.

I hold the doorknob to muffle the latch behind me, but Jasper stirs, squinting up at me with his curls squashed flat on one side. "You just now getting home?" I flinch a little; room 12 isn't a home so much as a place we happen to be, like a bus stop or a gas station.

"Frank kept us late."

Actually I'd spent an extra hour shivering on the old railroad bridge, watching the oily rainbow sheen of the water and wondering if I'd just done something incredibly stupid. In the end I decided I probably had, but that was hardly a first, and at least this time it might be worth it.

I flop beside him on the bed. "Did Miss Hudson get your book report back?"

"Yeah, I got an A." Jasper appears to struggle with himself before adding, "Minus."

"I assume you're trying to signal some sort of hostage situation. Blink twice if you're being blackmailed."

"It wasn't fair! We were supposed to say whether we thought it was a horror novel or a romance, right? And I said both, because it *is,* and she took off five points."

I offer to TP Miss Hudson's house, which Jasper feels would not affect his GPA favorably, so we compromise by calling her bad names until both of us feel better. Afterward he sinks into his amateur-filmmaker forums. (I used to worry about how much time he spent online. Last year I tried to bully him into joining the high school movie club until Jasper explained, patiently, that he'd been a member up until Ronnie Hopkins asked him to write the Spanish lines for a character in his screenplay listed as "CARTEL THUG #3." I said, defensively, that I was just trying to help, and Jasper said that would be the title of his next horror short. I surrendered.)

Now he scrolls contentedly while I open three packs of store-brand Pop-Tarts (dinner) and microwave tap water for hot chocolate (dessert).

For some reason I feel like singing, so I do, one of Mom's old sweet songs about apples in the summertime and peaches in the fall. I don't know where she was from originally—one of my earliest memories is watching the telephone lines lope alongside the car while Mom drove us from nowhere to nowhere—but her accent was green and southern, just like mine. Her voice was better, though: low, smoke-bitten.

Jasper slides me a look, but his mouth is too full to say anything.

We spend the evening cocooned in our sleeping bags, headachey and sticky-fingered from sugar. It's cold enough that frost spangles the window and the heater rattles, so I cave and let the hellcat inside, an act of generosity which she repays by slinking under the bed and hissing every time the mattress creaks. I plug in the Christmas lights and the room goes hazy gold, and I wonder what a stranger would see if they cupped their hands against the glass: the two of us huddled in our hideout like Lost Boys or Boxcar Children, a couple of homeless kids playing a defiant game of house.

Sometime after midnight Jasper switches to a playlist called "peaceful beach waves." It sounds like static to me, but Jasper's always wanted to see the ocean. And he will, I swear he will. Maybe I'll even go with him.

I try to picture it: shoving my clothes in a backpack and driving across the county line, leaving room 12 empty and anonymous behind me. It feels fantastical, unnatural, like a tree dreaming of ripping up its roots and walking down the highway.

Which is stupid because I don't have roots; I was born in the backseat of Mom's '94 Corvette. I remember bugging her when I was little, asking if we were going to stay in the motel forever, if Eden was our new home. I remember the brittle sound of her laugh, the hard line of her jaw when she stopped. *Home is just wherever you get stuck.*

I wait until Jasper's breathing rasps into snores before sliding the laptop off his bed. The hellcat gives a perfunctory hiss.

I click in aimless patterns for a while, as if there's someone watching over my shoulder and I have to prove how little I care. After the third game of Minesweeper I open a private tab and type two words into the search bar: *starling house.*

The image results are the same as always: mostly birds, vast murmurations hanging in the sky like desaturated auroras, with one or two grainy photos of the Starling House gates, or the historical plaque on the side of the road. Those pictures lead me to a haunted house blog that rates Starling House eight out of ten ghost emojis but doesn't seem to have much actual information, and the Kentucky State Historical Society, whose website is listed as "coming soon" as of four years ago.

Lower down in the search results there's an amber daguerreotype of a not-very-pretty girl wearing an old-fashioned wedding dress. A middle-aged man stands beside her with his hand on her shoulder, his hair a colorless gray that might be blond or red. It's hard to tell, but I think the girl might be leaning very slightly away from him.

My copy of *The Underland* doesn't have author photos, but I know who she is even before I click the link. It's the wild, abyssal look in her eyes that gives her away, and the ink-stained tips of her fingers.

The photo takes me to the Wiki page for Eden, Kentucky. I scroll through the history section, which gives me the story everybody already knows: the opening of the first mines; the founding of Gravely Power; the Ajax 3850-B, biggest power shovel in the whole world, called "Big Jack" by locals; seventy thousand acres dug up and wrung dry; that one Prine song that everybody still hates;[7] a few pictures of Big Jack digging its own grave in the eighties, with a huddle of smaller shovels gathered around it like pallbearers.

I remember once when I was hanging around the motel office as a kid,

---

7. Opal is referring to John Prine's 1971 song "Paradise," recorded on his debut album. Gravely Power took considerable offense to the line "Well, I'm sorry my son, but you're too late in asking / Old Gravely's coal train has hauled it away," resulting in several lawsuits and a brochure titled "Facts vs. Prine." "Ironically," the brochure begins, "we probably helped supply the energy to make that recording that so unfairly maligns us."

Bev told me about the time her daddy took her up to the top of Big Jack. She said you could see miles and miles in every direction, the whole county laid out like a patchwork quilt. Her face was soft and handsome for a minute, remembering, before she told me to go get the Windex and a roll of paper towels if I didn't have anything better to do.

E. Starling's name is linked only once, in the "Notable people" section.

Her page has a little exclamation point at the top advising readers that the article needs additional citations for verification. I read it with something strange and electric running through me, an itch I can't explain.

I open an empty document and the cursor blinks at me, an invitation in Morse code. I haven't written anything except résumés and forgeries in eight years—because Jasper deserves more than make-believe, and because even the Lost Boys had to grow up in the end—but tonight I'm tempted. Maybe it's the memory of Starling House, vast and ruinous against the winter sky. Maybe it's the bare facts of E. Starling's life, a dissatisfying arc that could be fixed in fiction. Maybe it's the damn dreams.

In the end I only permit myself to copy and paste the Wiki page into the document, telling myself it's research, before shutting the laptop so firmly that Jasper stirs in his sleep.

E. Starling (author)

From Wikipedia, the free encyclopedia

Eleanor Starling (1851–4 May 1886) was a nineteenth-century American children's author and illustrator who published under the name of E. Starling. Though initially poorly received, her picture book *The Underland* enjoyed a twentieth-century revival and is now frequently included in lists of America's most influential children's literature.

Biography [edit]

There is no record of Eleanor Starling's birth.[1] Her first appearance in the historical record is the announcement of her engagement to John Peabody Gravely, founder and co-owner of Gravely Bros. Coal & Power Co. (now Gravely Power).[2] The two were married in 1869, but John Gravely died shortly afterward, leaving the company to his surviving brother, Robert Gravely, and the fortune to his wife.

Starling, who never received formal training in art or literature, submitted the manuscript of *The Underland* to more than thirty publishers. Julius Donohue of Cox & Donohue recalled receiving a package containing twenty-six illustrations "so amateurish and upsetting" that he hid them in the bottom drawer of his desk and forgot them.[3] Several months later, when his six-year-old daughter begged for "the nightmare book" at bedtime, he realized the pages had been discovered.[3] Cox & Donohue offered Starling a modest contract and published *The Underland* in the spring of 1881.

Eleanor Starling never met with her editors or readers. She refused all interviews, and all correspondence addressed to her was returned unopened. She was declared dead in 1886. Her work was held in trust until it fell out of copyright in 1956. Her home in Muhlenberg County is marked by the Kentucky State Historical Society.

Critical Reception [edit]

The Underland was considered both a critical and commercial failure upon publication. A reviewer for the *Boston Times* described it as "deliberately unsettling" and "a transparent theft from Mr. Carroll,"[4] while the Christian Children's Union petitioned several state governments to ban the book for the promotion of immorality. Donohue defended it in an open letter, asking how a book could be immoral when it contained no nudity, violence, sex, alcohol, or profanity. In response the Children's Union cited the "horrific anatomy" of the Beasts of Underland and the "general aura of dread."[5]

The book developed a quiet following over subsequent decades. By the early 1900s a number of artists and writers were citing E. Starling as an early influence.[6] Her artwork, initially dismissed as clumsy and untrained, was lauded for its stark composition and intensity of emotion. Her sparsely told tale, which described a little girl named Nora Lee who fell into "Underland," was recognized for its engagement with themes of fear, isolation, and monstrosity.

Since then *Underland* has gained acclaim as an early work in the neo-Gothic and modernist movements, and is considered a cultural turning point when children's literature abandoned the strict moral clarity of the nineteenth century for darker, more ambiguous themes.[6] Director Guillermo del Toro has praised E. Starling's work, and thanked her for teaching him that "the purpose of fantasy is not to make the world prettier, but to lay it bare."[7]

Adaptations and Related Works [edit]

The Underland was adapted as a stage play of the same name in 1932 at the Public Theater in New York City, and revived in 1944 and again in 1959. The 1959 production ended after only three nights, and was the subject of a House Un-American Activities Committee report citing its "hostility to American values, traditional family structures, and commerce."

The Underland was produced as a feature film in 1983, but never released. A documentary about the filming of the movie, *Unearthing Underland,* was nominated for an IDA Award in 2000.

In 2003, the song "Nora Lee & Me" was produced as a hidden track on Josh Ritter's third studio album, *Hello Starling.* The bluegrass girl group the Common Wealth also cites the book as an influence on their 2008 alt-country album, *follow them down.*

The book was adapted as a serialized graphic novel in the 2010s.

The Norman Rockwell Museum organized an art exhibition in 2015 titled *Starling's Heirs: A History of Dark Fantasy Illustration,* which included works by Rovina Cai, Brom, and Jenna Barton.

Further Reading [edit]

- Mandelo, L. (1996). "Beastly Appetites: Queer Monstrosity in E. Starling's Text." In *The Southern Gothic Critical Reader.* Salem Press.
- Liddell, Dr. A. (2016). "From Wonderland to Underland: White Femininity and the Politics of Escape." *American Literary History.* 24 (3): 221–234.
- Atwood, N. (2002). *Gothic Children's Illustration from Starling to Burton.* Houghton Mifflin.

FIVE

I don't dream of the house that night. I don't dream at all, actually, which is weird for me; I often wake up with the taste of river water and blood in my mouth, broken glass in my hair, a scream drowning in my chest. But that morning, the first one after I set foot on Starling land, there's nothing but a deep quiet inside me, like the dead air between radio stations.

The gates of Starling House greet me with their empty iron eyes. My left hand aches, but this time I have the key strung around my neck on a red lanyard. The thunk of tumblers turning feels more dramatic than it is, a tectonic shifting I can feel through my shoes, and then I'm walking up the drive with the key knocking against my breastbone.

Starling House still looks like God scooped it up from the cover of a Gothic novel and dropped it on the banks of the Mud River, and I still like it far more than I should. I pretend the busted windowpanes are jagged little mouths, grinning at me.

Arthur Starling answers the door in a rumpled sweater that doesn't fit, his eyes the resentful red of someone who does not appreciate being conscious before noon.

I give him several thousand watts of cheery smile and a merciless "Good morning!" I squint up at the sun, gleaming reluctantly through the branches. "You said anytime after dawn was fine."

His eyes narrow to bitter slits.

"Can I come in? Where should I start?"

He closes his eyes completely, as if he is preventing himself from slamming the door in my face only through devout prayer, and steps aside.

Walking across the threshold of Starling House is like stepping from winter straight into summer: the air is sweet and rich and warm. It slides down my throat, goes straight to my head. The walls seem to lean toward me. My feet feel rooted in place—I have a vision of vines pushing up between the floorboards to twine around my ankles, nails driving up through the soft flesh of my feet—

The door snaps shut behind me, sharp as a slap. The walls straighten up.

I turn to see Arthur watching me from the dimness, his expression flat and unreadable, his palm flat on the door. This side is carved up just like the outside, except the neat rows of signs and symbols have been interrupted by a random crosshatch of deep, ragged lines, almost like claw marks.

I nod to the door, grasping at normalcy. "You got a dog?"

"No." I wait, hoping he's about to add some perfectly reasonable explanation about a rabid raccoon or an accident with a hatchet, but all he says is "Mother said we had enough to take care of without getting a pet."

"In my experience you don't get pets, they get you." When I left this morning the hellcat was watching me with her usual deranged intensity from under the dumpster. "Don't you ever have any strays turn up around here?" There are always strays in Eden, kittens with oozy eyes and yellow dogs with ribs like the tines of a pitchfork.

"No." His eyes flick over me, lingering pointedly on the holes in my jeans, and his upper lip curls. "At least, not until recently."

I don't have much of a temper. People like me learn to send their tempers down and inward, where they won't get you fired or arrested or cussed out. But the haughty curl of his lip sends a white lick of fury up my spine.

I'm opening my mouth to say something I'll regret—which begins *listen here, asshole*—when he sweeps past me and on down the hall. He lifts a lazy hand. "There's a broom in the kitchen closet and supplies under the sink. I'm sure you'll find your way around."

His steps creak and ache into the shadows, and then I'm all alone in Starling House.

The air hangs thick and expectant around me. A mirror watches me with my own eyes, spooked gray. I wonder what color Eleanor Starling's eyes were, and how she died, and how her husband died, and if their bones are buried now beneath the floorboards. Halfway down the hall a door opens with a Hollywood creak, and I swallow the urge to run screaming.

I raise both hands in the air. "Look, I don't want any trouble." I don't believe in ghosts, demons, possessions, aliens, astrology, witchcraft, or vampires, but I know that the person who walks into the haunted house and loudly proclaims that they don't believe in ghosts is the first one to get gruesomely murdered. "I'm just here to clean, okay?" I'm answered by a meek moan, like a stair beneath a tiptoed foot. I decide to interpret it as permission.

I spend the first hour or two just wandering. Rooms sprout from the halls at random, branching and splitting like the patternless roots of a tree: sitting rooms and parlors, cramped offices and tiled washrooms, closets beneath staircases and ballrooms beneath ribs of rafters. I've never been lost in my life—getting lost in Eden would be like getting lost inside my own skin—but I find myself wishing for a spool of red thread to string behind me.

The house is well past dirty and headed for derelict, the sort of filthy that blurs the line between inside and outside. Dust lies so thick on the floors that it gives beneath my shoes, like soil. Wallpaper bubbles and peels. Mold blooms like black eyes in the folds of curtains and corners of couches. Some rooms are torn apart—the furniture overturned and the rugs rucked, mirrors ripped from the walls and shattered, still surrounded by sharp skirts of glass—and some are perversely neat. On the second floor I find a dining room with the table still set for two, spoons and forks laid on napkins the color of lichen. Chicken bones smile up from the plate, thin and yellow.

I back quietly out of that room, pausing only to shove a set of tarnished silver spoons in my back pocket. I figure if you call someone a stray, you should expect a consequence or two.

Beneath all the filth there are problems no amount of housekeeping could address: cracked windowpanes, dripping pipes, floors slanted so badly I feel off-balance. In one room the plaster has fallen away like a calving glacier, so that you can see the studs and lath boards, crusted iron pipes and fat, flaky wasp nests. There are strange white cords wrapped around everything, like oversized cobwebs; it takes a moment for me to recognize them as roots. Those honeysuckle vines must have wriggled their way through the limestone.

The next room is small and bright, with pastel wallpaper and a squashy couch. There are portraits on the walls, their faces filmed with dust. If I squint it could almost be cozy, except for the dirt and mold and the drifts of cicada shells in the windowsills. The couch exhales a stale sweetness when I sit down, as if it remembers open windows and spring breezes.

I should probably be freaked out—this place is eerie and endless, a rotting labyrinth—but mostly I just feel sorry for it. Starling House makes me think of an underfed pet or a broken doll, a thing unloved by the person who promised to love it best.

I give the couch cushion an uncertain pat. "We'll set you right. Don't worry." It's probably a coincidence that a draft flutters the curtains.

The kitchen is just around the next corner: grimy tile with footprints smeared between the sink and the fridge, a rusted cookstove, a Paleolithic microwave set to the wrong time. The promised cleaning supplies consist of a half-rotten mop chewed into a mouse nest and a box of spray bottles that have melted into a single Chernobyl-like blob, so I end up tearing a curtain into rags and filling a bucket at the sink. The tap hiccups but the water runs clear. The Starlings must have a well or a spring; county water comes out brackish gray and leaves crusted chemical rings in the bathtub.

I return to the almost-cozy sitting room and run my rag over the wainscoting. In two swipes the wash water is black and silty, fly wings and pill bugs bobbing on the surface. I dump it and do it all again, and again, and again. The hours fall into a rhythm of scrubbing, wringing, dumping, filling, the hiss of the tap and the wet slap of the rag. My knees ache. My hands are scoured pink; the cut on my left palm shreds open again. The blood soaks into the floorboards before I can wipe it away.

I scrub the wavering glass of the windowpanes, the wallpaper, the floors; I wipe the rag lightly over the portraits, revealing a dozen mismatched faces.

None of the paintings are labeled or signed.[8] None of their subjects share even a slight family resemblance, but they still strike me as pieces of the same set. It's the intensity of their stares, the sense that they were each interrupted at a delicate and important task. It's the bare silver sword in every single portrait, held flat across their knees or hanging on the wall behind them, unchanged by the passage of time.

The oldest one shows a ghostly, dark-eyed Victorian woman who must be Eleanor Starling herself, much older than the picture on her Wiki page. There's a young man with strange white patches on his skin, like a human calico; an unsmiling pair of sisters with long black hair and striped blankets around their shoulders; a Black teenager in a Depression-era derby hat; two women with their arms around one another's waists; a whole family in crisp fifties outfits. The newest portrait shows a white couple: a broad-shouldered woman with a familiar lumpiness to her face, as if she was born with twice the usual amount of cheekbone, and a gangling man with an affable smile.

There's something ghoulish about the paintings, the way the faces of the dead are arranged like taxidermy on the wall, a museum exhibit of people who couldn't safely walk down the streets of Eden. I wonder how they ended up here; I wonder how they died.

I can feel their eyes on me while I work.

The sun is fat and low by the time I pause to crack my spine and eat a slightly squashed Pop-Tart. My heart sinks: less than half the room could be called clean, and only by someone with a very generous definition of the word "clean." Standing there with the shadows stretching long and my right arm swinging on the sore hinge of my shoulder, I understand that I wasn't given a job after all: I was given an impossible task, of the kind a king might set for his daughter's unwanted suitors or a god might give to a sinful soul. It would take fleets of professionals and several industrial dumpsters and possibly an exorcist to make this place livable, and I'm just a girl who cleans a couple of cheap motel rooms over the holidays, when Gloria and her mama fly back to Michoacán and Bev needs a hand.

I should quit. I should beg Frank for extra shifts. But I can't pay for Stonewood on minimum wage, and the gate key feels cold and sweet against

---

8. Despite exhaustive research, including consultations with art historians and curators, it has proven impossible to determine the original painters of these portraits. There are no records of commissions, no recognizable styles, no identifiable pigments. It is as if the paintings simply manifested, one by one, on the walls of Starling House.

my chest, and anyway I can't give the Starling boy the satisfaction of watching me run from him a second time.

I text Jasper—working late tonight, I hid the last picante chicken in the tampon box under the sink—and wring out my rag again. The house sighs around me.

Just before dusk Arthur finds himself standing alone in his mother's favorite room.

He didn't intend to be there; he left the library headed for the third-floor bathroom and wound up on the first floor instead, staring at the sagging couch his mother ordered from a catalog. She wasn't a person who permitted herself many indulgences, but sometimes after a hard night she would sit on that couch and wait for dawn to drive back the mist. Arthur knew she wasn't a pretty woman, but on those mornings—with her face golden and battle-weary in the rising sun, her knuckles bloody around the hilt of the Starling sword—she was somewhere beyond beauty, tilting toward mythic.

Arthur has let this room rot for almost a decade.

Now it shines fresh and bright, as if all those years were scrubbed out of it. As if his mother might step around the corner at any moment, smiling her soldier's smile, and his father might call from the kitchen. Arthur takes a step back and the eyes of the former Wardens seem to follow him from their frames, weighing him, finding him wanting.

The floor creaks behind him and Arthur whirls, one hand flinching toward his hip.

Opal is in the doorway, staring at him. Her hoodie is balled up under one arm and her T-shirt is smeared with grime. She's tied a scrap of something that looks like his kitchen curtain around her left palm, and her hair curls at her temples, dark as blood.

Opal's eyes flick to his hand, splayed at his hip, then away. She nods at the setting sun. "I'm heading out."

He tucks the hand very casually in his pocket and adopts his archest tone. "And what did you think of your first day?"

That wry twist of her lips, a glimpse of crooked teeth. "I think I'll ask Mr. Augeas if he needs his stables cleaned next. Be a piece of cake after this place."

Arthur blinks at her several times. He doesn't know what to say, so he says, obnoxiously, "It's pronounced *Aw-gee-us.*"

Her smile goes hard and fake. "Oh! My apologies. I must've dropped out before we got to ancient Greek." She shifts the hoodie beneath her arm. It makes a muffled clanking sound.

"I didn't mean—it's just that mythology is something of a . . ."—calling, duty, obsession—". . . hobby. In my family." Arthur finds he can't look at her. He withdraws a heavy envelope and thrusts it blindly in her direction. "Your pay."

Opal folds the envelope into her back pocket and holds her hand out flat for more. "I'll need extra for supplies." Her voice is syrup-sweet.

"So you're coming back. Tomorrow." Arthur tries to sound neither pleased nor sorry and winds up sounding bored.

"Yep."

He puts a twenty in her outstretched hand. The hand doesn't move. He adds another twenty.

The cash disappears into a different pocket and Opal gives him a switchblade smile as she turns away. "That's the thing about strays." Her voice echoes back to him over her shoulder. "We don't quit."

He'd said it because it was a cruel thing to say. Because it would hurt, and people hate what hurts them, and if she hated him maybe she would run before she got hurt much worse. So there's no reason regret should crawl up his throat. No reason he should swallow hard and say, far too quietly, "I'm sorry."

There's no reason he should wish she'd heard him.

He lingers, after she leaves, breathing in the smell of soap and clean wood. The House shifts subtly, the light tilting and the air chilling, so that the room is precisely as it was that last day. *Damn you,* he thinks, but the memory is already rising around him, closing like jaws.

He is fourteen. His mother is lying silently on her yellow couch while his father carefully stitches a flap of her scalp back into place. The battle had been a long and brutal one—had it always been this bad? was the mist rising more than it should?—and the skin over her cheekbones is white.

Arthur watches them for a while. His father's long-fingered hands—the hands of a painter or a pianist, bent instead to the bloody, endless work of keeping his wife alive. His mother, a knotted scar of a woman, already going gray. Her right hand is still resting on the hilt, restless, ready.

Without quite planning to, Arthur announces that he is leaving.

His mother opens her eyes. *How dare you,* she says. She's always been stern, but she's never spoken to him like this, with this furious contempt. *They took my home from me—you think you can just walk away from yours—this is your birthright—*

His father says her name, gently, and her mouth shuts as if sewn, the stitches overtight. *You're not going anywhere,* she says.

But Arthur had. That very night, he'd climbed out the library window and down the wisteria, while the House moaned and wailed. He thought it would try to stop him, but when his foot slipped, his fingers had found an old trellis in just the right place, and when he slid into his father's truck, he found a backpack full of peanut-butter-and-jellies.

He'd driven himself to the bus station with a heady, dangerous glee, as if he were a kite with its strings cut.

The next time he saw his mother, there had been a thistle pushing gently through the socket of her right eye.

The House shifts again and the memory falls away. Arthur is twenty-eight. He is alone, and he is grateful.

SIX

I toss the spoons on Jasper's bed when I get back to room 12 that evening. "Put 'em on eBay, please and thank you. The antiques account."

Jasper appraises the spoons with a clinical eye. He draws a finger down the silver and withdraws it, frowning. "You didn't get these at Tractor Supply," he observes.

It's my personal ambition never to set foot in a Tractor Supply again, actually.

As soon as I counted Arthur's money I texted Lacey tell Frank i quit :) and called Stonewood Academy to find out where I should send my first payment. The lady on the phone repeated "In . . . cash?" with audible ellipses and helpfully reminded me of the final deadline, as if I didn't already know it. As if I didn't repeat the date in my head every time I passed the smokestacks.

"Nope," I say.

Jasper looks like he might have a few follow-up questions, but we have a deal where he doesn't ask me anything he doesn't want answered, so he merely mentions his fervent hope that I'm not doing anything illegal.

I press a hand to my chest, mortally wounded. "*Me?*"

"Or dangerous."

He sounds worried enough that I give him my most earnest smile. "I'm not. For real." It might even be true. I mean, if houses can be haunted, Starling House absolutely is, but so far all it's done to me is moan and creak. And I'm pretty sure Arthur is just a garden-variety asshole rather than, say, a sexual predator, or a vampire. "Pretty please?" I nudge the spoons with my knee. "My phone camera sucks."

Jasper holds eye contact for another moment, just to let me know that he's not buying what I'm selling, before flopping dramatically back against the mattress. "I would, but Bev turned the internet off again."

"Did you ask her to turn it back on?"

He opens one scandalized eye. "I thought you loved me. I thought you wanted me to survive to my senior year—"

I whump a pillow at him and he wheezes theatrically. It sounds a little more real than he meant it to, the breath whistling in his throat.

I head back across the empty parking lot to the front office, where Bev is busy yelling at *Jeopardy!,* pausing only to spit tobacco juice into an empty coke can. She's probably not even fifty, but she has the social habits and haircut of a ninety-year-old man.

We have our traditional argument: she maintains that the internet is for paying customers and not for depraved freeloading teenagers; I swear at her; she threatens to throw us out into the street; I swear again; she flips me off and turns the power strip back on. I steal four packets of Swiss Miss from the folding card table she has the audacity to advertise as a breakfast bar.

"Those are also for paying customers, by the way."

"Yeah, but you don't have any of those, do you?"

Bev scowls at the TV and says, "Those Gravely Power people are back," which explains her sour mood. The only thing Bev hates more than me and Jasper are actual guests, who sometimes have the nerve to ask for things like reliable hot water and room service, and the only thing she hates more than guests is Gravely Power, which, as far as I can tell, she holds personally responsible for every social, environmental, and economic problem in the state. None of the executives actually live in Eden, obviously—Don Gravely has a brand-new house right outside the city limits, with seven bathrooms and white columns and one of those awful lawn jockeys out front, smiling a false red smile—but a bunch of them come into town every year for their annual meeting or whatever, and there's nowhere for them to stay except the Garden of Eden Motel. Bev's only comfort is that they always leave with a thick layer of bird shit caked over their windshields.

Bev looks away from *Jeopardy!* to glare between the blinds at the line of expensive SUVs in her parking lot. "They're talking about expanding, did you know that? One of them was going on about doubling capacity and opening new fields and all that. They're going to build a whole new fly ash pond, the woman told me." She adds, reflexively, "Goddamn vultures."

"Careful, that's Muhlenberg County's number one job creator you're talking about." I don't like them much either—maybe if they put filters on their smokestacks rather than just paying EPA fines every year, Jasper could actually breathe, and I wouldn't have to clean a haunted house so I could afford to get him out of here—but I like watching Bev's face turn red.

"We used to have luna moths when I was a kid. You ever seen one of them?"

"No?"

"Exactly." She seems to feel she's won the argument, because she thumps a pile of my mail on the counter and returns to her show.

There's a stack of library holds from Charlotte, which she doesn't have to deliver to the motel but does anyway; a couple of notices from debt collectors who are shit out of luck; some junk mail; and an envelope from the Department for Community Based Services with RETURN SERVICE REQUESTED printed in all capitals. That last one makes me swallow and tuck my hair behind my ear—my only tell, Mom used to say.

Trebek is sneering his way through a $400 question when I clear my throat. "Hey, Bev?"

She slides half a box of glazed doughnuts across the counter without looking away from the television. "They were going stale anyway."

"Actually, I was wondering—you know the Starlings?"

She turns away from the Daily Double, frowning. I have an encyclopedic familiarity with Bev's frowns, ranging from "turn that damn music down" to "have you been in the petty cash jar again, you reprobate," but this one is new. It's wary, almost worried, although the only things Bev typically worries about are bedbugs and tax audits. "What about them?"

"I was just thinking about them, is all. About that house."

She grunts again. "Been a long time since you bugged me about the Starling place, kid. You never used to shut up about it."

I remember myself as a girl, scab-kneed and quick, hungry even when my belly was full. Mom and me didn't always live in room 12—I remember other hotels, an RV or two, a couple of months sleeping on couches that belonged to men who liked the color of Mom's hair and the careless way she laughed, but never liked me much—but the motel was the first place we stayed for more than a few months.

Bev had mostly glared at me out the front office window until the day I poked a wasp nest and got stung twice, once on each arm. Mom wasn't around so I was just sitting on the curb, tasting tears in the back of my throat, when Bev strolled over and slapped a wet mat of chewing tobacco over the stings. She gave me a lot of shit about not having the sense God gave a flea, but the pain eased.

"Yeah, well, I googled it the other day, just out of curiosity, and didn't find much. I thought maybe you would know something about it."

Bev spits a black stream into her coke can and says, obliquely, "People talk. You know how it is."

I don't know how it is, actually, because people only talk to me when they're cornered. Small towns are supposed to be cozy and friendly, like perfect little snow globes, but me and Jasper have always been kept on the other side of the glass. Maybe because I only showed up at church for the pancake breakfasts and Thanksgiving dinners, or maybe because of Mom, with her lipstick and her shirts that didn't quite meet the top of her jeans and the pills she sold sometimes in little plastic baggies. Or maybe because people in Eden like to know your whole family tree for three generations on both sides and the only family we ever knew was each other.

I pick at a snowflake of doughnut glaze on the box. "Will you tell me what you know?"

"No." Bev heaves a sigh that bears an uncanny resemblance to Arthur Starling's before he offered me a job, infinitely harassed. The TV is old enough to make a faint electric pop when she turns it off. "But I'll tell you a story."

This is the story of Starling House.

People tell it different ways, but this is how my granddaddy always told it. He was a liar, but the best liars are the ones that stick closest to the truth, so I believe it.

It goes like this: Once in the wayback times there was three brothers by the name of Gravely who made a fortune digging coal out of the riverbank. They were good, honest boys, brought low by the same thing that always comes for honest men with a little money: a dishonest woman.

Eleanor Starling came from nowhere in particular and had no particular beauty, but she wormed her way into the Gravely household anyhow. She was an odd girl, silent and waifish, prone to melancholy, but the Gravely boys doted on her. It wasn't long after she arrived that they found the oldest Gravely facedown in the Mud River. There wasn't a mark on him, but they say his face was stretched and racked, like a man looking upon an unspeakable horror.

At the time it was considered a tragic accident, but when the middle brother announced his engagement to little Eleanor Starling a few weeks later, people started talking, as people will. They started asking themselves just how the oldest Gravely boy wound up in the Mud River, when he was known to be a sober and careful man. They wondered if perhaps he had learned something about Miss Starling that she didn't like, or simply resisted her wiles. But people kept their suspicions to themselves; Eden has always prided itself on its good manners, and good manners are mostly keeping your mouth shut and your mind on your own business.

John Gravely wouldn't have listened to them, anyway; he was thoroughly taken with Eleanor, or, it was murmured behind his back, taken *in*. On their wedding day she stood wanly at his side, too forgettable even to achieve ugliness, but John Gravely looked at her like she was ice water in July.

The fog rose that night, thick and sudden. When it burned away they found John Gravely lying dead down at the bottom of his own mine shaft, wearing an expression just as ghastly as his poor brother's. Eleanor Starling was nowhere to be found, but the men said they saw small bare footprints that led down into the deep dark and did not come out again.

Most people hoped she would have the good grace to disappear and let the last Gravely mourn in peace, but three days later Eleanor was seen wandering the hills and hollows of her husband's land, still wearing her wedding gown. The farmhands that found her said her skirt slapped heavy and wet against her ankles, the hem gray with silt, as if she'd walked straight out of the river. They said, too, that she was laughing, light and joyful as a child.

The new widow told the sheriff she went for a walk on her wedding night and got lost, and had no earthly idea what happened to her poor, poor husband. No one believed her, but no judge could convict her, so the town could only watch and whisper as she used up all her husband's money—and a hundred and sixty-six acres of his richest coal country, right across the river from the mines themselves—to build herself a house so vast it was written up in *The Courier-Journal* and *The Lexington Daily Press*.

She chose a strange site to build: a damp, low hollow so deep in the woods the house itself couldn't be seen from the road. The townsfolk knew it existed only by the workers that came and went: surveyors and architects, carpenters and masons, roofers and painters. She hired them and fired them within days—because she didn't want them getting too friendly with the locals, people said, or because she was mad. Why else would she hire four separate locksmiths, and order each of them to melt their molds afterward? The last person she employed was a blacksmith who came all the way from Cincinnati to hang the front gates.

Eleanor moved into the house the day after the gates were hung and was never seen again. For the following twenty years, the only sign of her continued survival was the shine of her windows at night, peering through the trees like the amber eyes of some restless animal.

The town thrived in her absence. They survived the Grant administration and the Freedmen's Bureau; they made peace with the carpetbaggers and war with the tax collectors. The youngest Gravely boy kept the family business afloat, opening new coalfields and laying railroad tracks across the river. He married well and smiled often, and people began to believe Eleanor Starling would leave him in peace.

But then, on one of those sickly spring nights when the fog comes off the river in great white curls like wood shavings under a knife, bad luck came for the last Gravely brother.

He told his wife he would be out late on company business, and rode off on his favorite horse, a glossy thoroughbred named Stonewall who cost more than most men made in a year. Stonewall was a sure-footed creature, but that night he must have caught a hoof between the railroad ties, or turned an ankle. Or maybe he saw something moving in the mist ahead and refused to take another step. All anybody knew for sure was that Stonewall and his rider were both standing on the tracks when the midnight coal train came through.

There was no proof it was the widow's work. But after that night, Starling House went dark.

There were several competing theories about this: maybe Eleanor had run away, her grim work finally completed; maybe the spirits of the three brothers had found some revenge of their own; maybe she hanged herself in sudden remorse, or maybe she simply fell down one of her own twisting staircases and lay at the bottom, broke-necked.

Eventually the sheriff took it upon himself to investigate—although whether he was more interested in discovering the state of Eleanor's body or her fortune, I couldn't tell you—but the gates were locked and the walls were high. He returned to town briar-bitten and muddy, with an expression of distant confusion, as if he'd walked into a room and couldn't remember why.

Eden might have forgotten about the widow and her strange house, given time, and returned their minds once again to their own business, but you already know they didn't. They couldn't, for three very good reasons.

The first was the unpleasant discovery that Eleanor had, without anyone's say-so or approval, become slightly famous. That book of hers—a morbid, unsettling thing that everyone did their best to ignore—made her name linger longer than anyone wanted, like an ill-mannered houseguest.

The second reason was the raggedy young man who arrived in Eden the following spring. He called himself a Starling, and maybe he was; all the town knew for sure is that the gates opened for him, and there were lights in the woods again, after that.

The third reason is rarely spoken of, and only slantwise, by suggestion and intimation. It's something about the way the shadows fell in Eden, after Eleanor died. It's the way everything soured: the river ran darker and the clouds hung lower; rich coal seams went dry and healthy children sickened; good luck went bad and sweet dreams spoiled. It's the way Starling House crouches just out of sight, watching us all.

It's the way the fog still rises, on chill and rotten nights. Some people think it's just weather, but my granddaddy always said it was her: Eleanor Starling, whittled down to nothing but malice and mist, still thirsty for Gravely blood, haunting the town that still hates her.

SEVEN

I didn't plan to stay up late again, but here I am: sitting with the laptop screen angled away from Jasper's bed, typing up a story that shouldn't matter to me at all.

I couldn't sleep, not even after reading six chapters of a racy "Beauty and the Beast" retelling I'd had on hold for weeks. Bev's story seemed to bleed through the pages, so that I saw a house swallowed by honeysuckle instead of a castle covered in roses. I could almost hear her voice: the rhythm of it, the slight slur of the tobacco tucked in her lip.

Eventually I gave up. I opened the file I'd saved as "document 4," buried in a series of folders with boring names, and typed it all out. I told myself that writing down somebody else's story wasn't as bad as making up my own, the way repeating a lie isn't as bad as telling one; I told myself it was probably all horseshit, anyway.

Before I had gone back to my room, I'd asked Bev if she thought any of it was true. She tilted her chin one way, then the other. "Enough, I'd say."

"Enough to what?"

"Enough to steer clear of those people. I don't think this town is cursed by anything but coal, and I don't know if all the Starlings are as bad as the first one was, but I'll tell you something: I don't trust the boy who lives there now."

A little chill ran down my breastbone. I kept my voice light and curious. "Why's that?"

Bev watched me closely when she answered. "His parents, they weren't too bad. People will tell you all kinds of nonsense about them—Bitsy Simmons swears up and down they kept Siberian tigers, says she saw a big white thing in the woods one night—but I don't believe it. The husband, he used to drive this beat-up old truck around, and he always waved when he passed the motel . . . Anyway, both of them turned up dead, eleven or twelve years ago. And the boy, he doesn't even call the police, not for days."

The chill settled low and heavy in my stomach. Bev continued, softly, "The animals had been at them so bad the coroner said he couldn't tell what killed them in the first place. Hell, maybe they did keep tigers. But the coroner said that boy didn't shed a tear the whole time. Just asked if he was finished yet, because it was past his suppertime."

After a long, unpleasant silence, I managed a hoarse "Huh."

Bev clicked the TV back on while I gathered up my books and junk mail.

She waited until I was halfway out her office door before she said, low and serious, "Stay away from Starling House, Opal."

I crossed the parking lot with my neck bent and my hands shoved deep in my pockets. The mist was just slithering up the riverbank, pooling in the potholes and dips of the road.

It's higher now. The streetlights have gone hazy and spectral, like low-hanging planets, and the fancy SUVs are animals crouched beneath them. By tomorrow, there will be little flecks of rust on the rims, and the fine leather seats will smell green and rotten.

Mom always said nights like this were unlucky. She wouldn't place a bet or cut a deal until the mist burned off the next day.

I don't believe in luck, but it was misty the night Mom died, and I sometimes think if it hadn't been—or if she hadn't had a few and announced, with her usual sincerity, that she was going to turn our lives around, or if I'd argued with her instead of pretending I still believed her, or if she hadn't been driving that damn Corvette, or if that whatever-it-was hadn't run across the road—well. Maybe she would be the one telling me to stay away from Starling House, instead of Bev.

And maybe she'd be right. I don't much like the idea of cleaning the house of a woman who murdered her husband for his money, or a pair of women who kidnapped a kid, or a boy who looked down at his parents' bodies with dry eyes. I have the sudden urge to take a shower, to scrub the dirt of Starling House out from under my nails and never go back.

A noise from the other side of the room: a high, wavering whistle. The note stops, rushes out, starts again. It sounds like a teapot just coming to boil, but it's not: it's a sixteen-year-old trying to breathe through bronchial tubes that are swelling shut.

The first time Jasper had an asthma attack I was twelve. It was three in the morning and Mom wasn't in her bed and I didn't want to call 911 because I knew ambulances were expensive. I turned all the faucets on as hot as they would go and shut the bathroom door. I held him in the steam—his ribs heaving, his muscles trembling under soft baby fat—until I realized he wasn't going to get better and Mom wasn't going to show up. When the dispatcher answered I said, calmly, "I don't know what to do."

I know what to do, now. I get out of bed and put an inhaler in Jasper's hand before he's fully awake. I count two pumps, five breaths, two pumps more. Jasper doesn't say anything, but his eyes are steady on mine.

I dump two scoops of instant coffee in a Waffle House mug and microwave it on high, then stir in all four packets of hot chocolate. Google says caffeine helps, but Jasper can't stand the taste.

He drinks it. We wait. Every five minutes or so I snap my fingers and he lets me check to make sure the beds of his fingernails aren't turning blue.

Eventually the whistle goes flat, falling down the scale until it's just air again, rushing in and out.

"I'm good." Jasper's voice is still a little strained, but he hates when I baby him.

I get back in bed and pretend to sleep, listening until his breathing turns deep. I think about the banner on Stonewood Academy's site: the clean blue of the sky, the healthful green of the lawn. I hold it in my head like a promise, like a map to the real Eden, until the colors oversaturate in my head, unreal.

I don't think about ghost stories or murder mysteries, sins or starlings, because none of it matters. I'm going back to Starling House, because I have to.

For Jasper.

The words are comfortable, familiar, the easy answer to every question I've ever asked myself. But for the first time they ring a little rote, a little thin, as if there's some shadowy part of me that doesn't believe them. That smiles and whispers in my ear: *Liar.*

I show up even earlier on my second morning, my wrists scored by the weight of shopping bags, my shoulders bruised by the handles of a broom and mop. I knock more times than is strictly necessary, loud enough to set the starlings screaming. Bev hates them because they eat her persimmons and sound like dial-up internet, but I've always liked them. Every now and then you see them at dusk, rising and falling in these grand, twisting patterns over the pits and marshes Big Jack left behind him, and you think if you stare at them long enough you'll make sense of them, read whatever it is they're writing on the sky, but you never do.

I jump when Arthur opens the door. He doesn't bother to speak this time, only stares at me with grim resignation. There's a line of fresh scabs along his jaw, and bluish hollows beneath his eyes, like he gets even less sleep than everybody else in Eden.

I hesitate on the threshold, wondering if I'm about to slide sideways into dreamland, sucked under the strange currents of this strange house, until Arthur sighs at me. I quash a strong urge to stick my tongue out at him. Instead I hand him the heaviest shopping bags and march past him to the kitchen. It takes an embarrassing number of twists and about-faces before I find it, Arthur trailing behind me like a mocking shadow, plastic bags shushing against his knees.

He piles his bags on the cookstove and looks almost fearfully at the bottles of bleach and borax and off-brand Windex. I stole most of it from Bev's supply closet—I consider Arthur's second twenty a tip for rudeness—but I bought the mop and broom brand-new at the Dollar General, along with an Ale-8 and a candy bar for lunch.

Arthur retreats upstairs to do whatever he does during the day, which I assume involves a coffin filled with grave dirt, and I set to work on the sitting room again. It looks better than I remembered, still shabby but approaching habitable. I spend the rest of the day scrubbing grime from the baseboards and rubbing oil soap into the floor, and if there's anything haunting Starling House it has the decency to let me work in peace. I go home sore and proud with another envelope in my back pocket. I mail the second payment to Stonewood that night.

The rest of the week goes the same way. On Thursday I fill three trash bags with mouse-chewed sheets and mud dauber nests, dragging them behind me down the long drive. On Friday I soak ten sets of yellowed curtains in bleach water and hang them to dry on the backs of dining room chairs, so that it looks as if a family of ghosts has come for supper. On Saturday—I hadn't asked if I was working weekends, but I need the money and Arthur doesn't seem to know what day of the week it is—I sweep out the pantry and find a trapdoor poorly hidden beneath a rug.

The handle is recessed into the floor, fitted with a cartoonishly large padlock, and there are symbols carved into the wood. It feels like discovering a clue in a video game, a giant glowing arrow inviting me to come closer, dig deeper, learn more. I lay the rug flat again and leave the pantry half-cleaned. I sing to myself all that afternoon, about dreams and thunder and old houses burning down.

On Sunday I wander up to the third floor looking for a stepladder and wind up in a high-ceilinged room full of armchairs and shelves and more books than the public library.

It's the sort of place I didn't know existed outside of movie sets, all mullioned windows and oak paneling and leather-bound spines. I see folklore and mythology, collections of fairy tales and children's rhymes, horror novels and history books and fat Latin dictionaries with half the pages dog-eared. My stomach twists with longing and resentment and wonder.

I snatch a book off the shelf, not even pausing to read the title.

It's a super old edition of Ovid, written in that awful verse where everything rhymes and "over" is spelled "o'er." The book falls open to a page titled "The House of Sleep," followed by a long passage about a drowsing god in a cave. The word "Lethe" is underlined more times than seems strictly sane, the page so deeply indented it's torn a little. In the margin beside it someone has written a list of Latin names: *Acheron, Styx, Cocytus, Pyriphlegethon, Lethe,* and then: *a sixth river?*

And I know without knowing how—unless it's something in the stark shape of the lettering or the black of the ink—that E. Starling wrote this note.

A throat clears behind me. I jump so badly I drop the book.

Arthur Starling is watching me, Bond-villain-ly, from the shadows of a wingback armchair. There are dozens of books piled around him, bristling with sticky notes, and a stack of neatly labeled folders. *Tsa-me-tsa and Pearl Starling, 1906–1929. Ulysses Starling, 1930–1943. Etsuko Starling, 1943–1955.*[9]

Arthur has a thick yellow pad of paper balanced on his knee. His left pinky is silvery gray with graphite, and his sleeves are rolled to the elbow. His wrists look stronger than I would expect from someone whose main hobbies are skulking and frowning, the bones wrapped in stringy muscle and scarred flesh.

"Oh, hi!" I reshelve Ovid and give him an innocent wave. "What you got there?"

His face twists. "Nothing."

I tilt my head to see the page better. There are notes at the top, tally marks and dates mostly, but the lower half of the page has been overtaken by crosshatching and graphite. "Looks pretty good from here. Is that the sycamore out front?"

He flips the pad over, glowering.

"Are those tattoos?" There are dark lines of ink slinking out from under the rolled cuffs of his shirt, tangling with the jagged lines of scars. I can't make out any images, but the shapes remind me of the carvings on the front door: eyes and open palms, crosses and spirals.

Arthur rolls his sleeves back down and buttons them pointedly. "I'm paying you for a specific purpose, Miss Opal." His voice is frigid. "Shouldn't you be cleaning something?"

That night I leave Starling House with a pair of candlesticks and a fountain pen rolled up in my hoodie, because fuck him.

At least I don't have to see him very often. Whole weeks pass without an exchange of words longer than "Good morning" when he unlocks the door, and "Well, I'm headed out" as I leave. Every now and then I take a wrong turn and catch a glimpse of hunched shoulders and uncombed hair, but

---

9. None of the persons mentioned were born with the name Starling, but all of them were buried with it. Though they were not related by blood, they all shared a tendency to keep excellent records, to which the present Warden of Starling House has been generous enough to grant me access.

usually the only sign that the house is occupied are the occasional thumps and murmurs from the attic above me, and the slow accretion of dishes in the sink. I might find a fresh pot of coffee or a soup pot still simmering on the stove, smelling wholesome and home-cooked in a way that's completely foreign to me, but I don't touch any of it, thinking vaguely of burrows and mounds and what happens to the idiots who eat the fairy king's food.

Time already passes strangely in Starling House. Sometimes the hours slouch by, and I find myself indulging in little-girl fantasies to occupy myself (I'm Cinderella, forced to scrub the grout lines by my evil stepmother; I'm Beauty, trapped in an enchanted castle by a Beast with a face like a crow's skull). Sometimes the hours skitter away into grimy corners and stained baseboards, and I look up from a gray bucket of water to find the sun hanging near the horizon, and realize the house has swallowed another day, another week.

The only reliable measurement of time is the state of the place.

By the end of February the first floor is almost livable. There's still a thriving population of spiders and mice, and I can't do anything about the hunks of plaster that sometimes fall from the ceilings, or the way the floors all seem to slant toward some central point, as if the whole house is collapsing in on itself, but walking down the halls no longer feels like touring a crypt. The tabletops gleam and the windowpanes wink. The rugs are red and blue and deep green, rather than gray, and the smell of bleach and tile cleaner has driven back the black smell of mildew.

The house seems to appreciate all the attention. The exterior is still stained and gloomy, but the vines are greening faintly, supple and alive, and there are fresh bird's nests in the eaves. The floor still provides an entire symphony of groans and creaks, but I swear it's no longer in a minor key.

Sometimes I catch myself humming along with it, weirdly content. Mostly it's just the money, which in my experience will solve all ninety-nine of your problems, but it's also Starling House itself: the way the walls feel like cupped palms around me, the way the doorknob fits in my hand, the absurd, childish feeling that I belong there.

EIGHT

B y the middle of March the sparrows are
bathing in the potholes and the daffodils
are peeking cautiously through the matted
leaves. It's still cold, but the world smells muddy and
awake, and I'm inspired to drag the rugs and couch
cushions outside for an airing. I prop them against
the biggest, oldest sycamore and beat them with my
new broomstick until dust fogs the woods and sweat
stings my skin, despite the chill.

I leave the cushions to air out and head back up
the steps, kicking aside the leaves and curled-up grubs.
It's only when I reach for the doorknob that I realize
it's locked itself behind me.

I pound on the door a few times, annoyed and embarrassed and wishing very much that I was wearing my hoodie rather than just a bleach-spotted Bible study T-shirt. The wind pokes icy fingers through the holes in the collar. I knock again.

After an amount of time that makes it clear Arthur isn't coming—either because he can't hear me or because he's a prick—I get more than annoyed. God, I hate the cold. It makes me think of the river closing over my head, the stars vanishing, the world ending. I haven't gone swimming in eleven years.[10]

Classic PTSD, Mr. Cole called it, as if that helped at all.

I stomp and swear at the house. I try my gate key in the lock, but it won't turn. I remind the house in a wheedling voice of all the hard work I've been doing on its behalf, feeling stupid for talking to a house but not stupid enough to stop. There's a shiver in my jaw, as if my teeth want to chatter, and the wind has turned my sweat clammy. The door remains serenely shut.

I flex my left hand. The cut is mostly healed now, and it seems a shame to split it back open, so I bite my lower lip until I taste salt and meat. My fingertips come away red.

I'm about to smear my own blood across the lock like some ancient cultist blessing a household when I hear boots on the steps behind me. I drop my broomstick and spin around to find Arthur Starling displaying his particular habit of turning up when I'm doing something especially embarrassing.

He's wearing a long dark coat of the kind I've only seen in spy movies and on the covers of pulpy mystery novels, his hair stuffed messily beneath a high collar, his face flushed with fresh air. He's looking down at me the way I look at the hellcat when she gets her claws stuck in the screen, as if he can't understand how he got saddled with such a piteous, hapless creature.

He sighs at me. "*Please* stop bleeding on my house."

I suck resentfully at my lip. "Where did you come from?"

"Walking the walls."

I squint around him at the winter woods, shadowed and empty except for the white bones of sycamores, and remind myself that this boy and his spooky shit are not my problem. "Of course."

"You're cold," he observes. He's mocking me, standing there all cozy in

---

10. In addition to its being several degrees cooler than the surrounding waters, there is a countywide advisory against swimming in the Mud River. The advisory cites the presence of mercury and arsenic, but there are also a statistically unlikely number of drownings reported each year. One survivor swore he felt a hand around his ankle, pulling him down; he said the fingers were small and fragile, like a little girl's.

his rich-kid coat, his shoulders safe and square against the winter light while I shiver in my secondhand T-shirt, remembering what I'd rather forget, and I'm suddenly, thoroughly, absolutely over it.

"No *shit*." I use my real voice rather than my cashier's chirp. His eyes widen gratifyingly. "See, when you get locked outside by a *haunted house* in the middle of *March,* and nobody is around to let you back in because they're busy doing *God* knows what—"

He moves past me in two long strides, keys clinking in his hand. He unlocks the door with his face half-hidden behind his collar.

I follow him back into the humid dark of the house, wondering if he's about to fire me and wishing I didn't have to care, wishing I'd stolen every last spoon in his stupid house.

But he doesn't say anything. We stand awkwardly in the hall, not looking at one another. The heat makes me colder somehow, the shivers moving from my jaw to my belly, rattling my ribs. He slides out of his jacket and makes an abortive gesture in my direction before folding it stiffly over his arm.

He scowls at the floor and asks petulantly, "Why can't you wear a *coat*?"

I repeat Jasper's name in my head three times to prevent myself from saying anything nasty. "Because," I answer, with only the slightest rasp of asperity in my voice, "my brother is using it."

Arthur's eyes cross mine, flashing with that terrible guilt. "You have a brother."

"Yep. Ten years younger."

His throat bobs. "And you, the two of you live with your father? Your parents, I mean."

"Oh, are we doing small talk now? Shouldn't I be *cleaning* something?" He flinches again, mouth half opening, and I cut across him before he can decide to fire me after all. "Last I heard my dad was driving trucks in Tennessee, but the Child Support people left him alone when I turned eighteen." I'd been fifteen, actually, but it was worth losing those checks to keep Jasper. "And we don't know about Jasper's dad."

Mom told us he was staying at the Garden of Eden for the summer. She said she liked him because he smelled like fresh-cut tobacco and always opened her beer first, like a real gentleman. Jasper used to ask around every August, until the lady who runs the Mexican place told him that the county sheriff started showing up in the fields and demanding H-2A visas. She heard Jasper's father went back to Managua.

"And our mom . . ." I look away from Arthur and let my voice wobble. "She's dead. Car wreck." Nobody fires you after you tell them your mom's dead.

I can't see his face, but I know how people look at you when they find out: with pity, and horror, and that strange, secondhand embarrassment, as if they've peeked inside your medicine cabinet and found something shameful inside it. Next will come the stilted apologies and the condolences, eleven years too late.

Instead, Arthur says, "Oh."

A small silence. For some reason, I fill it. "She wasn't drunk. I know what people say, but she was a damn good driver. Just—just unlucky, I guess."

She didn't think so; she used to list all her near-misses and close calls— the laced pills that landed her in the ER, the jealous boyfriend that barely missed, the fox she'd swerved to avoid—and say she was the luckiest woman alive. I argued that a lucky woman wouldn't have a list like that. I guess I won in the end.

Arthur has been working on a response for some time. Finally, he manages, "My mother," and stops. Then, "Her, too."

And then there's something sickeningly close to sympathy stuck in my throat, a terrible urge to reach toward him. I clear my throat. "I'm—look, I'm sorry—"

He interrupts, stiff and cold again, "I believe I pay you enough to buy a second coat."

I want to laugh at him. I want to explain about people like me, about the two lists we have to make and the one list we get to keep, the everything we give up for the one thing we can't. The way Jasper chews on one knuckle when he edits his videos and the way he stares sometimes at the horizon when he thinks I'm not looking, world-hungry and half-starved, and the email I received last night confirming his enrollment for the fall term. There had even been a personal note from the director of admissions, telling me how happy they were to welcome "students like Jasper" and asking me to send along a photo for their website. I'd sent an old yearbook picture, a few shots of him and Logan at their laptops, a hilarious one where he's leaning against the hotel in a hoodie, looking like an album cover.

I settle for a shrug. "The money's not for that."

"Not for what? Coats?"

"Me." I try to say it like a joke, but it comes out sounding like what it is: the flat truth. Arthur responds with a cold "I see" that makes me think he doesn't see at all, and stalks off, coat still trailing over one arm.

I don't run into him again for the rest of the day. Usually he turns up before sundown, but that evening the house remains hollow and quiet. I find my envelope waiting for me on the sitting room couch.

Beneath the envelope, neatly folded, smelling faintly of winter air and woodsmoke and something else, is a long woolen coat.

Arthur tells himself, firmly and repeatedly, that it doesn't matter. It's only a coat. So it was the last thing his mother ever gave him. So he had found her letter in its pocket after the burial, as if she'd climbed out of her grave and slipped it there herself.

(He knew it had been the House playing its little tricks, and in that moment he'd wanted to burn it to the ground for simply existing, for not fighting hard enough for what it loved. He'd torn the letter into two neat halves, instead.)

Still. It's only a coat.

But a sickly guilt trails him all evening, nipping at his conscience. He knows what to do with guilt.

He takes the sword to a large, empty room that only ever seems to exist when he's like this: restless and tense, his bones buzzing under his skin. He moves through his drills with a ruthless, graceless efficiency. His mother had been a natural to the sword, as if she had spent her whole life waiting for someone to put a hilt in her hands. She fought like an apocalypse, like a great and inevitable ending. Arthur fights like a butcher, fast and ugly. But still: he works until his shoulders shake and his tendons are hot wires around his wrists.

It isn't enough. He turns to books next, dragging himself through a tacky guidebook to European cryptids. He pauses to sketch an eighteenth-century headstone, engraved with a depiction of the twisted, sinuous animal that— one foggy night—supposedly dragged a woman to her death. The guidebook claims it was an enormous, bloodthirsty otter, but the locals used the word "*beithíoch.*"

Arthur opens a bound journal and records the coordinates, the proximity of the water, the fog, the symbols the natives carved above their doorways for good luck. There are hundreds of other entries, going back all the way to Eleanor Starling herself, generations of frantic research collected into an eccentric bestiary.

But Arthur has added a new column to his pages, titled "Present Activity." He refers back to the guidebook; the last reported attack was in 1927.

None, he writes, and feels a strange, sharp ache in his chest, almost like hope. Even bad stories end.

If he's careful—if he doesn't waver, if he isn't distracted—he will end this one.

Arthur opens his desk drawer and removes a glass jar of ink, a bottle of rubbing alcohol, a set of long steel needles with sharp starburst tips. He'd done his first tattoos with a ballpoint pen and a sewing needle, but he's more careful now.

He's running out of space. His arms and chest are crosshatched with stippled lines, the flesh knotted where he'd pushed the needle too deep. But if he rolls up his shirt and twists in the chair, he can reach a palm-sized stretch of skin between a pair of magpies, just below a set of crossed swords.

He chooses a Gorgoneion this time, a woman's face wreathed in serpents.

At first, tattooing was just another cold calculation, a logical piece of his plans. But he's come to enjoy it. The pop of parting skin, the sting of ink, the release. The feeling that he is slowly erasing everything soft and vulnerable, forging himself into the weapon he needs.

After a long time, he wipes the beaded blood away and checks his work in the mirror. He's copied the design well, except for a few accidental variations in the woman's face. Her chin is too sharp, and the hard line of her mouth ends in a wry, crooked twist.

I don't mind the walk to Starling House so much anymore. Wearing Arthur's coat is like wearing a small house, with shiny buttons for doorknobs and stiff woolen walls to keep out the chill. For the first time I understand how anybody could actually like winter; it's a delicious defiance to be warm when the world is cold.

I'm careful not to wear it when Jasper might see. He's good about not asking questions, but there's no reason to worry him, so I wait until the school bus is pulling out of the parking lot in the mornings before I slide my arms into the sleeves and square the collar against the late-March wind.

I'm just leaving the motel parking lot when a voice says, "Opal? Opal McCoy?"

I turn to find a pretty white woman striding toward me. She's smiling like she just caught me by chance, but her steps are hard and purposeful on the pavement. Her teeth look expensive.

"Yes, ma'am?" The words taste young and country in my mouth. "Ma'am" is for schoolteachers and hairdressers and harassed-looking moms at the grocery store; this woman is in some other category entirely. Her haircut is blunt and modern, and she wears a watch with the face turned to the inside of her wrist.

"I'm Elizabeth Baine." She pronounces every syllable of her name in a way that tells me no one has ever called her Liz. "I was hoping we could have a chat."

"Uh. About what? I'm headed to work right now, actually—"

"I'll be quick, then," Baine says, and smiles some more. It's a well-practiced expression, an efficient arrangement of muscles meant to make me smile back. *It's alright,* this smile says, *you can trust me.* The hair prickles on the backs of my hands. "You work at Starling House, don't you?"

I haven't told anyone where I've been working—not Jasper, not Bev or Charlotte, not even the hellcat—and the idea of Arthur gossiping casually about his new housekeeper makes my brain cramp.

The prickles spread up my arms and down my spine. "Maybe I do."

"Oh, don't worry." She steps closer and touches my shoulder. She smells like the JCPenney's in E-town: sterile, steam-pressed. "We keep track of things like that."

"Who's we, exactly?"

"Oh, of course!" A small, friendly laugh. "I'm with the Innovative Solutions Consulting Group. We're under contract with Gravely Power." She extends her hand. I'm aware that I should take it and tell her it's very nice to meet her—such a small lie, in the scheme of things. My arms remain at my sides, stiff in Arthur's sleeves.

Baine withdraws her hand smoothly, unoffended. "We were hoping you might be able to help us, Opal. We've been trying to get in contact with the current occupant of the Starling house for some time now."

"And why's that?" The question comes out before I can remind myself that I don't care.

"It's an issue of mineral rights and property lines—a lot of legal terms I don't understand." I bet she does; her laugh is humble, almost girlish, but her eyes are cut glass. "Mr. Gravely is always looking for new opportunities to invest in Eden, and we think the Starling property has a lot of potential. You know the plant is expanding?"

"I'd heard, yeah."

My tone must be off, because Baine says, chidingly, "It could be very good for Eden's economy."

"Sure." And then, because you can't grow up around Bev without picking up a few bad habits, I add, "They fix the leak in the fly ash pond yet? It's just everybody remembers what happened in Martin County. Massey paid what, five grand? And they still can't drink their own water over there—"

"Gravely Power is committed to the health and safety of the community," Baine says. "Now, what can you tell me about the Starling property?"

"I'm just the housekeeper." I do a friendly little shrug, trying hard to suppress Bev's voice in my head: *goddamn vultures.* "So you'll have to give Arthur a call about that."

"*Arthur* doesn't have a number listed." Baine puts a faint emphasis on his name, and I feel obscurely that I shouldn't have used it.

"So write him a letter."

"He doesn't write back." Her expression is still serene. "We just hoped you might convey the seriousness of our interest to Mr. Starling. This could be a very profitable arrangement." A precisely timed pause before she adds, "For all of us, Opal." This time her smile says: *I know how you work.*

And she does. I can feel my lips stretching in an ingratiating smile, my spine softening. I open my mouth to say, *Yes, ma'am,* but what comes out is "Sorry. Can't help you."

I can't tell which of us is more surprised. We stand blinking at one another, neither of us bothering to smile. Distantly, I notice my fingers are gripping the cuff of Arthur's coat.

I turn away, fighting the urge to run before I make any other bad choices or worse enemies.

Baine's voice reaches out after me. "Mr. Gravely knows about your situation." I stop walking. "It pains him." Her tone has a triumphal undercurrent, like she's pulled a winning card, except I don't know what game we're playing. The only Mr. Gravely I know is the man with hands like boiled eggs and hair the color of raw liver, the man who owns the power company and half the county. It's difficult for me to imagine that he even knows my name. Is this supposed to be another bribe? Or—my chest contracts—a threat?

I look back over one shoulder, hard-eyed. "I don't know what situation you mean, but we're just fine."

Baine makes a face that's probably supposed to be sincere. "He wants to help you, Opal."

"Why exactly would Mr. Gravely give a shit about me?"

"Because . . ." Her eyes move over my face, slightly narrowed. I have the impression she's performing a number of quick calculations. She swallows them with another smile. "Because he's a good man. He really loves this town, you know."

I doubt it. The Gravelys have that big house on the edge of town, but they're always vacationing and traveling.[11] I bet Don doesn't know which dogwoods bloom first or how the train whistle sounds at night, hollow and lonesome. I bet the tap water tastes like blood to him, because he's not used to all that metal in his mouth. I don't know if I love Eden, either, but I know it all the way down to its rotten bones.

I shrug one shoulder at Baine and say, "Sure," in a tone of voice that rhymes with *fuck off*. The fog swallows her silhouette before I hit the main road.

Arthur is even more sullen than usual that morning. The flesh beneath his eyes looks bruised and swollen, like overripe fruit, and he limps slightly when he walks away. I don't ask about it, and I don't mention Elizabeth Baine or her profitable arrangement.

It's easy to forget about her while I work. I bury myself in dusting and sweeping, scraping mold off window frames and dumping mud dauber nests out of drawers. The only thought that surfaces, again and again, is that I am no longer the only person interested in Starling House.

---

11. The original Gravely Manor sat very near the site of the power plant. It was abandoned following the death of the youngest Gravely brother in 1886 and caught fire shortly afterward. No member of the Gravely family has lived in Eden since, and few of them visit for more than a day or two.

NINE

I should head straight back to
the motel after work, but instead
I text Jasper working late again and take
a right before the old railroad bridge.
This is the best view of the power plant,
the towers lined up across the river like
the turrets of a castle, the ash pond
like a tarry black moat. After that there's
a pitted, scrubby stretch of Gravely
land, where nothing much grows.

Bev says that's where they buried Big Jack, because it was against twenty or thirty regulations to do it on company land.[12]

I make it to the Muhlenberg Public Library an hour before closing time.

Charlotte is bent over the computer banks, blond braid draped over one shoulder, glasses perched on her head, explaining to a patron that color copies cost twenty-five cents a page. The tone of her voice suggests she's explained this several times already, and expects to explain it several more, so I lurk in the New Arrivals section until she heads back to the front desk.

She greets me with a drawled "Well look who finally decided to turn up," but there's no malice in it, because Charlotte is constitutionally incapable of malice. She forgives late fees before the notices even go out and never calls the cops on drunks that fall asleep in the library armchairs; she personally tutored Jasper before his PSAT and she's the one who marched into the principal's office when one of his classmates told him to go back to Mexico. Even Bev sits up straighter and runs her fingers through her hair when Charlotte comes by.

"Hey Charlotte. How's things? School treating you well?" Charlotte has been taking online grad classes for years now. God knows why—they hired her with nothing but an English degree from Morehead State, and after more than a decade in Eden it seems unlikely that she'll be fired, no matter how many assholes complain about her rainbow decorations every June.

"Well enough. Where you been?"

I tuck my hair behind my ear. "Lots of extra shifts lately, is all."

"And how's Jasper?"

"Great. Fine." I elect not to tell her about the weird mood he's been in, or that we're in between inhaler shipments, so he's been waking up wheezing at two or three every morning, running salt water through his nebulizer until he can breathe again. Sometimes he can't fall back asleep afterward, and I wake in the morning to find him hollow-eyed and wan, hunched over his laptop. He still hasn't let me watch whatever he's working on.

"Anyway, I was just wondering . . ." I walk my fingers across the desktop and bounce them on the stapler.

---

12. The burial was, by all accounts, a frustrating event. The operator worried that the substrate was porous and friable, causing a series of small landslides that constantly refilled the grave. The reporters complained about the wait, and the weather. The fog wasn't good for their cameras.

Charlotte slides the stapler out of my reach. "Yes?"

"Do you have anything on the Starlings? Like, local history stuff?"

I'm expecting her to faint with joy—she's been working on a history of Eden for years now, and spends her weekends looking at microfilm and photographing old gravestones—but a pair of creases appears around her mouth. "Why?"

"Bev told me a story about it and I just got curious." I do a casual shrug. Her eyes follow the expensive lines of Arthur's coat, and the creases around her mouth are joined by a third between her brows. She taps a coworker's shoulder. "Morgan, can you cover the desk? Come on back, Opal."

I follow her to the oversized storage closet she refers to, somewhat aspirationally, as the archives. Craft supplies and book donations are piled between cardboard boxes and old issues of *The Muhlenburger* and the Greenville *Leader-News*.

Charlotte thumps a tower of plastic totes labeled *Gravely Estate.* "Do you remember when Old Leon Gravely died? It's been ten or eleven years now—liver failure, I heard. Pretty sudden. Anyway, when his brother took over the company he gave all his papers to the Historical Society, along with a generous donation. If we've got anything about the Starlings, it'll be in here. Both those names go way back."

I look from the totes back to Charlotte. "Okay. Would you maybe like to give me a hand? Or some tips?"

"I don't know, Opal. Would you maybe like to tell me why you've been working so much you can't stop by to say hi, and now you turn up wearing a man's coat and asking about the Starlings?" Charlotte is so sweet that I sometimes forget she's smart.

I consider. "No?"

Charlotte stares back at me, and for a short middle-aged librarian wearing glasses with salmon frames it's remarkable how much she resembles a concrete wall. "Then good luck." She edges around me. "Put everything back when you're done."

Within the first five minutes, I know I'm not going to find anything. The first tote appears to contain the entire contents of an old man's desk, only haphazardly gathered into folders. There are a lot of bills and letters between lawyers and accountants. There are stray buttons and family photo albums and corks that still smell faintly of Wild Turkey. There's a few framed photos of various Gravelys cutting ribbons and shaking hands with mayors, men with hair the color of raw meat and women with mean smiles. None of them include a pale girl with wild black eyes.

The second tote is the same, and so is the third. I don't even bother with the fourth. I'm shoveling everything back, feeling stupid and hungry, when I see it out of the corner of my eye: a wisp of paper poking out from between the pages of a Bible. It's a receipt from the Elizabethtown Liquor Barn. I hold it with my head tilted, wondering why the sight of it sent a jolt of electricity through my entire body. Then I focus on the phone number written across the top in shaky pen: *242–0888.*

I know that number.

My own breath rushes in my ears. It sounds a little like a river.

I fold the receipt in neat thirds and slide it into my back pocket. Then, very suddenly, as if I just remembered an important appointment, I leave. I shove out of the storage closet, leaving the totes open and messy behind me, fumbling with the doorknob to the break room. My hands feel numb and very cold, as if they've been submerged in ice water.

"Done already?" Charlotte is standing in the break room, pressing buttons on the microwave. Her eyebrows draw together as she looks me over; I feel like an animal caught clawing out of a trap, wild-eyed. "Opal, baby, what's wrong?"

"Nothing." The air is tastes thick and wet in my mouth. I can't seem to get enough of it into my lungs.

"It doesn't seem like nothi—" The microwave dings behind her, and I startle violently. We stare at each other for a long, taut moment before Charlotte says, even more gently, "Sit down."

I sit. I stare fixedly at the Reading Rainbow posters while Charlotte microwaves a second cup of coffee. It's all so normal—the clink of her spoon against the sugar jar, the slight stickiness of the tabletop—that I feel myself returning to my own skin. She sets a mug in front of me and I wrap both hands around it. The heat scalds the pads of my fingers.

Charlotte settles across from me. She watches me with her soft gray eyes. "Listen. I've written a whole chapter about Starling House. I can tell you anything you want to know. I'd just like to know what's going on."

I give her my best rueful, you-got-me-smile, but I can tell it comes out a little shaky. "The truth is that I've been taking a couple of online classes, too, and I want to write my final architecture paper on Starling House, and I need your help." It's a good lie because it's the one Charlotte wants to hear; she's always bugging me to get my GED or take some college classes.

Her eyebrows go very flat and her accent goes more eastern Kentucky than usual. "Oh, are we both telling stories now?"

"No, ma'am, I really—"

She holds up a single warning finger, the way she did when she caught me stealing out of the break room fridge as a kid. It means: *Last chance, bud.*

I scrub the heels of my hands into my forehead, but—for once—no better lie occurs to me. "Okay. So I got a job housekeeping at Starling House, which is a pretty freaky place, but that's none of my business because I'm just in it for the money, except now there's somebody asking questions about it"—Charlotte's eyes are widening with every comma—"and I want to know what exactly I've signed myself up for." I'm not used to telling the truth, the way it just comes pouring out of your mouth, unedited, unrefined. I could keep going. I could tell her that Arthur Starling gave me his coat, that he has strange signs tattooed all down his arms and I wonder sometimes where they end, that Elizabeth Baine knew my name.

That I just saw my mother's phone number written on a dead man's receipt.

I bite my own lip instead, hard enough to hurt.

Charlotte watches me calmly. If I told Bev everything I just told Charlotte she'd give me a ten-minute lecture about fast money and bad news and shut off the internet for a week, but Charlotte takes another drink of coffee and sucks the sugar off her teeth before she says anything.

"How did Bev tell the story of Starling House?"

"She said Eleanor Starling came to town and married this rich coal guy—"

"John Peabody Gravely."

"Yeah, and then murdered him for his money? And then built the house and disappeared."

Charlotte nods at her cup. "I heard that one, when I went asking about the Starlings. But I heard a lot of other stories, too. I heard they worshipped the devil and stole little children. I heard the house is haunted, that no Starling ever died of natural old age. I even heard they keep wolves on their property, great big white ones."

I feel a smile tugging up one side of my mouth. "I thought it was Siberian tigers."

"Well, Bitsy can't decide which one sounds scarier."

"You don't believe any of it, do you."

Charlotte lifts one shoulder. "I believe if somebody's just the littlest bit different, people will make up all kinds of nonsense." Her face shifts, sobering. "But then . . . remember I was doing all those interviews for my book? I ended up on the phone with a woman named Calliope Boone, who said her family had a history with the Gravelys."

"What kind of history?"

A certain degree of discomfort passes over Charlotte's face. "Miss Calliope is Black." She does not elaborate, inviting me to consider exactly what kind of history a Black family might have with a rich family just south of the Mason-Dixon Line.

"Oh."

"Yeah."

"She related to the Stevenses?" I know of exactly one Black household in Eden; their daughter was in my grade at school, before she left for Kentucky State.[13]

Charlotte shakes her head. "No. The Boones are up in Pittsburgh now. They left Eden well before the First World War—I'd say it was Jim Crow they were running from, but Miss Calliope said it was more than that."

"What else did she say?"

Charlotte takes off her glasses and rubs hard at her eyes. "She told me a different story about Starling House. Or maybe it's the same one, seen from a different angle, I don't know." She pulls out her phone and fiddles with it, frowning down at the screen. "She let me record it. I have a transcript, but it's not the same." She sets the phone between us, the screen staring up at the ceiling, and taps play.

I hear Charlotte's voice first. "Miss Calliope? Are you all set? Okay, whenever you're ready: You said you had a story to tell me?"

---

13. This should not be mistaken for a demographic accident. Kentucky—the thirteenth star on the Confederate flag, the birthplace of both Davis and Lincoln, and the home to over two hundred thousand enslaved men, women, and children—went unmentioned in the Emancipation Proclamation, and was later excluded from Reconstruction. Many freedmen fled, and Kentucky buried their tracks quite efficiently. Their names were forgotten and their homes were torn down; their graveyards were left untended, swallowed up by poison ivy and ironweed, until eventually they were paved over for used car lots or strip malls. Their memories are preserved only by their kin, in the stories told by those who stayed, and those who left.

"No." The voice is querulous, and very old. "I don't tell stories. I tell the truth."

W e sit in silence when the recording ends.
Eventually Charlotte goes back out front to hurry the last people out the door before closing, and by nine she's locking the doors. I follow her out.

We stand together in the white circle of a parking lot light, listening to the distant clatter of the coal train and the white noise of the river.

Eventually I offer, awkwardly, "I didn't know any of that."

"No," Charlotte agrees.

"It's . . . pretty awful." I'm thinking of the old mine shaft in the river-bank, the one the city boarded up. I'm wondering how many men died down in the dark before that one little white boy, and why his death is the only one we remember.

"Yeah." Charlotte blows out her breath in a long, sorry stream. "You know I started writing a history of Eden because I liked it here?" Well, that figures; Charlotte is the sort of person who would adopt the ugliest cat at the shelter. "I didn't think I'd stay long when I took this job, but I did, and I guess I wanted to show the world why. But sometimes it feels like I'm pulling up the carpeting in an old house, and finding everything underneath has gone to rot."

My mouth twists. "Most people around here would just staple the carpet back down and pretend they hadn't seen anything." They didn't like any-thing ugly or unfortunate, anything that took the shine off the story they were telling about themselves.

I must've sounded bitter, because Charlotte looks at me with concern, verging on pity. "I guess so," she says gently. "And maybe I'm no better. Maybe I'll just leave, and forget about the book. Go someplace none of it matters." She gestures at the rumpled black horizon. "Maybe you should go, too."

On any other night I'd lie to her, tell her I'm saving up money, dream-ing up some grand future. But maybe telling the truth is like any other bad habit, which gets harder to quit the more you do it. "Maybe. But Eden is . . ." I don't know how to finish the sentence.

"I know," Charlotte says, softly. "I thought I might set down roots here, too." When most people in Eden talk about their roots they're waving rebel flags and making bullshit arguments about the Second Amendment, but it sounds different in Charlotte's mouth. It makes me think of an apple seed spit carelessly by the side of the road, sprouting despite the bad soil and the fumes, clinging hard to the only patch of earth it was ever given.

She sighs. "But when I finish this degree . . . well." She exhales as she turns away. "People aren't trees, Opal." Her shoes tap across the blacktop.

"Hey. Could you send me that transcript, if you get a chance?"

Charlotte hesitates. She nods once. "Don't spread it around. I know where you live."

By the time I make it back to the motel I still haven't thought up a good story to explain how late I am, but I shouldn't have worried: Jasper's bed is empty. My heart seizes before I see the note on his pillow. *Went over to Logan's, will catch the bus with him tomorrow.*

Logan's dad is a roofer and his mom works in the county clerk's office, which means the Caldwells have a pool table in the basement and name-brand coke in the fridge. They're members of the PTA and the Rotary Club and they always bring tinfoil vats of mac 'n' cheese to the church dinners and send out color-coordinated Christmas cards full of foster kids, even though they're only a few years older than me.

I hate them.

The note ends with a cold *P.S. We're out of cereal* instead of his usual *x*'s and *o*'s, so I'm pretty sure Jasper's pissed at me. I should text him and find out why, but I'm tired and overcaffeinated and secretly relieved to have the room to myself tonight.

I don't have to wait for my brother to fall asleep before I can sit cross-legged on the bed and prop the laptop on the radiator. I close the open tabs—job search engines, a special effects tutorial, the Gravely Power website, for some reason—and open "document 4."

I wait. After a while, an email appears from the Muhlenberg Public Library staff account. The subject line reads: *Interview 13A—Calliope Boone.*

I open the attachment and read it again.

This is the truth about Starling House.

Once there were three brothers who made their fortune in coal, which is to say: flesh.

The Gravely brothers built themselves a nice big house on the hill, with two staircases and real glass windows, and then they built a row of rude cabins on the banks of the river. The first person they purchased was a man named Nathaniel Boone, from the Winifrede Mining Company. Nathaniel taught his fellows how to dig deep, how to shore up the shafts, how to wring coal from the earth like blood, and for a number of years the Gravelys did very well. But every mine runs dry, given time, and every sin comes home to roost.

By the middle of the century the easy coal was gone and profits had declined. The Gravelys might have scraped by another few years, making their living on the backs of better men, if it hadn't been for the election of 1860. If it hadn't been for Antietam and the proclamation that came after, and the way Nathaniel and the other miners paused sometimes at their work, as if they could feel the great gears of the world shifting beneath their feet.

The Gravely brothers determined to get as much coal out of the ground as they could before their time ran out. The oldest brother was the worst of them, a man with skin like sour cream and a heart like anthracite. Under his gaze Nathaniel and his men dug deeper and faster than they ever had before, driven down and down into the earth. When Nathaniel Boone spoke of those months, even decades later, his eyes would blacken as if he were still stuck in the lightless deeps of the mines.

They heard rumors, now and then, that the Constitution had been amended, but the Constitution didn't seem to apply in Eden. Each dusk Nathaniel went to sleep in the same rude cabin, and each dawn he shuffled into the same dark earth, so that the sun itself became a stranger to him, harsh and foreign. One of the younger men evinced his hope that someone would take note of the chains around their ankles and object, and Nathaniel laughed at him; there had been chains on his ankles for ten years, and nobody in Eden had ever objected.

There was nowhere to go but down, so Nathaniel kept digging. He dug so deeply and so desperately that he reached the bottom of everything, and even then he didn't stop. He kept digging until he fell through a crack in the underside of the world, straight down into Hell itself.

Nathaniel would never say what it was like down there, not even to his children or grandchildren. All he would say is that the Bible only got it half right: there were demons aplenty, but no fire at all.

The mist rose high that night, licking white up the bank, and the next morning the oldest Gravely was found bloated and blue in the Mud River. The men he owned, or thought he owned, were long gone.

Only Nathaniel Boone was still in Eden. He wasn't sure why; there was a missing place in his memory, as if he'd fallen asleep and dreamed dark and lovely dreams for days. When he woke he was climbing back toward the light, his hands slick on limestone and pale roots. He emerged from a crack in the earth and found himself in the low, wet woodlands to the north of town. He could have run then, but he didn't want to, or didn't want to have to, or maybe he just didn't want to leave Eden to thrive behind him, without any comeuppance at all.

So he took work on the riverboat that brought dry goods from Elizabethtown. And spent his days courting a freedwoman from Hardin County. She wanted to settle up north, and Nathaniel promised they would—but they lingered a long time after their wedding. They needed to save up a little more, he said. Or wait for the winter, or spring, or for her cousin's second baby to be born. Every night when they climbed into bed his wife dreamed of brick row houses and electric streetcars, and Nathaniel dreamed of the Gravelys.

He dreamed them falling down stairs and choking on chicken bones, drowning, dissipating, taking ill and never rising. He dreamed of himself, sometimes, riding the steam train out of Eden with his wife beside him, leaving behind nothing but gravestones.

But the Gravelys kept on living, the way men of their station always seemed to. Nathaniel was considering taking matters into his own hands, despite certain promises to his wife, when he saw a different possibility standing at the very edge of the Mud River: a white girl in a gray dress, the hem black with water.

He recognized her, of course. Miss Eleanor had turned up at the Gravelys' a little while back, big-eyed and thin, like a sickly songbird, and they'd taken her in. People said they did it out of the kindness of their hearts, but Nathaniel, who knew the Gravelys didn't have hearts, was less sure.

Now here she stood, looking down at the river like it was her long-lost lover. She took a single step forward into the water, and Nathaniel said, softly, *Wait.*

She looked up at him with a distant, harassed expression, as if he'd interrupted her hanging laundry on the line. He asked her what she was doing, and she answered that it was her wedding day. She said it as if that were a perfectly sufficient explanation, and Nathaniel supposed that it was; hadn't he himself dug a hole to Hell to escape the Gravelys?

He tied his flatboat to a leaning birch and waded ashore. He pulled Miss

Eleanor back from the water and drew the stones gently from her pockets, not because he pitied her—in his calculation, every bite of food and stitch of clothing the Gravelys gave her had been bought with his blood—but because he thought the two of them might briefly share a common purpose.

He asked Miss Eleanor if he could tell her a story, and if she still wanted to walk into the river after he told it, he swore he would not stop her. She agreed, so Nathaniel told Miss Eleanor a story about the hole in the world, and the place beneath it, and the things that lived there. He'd told this story once before, to the freedwoman he would one day marry, and she said if he loved her he would never go back to that place. But Miss Eleanor didn't love anybody, and nobody loved her.

She listened very carefully while Nathaniel spoke. When he was done, she did not walk back into the river.

Thus Nathaniel was not surprised to hear of John Gravely's death or the footprints they found in the mines. He was not surprised when the widow was found laughing among the sycamores on the north end of town, and he was not surprised that she built her great, mad house there.

He was only surprised once, many years later, when he came home to find a note slipped under his door, which advised him to leave Eden as quick as he could "in memory of an old kindness." It was signed with a small bird drawn in harsh black ink. A grackle, maybe. Or a starling.

Nathaniel left. When his wife asked him why, he told her there was no longer any reason to stay. Eden's comeuppance had finally arrived.

TEN

The town seems different the next morning. All the details are the same—the crooked awning of the pawnshop, the sour smell of the river, the faces staring out at me from behind cracked windshields, lips pursed—but now it all strikes me as purposeful, perhaps deserved, like the punishment for some grand sin. I know that part of the story must be made up, because there's no such thing as curses or cracks in the world, but maybe that's all a good ghost story is: a way of handing out consequences to the people who never got them in real life.

I walk to work with the collar of Arthur's coat turned up, thinking about Bev's story and Miss Calliope's truth, trying to decide if they're the same thing. It's like one of those optical illusions that's either a cup of wine or two faces about to kiss, depending which way you turn it.

The Gravelys are either victims or villains; Eleanor Starling is either a wicked woman or a desperate girl. Eden is either cursed, or merely getting its comeuppance.

It's none of my business, of course, but it's better than thinking about Jasper eating a hearty home-cooked meal at Logan's house, or Charlotte moving away. And it's a hell of a lot better than wondering why a rich old man kept my mother's cell number tucked in his Bible.

I'm more than halfway to Starling House when an engine hums somewhere behind me. I step well over the white line to let it pass.

Except it doesn't. It slows down, purring along beside me. For a wild second I think the Department for Community Based Services has really upped its game and they're coming to haul me in front of a judge for falsifying my birth certificate, among several other petty crimes, but nobody who works for the state of Kentucky has ever driven a car like this: sleek and low, with windows like polished black mirrors. My own face shines back at me, a pale oval caught in a scorched tangle of hair.

The back window scrolls down. My reflection is replaced by Elizabeth Baine's smiling face.

"Good morning, Opal. Let me give you a lift."

I have the sinking sense that this isn't the kind of offer you can refuse, but I try anyway. "No thanks."

Baine's smile widens. "I insist." She's already opening the car door. "You and I have a lot more to talk about."

"Do we?"

She slides across the black leather seat and gestures to the empty space beside her. I waver, caught between the satisfying choice (flip her off, keep walking) and the smart choice (play stupid, don't piss off the rich lady with friends in high places).

I get in the car. There are two men up front, both of whom are wearing dark suit coats, neither of whom looks back at me. I have the absurd sense that I've fallen out of Eden and into a B-rated spy movie, that someone is about to shout "Get her!" and drop a black bag over my head.

Baine merely leans across me to pull the door closed. "We're all set, Hal." The driver nods once and pulls back onto the road. An apple-shaped air freshener swings jauntily from the rearview mirror.

"So." Baine pivots in her seat. "Opal. I wasn't completely candid with you yesterday. I told you that my consulting firm was working for Mr. Gravely, which we are, but we have other clients who are very invested in our work here. The mineral rights to the Starling property are just one of several interests we're pursuing."

Each individual word seems sensible and reasonable, but they refuse to add up into sentences in my head. "Okay," I say.

"Our team identified some fascinating—maybe anomalous—data in this area, and we were hoping to interview some locals about it."

It's too hot in the car. I feel sweaty and stupid, bundled like a child in this ridiculous coat. The chemical taste of the air freshener fills my mouth. "Like what kind of . . . anomalous data?"

Baine twists her watch around her wrist. "Some of that is proprietary, of course, but some of it you could see on the census. The average life expectancy, the rates of heart disease, most kinds of cancer, addiction, asthma . . . fatal car accidents." Her eyes flick mildly up to mine as she says the last one. I hold my face still and think, calmly: *What the fuck.* "All those statistics are two or three times the national average, in Eden."

I lift one shoulder in the so-it-goes shrug everyone in this town learns before they start kindergarten. "Bad luck, I guess."

Baine tilts her head back and forth. "Bad luck doesn't usually have an epicenter. Here, let me show you." She bends to rifle through a plastic case at her feet and I look out the window. Hal is a slow-ass driver; we're still at least a mile from the front gates, and the fake-apple syrup of the air freshener is sliding down my throat, turning my stomach.

Baine slides a slick white tablet into my lap and scrolls to a satellite map in wrinkled greens and browns. I've never seen Eden from this angle, but I recognize the lush green of the Starling land, separated from Gravely land only by the muddy ribbon of the river. The power plant looks like a crop sign this way, a series of circles and scars. The ash pond is an ink stain on the blank page of Big Jack's grave. Bev says they buried him with all his guts and fluids still inside, which is why nothing will grow right on that land no matter how much fertilizer and fescue they spray at it.

There are little red dots spattering the image, labeled with long strings of letters and numbers. The dots are clustered more densely toward the north end of town, gathered like ants around an empty square of land. The picture must have been taken in winter, because I can see the pale bark of the big sycamore that stands in front of Starling House.

Baine reaches over to swipe sideways on the screen. There's a picture of a newspaper headline from the 2000s: FOUR DEAD IN PLANT EXPLOSION; INSPECTORS CITE MANUFACTURING DEFECT.

She swipes again. A screenshot from the Bowling Green *Daily News* describing a grisly incident at the strip mine, where the boom fell on four workers. She swipes again, and again, headlines blurring together into a litany of misfortune: CHURCH FIRE STILL UNDER INVESTIGATION; HISTORIC FLOOD LEAVES DEVASTATION; DEATH TOLL RISES AT GRAVELY SANATORIUM.[14] Wrecks and suicides, overdoses and cancer clusters, missing children and collapsed sinkholes and freak accidents. Some of them look brand-new, grabbed from online papers, and some of them are so old the paper is the color of weak coffee.

The screen swells and distorts in my vision. I close my eyes, suddenly carsick, and when I look back at the tablet there's a picture of the Mud River in winter. There are men in uniforms standing on the shore, their shoulders squared as if against a strong wind, although I know the air was perfectly still that morning. In the water behind them, just visible above the blur of the current, is the cherry-red bumper of a '94 Corvette.

She told me once I was conceived in the backseat of that car. God knows where it came from, or what she traded for it.

The headline seems to rise toward me, hovering above the screen in all caps: CONSTABLE MAYHEW SAYS MOTHER OF TWO DROVE INTO RIVER. Baine taps the first line of the article with the smooth arch of her fingernail. "Jewell," she says softly. "What a pretty name."

And then I'm drowning.

I'm fifteen and cold water is pouring through the windshield. The glove box is open, spewing pill bottles and plastic utensils. Mom is beside me, her limbs drifting gently, her hair tangling with the tacky dream catcher she pinned to the car roof. I'm reaching for her hand and her fingers are slick and limp as minnows and I might be screaming—*Mom, come on, Mom*—but the words can't make it past the river in my mouth. And then everything goes very quiet and very dark.

---

14. The Gravely Sanatorium was established in 1928 by Donald Gravely, Sr., as an ill-fated attempt to find profit in Eden's disused mines. After several obliging doctors testified to the healing properties of subterranean life, fifteen tuberculosis patients were lowered into the mines, where they lived in cramped underground huts. None of them survived the winter, but Donald Gravely never considered it a total failure, as he was then able to offer ghost tours for a quarter a head. Several participants claimed they could still hear coughing down in the mines, and heavy, panting breath.

I don't remember letting go of her hand, but I must have done it. I must have crossed her name off the list in my head and swum for the surface, abandoning her to the river bottom, because the next thing I remember is vomiting on the shore. Clay beneath my fingernails, grit in my teeth, ice in my chest. The shine of the power plant through the bare branches, a cold sun that refused to rise.

I drifted away from myself, dreaming, and in the dream I was not cold at all. I was not the bad-luck daughter of a bad-luck mother, an accident washed up on the shore of a poison river. In the dream I was held tight, safe and warm inside a pair of arms that didn't exist.

Later, the ER nurse told me that's how you feel right before you freeze to death.

They discharged me after forty-eight hours, but for weeks afterward I could feel this coldness in the middle of me, like something in my chest had never quite thawed. I even went back to the hospital and made them x-ray my lungs, but they said everything looked good. I guess that's just how it feels to find out what kind of person you are; to know, when it comes right down to the mean wire between living and dying, what you'll do.

"Opal?" Baine says my name gently, as if she's concerned about me, as if she didn't engineer this entire sick experience. I want to dig my fingernails into her cheeks. I want to open the car door and leap out rather than linger another second in the candy-apple stink of this car.

I keep my hands very still in my lap. I might be sick and dizzy and suffering from *classic PTSD,* but I still know better than to bleed in front of someone like Elizabeth Baine. "Yeah. Jewell." My voice sounds ordinary, almost careless. "I'm named after her, sort of. She picked my name off a list of birthstones, so we're both jewels. Get it?"

Baine sits back a little, studying my face. It's hard to focus on her features, so I close my eyes.

"Is that how she picked Jasper's name, too?"

His name runs through me in a dark current, tensing my jaw, curling my fingers into fists. When I open my eyes Baine is smiling again. This one says: *Bingo.* "There's no need to be alarmed. We're a research group. We just did our research." Her tone is soothing, hands palm up. "And we were hoping you would help us do a little more."

"I don't un-understand." My tongue feels foreign in my mouth, a wet muscle fumbling against my teeth.

Baine slides the tablet off my knees and swipes through several screens very quickly. "It won't take much of your time. We just want to know more about your employer and his residence. If you could just answer a few questions for us, keep in touch—maybe send a few pictures, tell us if you see anything interesting—we would be very grateful." On the word "grateful" she shows me the tablet again. The URL blurs unpleasantly in my vision, but I'm pretty sure I'm looking at my own PayPal account, except there's an extra comma in the balance. My stomach coils tight.

I don't know what she wants, but I already know what I'm going to say. When somebody turns up in a fancy car and knows way too much about you—where you work and how your mother died and your little brother's given name—you say whatever will get them to leave you the hell alone.

It shouldn't even be hard. What do I care if some out-of-towners get pictures of Starling House? What do I owe Arthur, other than forty hours a week of housecleaning?

But the answer gets lost somewhere between my brain and my tongue, caught in my throat. His coat feels very heavy on my shoulders.

Baine takes her tablet back. "Oh, and if you bring anything else off the property, we'd like to purchase it from you." The gate key burns cold against my breastbone. I'm careful not to reach for it. "There will be no need for Jasper to list anything else on eBay. Stonewood has very high standards of behavior, after all." Her voice is delicate, almost apologetic, as if she dislikes the game she is playing but is obliged to win it anyway.

Somewhere beneath the haze of panic and fury, I almost admire her efficiency. She might be a doctor reading an X-ray of my innards, pointing precisely to each wound and fissure. My answer comes out soft and easy, then. "Okay."

Baine pats my knee. Hal pulls over near the front gates and idles while I tell them everything I've seen or thought or guessed about Starling House. I do a pretty shitty job of it—telling things out of order and doubling back, stumbling over my consonants and trailing off, my thoughts derailed by the sour taste of betrayal and fake apple flavoring—but they don't seem to care. A little red light winks at me from the tablet.

Eventually I run out of words and sit swaying and blinking in the sickly heat. Baine reaches across me to open the door. "Thank you, Opal. We'll talk more soon." I scrabble back into the clean winter light, feeling the air like cold hands cupping my face.

The trees shiver above me. A cloud of birds rises from the branches, scatters, coalesces, screams down at us.

Baine leans out the window, watching.

"They do it to evade predators, apparently." I cannot, in that moment, imagine what she could be talking about. "The way they flock. We brought in an ornithologist, and he said these are a genetically distinct population, but not a remarkable one. Except that they do this"—a nod at the sky, where the starlings twist and wheel like smoke in the wind—"more often than is typical, given the low number of natural predators nearby."

I blink at her, swaying. "So?"

Her eyes move finally away from the sky to land on me. I can still see the dark, wild shape of the birds reflected in her sclera. "So we'd very much like to know if they have any unnatural predators." Baine gives me a false, concerned frown as the window glides up. "You don't look well. Take it easy, okay?"

I watch the car disappear over the crest of a hill. I try to count to ten in my head, but the numbers won't stay where they belong, so I give up and pull the key out from under my collar. It rests heavy in my hand.

The driveway feels shorter today, a quick twist through the woods that leaves me dizzy and panting on the front steps. I raise my fist to knock, but the door whips open before my knuckles land.

Arthur glowers down at me, heavy-browed and sullen, even more hunched-up than usual. There's a bruise yellowing along his jaw and a burst blood vessel in one eye. He gives me an insolent once-over, mouth twisting. "You're late."

The idea of him skulking on the other side of the door, waiting for me to show up just so he can give me shit about it, strikes me as very funny, so I laugh at him.

Then I puke across his shoes.

Arthur didn't sleep the night before. The mist had risen for the second time in a single week—an unsettling coincidence which had happened more and more often these last few years—and he'd spent hours stalking the halls, blade held high, listening hard for the sound of something that shouldn't exist: the susurration of scales against wallpaper, the tap-tap of claws across hardwood floors. He found it on the spiral stairs, still half-formed and weak, lost in the clever maze of the House, and sent it scattering into nothing once more.

After that he'd sagged onto his mother's couch, watched by all the Wardens that came before him, and waited for the sun to rise. For Opal to arrive with her overloud knock and her overbright smile, for the House to fill with her relentless humming.

The sun came, wan but warm; Opal did not.

He supposes it's possible that she's grown tired of wasting her days with housekeeping and petty theft, that she'd waltzed out the door the previous evening with her paycheck and her crooked teeth, never intending to return. This is, of course, his dearest ambition, and does not distress him in the least.

He begins to pace, glaring out windows, scratching at the scabbed lines of the Gorgoneion. The House is restless, too, settling and shifting beneath his feet. The fire won't stay lit and the forks clink tunelessly in their drawers. The light in the kitchen pops as he passes beneath it, the bulb staring down at him like a mournful gray eye.

He finds himself staring out a third-floor window, scowling at the horizon. A black rush of birds startles into the sky near the road, just above the gates. Arthur knows just by the shape of them, the outraged pattern they make against the gray, and that those people must have come back.

He's felt them circling, watching, buzzing like flies against the property lines. He's seen the vehicles idling at the gates and ripped out the sensors and wires they leave behind. He's found the elegant business cards wedged in the front gates and received the bland corporate letters, and he's burned them both.

Arthur has read enough records from the previous Wardens to know they aren't the first outsiders to come calling. There have been explorers and journalists, cultists and spies, generations of Gravelys and their damn lawyers. All of them want the same thing: to exploit, to extract, to profit, to throw open doors that should remain closed. So they followed the stories and starlings to his front gates.

They've never gotten any farther. Part of the duty of the Warden is to ward the walls, to feed the land a few drops of blood, fresh and hot, so that it never forgets who is and isn't a Starling.[15] Elizabeth Baine will never set foot on his property, unless she is much cleverer than she seems.

Or, he supposes, simply patient. She would have to wait until Arthur has found a way past that final door, the one that has no key. Until he's descended into the dark and done what none of the previous Wardens have ever managed. The gate would swing wide for her then, but it wouldn't matter, because the House would be only a house, with nothing beneath it but worms and wisteria roots.

The starlings settle back into the branches. The car is gone.

A moment later, Arthur feels the gates open. He presses his forehead hard against the glass.

A figure emerges from the woods, a scrawny shape swallowed by the black square of his coat, her face white beneath the red blaze of her hair. The sight strikes him as entirely and dangerously correct, as if she should always be wearing his clothes, walking toward his House. It's difficult to tell, but he thinks her face might be tilted up toward his; the possibility makes all his scars itch.

It's not an itch, of course. It's that tedious, boyish hunger, which he hasn't indulged since he returned from school. Luke sent a few letters, but Arthur burned them unopened. Luke had always been too soft, too sweet; after an hour in Starling House he would have run screaming and never come back.

He watches Opal walk closer and thinks, inanely: *She keeps coming back.*

The House sighs around him. He raps his knuckles against the sill hard enough to sting, unsure which of them he's trying to reprimand.

He tries to make himself as forbidding and unpleasant as possible when he opens the door, but Opal doesn't notice. She looks up at him with her eyes gone odd and dark, her freckles stark against bloodless cheeks. She laughs at him. And then—

Arthur stares down at his shoes, spattered with stringy bile.

---

15. In 1970, for example, a young man named Steve Burroughs became convinced that Starling House was a site of "significant spiritual energy." Having been rebuffed at the front gates, he attempted to tunnel beneath the eastern wall. He went missing for three weeks. Upon his return, he fulfilled his mother's greatest wish and joined the clergy. When asked why, he said that—having seen Hell—it seemed only fair to see Heaven. The relevant entry in Eva Starling's journal reads only, *House: 1, Jackasses: 0.*

Opal wipes her mouth on her sleeve, swaying a little, and whispers, hoarsely, "Sorry."

He gestures her wordlessly into the hall. She stumbles a little over the threshold and his hands give a traitorous twitch. "Bathroom?" His voice is indifferent. She nods, lips white.

Her footsteps are usually light and furtive, like those of an animal ready to bolt, but now she walks heavily, bones loose, shoes scuffing. Arthur's arm hovers at her back, not quite touching her.

"Sorry man. I mean Arthur. I mean Mr. Starling. About your shoes I didn't mean to." Her sentences run in a strange, flat rhythm, as if someone shook the punctuation out of them. "I'll clean it up just give me a sec."

There's an anxious note in her voice that makes his stomach twist with guilt. As if he cares about the state of the House, as if he hasn't purposefully overfilled the tub when it annoyed him, watching the water drip through the ceiling with black delight.

In the bathroom he settles her on the closed lid of the toilet and hands her a cup of tap water. She drinks and he kneels awkwardly on the tile, close enough to catch the sugary, chemical scent on her clothes. The room is much smaller than he remembers it; he grinds an elbow surreptitiously into the wall. It takes no notice.

"Thanks. Sorry about the mess. I'll take care of—"

He makes an embarrassed grimace. "Don't worry about it."

She nods sloppily, sloshing water. "Okay. Okay sure." Her forehead is sheened with sweat, her throat flushed.

"May I take your coat? Here." Arthur reaches up for the top button, but Opal jerks back so hard she rocks the porcelain tank behind her.

"*No.* It's mine." She frowns down at him, blinking as if she can't quite focus on his features. Up close her eyes look wrong, her pupils swollen and glassy, her irises reduced to slim rings of silver.

"Are you—are you *high*?" Arthur is almost relieved; so few of his problems are mundane.

She blinks, then she laughs again. It echoes off the tile, hollow and brittle, and leaves her panting. "Oh, go to hell Arthur Starling." She swallows hard. "Sorry sorry don't fire me I'm just a little carsick or something because Hal is a shitty driver and I had to read all those headlines. Which is funny because most of the bad luck in this town never even makes it into the headlines. In third grade the ceiling collapsed like three feet from

Jasper's desk[16] and the last time I went swimming I got my foot caught in an old trotline and nearly drowned and—" She's forced to pause for air. "—and I never looked at any pictures of the accident before—it was an *accident,* Constable Mayhew can go *fuck* himself—" She pinches her own lips together, hard.

Acid guilt rises from Arthur's stomach to his throat. There are no accidents in Eden.

Opal unpinches her lips. "I'm not feeling great. And I didn't really want to spend the morning playing twenty questions about you and your creepy-ass house."

The pipes whine in the walls and Opal pats the cast-iron lip of the bath-tub in absent-minded apology. Arthur pretends not to notice.

He takes the cup from her hands and says, mildly, "Someone was asking about me?"

"Yeah. I was walking along and this corporate lady pulls up in a nice car with a cheap air freshener and tells me—"

"You were walking?"

Opal gives him another unsteady frown. "I just said that."

"Why were you walking?" He doesn't know where she and her brother live, but the nearest house is at least a mile away, and it was chilly this morning.

"Be*cause,*" she enunciates very clearly, as if Arthur is the one who is drugged, "I had to get to work."

"Well why didn't you—" He feels suddenly very stupid. "You don't have a car."

Opal curls her lip. "Anyway this lady gave me a ride and then she gave me money to spy on you and that's why I'm late."

Arthur's fingers go numb. He thinks, distantly, that Elizabeth Baine must be cleverer than she seems.

He looks up at Opal, her hands gripping her own knees, her clothes reeking of something sick and sweet, her frown not quite covering the black memory of terror in her eyes.

He recalls in that moment the real reason his mother forbade him from

---

16. Jasper was actually in fifth grade when a portion of the Muhlenberg Elementary School roof collapsed. A state audit came to no definitive conclusions; they suggested that perhaps an animal had died above the fifth-grade classroom, given the degree of rot and mold present in the debris.

getting a pet: once you open the door, you never know what else might come in. Or what might get out.

As a boy he'd thrown fits over her rules, beating his heels against the walls, half mad with loneliness, but now—shaking with rage on his bathroom floor beside a girl who is not as brave as she pretends, who lies and steals and walks in the cold without a coat to earn money that isn't for her—he knows his mother was right.

He stands abruptly. The boundary walls will need walking, the wards tending. "I have to go."

Opal flinches back from the sudden grate of his voice. On any other day she would hide her feelings behind an artificial smile, but now she gives him an honest glare. There's reproach and betrayal in her face, as if she forgot for a few minutes to be afraid of him and resents the reminder. "I didn't—" She tucks a coil of hair behind one ear. "I didn't tell them anything. Promise."

The words sound cheap and plastic, like fake pearls; whatever they gave her must interfere with her natural talent for lying. He molds his face into a careless sneer. "Can't see why I'd care. Tell them whatever you want."

He tries very hard to mean it. To recall that it doesn't matter who they harass or drug or threaten, so long as the gates remain locked. That he is the Warden—the last Warden—and there is more at stake than the well-being of one girl, no matter how many times she comes back.

He leaves her sick and lost-looking in the bathroom, her arms crossed over her middle. Bits of plaster crumble from the ceiling, rapping against his skull like flicked fingers, and he digs his thumbnail into the wallpaper as he passes.

ELEVEN

I spend the next couple of hours laid out flat on the sofa, my face buried in the cushions, letting the springtime smell of the house drive the syrupy taste out of my mouth. I sort of hope Arthur will stomp back in to bitch at me, but he stays away. I hear the front door open two or three times, and the low rumble of his voice, as if he's speaking on the phone he doesn't have.

Around noon I get up, puke in the kitchen sink, and drag myself to the front hall with a bucket and a rag. But my mess has already been scrubbed away, leaving nothing but a damp spot and a faint lemony smell.

The rest of the afternoon passes slowly. I swipe half-heartedly at cobwebs and dust things I've already dusted. Mostly I just wander, leaning sometimes against the walls, running my palms along the banisters, as if the house is a pet or a person.

If the wall gives a little beneath my shoulder, if the wood feels warm under my hands, I tell myself it's a side effect of whatever the hell was in that air freshener.

I wind up in the library again. I often do, by the end of the day. It's the smell, all dust and light, or maybe it's the quiet I like. There are no echoes or creaks or sudden noises in this room; I have the sense that I could put two fingers in my mouth and whistle, and the room would muffle the sound before it left my lips.

I pick a book not quite at random. I've gotten into this weird habit of letting my fingers trail along the spines until one of them feels right, a sort of staticky heat against my palm. (Arthur caught me doing this once and said *What are you doing?* And I said *Nothing!* and he glared very hard at the bookshelf, as if letting it know he had his eye on it.)

I settle into the best armchair, the one where the sun always seems to be falling obliquely across the page, and let the book fall open.

It's a collection of Hopi folklore, printed on cheap yellow paper that flakes and cracks under my hands. The pages are heavily annotated, with the word "*sipapú*" circled and starred throughout.[17] I'm too tired and headachey to actually read much, but something slips out of the pages onto my lap.

It's a single sheet of notebook paper, pressed flat but deeply grooved, as if it was folded and refolded several hundred times. The handwriting is square and plain. The bottom half has been torn away.

The first two words on the page are *Dear Arthur.*

Later, I'll wish I hesitated. I'll wish I was the kind of person who thought about decency and privacy, right and wrong—but I'm not.

I slide my arms into Arthur's coat and shove the page deep into the pocket. I walk calmly to the sitting room to collect my pay, and then I leave. The air swallows the sound of my steps.

I pause only once, at the front door. I tell myself I'm just tired and dreading the walk back to the motel, but the truth is that I don't want to leave, don't want to step back into that map scattered with red dots, each one a disaster.

I call myself several bad names, including *chickenshit* and *fool,* and leave.

---

17. *Sipapú* is a Hopi word roughly translating to "the place of emergence," and is generally characterized as a hole in the earth, or a deep cave.

There's a dark shape waiting under the trees. I have a split second's impression of headlights and tires, Starling House reflected in a wide windshield, and very nearly panic—but the thing parked in the drive is not sleek and black. It is in fact the vehicular opposite of Elizabeth Baine's car: a prehistoric pickup, its hood dented, its paint gone a powdery periwinkle with age. The tires are matte black, brand-new, but there are orange patches of rust around each wheel well, and spidery lines of dirt crisscrossing every window, as if the entire thing had been overgrown with vines until very recently.

Arthur is standing by the driver's door, looking cross and bored in a puffy coat that shows several inches of bare wrist. He should be intimidating, blocking the drive with his face stark and half-shadowed in the setting sun, but intimidating men don't clean up other people's vomit, in my experience.

I stop when I get close, hitching my hip against the wheel well. "Hi."

A stiff nod.

I point my chin at the truck. "Whose car?"

His lips ripple. "My father's. He liked . . ." He trails away, apparently unable to tell me what his father liked. He adjusts the side mirror instead, his hands gentle, almost reverent. "I cleaned it up. Hasn't been driven much since . . ."

I consider waiting him out, letting the silence stretch him like a man on one of those medieval racks, but I find a small measure of mercy in my soul, or maybe I'm just tired. "What exactly is happening right now?"

Arthur exhales, abandoning the mirror. "What's happening is that I'm asking you not to walk home."

"It's not my ho—" I catch the word between my teeth, bite it in half. "So are you offering to drive me?"

His eyes meet mine for the first time, flashing with an emotion I decline to identify. "No." He holds out a stiff arm and something clinks in his fingers. It's another key, except this one isn't old and mysterious. It's cheap metal, with the Chevy symbol engraved on the head and a little plastic flashlight on the key chain. "I'm offering you a car."

My hand, half-outstretched for the key, freezes in midair.

This is not a candlestick or a coat, something a rich boy would never miss. This is a temptation I don't want, a debt I can't pay. Mom's entire life was a house of cards built from favors and charity, bad checks and pills. She never closed a tab or paid a parking ticket; she ripped the tags off in dressing rooms and owed everybody she ever met at least twenty bucks. When she died her house of cards collapsed around us: the junkyard took the Corvette, her boyfriend took the pills, and the state did its damnedest to take Jasper. All we had left was room 12.

But I'm trying to build something real for us, a house of stone and timber rather than wishes and dreams. I work for what I can and steal the rest; I don't owe anybody shit.

I slip my hand back into my coat pocket without taking the keys. The stolen letter gives a recriminatory rustle. "I'm good, thanks."

Arthur's eyes narrow at me, arm still stiff between us. "I didn't mean forever. Just until your work here is through." Another flash across his eyes, bitter black. "I don't like people asking questions about this place."

"Oh."

"And take this, too." He says it carelessly, as if it's an afterthought, but the piece of notepaper he pulls from his jacket is folded in a crisp square. He tips it into my hand along with the Chevy keys, fingers carefully not touching mine.

"I don't—is this a *phone* number?" The sevens are crossed with old-fashioned lines, the area code bracketed in parentheses. Hardly anybody in Eden bothers with the area code because it's 270 all the way to the Mississippi, and who would visit from farther than that? "Since when do you have a phone number? Or a phone?"

It's difficult to pull off a really convincing sneer after giving a girl your number, but Arthur makes an admirable effort. "Just because I didn't give *you* my number doesn't mean I don't have one." He slides a matte black square out of his pocket as proof, pinching it awkwardly between thumb and forefinger. There's a filmy look to the screen. He hasn't even peeled the plastic cover off yet. "If those people bother you again . . ." He shrugs at the paper in my hand.

"Okay." I blink down at the keys and the phone number, feeling disoriented, suspicious, as if Bev just asked to adopt me or Jasper brought home a B+. "Okay. But who are they? And why do they want—oh, come *on*."

But his shoes are crunching past me up the drive, his shoulders pinched tight. He disappears back into Starling House without looking back.

I slide into the driver's seat of the truck, hands strangely clammy. I never got my license—a fact I will withhold to share with Arthur later, whenever it seems funniest—but I know how to drive. Mom taught me. You'd think, the way she loved that Corvette, that she wouldn't have put a preteen behind the wheel, but she was the kind of person who didn't like to eat dessert unless you had some too. The last time I had my hands on a steering wheel she was in the passenger seat, head tilted back, eyes closed, smiling like nothing had ever gone wrong or ever would.

I look up as I turn the key in the ignition. There's a single light flickering from the highest window of the house, soft gold in the near night. A lonely figure stands silhouetted behind the glass, his back turned to the world.

Jasper still hasn't come back (I'd texted him hey lmk if you've been murdered or joined a cult, and he'd replied not murdered and then, by the grace of Lord Xenu), and room 12 is too quiet without him. I wake often that night.

The first time it's the sound of tires on wet pavement that gets me, and the sudden conviction that a sleek black car is pulling into the parking lot. The second time it's the old, bad dream, the one where Mom is drowning, her mouth open in a soundless scream, her hair drifting like red kelp, and I'm rising away from her, leaving her to the dark.

I turn up the heat and wrap myself in that ridiculous coat before getting back under the covers, driving back the cold memory of river water in my chest.

The third time it's the hellcat who lives under the dumpster. She wakes me with her usual strategy of sitting on the sill outside and staring at me with such predatory intensity that some ancient mammalian instinct makes the hairs stand up on the back of my neck. I ooch down the bed and kick the doorknob open with my bare foot, but she remains perched on the windowsill, looking out across the parking lot as if it's pure chance that she was staring holes through my screen at dawn.

I glare at her hunched-up shoulder blades, marveling that anything so desperately needy could be so willfully unpleasant, and then I fish Arthur's number out of my coat pocket.

The letter comes with it.

I hadn't forgotten about it; I just hadn't felt like reading it when I got back to the room. Apparently reading the stolen correspondence of someone who has just cleaned up your vomit and given you his father's truck was too low, even for me.

But now it's lying right there on the bed, a scrap torn from Arthur's vast quilt of secrets, and nothing's really too low for me.

Dear Arthur,

I hope you don't get this letter for a long time, but I know you will. I'm not much for reading, but I've read everything the other Wardens left behind, and they all felt like this at the end: worn down, wrung out. Like when you sharpen a knife too many times and the blade goes thin and brittle. And then one bad night, it breaks.

And there are so many bad nights. Seems like the mist rises more often than it used to, and the bastards go down harder than I remember. The floors are sagging and the roof leaks. Don Gravely's boys are pecking at the property lines again, like crows. You'd think a Gravely would know better, but he's a hungry one, and some mornings I'm too tired to walk the wards. Your father says I've been talking in my sleep.

I don't know. Maybe whatever's down there is getting restless. Maybe the House is weaker, without its heir. Maybe I'm just getting old.

What I know is that sooner or later—probably sooner—Starling House will need a new Warden.

This is your birthright, Arthur. That's what I told you the night you ran away, isn't

I reread the letter five or six times in quick succession. Different phrases seem to rise off the page each time, swelling in my vision: *mist rises; Gravely's boys; whatever's down there; birthright.* Then I just sit, staring at the blocky red numbers of the motel clock, thinking.

I think: He can't leave. It sounds like he tried, but he's bound to that house in some way I don't understand. Trapped in this town, just like me, making the best of the messes our mothers left us.

I think, jealously: But at least he has a home. A claim, an inheritance, a place he belongs. I've never belonged anywhere, and—no matter what I dream or pretend, no matter how dear and familiar it becomes to me—Starling House will never belong to me. I'm just the cleaning lady.

I think: How desperate must a person be, to be jealous of a cursed house?

But then I touch the page, a letter from a mother who cared enough to say goodbye, and think: Maybe it's not the house I'm jealous of.

My phone buzzes on the bedside table. It's a text from a number I don't recognize, with a faraway area code that makes my guts twist: Enjoyed our chat. We'll be in touch soon.

I go very still, then. The entire scene in Baine's car had acquired a wavering, bad-trip quality, extremely unlikely to my sober mind. But I remember what she wanted from me, and I remember the way she pulled Jasper's name like an ace out of her sleeve.

I raise my phone and take a single, slightly shaky picture of the letter.

It's exactly the sort of thing she's looking for. It's proof that there's something bad and strange going on in that house, something *anomalous*. I can almost see the letter being dissected fiber by fiber in some distant lab, distilled into a set of data points.

The hellcat saunters through the open door without looking at me, as if she hadn't been shamelessly begging at the window. She settles on a fold of Arthur's coat and begins kneading the fine wool, growling a little in case I try to touch her.

Without thinking about it, without deciding to, I delete the picture. I fold the letter back into my pocket and withdraw Arthur's number instead.

I am aware, on some level, that six A.M. texts are well outside the boundaries of the housekeeper-and-homeowner relationship, but I picture his face upon being woken even earlier than usual—the offended red of his eyes and the black weight of his brows—and can't help myself.

do you have canned tuna

Three little dots appear and disappear several times in response, followed by: Yes. He doesn't ask who it is, either because he has some spooky sixth sense or because—the thought feels sharp and fragile, like it ought to be swaddled in Bubble Wrap—he hasn't given this number to anyone else.

I don't write back.

Twenty minutes later the truck is parked in his driveway, ticking softly to itself, and I'm knocking on the front door of Starling House. The air has a sweet, green smell this morning, like running sap, and the birds are flitting bright between the trees. The vines on the house are covered in corkscrews of new growth, waving gently at me.

Arthur greets me with his customary glare, his features twisted and sour. I could almost imagine I hallucinated the previous day, the sight of him folded uncomfortably on the bathroom floor, looking up at me with his face young and uncertain, his hands scarred and huge around that ridiculous plastic cup. I'd almost forgotten he was ugly.

But it's too late for second thoughts, so I pretend I don't have any. "Morning! I brought you something." I open my coat and the hellcat explodes out of it like one of those aliens that pops out of people's chests. She hits the floorboards, spitting, and vanishes down the hall to flatten herself under a curio cabinet. She watches us yellowly, making a sound like an old-fashioned police siren.

Arthur stares down his own hallway for several long seconds, then looks back at me. "What." He says it with a period at the end. He tries again. "What—why—"

"Well." I give him a modest shrug. "I owed you. You did give me a truck."

"I did not give you a truck."

"Seems ungenerous. I gave you a cat."

The corner of his mouth twitches upward before he bends it back into a frown, and I think the pint of blood it cost me to get her in the truck cab was probably worth it. He crouches a little to look under his sideboard. The police siren sound goes up an octave. "*Is* it a cat? Are you sure?" He straightens. "Look, Miss Opal—"

"Just Opal."

That flash in his eyes, there and gone. "I am not interested in adopting any kind of animal, *Miss* Opal. I do not want any—"

"Strays?" I ask sweetly. I'm already waltzing past him into the house. "Feel free to toss her out yourself. I'd get a good pair of gloves, though."

I go straight up to the library, counting on the hellcat to keep Arthur busy. The book of Hopi folklore is right where I left it.

I tuck the letter back between the pages and return it to the shelf. I hesitate, feeling stupid, thinking about the way Arthur's mother had capitalized the word "House."

Then I clear my throat. "Just—keep this safe, okay? Hide it."

When I return to the library later that afternoon, the book is gone.

TWELVE

Despite daily threats to the contrary,
Arthur does not toss out the hellcat.

She spends the first day skulking from
room to room like a spy infiltrating an enemy camp.
I catch glimpses of iridescent eyes under couches
and dressers, a puffed-up tail disappearing behind
a headboard. At lunch I discover her in the kitchen,
hunched possessively over a small porcelain dish of
tuna. By the following morning a box of expensive litter
has appeared in the downstairs bathtub, complete with
a tiny plastic rake, and the hellcat has colonized the
most comfortable sitting room. By the end of the week
her empire includes every sunbeam and cushion in the
house—and I would swear there are more of those than
there were the previous week, as if the house has
rearranged itself specifically to please one deranged
cat—and she greets me with the insolent stare of a
countess facing an unwelcome petitioner.

I swat at her with the broom. "Scoot, Your Highness." She gives a luxuriant stretch, bites my exposed ankle hard enough to draw blood, and trots away with her tail standing straight up like a kitten.

The next time I see her it's in the third-floor library, where she's curled in an implausibly innocent ball on Arthur's lap. The fresh wounds across the back of his hand suggest that he made the critical error of touching her.

He's giving her a reproachful, we-talked-about-this glare. "*No biting*, Baast."

"I'm sorry, what did you call her?"

Arthur jumps several inches, winces as the hellcat's claws latch on to his legs, and glares at me. "Baast." He tries to say it snidely, but there's a faint flush along his neckline. "She's a guardian goddess from ancient Egypt."

"I know that, jackass."

The flush extends to his jaw. "I'm sorry, I shouldn't have—"

"You are aware that this animal spent most of her life under a dumpster. She once got her head stuck in a Pringles can." I still have a scar from rescuing her.

"Well, what did you name her?"

"I didn't name her anything. Bev called her the hellcat and so did we."

He looks so affronted that I laugh. He doesn't join me, but his face unsnarls very slightly. He stares hard out the window. "Who's Bev?"

"A pain in my ass." I fall into the chair across from him and hook one leg over the arm. "She owns our motel, and she's always giving me shit."

Black eyes slide back to me. "Your motel?"

His voice is neutral, but I've got a good ear for pity. My chin juts out. "My mom got us a room rent-free at the Garden of Eden. You're familiar with rent? The thing you have to pay if you don't inherit a haunted mansion?"

I'm being nasty on purpose, but he doesn't flinch. He just looks at me, eyes shadowed under those ridiculous eyebrows, a question working its way to the surface. "What—what's the money *for*, then?"

"Dirty magazines." I answer flat and fast, too quick for him to stop a huff of laughter from escaping. He raises his hands in surrender and fishes an envelope from his shirt pocket.

I take the money and stand to leave, but I find myself lingering, running my fingertips over the patterned upholstery, watching the woods descend into gold and gray. "It's for Jasper," I say abruptly. "My brother. He's—super bright, and really funny, and most high school art is embarrassing but his videos are honestly so good. *He's* good. Too good for Eden." The truth comes easily, sweet as honeysuckle and just as hard to get rid of. "He got offered a place at this fancy private school and I thought if I could send him there . . . His first semester is all paid up."

"Oh." Arthur looks like he would very much like to get up and stalk dramatically off into the shadows, but the hellcat makes a small noise of warning. His hands open and close a few times before he observes, with the stilted air of a spy participating in a formal exchange of information, "I went away to high school."

"Oh yeah?" I can't picture him anywhere but here, tucked away behind iron and stone and sycamore bones, but I remember the final, unfinished line of the letter: *the night you ran away.*

"My parents didn't—but I wanted . . ." It's not hard to imagine what a fourteen-year-old Arthur might have wanted: friends and video games and notes passed in class, cafeteria tables full of laughing kids instead of frozen dinners in empty rooms. I wanted those things, too, before I divided my life into two lists. "I was only there two years before I was needed at home."

I study his face, the hooked shadow of his nose, the bruised-fruit look of the skin beneath his eyes. I shouldn't ask, because it's not my business, but he looks lonely and weary and worn-out, and I've been all of those things for a long time. "Needed for what? What does this house need from you?"

He inhales, straightening his back against the chair. "You should go. It's getting late." I think he's trying for a cold brush-off, but he just sounds sad.

"Okay, be like that. Good night, Baast, Goddess of Dumpsters." I bow to the hellcat and catch the white flash of Arthur's teeth. I award myself a point, refusing to wonder what game we're playing or why I would get points for making him smile. "Night, Arthur."

The white glint vanishes, and he watches me leave in chilled silence. The floorboards moan an apology beneath my feet.

The evening air has a springtime hum to it, the silent sound of live things unfurling, emerging, surfacing, sprouting. I drive with the windows rolled down, letting the wild smell of it fill me up, pushing out the embarrassing ache in my chest. I don't know why I thought things would be different now, after puking on his shoes and driving his dead dad's truck and protecting his stupid secrets. Mom was always trying to turn frogs and beasts into handsome princes, but it never worked out for her. I should know better.

* * *

I don't head straight back to the motel. Instead I take an abrupt right turn, and another, until my headlights are coasting over eerily smooth lawns and concrete birdbaths.

Logan's an only child—*adopted,* his parents will tell you any chance they get, *our little miracle!*—but they live in a four-bedroom split-level on the curve of a cul-de-sac. The windows are muffled in lacy curtains, so that all you can see from the porch are the blurred squares of family portraits on the walls, the beige shapes of people around a table. The doormat reads *Blessed* in swirly cursive.

I knock, maybe a little too hard. There's a pause before I hear the re-proachful *ding* of silverware set down, the patter of footsteps down the hall.

Logan's mom is a wholesome blond woman with the bluish-white smile of a Realtor or a toothpaste ad. "Opal! We weren't expecting you!"

Eden etiquette demands a good seven minutes of seesawing pleasantries back and forth before either of us approaches the point, but I don't feel up to it tonight. Maybe Arthur is rubbing off on me. "Hey, Ashley. Can you tell Jasper to grab his stuff?"

A very slight tightening of the muscles around her mouth. "Oh, but Dan made chili! Why don't you join us?"

"No, thanks."

"But the boys are having such a nice time! They were working on those little movies of his . . . Logan's always so happy to have Jasper over." I bet he is; if Logan graduates high school, it will be because my brother carried him through every grade like a tiny, stoned baby bird. "And so are we. You know he's welcome to stay as long as he likes."

Her eyes are wide and sincere. They're always inviting Jasper on family va-cation and posting pictures on Facebook ("you have such big hearts 🙏" some-one comments) or coincidentally stopping by church functions and parading him around with whatever kids they're fostering lately, like items they won at a charity auction. Jasper says it's worth it for the high-speed internet and the full-size candy bars in the freezer; he also says I should mind my business.

I shrug at Ashley.

I can tell by the slight drawing-up of her shoulders that she would like to go coldly imperious on me—nobody on earth can do cold imperium like the girls in the county clerk's office—but she's never been quite sure where I stand in her personal chain of command. I'm neither a kid nor a parent, an awkward grown-up orphan who exists outside the comforting hierarchies of church and town, annual fundraisers and Avon parties.

I slouch uncivilly against her doorframe, still not speaking. She breaks. "I'll just—" She scurries off, calling for Jasper. Teenage moans rise in two-part harmony. Chairs scrape sullenly.

Ashley returns. "He's just packing up. Can we send you home with left-overs?" She extends a Tupperware with an air of aggressive largesse.

"No, thanks."

"You sure?"

"Yep."

She steps out onto the porch, plucking at the gold cross of her necklace. She nods at the truck parked crookedly in the drive. "That yours?"

"Yep."

"Oh, it's so cute! Me and Dan just love vintage. You know—" Her voice settles from bubbling to merely burbling. "You know, it looks sort of familiar."

"Does it."

"One of the Starlings—the one before the boy up there now—he used to drive around in a blue Chevy just like that."

And I know I should give her some vague nonanswer like *that so* or *did he now* but instead I let my eyes meet hers and say, "I know," just to watch her go pale.

"Oh, honey, I hope you don't have anything to do with that place. My uncle told me it's some kind of secret society, like a cult. I mean, it can't be a real family—he says back in his day a *Chinese* couple moved in!"[18]

"So . . ." I drawl the word out. "I shouldn't have anything to do with this house because your uncle said, quote, a Chinese couple, unquote, lived there. That right?"

Uneven patches of red bloom on her cheeks. "That's not what I—you've heard the stories." I blink big guileless blinks until she leans closer, her voice now a vicious whisper. "Listen. You might not believe everything people say, but my Dan saw something with his own two eyes." She pauses, as if hoping

18. Mrs. Caldwell's uncle might have been referring to Etsuko and John Sugita, first- and second-generation Japanese Americans who became Starlings in 1943. Etsuko drowned in 1955, and the rest of the family relocated to a modest cottage on the coast of Maine. Her daughters, now in their early seventies, remember the house fondly, but were never tempted to return. "No home," one of them told me, "should cost that much."

I'll ask her to continue. I don't, but it doesn't matter. "It was the night that turbine blew—eleven, twelve years ago now. Well, at the time Dan drove for Frito-Lay's—this was before we were even going out—and he refilled the vending machines at the plant. So he finishes up, he's crossing the parking lot when he sees that *very same Chevy*." She shoots my truck a hostile look. "And then, *boom*. The turbine blows."

I remember the boom. It was the sort of sound you heard with your bones rather than your ears, a great silent *heave* in the atmosphere. Jasper slept through it, but I sat up for hours, watching the sickly orange of the sky above the plant and wondering how many funerals it meant (four).

Ashley is leaning even closer, dark and eager. "And after all the fire trucks and EMTs cleared off, and it was just Dan in the parking lot again, he went looking for the Chevy. It was gone, but there was a trail of *blood* leading up to where it was, and a whole pool where it sat. Dan said it gave him a chill." A small silence, then: "And he said there were blackbirds everywhere, lined up on the light poles and power lines, watching him, dead silent." I bet they weren't blackbirds; I bet if you saw them in the light their feathers would have a queer iridescence, like used motor oil.

"It was a defect in the turbine." My lips feel stiff, strangely cold. "There was a whole report."

Ashley rubs a palm across the gold cross, smoothing it. "Dan saw what he saw. He reported it to the constable, but by the time they went asking around, both those Starlings were dead."

I've spent more time than is strictly rational studying the portraits in the yellow parlor of Starling House. Arthur's mother: hard-faced, strong, her knuckles scarred and swollen just like her son's. His father: long-lashed and over-tall, like a bashful greyhound standing on his hind legs. Neither of them struck me as ecoterrorists or mass murderers, but what do I really know about them? What do I really know about Arthur, with his cold silences and secrets?

Ashley is watching me with an awful compassion in her face. "I'm just trying to look out for you, Opal. I wouldn't trust a one of them. That young man—Alexander?—is likely just as bad as his parents, and twice as ugly, if you ask—"

"I'll wait in the truck." I walk back down the drive, berating myself. Why should I give a single lukewarm damn what anyone says about Arthur Starling? So he gave me a coat. So I'm driving his father's truck, which he cleaned up just for me, which he touched as if it were a poorly healed scar, still tender. He can't even bring himself to say *good night.*

Jasper slides into the passenger seat three minutes later, slamming the door hard enough to send paint chips skittering down the windshield. "Since when," he says, with frankly dangerous calm, "do we have a truck."

"Got it off the Rowe boys," I lie, blandly.

He looks pointedly at the broken handle of the glove box, the sun-faded dashboard, the seams of the bench seat, which are splitting to reveal crustaceous layers of yellow foam, lightly fuzzed with mold. "You got ripped off."

I turn the key in the ignition, already concerningly fond of the bronchial cough of the exhaust. "You don't even know how much I paid."

"You *paid* for this? Like, legal tender?" He cuts me off before I can make a case in the truck's defense. "Is there some kind of emergency? Did your appendix burst? Because I can't think why else you would see fit to drag me away from the dinner table—"

"I wanted pizza."

A small nuclear reaction occurs in my peripheral vision. "*Mr. Caldwell* made *chili*—"

I slide a twenty out of my back pocket. "*Real* pizza." Both of us are aware that this is a blatant and heartless bribe, that I am relying on his adolescent metabolism and the fact that Dan Caldwell uses bell peppers in his chili so it doesn't get "too spicy."

A moment of taut silence. Then, skeptically, "With wings?"

My phone buzzes halfway through the second box of pepperoni. It's that faraway number again. Please send interior photos of building to elizabeth.baine@iscgroup.com by 8:00pm on Friday. We look forward to working with you.

Jasper is watching me when I look up. He'd thawed somewhat beneath the sheer weight of calories, but his face is closed and tense again. "Who was that?"

I do a masterfully casual shrug. "Lacey. That guy asked for her number again at work and I told her to give him Bev's instead."

Jasper doesn't even pretend to smile. He nods at the grease spots on his paper plate. "Okay." He shoves the plate in the trash and slouches into the bathroom. A minute later I hear the petulant white noise of the shower.

I steal his laptop and waste a few minutes conducting a series of ineffective searches ("elizabeth baine isc," "isc group," "innovative solutions consulting"). All I get is a series of stock photos and corporate pages so devoid of actual information it feels like an elaborate joke. *The ISC Group is committed to finding solutions to every problem. Our consultants have a long history of bold strategies and innovative techniques.*

I pick up my phone. Set it back down.

I try to picture Arthur Starling the way I once did, the way everybody else still does—a ghoulish, shadowy figure, surrounded on all sides by sins and secrets. Instead I see him in the soft light of evening, determinedly petting a cat that has already bitten him once and will certainly do so again.

The laptop makes a soft ding. A new message notification appears in the corner of the screen, slightly transparent. I'm not generally in the habit of spying on Jasper's emails, but this one is from the Gravely Power HR department. I open it and read exactly two lines before my vision goes red and jagged.

Dear Mr. Jasper Jewell,
Thank you for your application to Gravely Power. We would love to schedule an interview at your earliest convenience.

I take two breaths, maybe three. I think about the seismic boom of the turbine exploding at the power plant. I think about the fly ash pond leaking slowly into the river, which is the reason why the health department says it's only safe to eat catfish once a year. I think about the greasy black dust that falls sometimes on close, windless days, and about Jasper's asthma attacks coming closer and closer together. The dark days and unlucky nights, the bad endings that wait for both of us, just over the horizon.

Then I think about Jasper, knowing all of that, filling out the application anyway.

Just yesterday Stonewood sent me a fat folder of forms and releases and bewildering orientation brochures. One of them showed a group of boys rowing a strange, flat boat, their uniforms perfectly ironed, their hair sandy and sideswept. There was a confidence to them, a vitality that I both hated and craved. I tried to picture Jasper sitting among them—brown and gangling, asthmatic—and felt the first breath of unease. For some reason I heard my own defensive voice in my ears: *I was just trying to help.*

But it wouldn't be like that. I was doing the right thing.

I mailed the forms back as requested, the signatures beautifully forged, and slid the folder itself into a sparkly gift bag for Jasper's seventeenth birthday, in June. I only have one payment left, which won't be a problem—so long as Arthur doesn't fire me and Baine doesn't sabotage me.

I drag the email from Gravely Power to the trash and empty the entire folder. It takes me a little googling to figure out how to block an incoming email address, but I do that, too.

Then I close all my tabs and text Baine two letters: ok.

Later—much later, after the steam from the bathroom has dissipated to a chill dampness throughout the room, and Jasper and I are both in bed, pretending to sleep—my phone buzzes again. I expect it to be Baine's reply, but it's not.

It says: Good night, Miss Opal.

Betrayal is just like shoplifting: the trick to getting away with it is not to think about it. You tuck the box of tampons under your left arm and keep walking, wearing an expression that suggests you're thinking about dinner or homework, because you are. No one ever asks what you're up to because you're not up to anything.

So I spend April doing exactly what I did during March—sweeping and dusting, scrubbing and polishing, bothering Arthur and dragging bag after bag of garbage down the drive—except every now and then I pause to hold up my phone and take a picture. At the end of each week I send an email to the address I was given, and the next morning there are questions and demands in my inbox. The foyer pictures are too blurry, please resend ASAP. Is that door locked? What's on the other side? Can you provide a rough sketch of the floor plan?

I write back at random, offering a careless bouquet of lies and half-truths and sullen *I don't knows,* provoking increasingly annoyed replies. The floor plan I draw them is laughably incomplete, and includes several rooms that don't exist. Or maybe they do—when I try to recall the precise order of halls and doors in Starling House the map twists and writhes in my head, snakelike, and leaves me dizzy.

But Elizabeth Baine and her consulting group must be getting something out of it, because they keep texting. In the middle of April I send a picture of the front door and get a flurry of emails in response: **We need better pictures of those symbols. Are there other objects like this in the house?**

There are. The place is full of the odd and uncanny: little crucifixes made of woven wood and tied with twine; silver hands with eyes in the middle; gold crosses with looped tops; sachets of dried leaves and salt, a dozen other charms and amulets strung above doorways and windows. At first I shoved them into dresser drawers and closets as I tidied, but the next day I'd find them right back where they'd been before.

Arthur had caught me once clearing a mantel into a garbage bag, swearing. He told me to leave it and I told him that lucky charms were, in my experience, total bullshit. I picked up a battered copper coin, a penny with a harp printed on one side. *Like, do you really think this will save you?* He'd answered, unusually earnest: *No, but it might buy you time.*

Then he'd stalked away, deploying his only known tactic for ending a conversation. I'd waited until I heard the clank of pots in the kitchen before slipping the coin into my back pocket.

Now I take pictures of the other objects I left on the mantel: a small mirror with eight sides, a silver heart pierced by a sword, a bundle of dried lavender. The digital shutter sounds much louder than it should.

Good work, Baine writes. **We're sending you a higher-quality phone tomorrow.**

I pick up the package in the motel office, and run into Charlotte. She's leaning over Bev's desk, her face intent.

"Oh hey, did my holds come in?"

Charlotte straightens very quickly. "No. I was just—"

She gestures at Bev, who says, shortly, "She was dropping off *my* books." She spins her office chair to face the television. "Not everything is about you, Opal."

"Oh my God, you can *read*?"

"Bite me."

Charlotte sighs a little harder than is necessary for what is essentially a civil Garden of Eden conversation. "I was just leaving." Those two little lines are framing her mouth again, and her glasses are slightly askew.

I sidestep in front of her. "Wait, I was wondering about that Gravely stuff. Do you think you could drop off one of those crates? I could help you catalog it all." I don't care about the Historical Society even a little bit, but I would like to know why a Gravely had my mom's phone number. It's probably nothing—she probably owed him money or flirted with him in the Liquor Barn parking lot or tried to sell his wife off-brand makeup—but I keep the receipt folded in my pocket anyway.

"What Gravely stuff?" Bev has spun away from a *Wheel of Fortune* rerun just to glare at me.

"Oh, did you think this was your business?" I make a sympathetic face. "Not everything is about you, babe."

This kind of overt obnoxiousness usually redirects her attention, but not this time. She shakes her head. "There's nothing you need to know about those people. Whatever it is, best leave it alone."

I'm opening my mouth to reply but Charlotte lets out a caustic little laugh. It barely sounds like it belongs to her. "Just leave it alone, huh? Just sweep it under some rug and hope nobody sees." She's looking at Bev with a degree of anger that strikes me as wildly disproportionate. She whips back toward me, braid arcing, eyes flashing. "I'll bring the first box down as soon as I get a chance."

She stalks out. The buzzer sings two flat notes as the door slams.

"Uh." I point to a crisp white box behind the desk. "That package is mine, I think."

Bev kicks it at me without looking away from the TV. I follow Charlotte out the door.

It's an overcast day, chilling toward evening, and the parking lot is full of birds. Grackles so black they look like bird-shaped holes cut in the pavement, a few crows, the speckled gleam of starlings. Charlotte cuts through them like a boat through dark water.

"Hey!" Charlotte stops but doesn't turn around, one hand fishing for her keys.

I catch up to her, shooing birds off the hood of her car. "I was just wondering. Do you believe Miss Calliope's story? Like, do you think there's really something awful under Starling House? Because I was talking to Ashley Caldwell the other night and she—"

"I don't know, Opal. Maybe. Not really." Her Volvo beeps once as she unlocks it. She slides into the front seat and pauses, looking hard at the closed blinds of Bev's office. "The only awful thing about this town is the people who live here, if you ask me."

She must mean Bev, and I experience a brief, unnatural urge to defend her. The slam of Charlotte's door saves me.

I open my new fancy phone and shove the packaging in the dumpster. If I thought about it much—the sleek, expensive shape of it, the weight of it in my palm—I might feel guilty, but I slide it into my pocket without thinking anything at all. The screen scrapes softly against the stolen penny.

THIRTEEN

April in Eden is one long drizzle. Moss sprouts in the sidewalk cracks. The river gets fat and lazy, rising until it licks the belly of the bridge and laps at the mouth of the old mine shaft. The seasonal plant nursery opens in the flea market parking lot and the ants make their annual assault on Bev's continental breakfast bar.

Starling House creaks and swells, so that every window sticks and every door is wedged tight in its frame. I expect an outbreak of mildew and weird smells, but the house merely acquires a rich, wakeful scent, like a fresh-turned field. I have the fanciful idea that if I dug a knife into the crown molding I would find green wood and sap. If I laid my ear on the floor I would hear a great rushing, like a pair of lungs drawing breath.

Even Arthur seems affected. He's altered his usual schedule of lurking and scribbling, spending more and more time outdoors. He returns with mud on his shoes and dirt beneath his nails, a healthful flush across his cheekbones that I find obscurely upsetting.

He frowns repressively if I ask what he's been doing.

"Careful, your face'll stick that way." When he doesn't answer, I make a stricken expression. "Wait, is that what happened to you? I didn't mean to be insensitive."

Arthur turns away so abruptly that I suspect the corner of his mouth is misbehaving again. He crosses to the stove to stir a cast-iron pot of something hearty and healthful-smelling. Eventually he asks, reluctantly, "What are you eating?"

I hold up a sleeve of powdered mini doughnuts from the gas station. "A balanced breakfast."

He makes a small noise of disgust and stalks away with his lunch, leaving the pot on the stove. There's a clean bowl and spoon set carefully beside it. Looking at the bowl gives me a weird, knotted feeling in my stomach, so I wad the doughnut wrapper in my pocket and get back to work. The next morning there's half a pot of coffee waiting, velvety and black, and a skillet of fried eggs on the stove. My phone hums against my hip. It's not poison, you know.

I waver, worrying about debts owed and the food of fairy kings. But would it be so terrible to be trapped forever in Starling House? The banisters gleam, now, and every windowpane winks as I walk by. There are fewer cracks in the plaster, as if they're sewing themselves shut, and just yesterday I found myself lying in one of the empty bedrooms, pretending it was mine.

I eat until my stomach hurts.

It's impossible not to feel guilty, then. I'm not used to it—guilt is one of those indulgences I can't afford, like sit-down restaurants or health insurance—and I find I don't like it much. It perches heavy on my shoulder, ungainly and unwelcome, a pet vulture I can't get rid of.

But I can ignore it, because I have to. Because I learned a long time ago what kind of person I am.

I've been checking Jasper's email every night, but there's been no follow-up from the power company. Just notifications from YouTube videos and promo emails from U of L. Jasper's been moody and evasive, always checking his phone and curling his lip when I ask him what's up, but whatever. I can ignore that, too.

I throw myself at my work, instead. By the beginning of May I've scrubbed and polished the entire second floor and most of the third, and Starling House is clean enough that I've started flinching when Arthur hands me my envelope at the end of each day, wondering if this will be the last time.

I work longer and harder, conscious that I'm inventing new tasks but unable to stop. I bleach yellowed bedsheets and beat rugs; I order polish online and shine all the silver I haven't stolen yet; I buy two gallons of glossy paint in a color called Antique Eggshell and repaint the baseboards and windows in every room; I watch a YouTube video on window glazing and spend three days fooling with putty and tacks before dumping it all in the garbage and giving the whole thing up. I even ask Bev how to patch plaster, which is a huge tactical error because she drags out a trowel and a bucket of mud and makes me practice by fixing the hole in room 8 where a guest punched through the drywall. She sits in a folding chair and shouts unhelpful advice, like a dad at a kids' soccer game.

I knock my forehead against the wall, not gently. "If you tell me to feather the edges one more time I swear to Jesus I will put another hole in your wall."

"Be my guest. Oh wait! You already are, forever."

"Not my fault you made a bad bet with Mom."

Bev spits viciously into her empty can, her lips pressed tight. "Yeah." She nods at the patch on the wall. "I can still see the edges. You have to *feather* it—" I throw my trowel at her.

Spring in Kentucky isn't so much a season as a warning; by the middle of May it's hot and humid enough to make my hair curl, and there are only two rooms in Starling House left untouched.

One is the attic with the round window—I started up the narrow steps one day with a bucket and broom, and Arthur opened the door with an expression of such profound spiritual alarm that I rolled my eyes and left him to stew in whatever nest he calls a bedroom—and the other is the cellar.

Or at least, I think it's a cellar—it's whatever is waiting beneath the trapdoor in the pantry, the creepy one with the big lock and the carved symbols. I haven't pulled up the rug since that first day I found it, but it tugs at me. It feels magnetic, or gravitational, like I could set a marble down anywhere in the house and it would roll toward it.

Elizabeth Baine seems to surmise its existence somehow.

Is there a basement or crawl space in the house?

I reply with that shrugging emoticon.

A terse silence of several hours, then: Please find out if there is a basement or a crawl space in the house.

I let her stew for a while before writing back, I'm really scared of spiders sorry. I add an emoji shedding a single tear, because if she's going to black-mail me into selling out a man who quietly doubles all his recipes for me, I'm going to make her regret it.

Baine replies with a string of annoyed texts, which I ignore. She mentions *karst topography* and *ground-penetrating radar* and includes several blurry aerial maps of Starling land.[19] I turn my ringer off.

The next time I check my phone there's a picture of the Muhlenberg County High School. It's an odd angle, taken behind the football field, where the bleachers back up onto a sea of feed corn. It wouldn't be remarkable at all, except that I know it's where Jasper eats his lunch every day—and so does she.

I stare at the picture for a long time, feeling that cold place in the middle of me.

The next day I roll back the rug in the downstairs pantry and send her a picture of the trapdoor. She's thrilled. Exactly where is it located? Is it locked? Do you know where the key is? And then, inevitably: Could you find it?

I'm not surprised by the request—you don't drug a person and threaten their only family member if all you want from them is a nice conversation and a couple of email attachments—but I'm a little surprised how much I don't want to do it. I delay as long as I can, backtracking and seesawing, sending back obnoxiously long lists of all the places I've looked for the key without finding it. She urges me to try harder and I send even longer lists in response, with footnotes. She suggests that perhaps I could pick the lock, making delicate mention of my school disciplinary reports; I reply that I was

---

19. Karst topography is characterized by large deposits of limestone and is very favorable for the develop-ment of caves and sinkholes. There have never been any significant caves discovered in Eden, but a local motel owner has no doubt of their existence: "Between the caves and the damn mines, if you yell at one end of Kentucky, you'll hear it on the other."

a shitty teen who knew how to open cheap doors with a credit card, not an old-timey bank robber.

In the end I receive a text that directs me very simply to open the cellar door by Friday. There are no threats or dire warnings, but I scroll back up to look at that picture of the high school until the chill spreads from my chest across my back, as if it's pressed against a stone wall.

The next day I wait until I hear Arthur's footsteps on the stairs. The sullen scrape of the coffeepot, the squeal of hinges, the squelch of boots on wet ground. Then I put down my paintbrush, thump the lid back on the can with the butt end of a screwdriver, and go up to the attic room.

It seems to take a very long time to get there: the staircase stretches end-lessly upward, doubling back on itself more times than is strictly logical, and I make a dozen false turns on the third floor. The fifth time I end up standing in the library I sigh very hard and say, to no one in particular, "You are being a real dick about this."

When I turn around, the narrow staircase is behind me. I brush my fingers along the wallpaper in silent thanks.

Arthur's room isn't messy after all. It's bright and clean and hot, floor-boards baking in the lavish light of May. There's a desk beneath the window and a bed under the eaves, quilt tucked neatly around the mattress because of course he makes his bed every morning. I consider rumpling his sheets just to be a pill, but the thought makes me feel suddenly sweaty and restless, and anyway the hellcat is curled in the middle of his bed giving me a one-eyed glare. I stick my tongue out at her and look elsewhere.

On the wall at the head of the bed, hanging in a heavy bracket, there's a sword. It doesn't look like a toy or a Ren faire prop. The blade is rust-mottled, chipped and scored, but the edge is sharpened to invisibility, like the point of a snake's tooth. There are symbols running from hilt to point, inlaid in soft silver, and I know with chilled certainty that Elizabeth Baine would have a seizure if I sent her a picture of it. I turn to the desk instead.

The surface is painfully tidy, all the pens nib-down in a coffee cup, all the books stacked and sticky-noted. The top drawer contains an array of overlong needles and pots of ink, a few paper towels stained a watery red. It should have occurred to me before now that the nearest tattoo place is in

E-town. That he must sit up here with his sleeves rolled high and his hair hanging in his eyes, pressing the needle into his skin again and again.

I shut the drawer too hard, feeling irritable, overwarm.

The next drawer is full of pencil shavings and little stubs of charcoal. The third drawer is empty except for a ring of keys. There are only two keys on the ring, both old and ornate.

Just as my fingers brush the iron, there's a muffled *thud* behind me. I flinch—but it's just a freckled black bird at the window. It flaps querulously at the glass, as if offended to find an entire house this high in the air, then vanishes. It leaves me with my heart ping-ponging against my ribs and my eyes very wide.

Every inch of the wall around the window is obscured by paper and thumb-tacks, as if an entire art museum had been crammed onto an attic wall. At first I think they must be early drafts of the illustrations for *Underland* and my stomach does a nauseous somersault—but no. Eleanor Starling worked in brutal black-and-white, her lines biting like teeth across the page, and these drawings are all gentle grays and soft shadow. There are Beasts stalking across the pages, but they're subtly changed. Arthur's Beasts have an eerie elegance, a terrible beauty that Eleanor's never did. They step gently through quiet woods and empty fields, obscured sometimes by graphite knots of briar and honeysuckle.

They're good drawings—so good I can almost hear the rattle of the wind through the branches, feel the give of the loam under my shoes—but the perspective is odd, tilted down instead of straight-on. It takes me a minute to realize this is how the world looks seen from the windows of Starling House.

I remember myself suddenly as I was: walking alone down the county road in my red Tractor Supply apron, looking up at this amber-lit window and hungering for the home I never had. Now I know Arthur was sitting on the other side of the glass, just as alone, dreaming of the world outside.

My throat tightens. I tell myself it's the dust.

There's a small sketch pinned just beneath the window, rougher and quicker than the others. It shows the woods in winter, the pale bellies of the sycamores, the doubled ruts of the drive. There's a figure emerging from the trees, her coat oversized, her face upturned. All the other pictures on the wall are strictly pencil and charcoal, but this one contains a tiny shock of oily color, the only bright thing in a sea of gray: a smear of rich, arterial red. For her hair.

Something small and delicate goes *ping* in my chest. I snatch the keys and run.

I clatter down the stairs and back into the hall, not thinking about the keys in my hand or the fancy phone in my pocket or the way his face might've looked as he drew me: half annoyed, half something else, dangerously intent.

On the first floor I get turned around and find myself in the chilly mud-room behind the kitchen, tripping over cracked rubber boots, and the next door I open takes me out into the humid light of spring.

The sky is hazy blue and the air is spangled gold, as if the sun is shining from everywhere at once. I peel off my tennis shoes—I would peel off my skin if I could—and step away from the shadow of the house, headed no-where, anywhere.

I walk, following a faint trail worn in the grass, studying the mad pattern of vines up the stone walls. There are leaves on the vines now, still translucent and damp-looking, and fat clusters of flower buds. The honeysuckle by the motel is already a ferocious, man-eating green, so this must be something else.

I turn a corner and stop abruptly, stunned by the sudden riot of color. Flowers. An uneven circle of lilies and daisies, lavender bursts of chicory and pale constellations of Queen Anne's lace. A hot red riot of poppies, wildly out of place among the gray stone and shadows of Starling House.

Arthur is kneeling among them. There's a pile of weedy green beside him and his hands are black with earth. Rows of gray stones surround him, stark and sinister among the riotous flowers. It's only when I see the name STARLING repeated on the stones that I understand what they are.

Arthur is kneeling beside the newest and largest gravestone. It bears two names, two birth dates, and a single date of death.

I should say something, clear my throat or scuff my bare feet on the grass, but I don't. I just stand there, barely breathing, watching him as he works. All the twist has gone out of his face, gentling the line of his brows and the arch of his nose, unpinching his lips. His hands are tender around the fragile roots of the flowers. The ugly, brooding Beast I met on the other side of the gates has disappeared entirely, replaced by a man who tends his parents' graves with gentle hands, growing flowers that no one will ever see.

The house exhales at my back. A sweet-smelling breeze pulls the hair out from behind my ear and bends the heads of the poppies. Arthur looks up then, and I know the second he sees me his face will rack and warp, as if someone turned a key in his flesh and locked him against me—except it doesn't.

He goes very still, the way you do when you see a fox at dusk and don't want it to disappear just yet. His lips fall open. His eyes are wide and black, and God help me but I know that look. I've gone hungry too many times not to recognize a starving man when he kneels in the dirt before me.

I'm not pretty—I've got crooked teeth and a chin like a switchblade, and I'm wearing one of Bev's old T-shirts with the sleeves ripped off and swipes of Antique Eggshell across the front—but Arthur doesn't seem to know that.

He looks at me just long enough for me to think, in desperate italics: *Fuck.*

Then he closes his eyes very deliberately, and I recognize this, too; this is what it looks like when you swallow all your hunger. When you want what you can't have, so you bury it like a knife between your ribs.

Arthur stands. His arms hang wooden and awkward at his sides and his eyes are a pair of sinkholes. The light is still warm and honeyed, but it no longer seems to touch him.

"What are you doing here." There are no question marks in his sentence, as if all his punctuation has calcified into periods.

"I didn't mean—are those—" My eyes flick to the gravestones at his back, then away. "I just got turned around in the house and ended up out here somehow."

The flesh of his face contorts, pulled taut across the bones. It's that same bitter fury I've seen so many times, but I'm no longer sure it's directed at me.

"I—" I don't know what I intend to say—*I understand,* or *I don't understand* or maybe *I'm sorry*—but it doesn't matter because he's already striding stiffly past me. He pauses at the wall of Starling House, his silhouette rippling in the window. Then, in a quick, passionless gesture, he puts his fist through the glass.

I flinch. Arthur withdraws his arm from the jagged hole. He stalks around the corner with his shoulders hunched and his left hand a mess of blood and dirt. A door slams, and the wind whistles sadly through the missing tooth of the windowpane.

I don't follow him. I can't stand the idea of being in the same room, facing him with the memory of his eyes on my skin and the weight of his stolen keys in my pocket. Betrayal works best when you don't think about it, and now I can't think of anything else.

I slip past the door to grab my shoes and slide into the cab of the truck. I press my forehead hard against the steering wheel, digging the plastic into my skull, and remind myself very firmly that I am in this for the money. That Arthur Starling and his mysteries and his stupid-ass eyes—however ardent, however ravenous—are not on my list. That today is Friday and Elizabeth Baine will be expecting a reply.

I pull out my phone and open her last email. *Sorry, tried my best!* I type back. *No luck.* I add an insincere frowny face and—before I can think twice, or even once—I hit send.

There's no response that night. For a little while, I can pretend there won't be one at all.

FOURTEEN

I've dodged enough consequences to know when there's one coming. I feel it as a weight in the air, a thundercloud massing above me, raising the small hairs on my arms.

I spend the weekend waiting for the lightning to strike, checking my phone too often and sniping at Jasper over nothing. I try to make it up to him by driving him to Bowling Green to see a movie, but he's fidgety and distracted the whole time, and when the credits come up he "doesn't feel like" sneaking into the new slasher movie playing on the next screen over, even though the poster is scary enough that I see a mom shielding her kid's eyes as they pass.

He makes me wait, blinking and sweating outside the Greenwood Mall, while he films some ants swarming over a half-eaten apple.

"How's the video coming? The new one, I mean," I ask.

"Is that really what you want to talk about?" His tone is perfectly neutral.

"Look, I don't know what's up with you, but—"

"Finished it last week." He passes his phone over, casually, as if he hasn't shown me all his other projects just as soon as he finishes them.

I step into the shade and hit play.

A young Black girl standing in the middle of the road, her back turned. The camera circles, bringing her face into view: eyes tightly closed, mouth seamed shut. I recognize her from Ashley Caldwell's Facebook posts—one of their foster kids, kept for a while and returned, like wrong-sized clothing. The camera gets closer and closer, until the girl's face fills the screen, her face tight as a fist.

Then she opens her mouth. I can tell she's screaming, hard and long, but no sound comes out. Instead, a stream of white smoke pours out of her mouth. It rises and thickens, obscuring her features, swallowing the frame until there's nothing but swirling white.

I wait, staring, nerves singing. Just when I've decided the video must have glitched, something moves in the mist.

An animal. A long jawbone, opening wide. A snap of teeth, and the screen goes dark.

I exhale for a long time. "Fuck, dude."

Jasper smiles for the first time all weekend, shy and pleased. "Yeah?"

"*Yeah*. I mean, how did you even—those effects were unreal."

The smile turns young and eager, the way it only does when he talks about film. "First I tried renting a fog machine, but it looked like ass. Dry ice was better, but in the end I just had to wait for actual mist. Making it come out of Joy's mouth like that was basically just trial and error—"

"No, I meant the thing at the end."

Jasper's smile fades. "What thing at the end?"

"The . . ." I don't know what to call it. I thought it was an animal, but the shape doesn't make sense in my memory. The neck was long and doe-like, but there were so many teeth, and the eyes were so far apart.

"Were you even paying attention?" Jasper takes the phone out of my hands, shoulders slouched again. "Christ, it was only like a minute and a half long."

"Yes I was—"

But he's already striding back to the truck.

We drive back in silence. I break it only once, to ask if we should stop for pizza rolls in Drakesboro. He shrugs with the perfect, insolent nihilism of teenagerhood, and I very seriously consider dumping the last of my Sprite down his shirt.

Later that night, Jasper makes a vending machine run and leaves his phone lying on the bedside table. I snatch it, tapping through folders until I find a file named "scream_FINAL_ACTUAL FINAL DRAFT.mov." I watch it on a loop, endlessly repeating. I don't see the animal again.

On Monday I approach Starling House more warily than I have in a while. I hold my breath when I knock, braced for some sort of excruciating scene of confession or accusation, but Arthur merely opens the door, gives me an unusually arctic "Good morning," and turns around without once meeting my eyes. I exhale at his back, unsure whether I'm relieved or annoyed.

I listen for his steps all day, hoping for a chance to stash his keys back in his desk drawer, but he remains locked in the attic like the mad wife in a Gothic novel. I don't see him again until evening, when he withdraws an envelope from his back pocket and hesitates. He rubs his thumb along the edge and says, abruptly, "I'm sorry. If I frightened you."

It should have frightened me—smashing windows is classically beastly behavior, of the kind that only men are allowed to indulge in—but all I felt at the time was an aching, echoing sadness, like grief. I had worried later whether he washed the dirt out of his cuts properly, which strikes me now as a pretty bad sign for Team I'm Just In It for the Money.

Today his left hand is a wad of gauze tied several inches up his wrist in a clumsy knot. I clear my throat. "I'm pretty good at that stuff, if you want help changing the bandages."

Arthur looks down at his own hand, then at mine, and visibly shudders. "*No.* God." Then, as if he'd prepared a script and refuses to be derailed from it, he says stiffly, "If you would like to end our arrangement, I understand. It's not like there's much left to clean, is there." Apparently his question marks are still lost at sea, all souls feared lost.

I search his face for regret or hope, not knowing which I'd rather see, but he's doing his best gargoyle impression, his eyes fixed stonily on the wallpaper. "Guess not," I say, and he nods twice, very quickly, in the manner of a man who has received a poor diagnosis at the doctor's office and refuses to have a single public emotion about it. He reaches the envelope at me, blindly, and it slips from his fingers to the floor.

Both of us stare at it for a charged moment before I pick it up and fold it carefully into my pocket. "But there's the window trim to paint." My voice is profoundly bland. "And I was planning to rent a power washer for the front steps. They're pretty gross, honestly." The overhead light gives a defensive flicker.

His eyes meet mine for the first time all day, a brief, striking look that reminds me for no reason at all of the scrape of a match against stone. He nods a third time. "Well. The vines need trimming. While you're at it."

I am tempted to ask him exactly what the hell his deal is. Why my picture is hanging in his room and why there's the tiniest, invisible hook of a smile on his lips right now and why he wastes his life locked up in this big, mad, beautiful house, so ferociously alone.

But what if he answered? What if, God forbid, he trusted me enough to tell me truth, and gave me some secret that would make the Innovative Solutions Consulting Group wet its collective pants? And what if—even worse—I was stupid enough to keep his secrets?

So I shrug, doing my best impression of Jasper, and leave him standing in the half-light with a tiny indentation in his left cheek which might, or might not, be a dimple.

I'm halfway down the county road that evening when the consequence finally catches up with me. It's standing a couple of feet past the painted white line, where the asphalt sags into dandelions and gravel, with its thumb pointed at the sky.

I hit the brakes so hard I smell rubber. "*Jasper?* What the hell are you doing here?"

He yanks open the passenger door and slides onto the seat with his backpack cradled in his lap and his hair standing in frazzled curls. He slams the door in a way that tells me he's progressed from *sullen* to *pissed* sometime in the last eight hours. "I might ask you the same thing, except you'd just *bullshit me* so I don't know why I'd *bother*."

A lot of good lies are wasted because people go belly-up at the first sign of trouble. I hold one hand up in a peacemaking gesture, speaking in the voice

I learned from the high school guidance counselor. "Okay, I can see you're upset." ("*Upset!*") "I don't know what's happened, but I—"

Jasper thumps the dashboard. "Let me tell you what happened, then. Today in fifth period I got called to the principal's office." This would not have been noteworthy for me, who spent at least thirty percent of my brief academic career in the principal's office, but the only time Jasper's ever been in trouble was when Mrs. Fulton accused him of cheating because he got a perfect score on her stupid math quiz. "But when I got there Mr. Jackson wasn't behind his desk. Instead it was this uptight corporate bitch"—a rushing sound fills my skull, along with the syrupy smell of fake apples—"who told me she was worried about you, and hoped I could, and I'm quoting here, 'remind you of your obligations.' What kind of mafia bullshit is that? Since when do schools let strange adults talk to students alone? She locked the *door,* for fuck's sake. And she had—she said she liked my videos." His outrage wobbles, tilting toward simple fear. "I haven't even posted that last one yet."

I put the truck in gear and pull back onto the road. I should be inventing some comforting cover story, but there are exactly two thoughts in my brain, swelling like tumors: first, that Jasper swears with significantly more familiarity than I'd previously suspected, and second, that I am going to dismember Elizabeth Baine and leave her remains for the fucking crows.

"What did you say to her?"

I'm not looking at him, but I can feel the seismic roll of his eyes. "I said *yes, ma'am, thank you* and booked it as soon as the bell rang. I'm not *stupid.*"

"Good boy." It occurs to me that he didn't run to, say, Tractor Supply Company. "And did she tell you where to find me? Where I'm working?"

His second eye roll would probably register on the Richter scale. "Did you really think I didn't know? One of those candlesticks had an *S* stamped on it, for the love of God. And you're always texting people who aren't me—why is there someone named *Heathcliff* in your contacts?—and you have like zero friends. So I called Tractor Supply a month ago and Lacey told me you hadn't worked there since *February.* She says she's praying for you, by the way."

"Wow, okay. *Wow.*"

"Anyway I thought it was really dumb, but like, you seemed happy and at least you weren't getting groped by Lance Wilson anymore."

"Hey, how did you know—it was a *mutual* groping, for the record."

"A good summary of every relationship you've ever had."

I feel dimly that the ref should blow a whistle and call foul on that one, because it's not so much a comeback as a disembowelment. I'm left scooping my guts off the floor, spluttering. "As if you have any idea—you don't know what you're talking about—"

"I am literally begging you not enlighten me. Jesus, Opal." Jasper sags back against the seat with a middle-aged sigh, infinitely wearied. A half mile passes in near silence, except for the rattle of the engine and the wet whine of spring peepers through the window. "I kept waiting for you to tell me what was up." Jasper says it to the roof, his neck draped over the headrest. "The night we got pizza. The day at the movies. I thought you were psyching yourself up for it, but you never did. Instead I had to hear it from a stranger in an ugly-ass pantsuit."

It's a cool evening, and the fog is already rising off the river in pale tongues, licking over the land. It looks strangely solid in the glow of the headlights, as if I'm driving among the slick white flanks of animals. "Look, Jasper." I wet my lips, dredging every ounce of sincerity out of my insincere soul. "I'm sorry. I'm really sorry."

I chance a glance at him at the next stop sign. He's still staring meditatively at the roof. "Are you? Or are you just sorry you got caught?" I don't answer. He sighs again, far longer than seems physically possible. "That house is bad news. You know that, right?"

"It's just talk." I do a gentle, condescending snort, like a skeptic making fun of a fortune teller. "I've been working there for months and the worst thing I've ever seen is Arthur Starling in a towel."

I'd opened a door I was positive had been a closet the day before and found Arthur toweling his hair in a second-floor bathroom. He'd made a sound like a wounded car horn, a sort of strangled bleat, and I'd slammed the door so fast I stubbed my own toes. I'd spent the rest of the afternoon blinking away the bright purple afterimages of his tattoos: crossed spears and spirals, a snake bent in a figure eight, a sharp-faced Medusa grinning between two birds.

Jasper's eyebrows are in danger of disappearing into his hairline. With the air of a person stepping carefully over something unmentionably gross, he says, "And what if it's not just talk? You know Mrs. Gutiérrez, at Las Palmas? She told me her brother-in-law was driving past the gates one night and he saw that guy in the driveway. Swinging a *sword* around, at *nothing.*

Looked right at him as he passed. And that same night, her brother-in-law has a *heart attack.*"[20]

I offer no comment, trying very hard not to think of the scars on Arthur's knuckles, the sword hanging in his bedroom.

"And that house is just—not right." A strange expression crosses his face then, rigid and inward-facing. I've sat through over a hundred horror movies with him, and I don't think I've ever seen him afraid.

"Look, it's nothing, okay? I should have told you, but I didn't want you to worry."

"Opal . . ." A considerable pause, then: "I'm not your son."

"First of all, *ew*—"

"And I'm not your job. Do you get that?"

"Yeah. Yes, I do." I'm not lying, but I can't seem to tell him the truth. How do you tell a sixteen-year-old that he was the only reason you got out of bed for weeks and weeks after the crash? That the whole world was sour and ashen except for him, so you committed every kind of forgery and falsification to make sure they could never take him away from you? That he is the only thing on the only list that will ever matter?

We're on Cemetery Road now, climbing the hill past the Dollar General and the funeral home. "It's just that you deserve a whole lot more than all this." I gesture out the window at Eden. At the flickering neon of the drugstore and the fog-choked sidewalks, empty except for mean bursts of thistles and the amber halos of streetlights. "You're so smart, and your grades are so good—"

"Why do you think that is?" Jasper straightens, staring at the side of my face with a strange, coaxing urgency. "Why do you think I work twice as hard as anybody else in class?"

"Because you want out of here. I *know.* I'm working on it, just give me a little more—"

Jasper shakes his head and thumps his back against the seat. His mouth is a furious slash in the rearview mirror. "You know what? I'm staying at Logan's tonight, stop here."

"Jasper, hey, come on—" But he's already fumbling for the latch. He

---

20. Mrs. Gutiérrez's brother-in-law made a full recovery. He ascribes his survival to his grandmother's crucifix, which he wears tucked beneath his collar on a slim gold chain.

stumbles onto the curb while the truck is still moving and gives the door a one-handed slap. He turns back once. "Oh, that lady gave me a message for you." He says it with the profound disgust of someone who is too old for secret messages and codes and can't quite believe he's being forced to participate. "The message is: ten, ten, ninety-three."

He leaves, hands jammed hard in his pockets, backpack slung over one shoulder.

I idle on the side of the road for so long that the cab fills with greasy fumes and the sky turns to star-flecked soot. I wonder how Elizabeth Baine found out, and if Jasper recognized the numbers, or if even he has forgotten my real birth date. I wonder if the state would let me appeal his guardianship now that I'm a legal adult, or whether they'd whisk Jasper away from me with bonus misdemeanors for forgery and identity theft.

These thoughts are idle, distant things, because I already know what I'm going to do. I've known since the second Baine said my brother's name in the back of her car, weeks ago. Everything since then has been playing pretend, dreaming about an old house and a grand mystery and a boy with secrets and scars. People like me should know better than to dream.

Sometime before midnight I pull away from the curb and make a wide U-turn in the empty street. I drive back to Starling House with Arthur's keys pressing against my hip like cold fingers.

During the day the House could be mistaken for a mere building; at night, it never could. It has the obscure topography of a dream or a body, with endless, sinuous hallways and stairs that climb at unnatural angles. The walls heave in and out, a vast rib cage, and Arthur suspects if he were to press his ear to the plaster he would hear the subtle beating of a heart somewhere beneath all the oak and pine and plaster.

Most nights Arthur finds it soothing—it's nice to imagine that he doesn't stand alone against the Beasts, even if his only ally is a foolish old house with ambitions of sentience—but tonight the House is restless. Every nail turns fretfully in its hole and the roof tiles clack like chattering teeth. A drainpipe bangs against the wall in the anxious rhythm of a woman drumming her nails on the table. Arthur soothes it as best he can, renewing wards and double-checking charms, but the weather is mild and the doors are locked.

He lies awake for a long time, listening, and falls asleep only when Baast curls on his chest.

When he wakes, Baast is standing over him with her back arched and her tail rigid. Arthur's skin is prickling, as if a chill draft has blown through, and he is suddenly aware that the front gates have been opened. So has the front door. He looks out his round window long enough to see the ghostly creep of fog along the ground, and then he's running barefoot down the steps with the sword aching in his bandaged hand.

There is nothing on the third floor, or the second. There's a tugging sensation in the back of his skull, like the trembling of a spider's web, that leads him to the kitchen, but it's empty except for the faint phosphorescence of the microwave clock.

Something clicks, like the shutter of a camera. It comes from the pantry.

He opens the door and light glances off rusted cans and old jars, their contents gray and glutinous. The rug has been rolled back, and beneath it there is a perfect square of darkness in the floor.

The trapdoor is open.

Arthur has seen it open only once before, when he was eleven. His mother had waited until high noon on the summer solstice before she knelt on the floor and unlocked it. Then she took his hand and led him down, down into the dark.

He remembers the steps, slick and endless. He remembers trailing a hand along the walls and finding them wet, weeping cold water. He remembers crying, and his mother noticing, but not stopping.

He doesn't understand how the door was opened again—he keeps the keys safe in his room, and these aren't the sort of locks that can be picked—but his thoughts have become very slow, very simple. He is the Warden of Starling House, and the locks have failed.

Arthur goes down beneath Starling House for the second time in his life, his heart beating evenly, his tattoos burning into his skin.

The walls are smooth limestone, untouched by picks or chisels; it's like the world split open and someone built stairs in the gap. It should be completely black, but the mist has its own ghostly fox-fire glow.

The sound comes again, that unnatural click. Arthur braces his sword before him and walks faster.

The stairs don't lead to a room or a chamber; they simply end, running straight into the great slab of the first door. He sees the chains still stretched taut across the surface, and the lock still shut, but there's a shape standing before it, pale in the mist-light.

Arthur does not hesitate. He lunges down the last few stairs and swings. It's an ugly swing, a woodcutter's downward chop, but it would have been enough to sunder a fresh-hatched nightmare. Except he slips on the damp stone, or the stone slides out from under his foot, and the sword goes wide. It skrees off the limestone in a spray of white sparks.

His body slams into the shape and he flinches, expecting rending teeth and gouging claws, the scuttling, scrabbling attack of a creature with too many joints and limbs—

It doesn't come. Instead, a voice says, fervently, "Christ on a *bicycle*."

Arthur doesn't move. He doesn't breathe. He is reasonably sure that his heart does not beat. "*Opal?*"

The pale shape lifts its head and he sees a pointed chin, a freckled pair of cheeks, gray irises rimmed with white. "*Opal.* God—are you alright? Did I—" His hand spasms and the sword clatters to the ground. He runs his fingers frantically up the bare skin of her arms, over her shoulders, dreading the tacky heat of blood.

"I'm fine. It's okay." It's only when she speaks, when he feels the warmth her breath on his face, that he realizes he has her pinned against the door. That his thumb is resting in the hollow between her collarbones, just over the wild rhythm of her pulse. That the expression in her eyes should be fear, but isn't.

He steps back, too fast, and something gives an expensive-sounding *crunch* beneath his left foot. "What are you doing here?"

His tone is menacing, but she answers easily. "Cleaning. You owe me overtime, bud."

Arthur decides the heat coursing through his limbs is anger. It makes his voice shake. "I told you never to come here at night. I told you—"

"You're standing on my phone."

He exhales. Bends to retrieve her phone from beneath his left foot. Looks down at the spiderwebbed screen, breathing hard.

"Give it here."

Her photos are displayed on the screen in a neat grid. One of them appears to be the front gates of Starling House. The next one is the front door, with several close-ups of the wards. Then the library, the sitting room, the kitchen, the mudroom. "What . . . what are these?" His voice sounds muffled in his ears, as if he's speaking under water.

"Pictures." He can hear the sullen set of her chin.

He scrolls up. There are pictures of every oddity in the House: claw marks scored in the wallpaper, books in dead languages, charms and spells. It's strange to see it this way, all the evidence of his family's long, mad war captured in bright arrangements of pixels. The most recent picture is a gray stone door crisscrossed with chains. There is a ring of three iron keys dangling from the padlock. One of them is jammed awkwardly into the keyhole, although he knows the lock won't turn. Arthur has wasted hours trying.

When his mother showed him this door, she asked him how many locks Starling House had. He counted in his head: gates, front door, cellar, and the stone door beneath it all. *Four,* he answered. Then his mother held up the ring of keys and asked how many keys Eleanor had made.

Three, he said. And then, daringly, he asked why.

Because this lock was never meant to be opened.

After nearly a decade spent searching for that fourth key, he has concluded that his mother was telling the truth. But he believes there is another way through. If he didn't—if he thought he and every Starling after him would be stuck forever fighting this foolish war—he isn't certain he would get out of bed in the morning.

Arthur exhales carefully. "You stole the keys. From my room." He doesn't know why his voice should sound so wounded. He knew what Opal was: a drowning girl who would do anything to keep afloat, a thief and a liar who owed him less than nothing.

Opal doesn't answer, but the skin of her throat moves as she swallows. His fingers twitch.

"You've sent all these pictures to them."

"So what if I did?"

Arthur doesn't like the look in her face—guilty and angry but still, even now, not quite afraid—so he closes his eyes.

Opal continues, gathering speed. "So what if people have questions about this place? I have a few questions myself, actually."

"Don't. Please." He isn't sure if he says the words out loud or merely thinks them.

"For example: Where the hell does this door lead? Why did I dream about it before I ever saw it? Why did you almost behead me just now?"

"I didn't mean—"

She drives forward, voice high. "Why do you have a goddamn sword in the first place? What happened to your parents? What happened to Eleanor Starling?"

"How in hell should I know?" Arthur's mother taught him very young how to keep secrets. How to discourage questions and prying eyes, how to drive away the curious and clever. She had not prepared him for Opal. "Do you think Eleanor *explained*? She disappeared and left her heir nothing but a sword and a fucking *children's* book."

He is surprised to find he is standing very close to Opal again, looming over her. The defiance in her face makes his voice crack. "I should never have let you into the House. I just thought—I thought—" He'd told himself at the time that it was guilt that made him do it, the memory of his second-worst failure and what it had cost her, but that was a child's lie: he just hadn't wanted to be alone anymore.

An awful tenderness crosses Opal's face, that soft streak she tries so hard to hide. "Arthur, I'm sorry. About the pictures. I didn't want to, but they told me—"

It's at that moment that Arthur hears another sound: a thin scratching, like nails on the wrong side of a door.

His left hand fists in the worn cotton of Opal's shirt. He feels the flesh of his palm splitting. She looks down at his hand and back at him, and he refuses to interpret her expression, refuses to think about the swell of her pupils or the infinitesimal slant of her face toward his.

He hauls her past him, away from the stone door, and shoves her roughly up the stairs.

"Okay, what the *hell*—"

"Get out. Go home. Don't stop, and don't look back." He retrieves his sword and sets his feet, facing the door with the blade half-raised.

Opal hasn't moved. She's looking down at him with the same beaten-nail eyes he remembers from the first night he found her outside his gates, like she doesn't know what's coming but she's ready to split her knuckles about it. There's a smear of his blood on her shirt.

For the second time, he summons all the malice and madness he can, and says, *"Run."*

For the second time, he watches her run away from him, and does not regret it.

FIFTEEN

I drive too fast and park shittily, cutting slantwise across two spots in the motel lot. I sit listening to the tick of the engine and the muffled screaming of the crickets, shaking very slightly. I say, softly, "What the hell." It feels good so I say it a couple more times with differing emphases. "*What* the hell. What the *hell*."

"Hey, you alright in there?" It's Bev, thumping on the hood, wearing boxer shorts and a ratty tank top. The mist laps at her bare ankles, thickening fast.

I consider telling her the truth, I really do, but at this point it would take a bulleted multilevel list to account for all the fuckery I have engineered and endured over the last eight hours.

1) My little brother yelled at me, which sucked, but he had a point, which sucked more;
2) I failed to accomplish the task Baine assigned to me, which means:
   A) She's going to do something slimy and awful that might lose me custody of Jasper, which means:
      i) I'll have a homicide to plan on top of everything else.
3) Arthur Starling almost murdered me and then almost kissed me and then tossed me aside like used gum, and I'm not sure which of those things upsets me more.

I settle for "I'm fine. Go back to bed."

Bev glares through the windshield for another second. "Okay." She thumps the hood again. "Learn to park, meathead."

There's a plastic crate waiting outside my door with a sticky note on top that says *Gravely collection, Box #1* in Charlotte's neat handwriting. I open the door and kick the box across the threshold.

Room 12 is stuffy and mildewy. There's a faint, hormonal funk in the air that tells me Jasper swung by at some point, either to make up or to grab his stuff, but I was busy housebreaking and getting busted and probably losing my job. The thought is sudden and chilling. How could Arthur keep paying me after he caught me stealing his keys and spying on the side? How could he ever let me set foot inside Starling House again?

It occurs to me that a normal person wouldn't have this number and intensity of emotions if they lost a housekeeping job. I tell myself it's just that the money was good and I don't know how I'm going to pay Jasper's tuition next year. It's just that I was going to power-wash the steps and trim back the vines, hang fresh curtains and patch the broken bits of crown molding. It's just that I'll miss the warm weight of the walls around me and the irritable sound of Arthur's footsteps on the stairs.

I want to storm back to Starling House and thump Arthur's head against the wall until he forgives me or apologizes or presses his mouth against mine just to shut me up. I want to drive over to Logan's and have a big, loud fight with Jasper, in front of God and everybody. I want to lean my forehead against Mom's breastbone and cry, and feel the slick lacquer of her fingernails against my cheek as she lies to me. *Everything's okay, babydoll.*

I open the storage crate instead, pawing through it at random. Somehow I end up cross-legged with the Gravely family photo album in my lap. I turn the pages slowly, feeling something sharp and green gathering in my throat. Envy, maybe. We never had a family photo album. I used to sneak onto Mom's phone and scroll back as far as I could in her pictures, but there weren't any from before I was born. It's like she sprang from the skull of the world, fully formed and laughing, a woman without a history.

The Gravelys have history. The whole town still tells stories about them, and the photo album shows me a parade of family dogs and Christmas trees and birthday cakes. Cousins and uncles and dour-looking grandparents all standing in front of that big brand-new house.

The last picture in the book is a teenage girl leaning against a car the color of a maraschino cherry. Her legs are long and freckled, crossed at the ankle. Her face looks different, younger and softer than I'd ever seen it, but her smile has a brazen, reckless tilt I know better than the backs of my own hands, and her hair—you don't forget hair like that. It's redder than the car, haloed gold by the sun, so that she looks like a woman on fire.

Mom. *My* mom. Standing beside the '94 Corvette that was always too nice for her.

It took me a couple of weeks after the funeral to make myself go out to the junkyard to collect her stuff. By then the inside of the car was black with mold, the seats lightly furred. Greasy brown water poured out of the glove box when I opened it. I grabbed the dream catcher and signed the rest over for scrap.

I find, somewhat to my surprise, that my hands are moving. They're sliding the picture out of the plastic and flipping it over. On the back of the photo someone has written *Delilah Jewell Gravely, 16* in blue ballpoint.

I think: *I always hated my middle name.* Then I stop thinking.

But my body is still moving. It's kneeling on the motel carpet, right on the bare spot where my feet land every morning. It's reaching under the bed, toward something I haven't touched in eleven years and—when did I lose track of the days? When did my life become more than a long tally of days endured?

The plastic bags have gone brittle. The dream catcher is cracked and broken, the beads dangling on loose threads. The book looks different than I remember, smaller and shabbier. There are fractal blooms of mold across the cover, bruise-black, and the pages have the rotten smell of clogged gutters. But the title is still stitched along the spine in bright silver—*The Underland*—and the initials on the inside cover are still the same: *DJG.*

I asked Mom once if she was DJG. She laughed and called me Little Miss Encyclopedia Brown, which is what she called me when I was being nosy. I asked what her real initials were, and she said *whatever the hell I want them to be* with such an edge to her voice that I shut up.

Now I kneel on the floor with names tumbling through my skull like dominoes, or Old Testament genealogies. John Peabody Gravely was the brother of Robert Gravely who begat Donald Gravely Sr. who begat Old Leon who begat Don Jr., brother of Delilah Jewell Gravely, who begat me, Opal Delilah—

I balk. I'm no Gravely.

I'm a cheat and a liar, a trickster and a tale-teller, a girl born on the ugly underside of everything. I'm nobody, just like my mother before me.

But that name would make us somebodies. I can feel my own story shifting around me, the arc of my life bending out of true.

Maybe that's why I turn the page. Maybe I'm looking for a story that still feels familiar, or maybe it's just muscle memory.

The next page is empty except for the dedication, which always felt like secret code, a letter written specifically to me:

> **To every child who needs a way into Underland. Befriend the Beasts, children, and follow them down.**

I turn the next page, and the next, reading until all I can see are monsters drawn in scrabbling black ink, until all I can hear is my mother's voice, soft and warm as cigarette ash.

Once there was a little girl named Nora Lee who had bad, bad dreams. The dreams were full of blood and teeth, and they frightened her very much, but I will tell you a secret: she loved them, too, because in her dreams the teeth belonged to her.

You see, Nora Lee had been left in the woods when she was a baby, where a wicked fox found her. The fox took her back to his home and fed her sweets and watched her with hungry eyes. She knew one day soon he would gobble her up.

Nora Lee begged the other animals to help her, but no one listened. The fox always wore a coat and tails when he left the house, and smiled often, and no one believed that the owner of such a fine coat and such a wide smile could have such unseemly appetites. They told Nora Lee to hush and be a good girl.

So Nora Lee, who was not a good girl, ran away.

She ran until she came to a wide green river. She didn't know how to swim, but she thought a wide green river must be better than a fox. Just as she was about to walk into the water, a hare passed by.

"Little girl," he said, "what are you doing?"

So Nora Lee told him about the bad dreams and the wicked fox.

As it happened, the hare did not much like the fox either. So he told her about a place—a secret place hidden way down deep below the world—where even the darkest dreams might come true. He called it the Underland.

She asked the hare how to find Underland, and he told her to follow the river down. "Follow it deeper than the deepest burrow," he said, "deeper than the longest roots of the oldest oak."

So Nora Lee followed the river to the place where it disappeared into the earth, and then she followed it further. And somewhere far below everything, south of the southernmost cellar, deeper than the deepest worm, she found Underland waiting for her.

For a moment she thought she had fallen asleep, because all around her she saw the terrible creatures from her nightmares, monstrous and wrong-shaped. But the beasts in her dreams were not real; the Beasts of Underland were as real as bones or dirt or foxes.

A good girl ought to be frightened of them. She ought to run away.

But Nora Lee, who was not a good girl and never would be, did not run away. She whispered her story to the Beasts of Underland, and they rushed past her into the night, baying for blood.

When Nora Lee climbed out of Underland the next morning she found there was nothing left of the wicked fox but a clean white skull, still smiling that wide smile. For the first time, she smiled back.

Nora Lee supposed this was the part of the story where she lived happily ever after, but she didn't seem to have a knack for it. She tried, truly she did. She kept quiet and minded her manners. She built a big stone house and a big stone door. She locked the way to Underland and then she buried the key by the sycamore tree.

But still, she slept poorly. She was waiting always for the next fox to find her.

When that day came, she knew what she would do. She would unbury the key and unlock the door and return, finally, to Underland.

The Beasts would greet her as one of their own, a thing with teeth, and curl tight around her. She would sleep then, and dream her bad dreams, and live happily ever after.

SIXTEEN

I dream again of Starling House that night.

It's been a while. I've been dreaming of that house since I was twelve, but this spring the dreams have receded like a long, slow tide. Instead I get memories, hazy and worn as old Polaroids—me and Jasper jumping off the old railroad bridge into the river, back when I could still stand the feeling of water closing over my head. The two of us taking turns pressing a can of coke against our foreheads until the chill of the mini-fridge fades. Mom driving too fast with the windows down, laughing.

I thought maybe I'd outgrown the house dreams, or made some private, inscrutable pact with Starling House.

But tonight I'm walking through the halls of Starling House again, and something is badly wrong. The doors are rattling in their frames and the pipes are howling in the walls. White fog is leaking up from the floorboards, rising fast, obscuring the windows.

A calico shadow slips around my ankles and the hellcat fixes me with urgent amber eyes before darting back into the mist. I run after her, twisting from room to room, faster and faster. I slip in puddles of something that leaves the soles of my shoes tacky and gummed. I can't see the floor through the thickening mist, but I have a terrible suspicion that I'm leaving a line of red footprints behind me.

I find myself descending stone steps. The mist parts, and I see a single figure standing in the room. The figure sags and staggers, terribly wearied. The tip of his sword hovers a bare inch above the floor.

I shout his name, running hard, and his head lifts. I get close enough to see the starless dark of his eyes, the desperate twist of his lips around my name, before the mist takes him. It drags him back with white claws, through an open door. The door slams in my face.

My own scream wakes me up.

There is a little pause here. A series of seconds or maybe minutes when I lie panting against the mattress, waiting for the nightmare to fade, for reality to reassert itself, for the motherly voice in my head to assure me that it was a dream, just a dream, go back to sleep. It doesn't come.

And then the truck keys are cold against my palm and the gas pedal is rough and alien against my bare foot. I'm pulling out of the parking lot, passing the Mexican place, rolling heedlessly through the ghostly reds and greens of stoplights.

The mist has risen like dough while I slept, creeping up to swallow streetlamps, trees, even the stars themselves. I drive with my knuckles hard and pale around the steering wheel, trying hard not to think about Jasper's stupid video, or the thing that ran across the road the night Mom died—ghostly in my memory, an apparition rather than an animal—or the second after the tires left the pavement but before we hit the river, when I felt my whole life splitting neatly into *before* and *after*.

I pull over at the front gates and fall out of the cab before the truck stops rolling, skinning my palms on the gravel. I fumble for the key but I don't need it: the gates of Starling House swing wide at the touch of my bloodied hands, hinges screaming.

"Thanks," I tell them, and from the corner of my eye I see the ironwork writhe, as if the beasts want to pull themselves free and run beside me.

The driveway is shorter than it's ever been, no more than a few pounding steps. I can almost feel the earth sliding beneath my feet, the wind rushing at my back, shoving me forward.

The house comes into view all at once, like it stepped out from behind a black curtain. It's more mysterious at night, more alive, maybe just *more*, full stop. There's a tension to the shape of it against the sky, as if it has to work hard to remember to be a house and not anything else. The vines rustle and tremble against the stone. Mist coils around every sill and eave. Every window is dark.

So it's only by the sallow sickle moon that I see him: Arthur, standing alone before the stone steps with his head bowed and his sword braced crosswise before him.

He should look like a fool—a boy standing in his own yard long after midnight, his shirt misbuttoned, one sock missing, wielding a sword against nothing at all—and he does, but the kind of fool that breaks your heart. I don't know what he's fighting or why, but I know he's losing.

"Arthur?" I say his name softly, carefully, remembering the chill of his blade passing inches away from my face.

His spine goes rigid. His head lifts, turns very slowly toward me. I expect him to be angry—I have, after all, trespassed on his property twice in one night, this time while wearing gym shorts and an undershirt—but he looks closer to despairing.

"No." He says it very firmly, like he thinks I'm an apparition he might banish with sufficient effort.

"Look, I know I shouldn't have come, but I had this dream and I thought—is that blood?" One of his sleeves is blotted black, the fabric clinging to his flesh. There's more of it shining down one temple, matting his hair, slicking his hands around the hilt.

"Opal, you have to go *now*—" His sword tip wavers as he says it, sagging slightly.

That's when it happens. A sudden, invisible strike, an attack from nowhere that sends him staggering to one knee. A fresh wound appears in its wake, four deep scores dug across his throat. Blood floods down his neck, a black sheet that soaks his shirt and pools in the hollow between his collarbones.

The sword makes a dull clatter as it hits the gravel. Arthur follows it, his body folding gently, his eyes on mine.

I think I must be screaming, but I can't hear it over the wild moaning of Starling House. It's as if every loose floorboard has creaked at once, as if every joist and rafter warped themselves against the grain. Shingles hit the ground like fists beating uselessly against the earth.

I am abruptly aware that my knees are studded with stones. That my hands are snarled in cotton, wet and warm. That I'm saying silly, useless things like "no, no" and "hey, come on" and his name, over and over.

I haul him onto his back and he blinks up at me, eyes fogged and faraway. One of his hands lifts sluggishly into the air and comes to rest against the tangled nest of my hair. He says, in a voice like a rusted saw blade, "Thought I told you to run." Surely, if he were truly dying, he could not manage to sound so profoundly exasperated with me.

I cover his hand with mine, turning my face in to the heat of his palm, aware that I am completely and permanently blowing my cover as a disinterested housekeeper but unable in this moment to care. "I did." I push harder against his hand, pressing our skin together. "You goddamn *fool*."

"Thought . . . never come back . . . was implied."

I shift so that I'm holding his hand in mine, our thumbs hooked around each other's wrists. The salt of his blood stings my scraped palms, but I don't let go. "You're coming too. I don't know what the hell is going on, but—"

I stop talking, because something strange is happening to me. It begins in my palm, at the precise place where my blood mingles with Arthur's: a spreading chill, a deadening cold. It flows up my wrist, laps across my sternum. I feel like I'm walking slowly into a cold river, the water rising fast.

Arthur is saying something, pulling weakly at my shoulders. I hardly hear him. I'm too busy staring at the mist that surrounds us, which is suddenly much more than mist. Somewhere beneath the terror I feel a distant, childish disappointment; I'd always thought Eleanor Starling was a writer of pure imagination, a liar of the highest order, just like me.

Now I know she never told anything but the truth.

I used to have nightmares about the Beasts of Underland.

Honestly, who didn't? I read somewhere there was an animated adaptation in the works back in the eighties, but little kids puked during the early screeners so the whole project was pulled. I don't know if that's true, but I know I used to stare at E. Starling's illustrations and imagine that the Beasts had moved since the last time I'd looked, as if they might creep off the page on those racked and tortured limbs.

The creature that crouches on the steps of Starling House—its body the color of mist, its eyes the color of midnight, its legs bent beneath it like fractured bones—is far worse than any of my nightmares or daydreams. It's as if someone had given a child a piece of white chalk and told her to draw a wolf, but the only thing she knew about wolves was that they frightened her. There are teeth. There are claws. There is a long, lupine skull. But the spine is warped, and the fur drifts and twists like mist in a gentle wind, faintly translucent. Also, it's way, way too big.

I don't understand how a picture-book monster came to be standing in the ordinary springtime moonlight of Eden, Kentucky, but I know this is when I run. This moment, right here—as the Beast is gathering itself, as its lips peel away from its canines and its tendons flex beneath translucent flesh—is exactly when a girl like me splits. This is the river closing over my head, the cold filling my lungs, my own death staring at me with black and pitiless eyes. Last time I let go of my mother's hand and left her to die alone, and I know with weary certainty that I'm going to do it again.

I pull my hand away from Arthur's. Our blood separates with a faint, gluey pop.

I rise to a crouch. The Beast lowers its head, shoulder blades high and jagged on either side of its spine. There's a wariness to it, as if it doesn't much like Arthur or his sword. For the first time I notice the wounds along its flanks, and the mats of silvery fur caught around the doorway. There's a pool of pale mist spilled across the threshold, as if the Beast had to fight its way free of Starling House. Even now I see vines creeping across the steps, coiling around its claws only to be ripped away.

"You have to go." At my feet Arthur rolls to his stomach and scrabbles blindly for the hilt of his sword. "Run." His fingers find the blade. He drags it to him, surging to his knees with terrible effort. He sways, bloodied and pale, unable even to lift the tip of the sword from the ground but still glaring up at the Beast as if he intends to stop it with the sheer power of his scowl. It occurs to me that this lonely, beastly, bleeding boy is the only person who has ever fought for me, ever stood between me and the dark and told me to save myself. I feel like laughing, or maybe screaming.

The Beast takes a silent step toward us. The grass dies where its foot lands, going from green to brown to rotten black. The crickets and night birds have gone quiet, the air dead and dreaming around us.

Now, I think. *Run now.*

"Now," Arthur echoes. "Please—Opal—" His voice shivers very slightly around my name, trembling under the weight of unsaid things, and I think, very clearly: *Goddammit.*

Then I step in front of him and take the sword from his shaking hands. It's heavier than I imagined. I can feel my joints protesting, the small bones of my wrists grating together. The symbols etched into the blade have an odd, phosphorescent glow, like fox fire.

"No, stop, you can't—"

"Arthur," I tell him, and if my voice trips over the shape of his name, I'm sure it's just the effort of holding the sword in the air. "Shut up."

Arthur shuts up. I hear his breath behind me, ragged and uneven.

Maybe, if I'd had more than a half second to think about it, I'd have chickened out. Maybe I would have remembered that I have one list with one name on it, which sure as hell isn't Arthur Starling. Maybe that cold thing inside me would've won, and sent me running.

But the Beast strikes before I can even brace my feet. One limb unfurls, snakelike, obscenely fast, and I'm flung sideways. My face scrapes damp grass. The sword spins away from me, skidding far out of reach.

I look up and see nothing but teeth, white and wicked, and a single eye so filled with malice that my heart seizes. It's the kind of hate no natural animal has ever felt, a mad, howling, frothing fury, the kind that only comes from unrighted wrongs and unpunished sins.

The maw opens wide above me. There are claws on either side of my body, and the putrid, fungal smell of dead grass. Someone is screaming, a hoarse, grieving sound, as if they've seen this movie before and know how exactly how it ends.

I'm flailing, scrabbling, reaching, still hoping, somehow, to live. The ground ripples weirdly beneath me, and my fingers close around cold iron. It's not the sword, but it's good enough for me. I twist the metal between my knuckles without thinking, the same way I do when I walk alone across a dark parking lot or shout back at catcallers.

The Beast strikes again, except this time it's a killing blow, teeth heading straight for my sternum. And this time I roll aside at the last moment, and punch the gate key three inches into the black pulp of its eye.

There's no blood, no thrashing, no animal screaming. The Beast simply comes undone, disintegrates back into lifeless mist and leaves me lying bruised and alone on the cold earth, still stubbornly alive.

I spend the following seconds reveling in the itch of grass on the back of my neck, the smeared shine of the stars, the miraculous rise and fall of my own chest. I don't remember crawling out of the river that night—nothing but clay in my fingernails and heat against my back—but I remember this feeling, the quiet delirium that comes from not dying when you absolutely should have.

Normal night sounds return: spring peepers, crickets, a couple of chuck-will's-widows chirping brainlessly to one another. And an awful, racking sobbing from somewhere nearby.

"Arthur?" The sobbing stops.

There's a pause, followed by a thrashing, dragging sound, and then Arthur Starling's face is hovering inches above mine, blotting out the stars. His skin has gone a sickly, waxy white and his hair is matted with gore and sweat. His collar has stiffened into ragged black peaks beneath the oozing wounds of his throat, and his eyes are ringed in wild white.

He looks like a werewolf that turned accidentally back into a man, mid-meal. He looks like a character invented during a late-night back-porch ghost story, a human collage of every dark thing anyone has ever whispered about the Starlings.

He looks like shit, so I say, laughing a little, unreasonably delighted by the shape he makes against the sky, "You look like shit."

He makes a small, harassed sound. Then he kisses me.

If I had ever imagined Arthur Starling kissing me (I have), I would have thought it would be quick and awkward: a passionless, pent-up affair that would leave me irritable for a week but otherwise cold. This is, after all, a man who put his fist through a window rather than have an emotion about me.

At first, going by the taut lines of his face, I think I'm right. But then his hands find the sides of my face and his lips crush into mine with a bruising, furious heat, almost cruel in its intensity, and I think: *I should have known.* I should have known that he would only touch me if he'd come to the end of all his tight-held restraint. I should have known there would be no sparks between us, only a conflagration.

I could stop it. I probably should, rather than go up in flames—but it feels so good and both of us are so beautifully, absurdly alive and I don't know who

I am or where I come from but I know, right now, what I want. I push toward him instead, just as hard, twice as hungry.

His hands tighten, fingers fisting in my hair, pulling right at the raw edge of pain—I gasp—

And he breaks away, panting, wild-eyed. "Sorry, I'm sorry. I'm—" He straightens, burying his hands in his own hair and pulling hard. "It's just—I thought you were—just like *them*—" His sentence falters beneath the weight of em dashes.

"No, it's . . ." My lips sting. I press them together, hard. "I'm okay."

I am not okay. I have rarely been less okay in my life. I just found out my family name and fought an imaginary creature with a magic sword and I am very, very close to grabbing Arthur by the collar and sinking my teeth into his bottom lip. "I mean like in general you should probably *ask* first, but . . ." I give him a lazy, devilish smile, as if this is nothing to either of us, as if my pulse is not pounding in my ears.

He scowls at me. "Stop that. It's not—I can't—" He tugs harder at his hair, looking thoroughly wretched, and I cannot honestly believe I am harboring any feelings at all for someone this absurd.

I fold my smile away. "Okay, whatever. Let's get inside, get you cleaned up. Do you have your phone on you? It's so dark—" Before I can finish there's a faint, electric snap and the lights of Starling House flick on all at once. The windows cast long bars of gold across the drive, burning through the last wisps of fog. I observe, conversationally, "You know, somebody told me once the house was never hooked up to the grid."

Arthur is still shaking, but his fingers have unwound from his hair. "It wasn't." He gives a jerky shrug. "Light switches started turning up sometime in the early fifties, my mother told me, and an electric stove. Just like the plumbing did in the thirties."

I should probably freak out. I should have at least one small crisis about the existence of actual, honest-to-Jesus magic in the world, but I'm really tired and the sword is still glowing faintly in the grass, and anyway it's not like I thought Starling House abided strictly by the laws of reality. So I just say, in a carrying voice, "Any house that can grow its own light bulbs shouldn't need a housekeeper."

The windows flicker, like rolled eyes.

"I think it just likes the attention," Arthur mutters. I nearly laugh, and he nearly smiles, but the motion wrenches the torn flesh of his throat. He winces instead.

"Alright, come on." Standing up hurts more than it should. There's something messed up in my left side, a splintery sharpness that makes me swear as I haul Arthur to his feet. He tries to pull his hand away from mine but I pull it over my shoulders instead, ignoring the silent shriek of my ribs.

Arthur tries to hold his body away from mine and I elbow him. "Don't be weird, just do it." His protest strikes me as half-hearted.

We lurch together into Starling House, the sword point striking sparks against the stone. The front steps are somehow only two or three stairs long and the front door swings open before I can touch it. I stroke the frame as we pass and the wood creaks worriedly at me. The carved symbols are still very slightly luminescent, like glow sticks the day after a sleepover.

I don't know where we're headed or which of us is steering, but the first room we stumble into is the cozy parlor with the squashy couch. I dump Arthur on the cushions and his palm skims the back of my arm as we part. I walk away without looking at him.

There are an unlikely number of freshly laundered washcloths in the kitchen. In the bathroom, the medicine cabinet is already open, displaying a slightly frantic array of antibiotics and disinfectants. "It's alright," I say. "He'll be okay." The ceiling shudders.

Arthur does a very unconvincing I-don't-need-you-I-can-do-this-myself act when I return to the parlor, but his skin is the color of old mushrooms and his pupils are swollen and shocky and there are bruises blooming beneath his tattoos. The hellcat ends the argument by materializing on his lap and curling into a ball, like a furry land mine.

I slap Arthur's hand away from my stack of washcloths and shove him back against the couch. Maybe I should be a little gentler but he did recently kiss me with ardent desperation before suffering a sudden change of heart and *apologizing* for it, so the way I see it he's lucky I'm not scrubbing salt in his wounds.

I begin roughly, sitting on the coffee table while I swipe ruthlessly at dirt and blood, wringing gory brown water back into the bowl. Arthur bears it with perfect stoicism, his breath barely hitching even when I drag the cloth over the tattered skin of his throat. The only time he flinches is when my knuckles brush the underside of his jaw.

"Sorry," I say, not meaning it. He makes a hoarse, wordless sound and tilts his head against the couch with his eyes firmly closed. His pulse is quick and uneven beneath the rag.

Under the blood I find other, older marks. Scars, jagged and knotted; yellowed bruises and lines of scabs like scattered ellipses; tattoos he inked himself, the lines shaky over the bones, where it must have stung most. There's a crooked cross visible beneath his torn collar, a constellation on his left shoulder, an open eye where his collarbones meet. That one must have hurt. All of it must have hurt: his skin is a map of suffering, a litany of pain. I'm plenty familiar with pain, with scars that never heal quite right and still ache sometimes on misty nights, but at least I've always had Jasper. At least I've always had a reason.

My hands are slowing, gentling against my will. "Jesus, Arthur. What have you done to yourself?" He doesn't answer. I want to shake him, hold him, touch him. I unscrew the cap on the hydrogen peroxide instead. "Why don't you *leave*?"

"I did, once." He's speaking to the ceiling, eyes still closed as I dab peroxide on his throat. It hisses and bubbles, foaming pink. "I came back. Not that I don't dream about selling this place and getting an apartment in Phoenix." The curtains give a small, offended huff.

"Phoenix?"

He must hear the laugh in my voice because he shrugs defensively. "It seems nice. Hot, dry. Bet there's never any fog."

"So what are you still doing here?"

He straightens and opens his eyes, but can't seem to look me in the face. His gaze lands to my left, where my hair corkscrews past my ear, and his face twists with that awful guilt. "I have . . . responsibilities."

It's a statement that would have been obnoxiously cryptic before I saw him bloodied and beaten, brought to his knees but still trying desperately to protect me from a creature that shouldn't exist at all. The memory of it—the unwavering line of his spine, the way he glared up at the Beast as if he would fight it with his bare teeth before he let it past him—does something painful to my lungs. "I . . . thanks. Thank you."

"You should go. *Please*, go." His voice has none of the snarling, theatrical fury it did when he told me to run earlier. This isn't a command or a scare tactic or a show; it's a plea, weary and sincere, which any decent person would honor.

I laugh in his face. "Absolutely the fuck not."

"Miss Opal—"

"If you call me that again, I will do you a harm."

That treacherous not-quite-a-dimple crimps the corner of his mouth. "You wouldn't hurt an injured man."

"I would change your ringtone to Kid Rock and call you every day at dawn for a decade. My hand to God."

"I would simply turn it off."

I tilt my head. "Would you?"

His eyes move to mine, then away, dimple vanishing. "No," he says quietly. "God, just go *home*. Please"—his throat moves—"Opal."

I settle on the other side of the couch and pull my feet up on the cushions. "Number one, I don't have a home." I wonder suddenly if that's still true, if the Gravely name could change more than my past. I imagine squashing that thought into a grocery bag and shoving it very deep under my bed. "And number two, I'm not leaving until you explain."

"Explain what?" he asks, which is weak even for him.

I gesture at the sword lying on the floor, the bloodied rags, the mad, impossible house all around us. "Everything."

He looks like he's planning to say no. To tell me that he can't, or it's none of my business, or make some snide comment perfectly calculated to send me storming out of the house. I can tell by the set of his jaw that he won't be swayed by lies or wiles or charming smiles.

So I tell him the truth. "Look, both of us almost died tonight and I don't know why or how. I'm sure you've got your reasons for keeping secrets and God knows I'm not trustworthy, but I'm pretty freaked out right now. I'm confused and angry and"—admitting it feels like calling my own bluff, like laying out a pair of sevens after talking a big game—"scared."

A ripple moves through his limbs. The hellcat extends her claws. Arthur places his hands carefully on the cushion, palms down. "I'm sorry." He slants me a look of such grievous bafflement that I almost laugh. "You know, usually when people are scared, they *leave*. Why won't you? Why haven't you?"

"Because . . ." Because the money is good. Because I had to, for Jasper's sake. The answers come to me quick and easy, but then, lying always has.

The truth is harder: Because I dreamed of Starling House long before I ever saw it. Because sometimes when the light slants soft through the west windows and turns the dust motes into tiny golden fireflies I like to pretend the house belongs to me, or that I belong to it. Because Arthur Starling gave me a coat when I was cold and a truck when I was tired and he uses way too much punctuation in his texts.

I hitch a smile at him, too crooked to be charming. "Because I'm a meathead, I guess."

He looks at my mouth, then away. "Alright." He sighs for a very long time. "Alright. How much do you know already?"

"I've done some googling, heard some stories." The narratives run together in my head like a song sung in the round, different words to the same tune. Starlings and Boones and—the melody sours in my head—Gravelys. "I'd like to hear yours."

"I'm sick of stories." Arthur's voice is distant, a little dry. "My . . . antecessors were obsessed with them. Myths and fairy tales, folklore, parables. What I've been studying—what I've been assembling—is *history*. The *facts*."

"So give me the facts."

"Oh, it's not—" He fidgets, looking suddenly like Jasper when I ask to see the first draft of an essay. "There are still some gaps, and I haven't got it all organized yet—" He's interrupted by the drawer of the end table beside the couch, which has suddenly fallen open at his elbow. A stack of folders rests neatly inside. There's a thick yellow pad of paper on top, covered in Arthur's precise handwriting.

Arthur frowns repressively at the end table. I make a grab for the notepad but Arthur beats me to it. He clutches it close to his chest, looking thoroughly harassed. "Alright! Fine."

"Is that, 'Alright, fine, I'll tell you everything'?"

His eyes don't meet mine. He flips fastidiously through the pages instead. He wets his lips once, and then he tells me everything.

This is the history of Starling House.

On May 11, 1869, a young woman named Eleanor Starling was married to a local businessman named John Peabody Gravely. The morning after their wedding, John Gravely was found dead. The coroner listed the cause of death as heart failure, but noted that he was a healthy man of no more than forty-five. From this, and from the subject of Eleanor Starling's later obsessions, we can surmise two things: that his death was not a natural one, and that Eleanor knew it.

Historical evidence cannot tell us whether the young widow mourned her husband, but grief would explain several of her subsequent actions. She chose to remain in Eden, despite having no blood relations or family ties in the area. She never remarried, despite her youth. And she built Starling House on her husband's property, in close proximity to the mines, and directly above the source of his death.

Construction began by the summer of '68. The original blueprints were either burned or never made in the first place; several later Starlings have attempted to map the House, but none of their drawings are in agreement, and several of them appear to have changed over time. Eleanor Starling left no record of why she built such a vast and strange house, but the oldest and best-loved book in her collection was a copy of Ovid's *Metamorphoses*. It has been suggested by subsequent Starlings that she was not building a house but a labyrinth, for much the same reason the King of Crete once did: to protect the world from the thing that lived inside it.

When the house was complete, in February of 1870, Eleanor Starling took up residence and stayed there until her death in 1886. There is substantial evidence that she devoted the remaining years of her life to the study of the place she later called "Underland." She believed, according to the notes and journals found by her successors, that there was another world beneath, or maybe beside, our own—a terrible, vicious world, populated by monstrous beings. She believed that there were cracks between that world and our own, places where things might leak through, and that one of these rifts lay underneath Eden, Kentucky.

It was not the only such place, by her reckoning. She was convinced that these holes in reality were the source of every ghost story and monster tale, every legend about creatures that crawl out of the dark. She filled her library with folklore and fables, rhymes and songs. She studied them not as fictions, but as records, hints, the faded footprints scattered across time and space.

From her studies she learned that Beasts might be fought. Every culture seemed to have its own defenses against them: silver bullets, crosses, holy words, hamsas, circles of salt, cold iron, blessed water, wards and runes and rituals, a hundred ways of driving back the dark.

In 1877, she was confident enough in her research to commission the making of a sword. It was forged from pure silver by a blacksmith who claimed to have once served the King of Benin. She had it stamped with a dozen different symbols and quenched in water from St. George's Well and the Ganges. In her papers there was a letter from a convent in France suggesting it had been blessed by a living saint.

From the existence of the sword we can surmise that she planned a great battle. From her sudden disappearance in 1886, we can surmise that she lost. While it's possible that she ran away, it seems likelier that she was finally taken by the very Beasts she had studied for so long, leaving Starling House empty behind her.

But Starling House was no longer just a house. What had begun as stone and mortar had become something more, with ribs for rafters and stone for skin. It has no heart, but it feels; it has no brain, but it dreams.

In the census of 1880, Eleanor Starling listed her occupation as "Warden of Starling House." When she died, the House chose a new Warden for itself.

Less than a year after her death, a young gentleman named Alabaster Clay arrived at Starling House. In his letters to his sister he recounted the bad dreams that plagued him, full of hallways and staircases and black birds with black eyes. He said he woke every morning full of yearning for a house he'd never seen.

Eventually, he followed those dreams to Eden. The gates opened for him, and so did the doors. Inside he found a deed in his name, a ring of three iron keys, and a sword. All his subsequent letters to his sister were signed *Alabaster Starling*.

After Alabaster's tenure ended, others came. Whenever one Warden fell, another was chosen to take up the sword. Some of them found something like happiness, at least for a while. They've married, raised children, watched the passage of time from the windows of Starling House: the building of the power plant across the river, the veins of telephone lines spreading across the county, the rise and fall of Big Jack. They've walked the wards and kept the Beasts at bay.

But the Beasts always take them, in the end.

The most recent Warden arrived in 1985, all the way from North Carolina. She and her husband met at a pork-processing plant—Lynn Lewis worked on the kill floor and Oscar was a janitor. But Oscar was let go after he hurt his back and, following some sort of violent altercation with management, so was Lynn. The two of them lingered as long as they could, until the electric company shut off the lights and the bank boarded up the windows, and then they drifted from job listing to job listing, aimless and homeless. A few months later the Warden began to dream of a big house behind high iron gates. They followed the dreams west, and when they arrived they found a ring of keys and a deed waiting for them.

The House thrived under their stewardship. The floors didn't creak and the windows didn't whistle in winter; the kitchen always smelled like lemons and the wisteria was always in bloom. Lynn and Oscar loved Starling House, and they fought for what they loved.

Their son was less worthy. He was a weak and selfish young man, given to fanciful drawings and silly daydreams. He denied his fate as long as he could. He thought for a while the House would find someone else, someone braver— until he saw the cost of his cowardice.

Lynn and Oscar Starling died in 2007. That very night he made his oath and became the new Warden of Starling House.

But he swore a second, private oath: that he would be the last.

SEVENTEEN

I saw this old map of the Mississippi once. The cartographer drew the river as it actually is, but he also drew all the previous routes and channels the river had taken over the last thousand years. The result was a mess of lines and labels, a tangle of rivers that no longer existed except for the faint scars they left behind. It was difficult to make out the true shape of the river beneath the weight of its own ghosts.

That's how the history of Starling House feels to me now, like a story told so many times the truth is obscured, caught only in slantwise glimpses. Maybe that's how every history is.

The Starlings are watching me from their portraits, unalike but all the same. Each of them drawn here by their dreams, each of them bound to a battle I still don't understand. Each of them buried before their time.

Arthur is watching me, too. His eyes are red, sunk deep in the uneven planes of his face. Watery blood is seeping from his throat again but he keeps his chin high and his spine stiff. He looks cold and a little cruel, except for the slight tremble in his hands. His tell, Mom would call it.

"So, the last Warden. That's you, isn't it?" My voice is loud in the hush of the house. "What did you mean, last?"

"I meant," Arthur says, "that there wouldn't be another Warden after me."

"Oh? You don't think there's anybody out there having strange dreams about a big empty house?" Arthur was born to this house, but maybe I was chosen for it. Maybe I don't have to be a Gravely, after all. "You don't think maybe somebody will come along after you—"

"The Starlings have been fighting this war for generations!" His hands are shaking worse, his tone vicious. "They've bled for this place, died for it, and it's *not enough*. It's getting—" Arthur bites the sentence off, looking up at the portraits with his lips pale and hard. "Someone has to end it."

"And that's going to be you." As I watch, a little blood drips from his collar onto the hellcat. "And what army?"

Arthur's lips go even paler, pressed tight. "I don't require an army. Every Starling has found new wards and spells, weapons that work against the Beasts. I've taken their studies further." He rubs his wrist as he talks, thumb digging into his tattoos hard enough to hurt. The wind moves mournfully under the eaves. "All I need is a way through that damn door."

There are dozens, maybe hundreds, of doors in Starling House, but I know which one he means. "And you don't have the key."

"No."

"And you can't pick the lock."

"No."

"And you can't, I don't know, blow it up?"

His mouth ripples. "I would think, by now, that you would know the laws of physics do not always apply in this house."

I'm about to ask if he's tried "open sesame" when a rhyme goes lilting through my mind: *she buried the key by the sycamore tree.* "Have you dug around the sycamore? That big old one out front?" I regret the question as soon as I ask it, because what if I'm right? What if I've just handed Arthur the key to Hell? I have a sudden, mad urge to circle my fingers around his wrists, to hold him here with me in the world above.

But Arthur makes a small, exasperated noise. "Eleanor Starling left all her drafts and sketches of that book in this house. I've read each version fifty times. I've examined the drawings under microscopes and black lights. *Of course* I've dug around the sycamore." The exasperation subsides. In its absence he merely sounds tired. "There's nothing there. If there ever was a key, Eleanor must have destroyed it. She wanted the way to Underland to remain closed."

Relief moves through me in a searing wave, far too intense. I swallow and say, somewhat at random, "I don't know. What about the dedication?"

Arthur is frowning at me. "It doesn't have a dedication."

"Yes it—" I close my mouth. Maybe Eleanor Starling's drafts and manuscripts didn't include the dedication; maybe Arthur hasn't read the later editions. I hope, suddenly and desperately, that he hasn't. "I still don't understand why you'd want to go down there in the first place. I mean, *look* at you." I let my eyes move over him, lingering on the oozing red furrows along his neck, the rusty patches on the couch where blood has dried and flaked from his skin. "Why are you doing any of this?"

The small muscles of his jaw clench. "It's the duty of the Warden to wield the sword," he says stiffly. "To keep the House and ward the walls and do your damnedest to keep the Beasts from breaching the gates."

He makes it sound so noble, so tragic, like one of those medieval ballads that ends with a knight lying dead on the field of battle with his lady weeping over his broken body. I picture myself finding him slumped in the hall or sprawled on the driveway, his throat torn out but his sword still in hand, and a panicked, senseless fury boils up my spine. "Oh, right, you're the *Warden*, of course."

I'm aware that my tone has edged away from sarcastic and toward genuine outrage, that I'm giving away a game I shouldn't even be playing, but I don't care. "It's your *birthright*, I forgot." He flinches from the word, eyes white-ringed. "Did you have to swear it on the full moon? Was there a blood sacrifice? Because I'd hate to hear Lacey Matthews say she told me so—"

"Stop it." He says it very quietly, face turned as if he's speaking to the hellcat still curled in his lap.

"Do you want to die, is that your deal?" I'm mildly surprised to find that I'm on my feet, fingers curled into fists, ribs screaming. "Because it sure

looks like it. You could have *called* me, you could have—I don't know—
hidden in a closet, or run away—"

"*I did.* I told you." He doesn't shout, but his voice has a rasp to it that
makes me think he'd like to. His features are white and contorted, aggres-
sively ugly. I make a distant note that this is what Arthur looks like when he's
actually angry, rather than just pretending. "My parents didn't let me go off
to school, I *ran away.* Because I was tired of living in a ghost story, because
I wanted a nice normal life with lockers and—and stupid worksheets—
and for a while I thought I'd done it. Made a clean getaway. For two years,
I didn't dream at all."

It occurs to me that I would have been about twelve when he ran away
to school. That my dreams began just when Starling House lost its heir. A
whole string of what-ifs and might-have-beens unfurls in my head, an alternate life where I took up the sword instead of Arthur. I stamp on it.

"I came home because the town commissioner called me to complain.
My parents had stopped picking up the groceries, see, and it was all rotting
outside the gate, attracting vermin. It was a public nuisance, he said."

I remember—in a cold, unwilling rush—what Bev said when I asked
her about the Starlings. How the boy didn't call the police for days after his
parents died. How he didn't shed a tear, but just told the coroner it was past
his suppertime.

At the time, the story scared me. Now I feel nothing but terrible, familiar
grief. I remember my first meal after the crash: the constable brought me a
Happy Meal and I sat staring at the bright-colored box in my lap, printed
with smiling, bumbling cartoons, and realized all at once that I was too old
for it. That I'd spent the last minutes of my childhood dying on a riverbank in
the cold light of the power plant, dreaming there were warm arms wrapped
around me, and when I woke up the next morning I had outgrown such
youthful fantasies.

My temper rushes out of me in a long sigh. I take a step back toward the
couch. "Oh, Arthur."

He's looking down at the hellcat again, eyes glassy, stroking her spine
with a single, miraculously unharmed finger. "They must have been in the
middle of dinner when the mist rose, because there was still food on their
plates. The Beast breached the gates, and they took the truck, followed behind. I don't know how they made it back after, the state they were in. I
found them crawling back toward the house, right where you—"

He's interrupted by a sound like gravel in a dishwasher. It takes both of us a moment to realize it's the hellcat, purring. Arthur's hands unclench on the couch and the knot of his face loosens very slightly.

He looks up, finally, to meet my eyes. "I'm going to make it stop. It's not a choice. I have to."

There's an urgency to his voice that I know very well. Arthur has been many things to me—a mystery, a vampire, a knight, an orphan, a real dick—but now I see him for what he is: a man with a list just like mine, with only one thing on it.

And that should warn me away, because I know a person like that doesn't have room for wanting, for wishing, but my body moves of its own accord. I step closer, too close, my feet small and bare between his. He tilts his head to look up at me and his wounds gape wide. He doesn't flinch.

His hair is matted to his throat with sweat and gore. I brush it aside. He shivers but his skin is hot, almost feverish beneath my fingers, and I think dizzily that I know exactly why Icarus flew so high: when you've spent too long in the dark, you'll melt your own wings just to feel the sun on your skin.

My fingers find the collar of his shirt. I lean closer, not smiling at all now. "And do you have to do it alone?"

"Yes." Arthur's voice is ragged, as if it caught on barbed wire and ripped itself free. "Yes, I do," he says, but he's reaching for me and the hellcat is clawing out of his lap with an aggrieved hiss and his eyes are wide and dark on mine.

"Horseshit," I say, and this time, I'm the one who kisses him.

A rthur Starling considers himself a strong-willed man. He has, after all, spent most of his life locked in a one-man war against an ancient evil with nothing but a sword and an opinionated House for company. He has stood against a hundred nightmares and lain alone for a thousand nights, dry-eyed; he has scrubbed his own blood from the floors and stitched his own wounds with steady hands.

And yet he cannot seem to push Opal away. His hands are tangled in the bloody red of her hair and she is kissing him with a heedless, reckless hunger, her mouth like a match against his, burning every dark thing away. Her hands are fisted in the collar of his shirt and she is so vital, so furiously alive that Arthur understands for the first time why Hades stole Persephone, why a man who has spent his life in winter might do anything at all for a taste of spring.

But he will not bring Opal down into the dark with him. He is not, perhaps, as strong as he hoped, but he is not that weak.

He breaks away. He can't quite make himself let go of her hair, so he presses his forehead against hers, their breath mingling. He says, hoarsely, wretchedly, "You don't understand."

She pulls back so fast he feels hairs snapping around his fingers. She crosses her arms over the tired cotton of her shirt and presses a palm hard to her rib cage, like she's trying to hold herself together. "Hey, you're the one who kissed *me* like ten seconds ago so excuse me if I got mixed signals." Her voice is caustic and careless, the way it always gets when she's scared. He pictures her planting her feet in the grass, wrists straining beneath the weight of the Starling sword, telling him to shut up.

He reaches up to her a little helplessly, wiping a smear of dirt or blood away from the harsh angle of her elbow. "It's not that I don't—it's just—"

Opal flinches back from his touch, then pauses. Her eyes narrow in sudden suspicion. "Wait. Have you done this before?"

"Done what before?"

"I just—I mean, I'd understand." She shrugs, not unkindly. "You've spent your whole life locked in a haunted mansion, so it's not like you've had many chances to . . ." She drifts into tactful silence.

Several seconds later, Arthur grates, "I went away to school for *two years.* I *dated.*"

"Oh yeah?" A sliver of that mocking, too-sharp smile. "What was her name?"

"Victoria Wallstone," he says stiffly, a little surprised he remembers her surname. Victoria had been a loud, likable girl who asked if he wanted to have sex with the disarming ease of someone asking for a stick of gum. He hesitates before adding, "And Luke Radcliffe." He has no difficulty remembering Luke's name.

He half hopes that Opal is a secret bigot who will be frightened off by the implication that he spent a semester sneaking into another boy's dorm room, but she merely rolls her eyes and mutters "Rich kid names" in a tone of mild disgust.

"So then . . ." She looks away from his face, as if the next question doesn't much matter. "What's your deal?" The mocking smile has wilted very slightly, leaving her looking young and wounded, almost vulnerable. Arthur traps his hands between his knees and presses hard.

"It has nothing to do with you. I mean it does, but it's not—you don't *understand*." It sounds pathetic even to him.

"Jesus, fine. It doesn't matter." She tucks her hair behind her ear. "I'm tired, and you're probably not going to bleed out overnight. Could you dig up a spare blanket somewhere?"

She tries to throw herself defiantly onto the couch, but she stiffens as her body hits the cushions. It's a tiny motion, less than a wince, but Arthur hears the hitch in her breath. He notes that her palm is still pressed to her left side, that the pads of her fingers have gone white.

And it's just like that night on the riverbank: the sight of her pain sends a hot tide of guilt through his body, fills him with an urgent, animal desire to make it stop. He finds himself on his knees, folders and notes scattered around him, reaching for Opal as if she belongs to him.

But they were children back then, and Opal was too busy dying to notice him. Now she watches him warily, her body held stiff and upright. He wonders when she learned to hide her wounds from the world, and why the thought makes his throat tight. He stops his own hand in midair, an inch above hers.

After a moment he manages to say, more roughly than he intended, "Let me." He is distantly aware that it should have been a question. He scrapes up the ragged remains of his decency and adds, "Please." Opal watches him for another uncertain second, searching for God knows what in his face, before lowering her hand slowly to the couch. It feels like surrender, like trust; Arthur deserves neither.

He runs his fingers over each rib, pushing through the soft heat of her skin to feel the bones beneath. He wishes he couldn't feel her heart beating on the other side of her sternum, quick and light. He wishes she weren't watching him with that foolish trust in her eyes, as if she's forgotten it's his fault she's hurt. He wishes his hands weren't shaking.

But he finds no cracks or splinters. The terror recedes, leaves his voice hoarse. "Just bruised, I think. Not broken."

"I'm lucky like that." Opal is aiming for sarcasm, but her ribs are rising and falling too fast beneath Arthur's hand. He reminds himself that there is no medical emergency, that he should absolutely stop touching her now. The desperate, animal feeling should fade away, but instead it turns hot and languorous, coiling in the pit of his stomach.

He feels Opal swallow. Her voice is an exhalation. "Are you really going to kick me out again?"

God, he doesn't want to. He wants to push up her shirt and press his lips to the hollow place between the wings of her ribs. He wants to make her spine arch against the couch. He wants her to stay, and stay.

So does the House: the room is warm and wisteria-sweet around them, the light gentle amber. He wonders if Opal has noticed that the water comes out of the faucet whatever temperature she wants and the cushions are always precisely where she likes them best. That she never trips on the stairs or fumbles for a light switch, that the sun follows her from window to window, room to room, like a cat hoping for affection.

Arthur knows she would make a good Warden, much better than himself. He was born in the House, but Opal was called, and the House calls the homeless and hungry, the desperately brave, the fools who will fight to the very last.

For a dark, tilted moment he can almost see her as she would be years from now, if the House had its way: scarred and war-weary, smiling that crooked smile over her shoulder at him. The Wardens don't last as long as they used to, but Opal would. She would make a war of her life, would fight so long and fiercely that Hell itself would tremble.

Until the day—perhaps a long time from now—when she would fall, and would not rise again. Then a new headstone would join the others, and a new portrait would appear on the wall, the latest addition to a gallery of stolen years. Somewhere, another homeless bastard would begin to dream of staircases and hallways and black eyes that watched through the mist.

Unless Arthur stops it all.

He takes his hand away from her side. The air chills several degrees. A floor nail worries itself loose from the wood and jabs into his right knee. Arthur relishes it. "Opal." He says her name slowly, savoring it the way you might linger over a last meal. "Here's what's going to happen: I am going to explain about the Beasts, about me, and then you are going to run. And this time you will not come back."

"Well, third time's the charm," she says. She is looking down at him with fond exasperation, as if he is a child who has announced, once again, that he's running away from home.

Arthur closes his eyes. He has to make her understand, but surely he doesn't have to see her face when she does.

He hammers his voice flat. "When those Beasts get past the walls—when I fail to stop them—they run until they find someone else to hurt. Only Starlings can see them, but anyone can suffer." He thinks of generations of newspaper clippings and journal entries, all those fires and floods and freak accidents, sudden deaths and strange disappearances, centuries of sin mistaken as bad luck. "And certain people . . . draw them."

"Which people?"

"The Gravelys. Above everyone else, they'll go after Gravely blood. I don't know why."

Opal goes very, very still, then. Arthur is grateful.

"The night my parents died was the night the turbine blew at the power plant. Four people died." Arthur had torn the story from the paper with clumsy fingers, understanding for the first time that his life did not belong to him, that even his tragedies were not entirely his own. "I was so careful after that. I kept up the wards and patrolled the halls. For a whole year, I was vigilant, attentive. Until I wasn't."

It was Christmas that got him, the first one since he buried his parents. The House produced a few sad clumps of tinsel and mistletoe, but he ripped it all down in a fit of petulant grief. After that he had locked the sword in an old trunk, ordered a case of cheap whiskey using his father's ID, and spent a week on the run from his own conscience. He found that, if he began drinking straight after breakfast, he could achieve a weightless, careless state by midday, and complete unconsciousness by dinner.

And then one night he'd woken up with his forehead smeared against his mother's grave and tear-tracks frozen on his cheeks, feeling dramatic and slightly ashamed and extremely sick to his stomach. It took him far too long to notice the mist had risen.

He doesn't tell Opal any of this; he doesn't want to temper her fury with pity. "I saw the Beast rise. It looked at me, right at me, and I . . ." He'd looked straight back into its eyes, a pair of open wounds teeming with terror and fury and barren grief. He hadn't been scared. How could he be scared of the eyes he saw in the bathroom mirror every morning?

Arthur doesn't tell her that, either. "I didn't even try to stop it. I just let it go. I ran after it, once I'd realized what I'd done. Through the gates, across the old railroad bridge. But I was too late. There were tire tracks running off the road, headed down the riverbank . . ." Arthur swallows, savoring this last moment before she hates him, before she knows what his cowardice cost her. "It was New Year's Day."

Her breath stops. He wonders if she is feeling the water close over her head again.

"I saw in the paper they said she drove into the river on purpose. But I knew it wasn't her fault."

Opal is breathing now, hitched and jagged.

Arthur keeps his eyes screwed shut. His voice scrapes out of his throat. "It was mine."

Silence, thick and cold. Arthur thinks of food congealing on a plate.

He doesn't expect Opal to speak to him again—what is there to say, after all, to the man who murdered your mother?—but she does. "You should know. Eleanor dedicated her book to 'every child who needs a way into Underland.'"

Opal has puked on him and kissed him and told him to go fuck himself more than once, but she's never spoken to him like this: cool and distant, perfectly detached. "She said to befriend the Beasts and follow them down. Maybe you should try it." Her voice betrays her on the last sentence, a fatal, furious shake.

Arthur doesn't know what she's trying to tell him or why; he's expending all his attention on keeping his eyes shut and his hands still.

He hears the couch creak, followed by a metallic clink and then, finally, the slap of bare feet on wood floors.

When Arthur opens his eyes several minutes later, his gate key is lying on the floor in front of him, and he is alone. She has run from him a third time, and God, he regrets everything.

EIGHTEEN

The thing is: I already knew. I may not have known where Mom was headed that night or who she really was, but I knew she didn't do it on purpose. I'd seen something wrong-shaped in the white flash of the headlights. *A deer,* I told the officers, *or maybe a coyote,* but I knew it was neither. I knew it was bad luck on four legs, a nightmare set loose by whatever petty and careless god rules over Eden.

But I didn't know I'd been cleaning his fucking house for four months. I didn't know I'd betrayed him and bled for him and kissed him, that one day he would be on his knees, neck bowed, eyes closed, speaking in a voice like a shovel biting into earth.

So: I run. Just like he said I would.

The hall is short and straight, but the front door is locked. I rattle the knob and the house moans at me. "Don't." My voice sounds thick and wet; I think I must be crying. *"Please."*

The door opens.

I run down the steps and along the drive, ribs aching, the gravel leaving teeth marks in my feet. I slip out the front gates and circle wide around his truck. I don't want to think about the truck or the phone number, the too-high pay, the too-nice coat—so many things I thought were gifts, but which strike me now as desperate attempts to pay down a blood debt. But he's shit out of luck, because my mother was worth more than he could afford. She was feckless and foolish and beautiful, she drank and she lied and she had a laugh like the Fourth of July and I *needed* her.

I've never stopped. I tried to cross her off my list that night in the river, but if I ran my fingers across the page I know I could still feel the shape of her name, indelible.

By the time I get back to the motel the sky is the color of old denim and the stars are faded flecks of bleach. The crickets have screamed themselves out and the only sound is the river, like the static between radio stations.

My feet hurt. My chest hurts. My eyes hurt. I feel like an open wound, a bruise.

The Underland is still lying open on my bed, bristling with ghosts and beasts. I crawl onto Jasper's mattress instead.

I dream of Starling House again—an endless, arterial map of hallways and open doors, stairs and balustrades—and I'm grateful. At least I'm not dreaming of the river.

I've never really had the chance to wallow. Wallowing is an indulgence you can't afford if you have thirty dollars left in your checking account and a baby brother watching you like you're his personal sun, sure to rise. But now I find myself jobless and aimless, with no one counting on me and no-where to be, so I figure: screw it. I wallow like I'm making up for lost time, like I'm going for the gold in self-pity.

I burrow deep into Jasper's bed and spend three days in a sweaty cave of sheets and stale deodorant. I wake up to eat and piss and shower, and afterward I sit wrapped in my towel for so long it leaves bumpy pink imprints on the backs of my legs. I watch the tidal motions of the sun across the floor. I study the alluvial stains on the ceiling. I dig my fingers into my bruised ribs, thinking of other, gentler hands, and then I close my eyes and bully myself into a restless sleep.

I dream, and every dream is a bad one. The mist rises. The house falls. Arthur follows the Beasts down and down, just like I told him to, and I wake with wet cheeks. Sometimes I wish I hadn't told him; sometimes I wish I'd fed him to the Beasts myself.

My phone buzzes every now and then, like a carpenter bee thumping senselessly against a window. I look at the screen the first couple of times, but it's just the library letting me know my holds are available, or Jasper saying he's spending another night at Logan's (fuck Logan), or Elizabeth Baine asking if I received her message. That last one almost provokes an emotion, so I shove the phone under the mattress. I figure if they're good enough to find my real birth certificate, then surely they can figure out that I'm not working at Starling House anymore.

Eventually the phone goes quiet.

A distant, rational part of me thinks: *You know she won't give up that easy.* She'll never give up, because she's like me: willing to break every rule and cross every line to get what she needs. An urgency moves through me, a desire to call Arthur, warn him about her—

But then I think of the river. The mud under my nails. The cold place in my chest. I think of all our other close calls and bad nights. All Jasper's ambulance rides and steroid shots, the ugly bike crashes and the time I tangled my foot in old fishing line and nearly drowned. The time Jasper chased a stray dog into the woods and a hunter's bullet missed him so narrowly it left a purple welt on his right ear.[21]

I think about cursed towns and cursed families. I think: *Above everyone else, they'll go after Gravely blood.*

I don't think anything after that.

* * *

21. The hunter, Dennis Roark, later claimed he was shooting at a doe and missed, and further alleged that it was Jasper's fault for going out in deer season without wearing orange. Dennis's mother, Mrs. Roark, said she told him not to go out hunting on such a foggy evening.

On the third day a fist slams against the room 12 door with an aggression suggesting I am about to be dragged off by men in jackboots.

"Hey kid, you dead?" Bev sounds as if she doesn't care much either way, but wants to know if she'll have to rent a steam cleaner. I wonder if she's already planning to add me to her list of ghost stories—the girl who died of a broken heart and stank up room 12. The meathead who still haunts the motel.

More thumping. "I turned the internet off *two hours* ago. What's going on?" There's a strained note in her voice, perilously close to concern, that sends something white-hot licking up my spine.

I thrash out of bed and whip open the door so fast that Bev says, "Jesus H.—"

"Did you know?" My voice sounds like it's coming out of a rusted gutter pipe.

She squints at me, hands on her hips. "You look like hot hell. You been eating right? Not that gas station garba—"

"Did you *know*?"

A flash of wariness, covered by flat irritation. "Did I know what?"

It takes me a second to unwedge the words from the small, dim place I've been keeping them. "Did you know her last name? *My* name?"[22]

Bev doesn't answer, but she goes very still. My cheeks sting as if I've been slapped. "You did. The whole time, and you never—" I stop speaking before my voice can do anything embarrassing, like crack or wobble.

Bev scrubs her hand hard over her face and says, "Hon, everybody knew." She sounds almost gentle. I wonder how bad I must look, to squeeze pity out of Bev. "Everybody knew Old Leon Gravely, and everybody knew his little girl. The day she got that Corvette was the last day of peace and quiet in this town."

I swallow the phrase *everybody knew*. It ricochets around inside me, bruising bones. "Did Charlotte know?" The question feels desperately important.

Bev shakes her head quickly. "I never said anything, and she didn't grow up around here."

---

22. There is an ongoing and extremely contentious legal case debating whether Opal has a genuine legal claim to the Gravely name. On the one hand, Jewell Gravely never used the name after she left her father's household—the Corvette was registered to Jewell Wild, and the motel room was originally booked under a Jewell Weary—and marked an *X* on Opal's birth certificate. On the other, as several witnesses testified, "She's a Gravely, alright. Just look at that damn hair."

A tiny ray of relief, that at least one person in my life wasn't lying to me. I lick cracked lips. "So then do you know why my mom didn't—how she wound up here?"

"Your mama had a wild streak a mile wide. Eventually I guess she finally crossed the line and her daddy threw her out. She dropped out of school, left town, and when she came back—there you were. With that Gravely hair." Bev's eyes flick up to my greasy red curls.

"And Old Leon." The man in the mansion, the reason there's no luna moths or unions in Muhlenberg County. *My granddaddy.* "He didn't take her back?"

Bev shakes her head once. "He might have, if she turned respectable, begged a little bit. But your mama was stubborn."

She says it admiringly, but it sounds to me like Mom was just a rich-kid rebel, one of those spoiled children that break rules out of boredom. And then she wound up with two kids and too much pride to ask for help. Instead, she taught us to scrabble and steal. She raised us in parking lots and motel rooms, hungry and lonely, chased by Beasts we couldn't see.

And nobody in this whole damn town did anything about it. They turned their backs and looked away, just like they always have and always will.

Even Bev, who could have told me the truth anytime, who I trusted.

She's not looking at me now, tonguing the tobacco in her jaw. "Listen, I should have—"

"Did Charlotte bring my library holds by?" My voice is cool, serene.

I see Bev flinch a little from whiplash. "Charlotte's not—" She clears her throat, falls back into her usual aggression. "If you want your smut you'll have to walk your ass over to the library just like everybody else."

"Okay," I say calmly, and then I slam the door in her face.

"Opal, hey, come on." I hear her feet shuffling on the other side of the door. "Fine, be like that. But I'm not turning the internet back on until you take out the trash."

Her boots scuff the pavement as she stomps away.

I go all the way under, after that. No longer drifting but diving down, kicking hard toward the riverbed. I lose track of the days and nights, existing in the changeless twilight of deep water. I don't have to dream because I never sleep; I don't have to think because I never wake up.

At some point, the door opens. I don't roll over, but I can smell the warm blacktop of the parking lot, feel the aggrieved tumble of air disturbed after a long stillness. I hear Jasper's voice. "Hey," he says, and then, after a while, "Okay, whatever."

I think he leaves then, but he comes back later, and then again. He gets louder and more annoying each time. *Opal, are you sick? Opal, what's wrong with you?* I feel like one of those eyeless fish who lives in the deep pools of Mammoth Cave, too canny to be caught and dragged out into the light. I stay safe and deep, even when I feel the ghastly chill of blankets torn away, even when I hear the shift in his voice, the teenage crack at the end of my name. *Opal, what the fuck? Opal, why are your ribs that color?*

He keeps at it for a while, but eventually he gives up and leaves me to decompose in peace. Some small, wakeful part of me wants to feel sad about that—is this how it feels, to be crossed off somebody's list?—but most of me is relieved. It's easier to fall apart when no one is watching you.

Arthur Starling becomes aware—gradually, in reluctant stages—that someone is watching him. His first clue was the nervy shiver at the back of his skull that told him there was a stranger on Starling land. He ignored this on the grounds that it was impossible, as he was in possession of all the keys again, and as the only person who could theoretically gain entry without a key was never coming back.

His second clue was the physical sound of his front door opening. He had ignored this on similar grounds. The House had been displeased since Opal left—none of the faucets worked and the windows were all jammed, and everything in the fridge had molded to spiteful green sludge overnight—but it wouldn't yet betray him by opening for his enemies. And, furthermore, Arthur had been drinking with such unflagging dedication that he was simultaneously still drunk and already hungover, and couldn't be sure he'd heard anything in the first place.

His third clue is the sound of a bourbon bottle shattering several inches away from his head. This, he finds, he cannot ignore.

Arthur opens his eyes—a process not dissimilar from prying open a pair of crusted paint cans—to find himself on the library floor, which is something of a surprise. The afternoon air is gluey and hot because none of the windows will open, and there's a young man watching him. Glossy curls, rangy brown limbs, a surplus of eyelashes. There's nothing even slightly familiar about him—except for his expression.

Only one person has ever regarded Arthur with that particular canny, cornered-animal fury.

"Oh God, there's another one." The words come out smeary and flat, which tells Arthur that his face is still adhered to the floorboards. He closes his eyes again and hopes Opal's little brother will leave, or perhaps dissipate, like a bad dream.

A second bottle hits the floor, a little closer.

"Is there something," Arthur asks the floor, "I can do for you?"

"I'd say 'die in a ditch,' but it looks like you're halfway there."

From the way she talked about him, Arthur had formed an idea that Jasper was a sheltered, delicate creature, in need of constant protection. But he is, in fact, a sharp and resentful sixteen-year-old from Muhlenberg County, whom everyone else needs protection *from*.

Arthur detaches himself from the floor in unpleasant stages, pausing several times to reacquaint his stomach with vertical gravity. Eventually he achieves a slouched sitting position, his back braced by a bookshelf, and tries again. "Why are you here?"

Jasper, who had apparently grown bored while Arthur wormed himself upright, is leaning over a desk, perusing Arthur's notes and folders. They're in a state of fantastic disarray, folders emptied, papers crumpled, his yellow notepad teetering precariously on the edge with half its pages torn out. Arthur has an embarrassing suspicion that he removed them in a fit of impotent temper.

"Opal left her favorite hoodie here," Jasper says, without looking away from the desk.

Arthur grunts. "Your sister's a better liar."

"Yeah, but I'm smarter." Jasper looks away from the notes and meets Arthur's eyes, flatly threatening. "I came to tell you to leave her alone."

Arthur feels infinitely too old for this conversation, and also too drunk, too sober, and too wretched. "I've been *trying*. You're the ones who keep turning up at *my* House."

"Tell it to leave us alone, too."

Arthur is about to reply that if he could make the House behave as he liked then Jasper wouldn't be standing in his library, when the plural pronoun penetrates the haze of nausea. He forces both his eyes to focus on Jasper— lean and dangerous in the afternoon light, brave or stupid enough to face a monster for his sister's sake—and repeats, softly, "Us?"

Opal would have smiled or lied or cheated her way out of the question. Jasper just lowers his head, a boy with the bit in his teeth, and ignores it. "She's not eating. She's not sleeping. I don't even think she's *reading*." The slightest, most awful break in his voice. "I've never seen her like this."

The weight that has been hovering above Arthur for days now—the suffocating guilt he's been holding off with sheer volume of alcohol—descends upon him then. It lands like cannon shot, smashing through him. "Is she— someone should look at her ribs—" He hears an unhealthy wheeze in his own voice, swallows twice. "Is she alright?"

Jasper is perfectly cold, not scathing so much as searing. "It's none of your business, because you're never going to speak to her again, are you?" Jasper steps closer, crouching among the glittering teeth of broken bottles until his face is level with Arthur's. "I don't know what happened. But if I see another bruise on my sister, I'll know who to blame."

It occurs to Arthur, with the painful clarity that follows a long period of stupidity, that Jasper would be entirely correct to blame him. The mist could have risen any night in the past week and the Beasts would have found the Warden insensate, mired in self-pity. They would have been free to roam as they liked, sowing their bad seeds, perhaps sinking their teeth into a pale throat, raking their claws across a freckled face.

The fumes from the bourbon bottles make Arthur suddenly, violently sick.

Jasper watches impassively. He stands, looking down at Arthur with a disgusted, almost pitying expression, before turning away. His shoes crunch across the glass.

"Jasper." Arthur's eyes are closed, his head propped against the bookcase. "You should leave. Get out of Eden."

Jasper turns slowly back, hands jammed deep in his pockets. Arthur can see the outline of fists through the denim, but his voice is flat and bored. "People have told me that my whole life, you know that? People who love me, people who hate me. All of them seem to agree that I don't belong here."

Arthur begins a garbled, embarrassed denial but Jasper cuts him off. "The hilarious thing, the real fucking joke of it all, is that my family's been here longer than any of them, and they know it. I think it drives them crazy, actually."

Arthur tries to imagine how the son of a part-time dealer living in a motel and a migrant worker could have a claim on that kind of old Kentucky legacy; he fails. "What do you mean?"

"Opal always got by on forgeries and bullshit and everyone feeling sorry for her, and never once wondered what it was like for me to walk around with faked papers. I used to have these nightmares . . ." Jasper's flat affect has cracked. Through the fault lines, Arthur sees something familiar: a lonely, tired boy who is too young to have this many secrets. "But did you know if you write the Department of Health they'll email you an index of every birth certificate in the county? If Opal had ever really wanted to know where Mom came from, she could've figured it out, too."

He asks, carefully, "And where did your mom come from?"

"The same place everything in this town comes from." And then Arthur knows, oh Jesus, why didn't he guess? No wonder the mist had risen so often this spring; no wonder Opal and her brother had such accursed luck. The only surprise is that their mother made it as long as she did.

Jasper shrugs, a hard jerk of his shoulders. "The goddamn Gravelys."

Arthur pushes the heels of his hands into his eye sockets, pressing until fireworks burst in the black. "Jasper. You *have* to get out of this town. Now. Tonight."

"I literally *just* told you how sick I am of hearing that."

"You don't understand. The Beasts—the curse—" Arthur pauses to reflect on all the poor life choices that led him here, sitting in his own sick, speaking freely of his family's secrets to a boy who wants him dead, or at least maimed. He swallows. "Haven't you ever wondered why no Gravely stays longer than a night or two in this town? Even if they don't know the whole truth, they know what happens to the ones who stay."

Jasper's eyes have widened, very slightly. Arthur can almost see the machinery of his mind working, recalling every near-miss and brutal accident, all the times the mist rose and he felt the weight of black eyes on the nape of his neck.

Then Arthur watches him gather it all up and shove it someplace cold and private. He arranges a sneer on his face. "You think it's news to me, how much my life has sucked?"

"But it's getting worse. You have to leave—"

"I will." Jasper turns away again. This time he makes it all the way to the door before he pauses. In a much softer voice, he says, "But she won't. So if you can stop this, whatever it is—now's the goddamn time."

It's past time. Opal handed him a vital, final clue—*befriend the Beasts*—and he spent a week pickling himself in self-pity and booze, just because he was too cowardly to pursue it. To unlock the door he's been trying to unlock for his entire adult life, and follow the Beasts down into Hell and make war on whatever he finds there.

He doesn't know what it is. He suspects there's a locus or a source, something that sends the Beasts up to do their bloody work, and he hopes that it's mortal enough to be stopped by a sword through its heart. All he knows for sure is that there have been other places plagued by foul mists and invisible Beasts—until they weren't. Until someone stopped them.

Even now, Arthur should be arming himself, pursuing that dedication, making ready. Instead, he's been delaying. Drinking, because then he would sleep, and when he sleeps the House sends him dreams of her, of them, of a future they won't have.

How selfish, how fundamentally silly, that he should start wanting to live right when he ought to die.

When Arthur finally looks up, Jasper is gone.

It's only much, much later—after Arthur has swept up the glass and puke, emptied the rest of the bourbon down the bathtub drain, opened the fridge, puked again, and begun to assemble everything he'll need for his final descent—that he realizes: his notepad is gone, too.

NINETEEN

I must fall into actual sleep at some point, because I dream of the house again. Except— for the first time—Jasper is there. He's standing in front of the gates, eyes accusatory, both palms red and wet. As I watch, the wrought-iron beasts of the gates begin to move. They coil and writhe, reaching for Jasper, wrapping their metal limbs around him, opening their rusted mouths to swallow him whole.

My own scream wakes me up. The dream fades, but I remember snatches of Jasper's real voice, the worry and fear in it, and think, with disgust: *Enough.*

I take the trash out that evening, embarrassed by the flaccid, stringy feeling of my muscles. On the way back from the dumpster I lift two middle fingers in the direction of Bev's office. The blinds snap back into place.

The next morning I shove my feet into my tennis shoes, trying not to notice the drips of Antique Eggshell scattered over the tops, and slouch across town.

The air is wet and vivid and the sky is a cheery almost-summer blue that makes me want to crawl back to room 12 and hibernate. But the light sinks determinedly into my skin, driving out the gloom of the last week and leaving a slightly depressing normalcy in its place. Everything I know about myself and the world itself has shifted, but nothing's really changed. I know my name, but I'm still nobody; I know where my nightmares come from, but I can't make them stop; I know how Arthur tastes, how his hand feels at my waist, but I can't have him.

Charlotte is peeling pastel flower decorations off the library windows when I turn up, and it occurs to me that I missed Mother's Day. Jasper and me usually play cards and split a cigarette on the riverbank, in memorial. I wonder if he was with the Caldwells this year, if he picked flowers or made pancakes or whatever kids are supposed to do on Mother's Day.

Charlotte beams when she sees me. I feel like a grub exposed to strong sunlight. "Hey."

"*Hey.*" She says it low and sullen, the caricature of a teenager. "It's business hours. How come you aren't housekeeping for Sweeney Todd?"

"How come you aren't bringing my holds to the motel anymore?" It's a clumsy dodge, but it works.

Charlotte sets her box of decorations on the sidewalk and crosses her arms. "Oh, I didn't realize I worked for you! I haven't got a paycheck yet so maybe you should figure that out and get back to me." Her voice is two degrees past teasing, sharper than I'm expecting.

I fiddle with a stray thread on my shirt before muttering, "Sorry," and going inside. I get my holds from the high school volunteer behind the desk, who greets me with a youthful effervescence that ought to be criminalized, and slink back out the double doors with my shoulders hunched around my ears. My reflection looks like someone else. I refuse to consider who.

"Opal." Charlotte stops me before I can stalk dramatically past her.

"Yeah?"

"You know I'll have my master's degree by the end of the month."

"Congratulations." The word comes out sour, teetering on the edge of sarcasm. If Bev were here she'd throw something at me. I'd deserve it.

Charlotte runs her tongue across her teeth. "I wanted you to know that

I've been applying for other positions. In other counties." My guts twist. If I were a cat my spine would be hunched, my fur poofed out. "I thought, if I get a call back . . . I thought maybe you might want to move with me. We could split rent, for a while."

I am aware, in a distant, intellectual way, that this is an act of kindness. I should be flattered and warmed by it. I should be relieved, to be handed a way out of a town that's trying to kill me. I shouldn't want to put my fist through the glass at all.

When I fail to answer, Charlotte adds, "You could do better than this place. You know you could."

I know she's right. When people drive through Eden—and they rarely do—all they see is a little bad-luck town scrabbling on the surface of Big Jack's bones, like a parasite on the carcass of a whale. They don't know about the Gravelys or the Starlings or the things that prowl in the mist, but they sense something off, something spoiled. They keep driving.

Anywhere would be better. But: "Maybe I don't want better." Charlotte opens her mouth. I cut her off. "Anyway, Jasper's still in school. He needs me."

She looks at me with that gentle, insufferable sympathy and asks, softly, "Does he?" and I am amazed how much a question can feel like a sucker punch.

It leaves me panting, reeling. "He does, he *needs* me. I can't *leave*. This is my—" The word catches in my throat and burns there, a choking sweetness, like wisteria in bloom.

It's funny: I always wanted to be from somewhere, to come from something other than a red Corvette and a motel room, and now I do. I'm a goddamn Gravely—my ancestors have been here for generations, digging their roots deeper and deeper into the earth. They've written the history of this town in blood and coal, and the town has buried them, one by one.

So how come I can't say the word? How come it still tastes like a lie?

There are no more flowers left on the front doors. Charlotte tucks the cardboard box under one arm and studies me with a tired sort of pity. "Home is wherever you're loved, Opal."

"You come up with that yourself or did you see it on some soccer mom's Instagram?" I'm all spite now, hissing and spitting. "So, what—you aren't loved enough around here? Is that it?" I try to make it mocking but I wonder if it's true, if that's why everyone keeps leaving me.

For a moment Charlotte's calm cracks and I see the wound running beneath it, raw and red. She stitches it closed again. "Apparently not. Just think about it, alright?"

"Sure," I say.

But I won't. I've made it twenty-six years—despite the Beasts, despite Baine, despite everything—and I'll be damned if I'll cut and run now.

I fully intend to go back to room 12 and continue wallowing at an Olympic level, but when I open the door it strikes me less as a room and more as a den. The floor is scattered with the plastic carcasses of a dozen meals and the sheets have a greasy sheen, like hides. The air is still and meaty.

Room 12 has never meant much to me, but it doesn't deserve this. I rest my head on the sun-warmed metal of the door, wondering if Starling House is falling into decay in my absence and reminding myself firmly that it isn't my problem and never will be, before sighing and stripping the sheets off both beds.

In the movie version of my life the scene would collapse here into a cleaning montage. You would see me rolling up my sleeves and hauling wet laundry out of the washer, dragging the motel cleaning cart across the parking lot, discovering half a granola bar stuck to the carpet and shoving it furtively in a trash bag. The soundtrack would turn peppy, indicating the heroine's renewed resolve. But reality never skips the boring parts, and I'm not sure I have renewed resolve so much as a real stubborn streak, just like Mom. Survival is a hard habit to break.

By the time Jasper turns up the room smells like bleach and Windex and there's a feast laid out across his bed like an apology: canned peaches and gas station pizza, a pair of Ale-8s, a king-sized Reese's to split. I know it's not much, but maybe it's enough, because maybe home is wherever you're loved. The worst thing about cheesy slogans is that they're mostly true.

Jasper dumps his backpack with a seismic thud and stares at the food, then at me—upright, showered, coherent—then back at the food. He eats two slices of sausage-and-pepperoni in showy silence, chewing with the expression of a young god weighing an offering at his altar. Eventually he grants me a measured "Thanks."

"Sure."

He rubs cheese grease on his jeans. "So. You're back. What's up?"

"Nothing," I say, and burst into tears.

I wasn't planning to. I had a whole set of slick lies about how I'd finished my contract at Starling House on good terms but then Lance Wilson gave me mono and I was really sorry I'd been so out of it, but I can't get the words out around the sobs.

The mattress dips and Jasper's arm settles over my shoulders and I know I should push him away and pull it together because kids shouldn't have to take care of adults, but somehow I don't. Somehow I'm smearing snot all over his shoulder—Christ, when did he get so tall—while he gives me tentative pats and says "Hey, it's okay, it's okay" even though it obviously isn't.

I don't stop crying so much as run dry, hiccupping into silence. "So," Jasper says casually, "what's up?"

My laugh is gluey and wet. "I got fired, I guess. A couple of times. And then I quit? It's complicated."

"Did you find a dead body? Or like, a murder dungeon?"

"God, I let you watch too much creepy shit when you were little. No, nothing like that. He just—we just—" I can't think of a succinct or sane way to say *we fought an eldritch beast and briefly made out before he ruined everything by revealing his complicity in our mother's death* so I finish, "Disagreed."

"He's a real asshole, huh."

"The *worst*." I straighten up and tuck my hair behind my ears. "He's rude and weird and his face is all"—I make a violent twisting gesture in midair—"and you know I like tattoos but there's an upper limit. And he's so full of shit, and so *arrogant* about it, like he knows what's best for everybody else—what?"

"Nothing," Jasper says, but he gives me the sideways, shit-eating smile of a kid who's about to break into the K-I-S-S-I-N-G song.

I jam my elbow between his ribs and both of us lose it, laughing in the abrupt, overloud way you do when you haven't laughed in a long time. I have a split-second vision of an alternate world, where monsters aren't real and Starling House is just a house, where Mom never died and I never dropped out and my brother and I were allowed to be dumb kids together.

When we stop laughing, I say, quietly, "Hey. I'm sorry."

"It didn't hurt. You're like, super weak."

"I mean for being such a baby about everything and for ignoring you earlier and for—before. For not telling you what was going on." There's a whole lot more I could and probably should tell him, but I chicken out. My whole body feels raw and weepy, like a skinned knee.

Jasper sobers. "It's okay. I mean it's not, but it is." An unfamiliar weight drags at the corners of his mouth, a hint of confessional guilt. "Look, Opal, I . . ."

He draws a deep breath and I'm struck by the suspicion that he's going to say something heartfelt, that he loves me or forgives me, and I'm too dehydrated to do any more crying. So I say, "Been working on any new videos?"

He closes his mouth. Opens it. "No."

"Why?"

"Just over it, I guess." Jasper shrugs. I'd would call it his tell, except his entire body is comprised of tells. He looks out the window; he fidgets guiltily with the wrapper on the peach can.

A sudden thought knocks the smile off my face. "It doesn't have anything to do with Baine, does it? She hasn't been bothering you?"

A sharp look through his lashes. "No," he says slowly. "She hasn't. And she won't, because you don't have anything to do with that house anymore."

"No. Yeah, I mean, I don't." It's not even a lie. I'm through with Starling House and its Warden, with Elizabeth Baine and her cut-glass eyes, with the whole ugly mess of debts and desires, sins and stories.

I just can't swear they're through with me. *Gravely blood.* "But call me if you hear from her, okay? And"—I reach into my back pocket and withdraw the copper penny I stole weeks ago, which I never quite managed to sell or give back, because I liked the feel of it, the round print it left on my skin— "take this, will you?"

Jasper takes the coin gingerly. He studies the swirling lettering, the faded harp. "Why?"

"For luck." I say it lightly, but I hold his gaze until he slides the penny into his pocket. Maybe when he falls asleep I'll stitch an Eye of Horus into the lining of his backpack; maybe I can find a horseshoe somewhere to hang over the door to room 12. Maybe all Mom's stupid little charms and superstitions were the reason she made it as long as she did.

I have a sudden, sick memory of her hair tangling with the plastic beads of that dream catcher, the night her luck ran out.

"So." Jasper makes a visible decision to sidestep all my weird shit. "What'll you do now?"

Get you the hell out of here. Before Baine gets creative, before Arthur throws open the gates of Underland, before the mist rises again. Which means cash.

Which means—"I'm going down to Tractor Supply in the morning. Figure I'll get my old job back from Frank."

Jasper swallows and the whatever-it-was vanishes. "Didn't you quit without notice and text him a middle finger when he asked where you were? You think he'll hire you back?"

I smile one of my least charming smiles, all sharp angles and teeth. "Yeah. I think he will."

H e does. I mean, the first thing he says when he sees me walk through the door is "No," followed shortly by "Absolutely not," and then "I will call Constable Mayhew and have you removed from the premises," but he comes around. All I have to do is mention my familiarity with child labor laws and the documented fact that he paid me for more than thirty hours per week while I was a minor. His face goes blotchy pink and he disappears into the back office. He returns with a contract balled in his fist and warns me that he'll call Constable Mayhew anyway if I try any more "funny business." He finishes with an admirable attempt at an intimidating glare, and I pay him the courtesy of not laughing in his face. I've gotten used to a higher class of monster, this spring.

I spend the next two weeks wearily reassembling the life I'd had before Starling House, like a hurricane survivor returning home after the water recedes. I open the laptop and drag "document 4.docx" to the recycling bin. I wrap *Underland* back in its shroud of grocery bags and shove it deep under the bed, except this time I add a long woolen coat. It's too hot for it, anyway.

I charge my phone and make a call to Stonewood Academy to confirm that they received my final payment. I ask about summer courses and discover that, for some reason, room and board is twice as much as the regular term. The bursar suggests, delicately, that we might consider an installment plan. I agree, even though I have no idea how I'll make the payments. Then the bursar suggests, even more delicately, that Jasper might want to enroll in noncredit courses the first term. "They're designed to help students like Jasper catch up to their peers."

"Oh, no, his grades are great."

"I'm sure they are! Stonewood only accepts the best, after all." But she keeps talking, circling and insinuating. She mentions *culture shock* and *his background* and how hard they're working on their retention rates for *under-represented demographics.*

I find myself picturing those boys on the rowboat, the oversaturated blue of the sky behind them. I bet none of them ever took a noncredit course; they were the lesson Jasper was supposed to learn, the blueprint he would spend the next two years studying.

Eventually I manage, through a suddenly tight throat, "Thank you, we'll look into that."

I go through my missed texts, including six or seven from Bev asking if I've talked to Charlotte lately and telling me the guests in room 9 left half a pizza behind if I want it. I don't reply.

I block Elizabeth Baine's number without responding to her last message. I make sure to walk fast across the motel parking lot. I never see her, but sometimes I feel the sharp press of eyes on the back of my neck.

I hesitate before tapping the conversation labeled *Heathcliff,* my chest seizing with hope or hate or maybe simple hunger, but his last message is weeks old. Good night, Opal. I wonder if he's sitting in that big empty house, just waiting for a misty night. I wonder if he's been sleeping at all. I wonder if I'll ever see him again.

I take the long way to work. At least it isn't cold anymore; by the end of May the air pants against the back of your neck and the sun lands like a slap.

I pass white crowns of honeysuckle and don't wonder whether those vines are blooming at Starling House. I kick dandelion heads by the side of the road and don't see animal shapes in the pale clouds of seeds. I eat my picante chicken ramen in the break room and don't remember the warm smell of soup simmering in a cast-iron pot. When I see starlings flocking, I don't try to read the shapes they make in the sky.

It's only the dreams I can't get rid of, like stains left behind even when the floodwaters recede. My nights are full of dark corridors and twisting staircases, rooms I remember and others I don't. Sometimes the hallways turn into caves and I realize too late that I've wandered into Underland, that the mist is coiling into spines and skulls. Sometimes the house remains merely a house, and I spend hours running my fingers along the wallpaper, looking for someone I can't seem to find.

Either way, I wake up with his name in my mouth.

"You could take something," Jasper says one morning. "To help you sleep." His eyes are fixed carefully on the back of his cereal box.

"Yeah, maybe I will." And maybe I would, if I wanted the dreams to stop.

My life is already so much dimmer without Starling House. I feel like one of those maidens stolen back from the fairies, blinking the glamour from her eyes to find that her silken gown was made of cobwebs and her crown was nothing but bracken. Or maybe like one of the Pevensies, an ordinary kid who was once a king. I wonder if the feeling will fade. If the memory of a single season will be buried beneath the weight of ordinary years, until it is just a story, just another little lie. If I will learn to be content with enough, and forget that I was ever foolish enough to want more.

I buy a bottle of Benadryl at the gas station the next day. It sits on my windowsill, unopened.

TWENTY

The last week of May is so hot that the mini-fridge sweats and the soles of my shoes stick to the asphalt. Jasper and me take cold showers before bed and wake up with salt crusted to the collars of our shirts. It gets bad enough that Jasper threatens to go live with Logan, so I drag myself over to the front office for the first time since I slammed the door in her face.

Bev is sagging in her chair, a box fan pointed directly at her face and a cold soda pressed to her forehead. A small pool of sweat has gathered in the divot of her throat. "Well, well, well. If it isn't Little Miss Cold Shoulder."

"You've got to turn the AC on, Bev. It's a human-rights issue."

Bev asserts that I'm being dramatic, and furthermore that her granddaddy didn't turn the air conditioner on before June and neither will she.

"Your granddaddy didn't live to see global warming."

"No thanks to the Gravelys." A chill falls between us. If I squint I imagine I could see frost sparking in the air. Bev grunts, "Mail came."

She tosses a rubber-banded roll of mail at me and I turn on my heel, flicking through life insurance ads and threats from debt collectors. There's a cream-colored envelope addressed in handwritten ink that causes me to stop breathing very briefly, but it's not his handwriting. It's swirling and feminine, and there's an embossed seal on the back with the words "Stonewood Academy" circling the edge.

I rip it open in a fumbling rush—did my last payment get lost in the mail? did Elizabeth Baine pull something dirty?—but it's just a card with *thank you* printed across the front in elegant gold.

Dear Mrs. Gravely,

As the principal of Stonewood, I would like to extend my personal thanks to you for making such a generous long-term commitment to our school. Jasper's tuition has been paid in full, and the additional funds will be made available for room, board, and medical needs, as per your request. We can't wait to welcome Jasper this fall!

The card ends with a heartfelt request that I call on the principal personally if Jasper or I need anything at all, and a flourishing signature. I have to read it several times before I understand what must have happened, and then several more before I understand who must have done it.

The card crimps in my hand. "Oh, that *jackass*."

Here I am, doing my damnedest to fold myself back into the grim dimensions of reality, to forget him and his crooked face and the cold taste of the river in my mouth—here I am trying to wake up from the wild dreams of the spring because dreams aren't for people like me—

"You alright?" Bev is squinting at me from under the coke can.

I bite my tongue, very hard, and give her a big, mean smile. "Just fine."

"You don't look fine."

"Neither do you, but I didn't like to mention it."

"Look." Bev smacks the can on the counter. "I know it's a shock finding out who your mama was, but you been walking around like your best friend ran over your dog and now you're crying over a thank-you card—"

"*Jesus,* mind your own *business*!" I slam the door as I leave, because if you're going to act like a hormonal teenager you might as well commit to the role.

I make it two steps out of the office before my legs go. I sit hard on the curb, pressing the tears back into my eyes with the heels of my hands, wondering why Arthur keeps trying to pay that unpayable debt, and why it hurts so much to see him try. And why I'm so damn relieved that he hasn't fallen into Underland, at least not yet.

A shoe scuffs beside me, and I smell tobacco and Febreze. Bev settles on the curb next to me with the harassed sigh of someone whose joints no longer appreciate low seats.

We sit in sweaty silence for a minute before she says in a rough voice, "Remember when I first met you?" I shrug at the pavement. "You got yourself stung by a wasp, one of those nasty red ones. What were you, seven?"

I unpeel my palms from my face. "Six."

"But you didn't cry. You just sat there, biting your own lip, waiting it out." Denim scrapes on concrete as Bev turns to face me. "It didn't even occur to you to ask for help."

"I was an independent kid."

"You were a *stupid* kid, and now you're a stupid woman." Bev has called me stupid at least twice a week for most of my life, but she's never done it with her jaw squared and her eyes pushing hard into mine. "How in hell is anybody supposed to help you if you won't ask?"

Because asking is dangerous, I could tell her. Because to ask is to hope that someone answers, and it hurts so bad when nobody does. I stiffen my spine instead. "I take care of my own shit, okay? I don't need anybody's charity."

Her lip curls. "That so?"

"Yes."

She huffs like I hit her and I think: *Finally.* If I can't shout at Arthur Starling then a good old-fashioned parking lot slap-fight with Bev will have to do.

I'm tense and ready, darkly eager, but Bev just watches me with that weary disgust. "Do you still think," she asks, and I've never heard her sound so tired, "at almost twenty-seven years old, that I let you stay here all this time because I lost a *bet?*"

If this was a fight, I lost it. I'm laid out flat, gasping for air, feeling furious and ashamed and everything except surprised. Because I guess this is another thing I already knew. I knew Bev didn't let me stay because she had to. She did it for the same reason she slapped wet tobacco on my wasp sting as a kid: because I needed help, even if I never asked.

I'm bent over, arms crossed around my own chest, as if I might come apart at the seams if I don't hold myself tight. "Why didn't you tell me? That I was—that Mom was a Gravely." My voice is small in my ears, very young.

Bev sighs beside me, and her body sags into it. "I don't know. Never seemed to be a good time for it, I guess." She wipes sweat off her upper lip. "Or maybe I just didn't want to tell you. Your mama was the only Gravely I ever met that was worth a damn, and they cast her out, and you too. I took you in." I risk a look at her face and find it just as hard and mean as always. But she scoots her foot toward me until the sides of our shoes are pressed together. "Finders keepers."

A weird warmth moves from her shoe to mine, chasing up my limbs, settling in my chest. It occurs to me that I was wrong, that Bev never looked away. She helped us even though we never asked. And if home really is wherever you're loved—

I can't finish the thought.

Bev is speaking again. "You should know. The day before your mama—on New Year's Eve, she came over. We split a bottle or two and she told me her daddy was dying. She said she was going to talk to him, to make things right for you and Jasper. She said she'd pay me back for all those years in room 12."

I exhale, not quite a laugh. "She said a lot of things." I remember all the big talk, and all the broken promises that came after. It occurs to me, for no good reason, that Arthur has never broken a promise to me.

"I know, but this time seemed different." Bev shakes her head and stands. Her knee joints sound like cap guns. "I don't know what all's going on with you, kid, but if you ever . . ." She trails into a sigh, having apparently exceeded her annual quota of public emotions.

She reaches for the office door with her neck bent and her shoulders heavy, and it strikes me that it's been a long time since I saw her with her chin held high. The buzzed sides of her head have gone shaggy with neglect and the shadows under her eyes have deepened to a sleepless mauve, and I didn't notice because I was too busy wallowing.

"So what about you?"

She pauses with the door half-open. "What about me?"

"Do you ever ask for help?"

She very nearly smiles. "Mind your own business. Meathead."

The CLOSED sign jangles against the glass as the door shuts behind her.

I sit on the curb, letting the sun bake the hate out of me, feeling like a rug dragged out for an airing. I reread the thank-you note a few more times and try to picture it: Jasper in a crisp navy uniform, sitting at a desk without cuss words carved into it, breathing air without coal dust in it. Jasper, all taken care of, launched like a ship onto the bright seas of a better world.

I want it, I swear I do. It's just that I can't see myself in that picture. I'm somewhere else, off-screen or under water, drifting in whatever abyss waits for you when there's nothing left on your list. I wonder if I'm truly angry, or just scared.

I slide my phone out of my back pocket and type why did you do it.

He might not answer. He might pretend not to know what I mean. He might have smashed his phone to pieces and gone to make war on Hell itself, because that's the kind of dramatic fool he is. But I wait, sweating into the sidewalk, phone held too tight in my hand.

Because I didn't want you to come back.

I type a reply but don't send it. It sounds too much like asking a question, and to ask is to hope.

But later, when I wake from a tangled nightmare of mist and blood, with the taste of river water in my throat and the shape of his name on my tongue, I press send. i think you do.

He doesn't answer.

It takes three days before I stop checking my texts every ten minutes, and even then I don't really stop. I keep my phone tucked beneath the counter at Tractor Supply, hidden behind a roll of paper towels, and my heart seizes every time the screen lights up. (It's only ever Jasper texting me pictures of friendly dogs or early tiger lilies; he seems to think I need cheering up.)

I don't even know what I'm hoping for—an apology, a plea, an excuse to go marching up to his front door and ask him how the hell he could let me work under his roof for four months without mentioning the monsters under the floorboards which, by the way, are the reason my mom is dead.

But I suppose he has nothing to say to me, after all. He's alone in Starling House again, just like he wanted, a mad knight readying himself for a battle he's bound to lose.

Honestly, I'm lucky I made such a clean getaway. I check my phone again.

"You waiting on a text?" Lacey asks over my shoulder.

"Tell Frank I'm taking lunch early." I shove the phone in my back pocket and slide out from behind the cash register.

I used to time my breaks to overlap with Lance's so we could get high and make out behind the Tractor Supply dumpsters, but it turns out the availability of the weed was dependent on the making out, so now I spend my breaks stalking restlessly around town. Today I find myself passing the high school just as kids are shuffling toward the cafeteria, gossiping and bitching and flirting.

Technically you're supposed to sign in at the front desk and get a guest pass, et cetera, et cetera, but Jasper won't be in the cafeteria.

I cross the crisp white lines of the football field, sweating, fighting the dizzy time-warp sensation of visiting your old school: a glutinous sucking at the soles of your feet, as of quicksand, and the nagging suspicion that you never really left and never will.

Everybody else in my grade is either married with two kids or long gone, and here I am, spending my lunch break with a brother who won't be here for much longer, hunted by hungry Beasts, waiting for a text I'll never get and shouldn't want. No wonder I still dream of Starling House; even a bad dream is better than nothing.

Jasper is alone, an empty blue plastic tray beside him in the grass. He must be catching up on homework—nerd!—because his laptop is open and he's frowning down at a yellow notepad full of cramped writing.

I stare very hard at the notepad, neurons screaming. I know exactly who it belongs to, but it seems to take my brain a long time to accept its existence here, now. It's like seeing a teacher at the grocery store or a cat on a leash, something inimical to the order of the universe.

"Jasper?"

Jasper startles, sees me, and startles worse. He shoves the notepad under his backpack, centuries too late.

"Where did you get that?" My voice sounds ominous in my own ears, like the cool rush of air before a good summer storm.

Jasper tries out several different expressions—guilt, denial, pure panic—before settling on a tired honesty. "Where do you think?"

"But you didn't go there. You wouldn't. Or—did he give it to you? Because if he did I'll—"

Jasper shakes his head once. "No, *he*"—he says it with audible italics—"didn't give it to me. I stole it."

"*Why?*" Somewhere underneath the panicked shrieking sounds in my head, a more detached part of me would also like to know *how*. (A less detached part of me wants to know if he saw Arthur, if his wounds are closing up right, if he asked about me. I smother that one in the cradle.)

Jasper does not look like any part of his brain is panicking or shrieking. He looks resigned. "Because I wanted to know what happened to you, and what the hell is up with that house."

"So, you decided to commit a crime about it, and hide the evidence in your backpack. Do you have any idea what kind of people are watching the Starling place? What they'd do to you? Were you ever planning to tell me, or—"

"Surely"—for the first time in this conversation, there's a hint of heat in his voice, a dangerous aridity—"you don't think you have the moral high ground here."

A half second's pause here, while I shore up my crumbling defenses. I fall back on the oldest line, the one I could say in my sleep: "Everything I did, I was doing for you."

He looks at me with an eerie clarity, as if he's reading a map of me, with every fault line and fissure in my character clearly labeled. "Okay," he says, gently and tiredly. I think, for no reason, of that video he made of the bloody-handed girl mouthing *I love you* at the camera.

"Okay," he says again. He looks back down at his laptop, scrolling and clicking. "But would you like to know what I found out?"

I cross my arms, feel the chill bumps prickling beneath my T-shirt. "Arthur already told me."

"You think he told you everything?" Jasper asks, mildly.

I hesitate. It's just a fraction of a moment, but he sees it. He smiles, not particularly happily, and gestures to the grass beside him.

I don't sit down so much as cave in. Jasper looks out at the cornfield, the sharp lines of new shoots warped by noon heat, and tells me a story.

This is not the story of Starling House.

I mean, it sort of is, but it's not about Eleanor or her husband or whoever else. I don't care about who built the house or why, or whether they were good or evil or insane. I care who came after and what happened to them, and making damn sure it doesn't happen to anyone else.

This is the story of the Wardens of Starling House.

The first one after Eleanor was a guy named Alabaster Clay—do not shush me, Opal, how many of your stories have I sat through—who showed up in 1887. Alabaster was from Crow County, way east of here, and he'd been born with a rare skin condition where all the color drained out of him in big, milky patches. Which wouldn't have been a big deal, except that the local preacher apparently accused him of devilry or witchcraft or something, and Alabaster was driven out of town. A little while later he started having these dreams—I won't describe them, because I know you know what kind of dreams I mean—and eventually he showed up in Eden. He wrote to his sister that he "followed the starlings."

And then in 1906 they found old Alabaster hanging on the front gates of Starling House with his throat ripped out. I looked up the date in Charlotte's newspaper collection. They blamed it on wild dogs at the time; seems they'd attacked several people that same night.

After Alabaster came two young Osage women, Tsa-me-tsa and Pearl. Their family was originally from somewhere on the Ohio River, but they'd been driven west, and then farther west, and then came the Indian Appropriations Act and they were left scraping a living out on the big flat hell of Kansas. Pearl and Tsa-me-tsa were orphaned and sent off to one of those fucked-up boarding schools, but then Pearl started having these dreams. (This is what we might call a *pattern*.)

If you look their names up in the school records, it says they both died in a typhoid outbreak. That must have been some administrator trying to cover his ass, because they lived in Starling House for more than twenty years before they died.

Nobody ever found their bodies, but according to your boyfriend's notes—ow! Jesus, it's called a *joke*—they have headstones side by side on Starling land.

Then came Ulysses Wright, the son of Tennessee sharecroppers. He and his parents arrived in the early thirties, after their employer sold the land out from under them. His parents died of regular old age, but Ulysses was found with the sword still in one hand. Next were Etsuko and John Sugita in '43. They were originally from California, but met in Jerome, Arkansas. After about six months of unlawful detention they climbed the camp fence and followed the Mississippi north. They had two daughters in the house before Etsuko was found floating down the Mud River. After them came Odessa Dixon and her wife, then Eva Jackson, then Lynn and Oscar Lewis.

Can you guess what happened to all of them? Are you starting to see the pattern?

A Warden falls. The house calls someone new—someone lost or lonely, someone whose home was stolen or sold or who never had a home in the first place. It calls them, and they come, and they are never homeless again.

All it costs is blood. I mean that very literally—Arthur's notes mention some kind of **blood oath** (God, that's embarrassing to say) to become Warden.

But it doesn't stop there, does it? It takes more blood, and more, until another Warden is dead and some other poor bastard starts to dream of staircases and hallways and locked doors. Again and again, faster and faster.

It sounds okay at first, even sort of noble: a house for the unhoused, a home for all the people whose homes were stolen from them. It's like a fairy tale, a dream. But then it eats them alive.

In her diary Etsuko called Starling House their "sanctuary." But it's not a sanctuary. It's a grave. And Opal: it won't be yours.

TWENTY-ONE

The last time I heard a story about Starling House I was sitting inside it. The night pressing at the windows, Arthur's blood on my hands, his eyes wild on mine. It had all sounded so grand and so terrible, like a modern-day myth.

Told here, sandwiched between the cornfield and the football field in the mean light of noon, it just sounds sad and strange.

Jasper is watching my face closely. "Well?"

"Well, what?" I lift one shoulder and let it fall, showily unconcerned. "I got fired, remember? Haven't been back since. I appreciate your concern, but this is all extremely old news."

"Have the dreams stopped?"

I tuck my hair behind my ear. "What dreams?"

Jasper rubs his face so hard it looks like he's trying to physically mold it into an expression of patience. "There are two more things you should know. The first one is that whatever's going on in that house is getting worse. I looked at all the dates, went through more newspapers . . ." He rubs his face again, this time like he's trying to remove something from it. "The Wardens are dying faster."

My own pulse is suddenly loud in my ears. "Since when?" Screw waiting for a text, I'm going to call Arthur over and over until he picks up, warn him—but then I remember Arthur's oath to be the last Warden, the pure panic on his face when I mentioned my dreams, and realize: he already knows.

"I don't know, like the early eighties? But here's the second thing." Jasper turns until he's facing me, his eyes heavy on mine. "All these people, every Warden, had a *choice*. They chose to act on their dreams, to follow the fucking starlings or whatever. They *chose* to swear themselves to that place—even Arthur."

"Maybe."

"No, not maybe. Look, there was something else tucked in the notes." For the first time in this conversation, Jasper looks a little guilty. "I know I shouldn't have read it, because of privacy or whatever, but . . ."

He pulls his Algebra II textbook out of his bag and withdraws a very familiar piece of notebook paper. I recognize the faded blue of the lines, the plain handwriting, the torn edge. But this isn't the page I found before, the one that ended midsentence: *This is your birthright, Arthur. That's what I told you the night you ran away, isn't—*

This is the other half of the letter. I take it from Jasper without speaking, and read.

it? But—God forgive me, because I doubt you can—I was wrong.

There's no such thing as a birthright. All you have inherited from us are your cheekbones and your stubbornness. You are free to make your own life, build your own home, fight your own battles. This House has no heirs; the next Warden will be whoever takes up the sword.

I'm sorry. I have loved this place for so long, and fought so hard for it, that I got all confused. I thought I was fighting for a home; I was only ever fighting for you.

Back in North Carolina, the dreams didn't come to me when the bank took the house away. They didn't come when we missed rent in the trailer park, either. It was only when I knew you were on the way that I started dreaming of Starling House, because that's when I decided I needed some-place nobody could take from me.

I chose. So will you.

I love you.
Mom

P.S. Your father wants me to remind you to trim the roses before the last frost and stake the foxgloves by June. I told him you weren't coming back and he said that's fine but I should tell you just in case.
P.P.S. Wherever you go, I hope you're not alone. If I was ever strong—if I ever did a single good or brave thing in my life—it was only because I had you and your father to be strong for.

The letter leaves a catch in my throat, an ache in my chest.

All this time, I still thought Arthur was trapped, cursed to carry on his mother's work. But he wasn't. He came home to bury his parents and found a letter setting him free. He never had to take up the sword.

Right now, he could be living in a cute two-bedroom apartment in Phoenix, haunted by nothing more alarming than mice. He could be working nights and dating a dental hygienist. He could be a professor or a happily starving artist or anything he wanted.

But he's here, all alone, paying a terrible price so that no one else has to. And if he has made mistakes—if he let a monster slink out into the night, hunting Gravely blood—hasn't he paid enough for it?

I fold the letter carefully along the tattered lines and slip it in my pocket. I swallow twice. "You're right. You shouldn't have read that."

Jasper's eye roll is almost audible. "Okay sure, but I did, and so did you, and now we both know the truth."

"That we are criminals and degenerates?"

"That every Warden makes a choice. It's not inherited or destined or what-ever. A few of them had families, right? And do you know what happened to their kids? They moved away and got married and had normal lives! Noth-ing kept them here, not fate, not blood." Jasper is leaning toward me now, speaking clearly, like a teacher talking to a sullen and slightly slow child. "The Wardens *chose* that place. And that means we can choose, too."

"I get what you're saying but"—someone hits the brakes in my brain, tires squealing—"*we?*"

Jasper looks at me for a long time then. Long enough for me to notice the spongy, sleepless bags beneath his eyes, the new lines carved beside his mouth, the wispy not-quite-stubble of an unshaven teenager. Then he says, horribly slowly, "You aren't the only homeless kid in this town, Opal." In his eyes I can see the reflections of doors and stairs he's only seen in dreams, the ghostly map of a house that isn't his.

All the air seems to evaporate out of my bloodstream. I'm dizzy, breathless with emotions I can't even name. Fury, maybe, for the years of secrets between us, and fear for what happens next. But also something acid and viscous, bubbling noxiously in my throat: *envy.*

"You can't ever go back there. Promise me you won't." My fingers are biting into the turf, ripping roots.

Jasper is closing his laptop, sliding it between the textbooks in his backpack, zipping it shut. He stands, looking at me with that tired, distant expression back on his face. "Why? Because you want me safe, or because you want the house for yourself?"

"Oh, go to *hell*—"

"You haven't been able to make up your mind, have you? But I have." His smile is strangely gentle. "Nobody—not you, not that house—is going to tell me what to do with my life."

Jasper picks up his blue plastic tray and leaves me alone at the edge of the field.

I waste the rest of my lunch break kicking rocks at the Tractor Supply dumpsters, periodically shouting swears. It doesn't help; by the time I clock in I'm still so mad that Frank opens his mouth to bitch at me for being late and then slowly closes it and scurries down the cat toy aisle instead.

I ring up four customers without making eye contact. I don't look up until a cool, not-from-around-here voice says, "Good evening, Opal."

I hadn't seen her approach the counter: a pretty woman with her watch turned to the inside of her wrist and a smile that looks like it was clipped out of a magazine and glued to her chin.

I'm not surprised; I always knew Elizabeth Baine wouldn't give up easy.

I greet her with the aggressive apathy of a cashier on the sixth hour of her shift. "Find everything you need, ma'am?"

"Yes, thank you." She places a pack of gum and a matchbook on the counter, one of those embarrassing souvenirs that says *My Old Kentucky Home* in blue script. I ring her up and she draws a matte black card out of her purse. She doesn't hand it to me.

"Anything else I can help you with?"

She taps the card on the counter. "We've been trying to get in touch with you."

"Well, here I am." If she's trying to rattle me, she shouldn't have tried it here. I've stood behind this counter and smiled down eight years of lewd suggestions, one attempted robbery, and more than a hundred 4-H-club moms with highlights and out-of-date coupons.

"Can we talk privately? You're off at six."

Frank is lurking in the lawn mower belts now, watching us, so I give her an extra big smile when I say, "Fuck off."

A muscle moves in her jaw. "Then I'll be quick. Our group has determined, thanks to your *cooperation*"—she wields the word like a knife, looking for a soft spot—"that it's worth pursuing the phenomena at Starling House."

My heart gives a guilty flinch, but my smile doesn't twitch. "Best of luck."

"We believe—" Baine inhales, her nostrils pinched white. "—that we need the keys. We are willing to pay you a substantial sum for them."

"Oh, gee, that's awful nice of you, but I don't have them." I make the same face I use when I'm telling someone their brand of dog food won't be restocked until Wednesday. "And, as I don't work for Mr. Starling anymore, I'm afraid I can't help you."

Her magazine smile is wadded up now, all edges and angles. "Can't or won't?"

This is the moment to cover my ass, to assure her that I'm still the spineless money-grubbing double-crosser she thinks I am. It wouldn't even be a lie.

But maybe I don't want it to be true. Or maybe I just don't think Stonewood Academy would kick Jasper out after cashing the check Arthur sent them; it's easy to be brave when it won't cost you anything.

Or maybe I've just had a very shitty day. I bare my teeth at her, brazen and stupid, and don't answer.

She waits, then says, "I see," and slides her card across the counter.

I tuck her receipt in the bag and hand it over. "You have a nice day, ma'am."

Baine lingers, studying my face as if she's looking for the error in an equation. "I misjudged you, Opal." She says my name like she owns it. "I thought you loved your brother."

She unfurls a new smile as she says it, the bright white sneer of someone who has never spent a single week without dental insurance, who wins every hand because she has all the cards. It's designed to put me in my place, to bend me.

Instead, I break.

There's a hitch in my vision, like a skipping track, and then Elizabeth Baine isn't smiling anymore. She's bent double with her hands pressed over her mouth, making a sound like a rusty hinge in the wind. My knuckles are split, throbbing sweetly, and Frank is pointing at me in red-jowled triumph. My hearing has gone funny, but I can read his lips beneath the flying spittle: *Get out!*

Which is either the second or third time I've been fired this month, depending on how you count it.

This time I don't run. This time I tuck my phone in my pocket and grab a candy bar from the rack. I touch the Butterfinger to my forehead in mocking salute and saunter out into the ripe spring sun.

Jasper and me used to jump off the old railroad bridge when we were kids. Everybody did, even though half the time the water left your skin rashy and red. It was the only satisfactory ending to a summertime double dare, high enough to scare you but not high enough to hurt, close enough to Starling House to send goose bumps down your spine but not close enough to stop you.

I used to like it: the curl of my toes over the edge, the rush of wind, the clap of skin against water and then sudden, plunging silence. It was like falling into another world, escaping the noisy gravity of reality, just for a little while. It was like dreaming.

I haven't done it since the accident, of course. I've cuffed my jeans and gone wading once or twice, but never for very long, and only ankle-deep. The water is always too cold, even in summer, and I have this stupid conviction that I'm going to trip and go under and not come up. *Classic PTSD,* I guess.

But every now and then I come sit on the bridge. It's a good time for it: the glazed hour right before sunset, when the heat fades and the shadows stretch like tired dogs across the ground. The first fireflies are pulsing above the river, visible only by their reflections in the dark water, and the steam from the smokestacks is ribboning into the sky. I don't look at the power plant, because I don't want to think about who it belongs to.

I look at the old mines instead, almost invisible beneath the kudzu, boards black with rot, before it occurs to me that they're owned by the same family: mine.

A wave of something like nausea moves through me. I wonder if Nathaniel Boone dug that very mine, and if he really found a way into Hell to escape my great-great-whoevers. I wonder if Eleanor Starling hated her husband or mourned him. I wonder why she put stones in her pockets, or if that's just what happens when you run out of dreams and have nothing left but nightmares.

That's how I knew Mom didn't drive into the river on purpose, no matter what Constable Mayhew thought: she had enough dreams for a dozen people. She was an appetite on two legs, always running from one scheme to the next. Instead of bedtime stories she told our fortunes, with the starry-eyed conviction of a kid with a cootie catcher. She'd marry a pharmacist and we'd live in a big brick house with two bathtubs. She'd win the scratch-off and we'd buy a cottage on the seashore. She'd become a big-time music star and they'd play her songs on 94.3 (The Wolf: Country That'll Make You Howl) and the three of us would move to one of those fancy suburbs where you have to enter a code to get past the gates.

I guess that's what she was doing the day she died. Rolling the dice, taking a chance, chasing a dream. She told us she was finally going to turn our lives around, and I guess she meant it—I guess she was going to talk her way back into her daddy's good graces and give us a last name and a family fortune, make us somebodies after years of being nobodies—but at the time I didn't believe her. The last thing she said to me, before the wheels screamed sideways across the asphalt, was: *You'll see.*

I saw plenty. I saw the mist cleave. I saw the river rise. I saw that dreams were dangerous, so I folded mine up and shoved them under the bed along with the rest of my childhood.

I barely even remember what they were, now. I close my eyes and let the sound of the river fill my skull, trying to imagine what I wanted before I made myself stop wanting. At first all I can think of are little-kid dreams: cakes with thick frosting, matching sheets, that one baby doll that ate plastic cherries off a plastic spoon.

And then: a house that feels like a home. A boy, kneeling among the flowers.

A boy who grew up in a hurry, just like me, who spent his life doing what was necessary instead of what was nice. A boy who wanted me—look, I know he did—but not as much as he wanted to keep me safe.

I remind myself firmly that Arthur Starling is also a liar and a coward, responsible for my mother's untimely death, et cetera, et cetera, but my own voice sounds unconvinced in my head. He couldn't have been more than sixteen or seventeen when it happened. All alone except for the awful weight of his choices, the endless halls of his labyrinth.

It was an accident, plain and ugly, and he blamed himself so thoroughly that even I believed him. And now—while I sit here wishing and wallowing—he's going to follow the Beasts back into Underland. He's going to be the last Warden and the newest grave.

Unless I do something.

I slide my phone out of my pocket and run my thumb across the cracked screen. I text Jasper first, because a person should have their affairs in order before they do something really stupid, and I don't want the last words between us to be lies and accusations. hey, we have to talk.

All this time I told myself I was saving him, shielding him from the messy shadow of Starling House, but apparently he's already in it neck-deep, and the only person I was saving was myself. I didn't want to tell him he was actually a Gravely, or even a student of Stonewood Academy. I didn't want him to belong to anybody but me.

I guess I understand, a little, why Bev never told me the truth.

I wait, listening to the green hum of the trees and the throttled song of the river. The sun disappears behind the western bank and the air follows it in a rush, lifting the hair from my neck, cooling my swollen knuckles.

Jasper doesn't write back, even though I'm pretty sure he's hanging out with Logan doing exactly fuck all, because school lets out next week and he finished all his finals early.

I call him instead, feeling a little cruel because we generally only call each other when there are legitimate medical emergencies, but it's his fault for ignoring me. He doesn't pick up. I wait some more.

The dusk deepens. The stars quicken. The power plant glows hot orange. There's a gathering weight in the air, like rain. Like a consequence, coming straight for me.

I call Jasper again, counting each ring before a cool voice tells me the owner of this number has not set up a mailbox. I'm telling myself firmly that there's no reason to panic, nothing to worry about, when I see it: a wisp of mist rising up off the river.

My feet go numb, like I'm walking into cold water. I watch another milky curl spiral upward, reaching toward my ankles.

I call again. The water reaches my belly, a sick chill.

Again, and again, and I feel myself going under.

TWENTY-TWO

When Arthur's phone rings, he assumes he is dreaming. It's happened once or twice (or maybe three times, or four) recently. It's a stupid dream, because only one person has this number and she has no reason ever to speak to him again. Still: he keeps the phone in his breast pocket, and never lets the battery dip below twenty percent. He lingers by the socket while it charges, just in case.

But now he can feel the buzz of the phone against his chest and Baast is staring at his pocket with a disgruntled expression. He fumbles it out of his pocket and answers without pausing to look at the screen.

"Yes?" He hopes she can't hear the foolish gallop of his pulse.

"Arthur Starling?"

There is a pause while Arthur's heart sinks and he berates it for rising in the first place. "Who is this?"

"My name is Elizabeth Baine. I'm with the Innovative Solutions Consulting Group, calling on behalf of Gravely Power. We've been trying to contact you for some time."

Arthur supposes he should have expected this. They no longer have a spy, so they must resort to less-elegant strategies—bribery, blackmail, various unlikely legal threats designed to frighten people into compliance. But you can only be frightened if you have a future to lose, and Arthur doesn't.

The morning after Jasper's visit, Arthur called Eleanor's publisher. The first person told him chirpily that she didn't know who to ask about the source of a nineteenth-century dedication, but she'd get back to him! (She did not get back to him.) The next person asked him if he knew there was a recession on and that everyone was stressed and overworked and did not have time to pursue the eccentric requests of a dead author's not-quite-descendant. The next person hung up on him.

But Arthur persisted, and eventually he spoke to the great-nephew of Eleanor's first editor, who consulted the family archives and confirmed that the dedication was added in the seventh edition, in accordance with the will Eleanor Starling wrote just before she disappeared.

Arthur had thanked him and hung up knowing that Opal was right, and that Eleanor had left instructions for finding Underland.

Since then he's been readying himself, waiting only for the mist to rise.

"So, Mr. Starling—"

"Fuck off."

He's pulling the screen away from his ear when the voice sighs and says, tinnily, "That's the second time today I've been told to fuck off."

The tendons go taut across the back of Arthur's hand as he presses the phone back to his ear. "You've spoken to Opal."

"Who do you think gave us this number?" Of course she did. Arthur doesn't blame her; he deserves worse. "We expected a little more from her, if I'm honest. But she proved uncooperative."

"What does that mean?" Somewhere inside Arthur there is a leash, badly frayed. He hears invisible threads snapping. "What did you do to her?"

"We didn't do anything *to* her." It's her mild amusement that does it: the leash breaks.

His voice emerges as a glottal rasp, fury-choked. "If you're lying, if you've hurt her, I swear I'll—"

"You'll what?" She asks it quickly, almost greedily, as if she knows precisely what violent delights he is imagining. The cellar door, thrown open. The Beasts running loose, clotting her arteries or crashing her car, raining a thousand calamities on her miserable soul—

Arthur swallows savage bile and does not answer, fumbling for the ragged remains of that leash.

"Did you think we took a bat to her kneecaps? We're corporate consultants, not mob bosses." Elizabeth Baine laughs, artfully. It's supposed to make Arthur feel a little chagrined, quietly reassured.

Arthur is neither. "You drugged Miss Opal without her consent or knowledge." He remembers the way she looked—sick and reeling, unwillingly vulnerable, like a knight stripped of her armor; he wonders where Baine is now and how quickly he could get there. "Then you questioned her, you must have threatened her—"

"We found the right incentive for her cooperation, that's all. Or I thought we did." There's a shrug in her voice. "Apparently I was mistaken."

Had Opal refused them, in the end? His heart lifts, and he tries hard to stamp it back down. "That's too bad."

"It is. So, we were going to approach you directly. Starling House isn't the only place we're investigating, I hope you know. It's one of several unique sites—we're calling them anomalous apertures, in the reports—but it seems to be the most active. I was going to offer you a fairly absurd amount of money for your property. I imagine you would have refused—"

"Yes."

"—forcing us to work with Mr. Gravely to pursue the mineral rights to your land which, as I suspect you already know, do not belong to you."

A little chill slicks down his spine, dampening the pleasant heat of hate. He thinks of all the notices and letters he's received from Gravely Power, the font growing larger and redder with each missive. He'd forwarded them to the family lawyer without opening them, and been assured that no one could mine his property without his written consent, as it was no longer the 1940s. But if there's anyone with fewer scruples and more connections than a coal company, it's surely Elizabeth Baine.

Arthur swallows a vision of strangers digging and pawing through his earth, pretending to look for coal until they found something much worse.

Arthur decides it's a helpful reminder of what will happen if he fails, if he lingers up here in Eden, rather than going down to Underland.

"I hope you're prepared to spend the next decade in court, then," he says into the phone. He hopes his growl is convincing. "I promise I'll make you regret ever setting foot in Eden."

A sigh gusts through the speaker. "I'm sure you would have." Only then does Arthur hear her odd choice of tenses: *would have, was going to.* "But I don't think it will come to that. I've found what I need."

The chill thickens, congealing in his stomach. "And what's that?"

He can see her smile hanging before him, a sickly Cheshire grin. "The right incentive."

The line goes dead.

Arthur is almost at the front gates when he realizes he cannot see his own feet, because he is running through a thin veil of mist.

TWENTY-THREE

I call Jasper nine more times on the way back to the motel, hanging up before the automated message begins and forcing myself to take ten steps before I call again. No answer.

I don't have Logan's number in my phone, so I call the high school counselor and ask him to look it up for me. Mr. Cole tells me he can't do that due to student confidentiality or whatever and I put a tremor in my voice, which isn't hard, and say, "Please, sir. I'm worried about Jasper."

Ten seconds later Logan answers his phone and says "Hi?" with the ponderous wonder of a teenager who has spent the last week marinating in weed and video games.

"Hey, tell my brother to pick up his phone."

"Opal?"

"No, it's Dolly Parton." I can almost hear the gears of his brain grinding, like nachos in a blender. "Yes, Logan, it's Opal. I want to talk to Jasper."

"Uh, he's not here?" He doesn't sound very sure.

I exhale slowly through my nose. "Logan Caldwell, are you lying to me?"

I hear the click of his throat as he swallows. "No, ma'am."

"Well then where is he?"

"Home, I guess? He said he had that interview thing to get ready for, but he was supposed to come over later, my mom's making wings—"

I hang up before I say something I'll regret. Like: *What interview,* or, *How come he told you and not me, you little shit?* The power company people must have gotten ahold of him somehow, and he didn't have the guts to tell me. I have a guilty flash of the Stonewood acceptance folder waiting under my bed in its sparkly gift bag; I walk a little faster.

The air is hushed and the fog is thickening fast. The leaves are thrashing above me, white-bellied, and the wind tastes bitter in the back of my throat. Dark, oily clouds boil on the horizon.

Maybe Jasper just turned his phone off for his interview and forgot to turn it back on. Maybe he fell asleep with headphones on. Maybe Arthur is drawing the Starling sword even now, standing between the Beasts and my brother.

Or maybe he's waiting to befriend them, empty-handed, leaving Eden to fend for itself. I walk a little faster.

I'm getting close when I hear the sound of sirens. High and distant, howling closer.

I look up at the sky and realize that it isn't thunderclouds massing overhead, eating the last of the light: it's smoke.

I stop trying to call Jasper. I run, shoes slapping the road, lungs aching. The sky darkens. The smoke thickens, pooling and coiling above the fog, nothing at all like the honest gray of chimney smoke, or even the bleached white clouds from the power plant. It's black and sour, littered with greasy flakes of ash and the chemical remains of things that were never meant to burn. It tangles with the mist, forming dark shapes that make my eyes sting.

All the Gutiérrez kids are out on the sidewalk in front of Las Palmas, coughing into their elbows, their faces blurred by mist and smoke. One of their aunts shoos them back inside as I pass, casting worried looks over her shoulder. Her face appears at the old drive-thru window, watching the sky. She pulls a charm from her blouse and kisses it three times.

Four fire trucks scream past me, cutting through the haze. I stare after them, willing them to keep going straight, as if my will matters at all, as if anything in this damn town has ever gone right.

The trucks turn in to the motel parking lot. My jaw twinges, the way it does when I'm about to puke.

I run faster.

I make the last turn and the heat hits me. It boils off the motel in an acrid wave, drying my eyes and cracking my lips, burning the mist away. I shove past knots of onlookers, knocking phones out of hands, taking an elbow to the corner of my mouth and not caring, not even feeling it. I trip over a canvas hose and lurch back up, coughing hard, lying to myself as hard as I can.

Maybe Bev tried to reheat her pizza in the toaster again. Maybe a guest stubbed their cigarette out on their mattress. Maybe it was just regular bad luck, rather than a Beast with a taste for Gravely blood.

It'll be fine. Everything's okay.

Then I make it around the last car and see that nothing is okay, that it might never be okay again, because the Garden of Eden is burning.

The Garden of Eden is burning—flames blooming from the rooftop, shingles melting and oozing into the gutters, guests huddled beneath shiny emergency blankets—and I don't know where my little brother is, and it's all my fault.

Someone is shouting at me. I ignore them, squinting through the smog, blinded by the blue strobe of police lights and the sting of smoke. I'm looking for that brass number 12, that not-quite-a-home, that one safe place—but it's gone. There's nothing but a gaping hole where our door used to be, a black throat spewing smoke. The window is gone, too, the sidewalk glittering with glass. Flames lick over the sill to lap at the eaves.

I run. A hand grabs my shoulder and I bite it, quick and vicious. The hand disappears. I taste someone else's blood.

I'm yelling now, my voice swallowed by the hungry roar of the fire, close enough to feel the bite of cinders through my jeans. They get me right before I dive through the hot maw of the door.

I don't go down easy. It takes two volunteer firefighters and a state trooper to pin me and get the cuffs around my wrists, and even then I'm still kicking and clawing, because once I stop fighting I'll start screaming.

I should have gotten him out of Eden. I should've known a lucky penny and a mad Warden weren't enough to keep him safe. It's only now, thrashing on the hot pavement, that I realize how much I still trusted Arthur Starling. He failed my mother, but I never really believed he would fail me.

"Let me go, let me *go*, where is he? Did you get him out?"

They don't answer. Someone steps through the smoke and stares down at me with his thumbs hooked in his belt loops, and of course Constable Mayhew would be here. Of course the two worst moments of my life would be overseen by a saggy old man dressed like an extra from the set of a direct-to-DVD Western, his ten-gallon hat held up by the sheer density of his eyebrows.

I laugh at him, and note distantly that it sounds like sobbing.

He points at me with the waxed tip of his mustache. "This her?" It takes me a dizzy second to understand that he isn't speaking to me.

He's speaking to the man just behind him, a hulking figure in a sharp black suit. His face is unpleasantly familiar; I remember those eyes staring at me from the slanted surface of a rearview mirror.

It occurs to me that not every Beast comes crawling out of Underland. That some of them live up here, and walk around in expensive suits and pencil skirts.

That Arthur didn't fail us, after all.

"Yes, sir," the man says earnestly. His accent is local but overblown, a step away from caricature. "I saw her acting funny this evening. She dropped this."

He hands the constable something small and square, and Mayhew squints down at it. It's an old-fashioned matchbook with something written across the front in blue cursive. I can't read the words by the flare and flicker of the firelight, but I don't have to. I already know what they say.

My Old Kentucky Home.

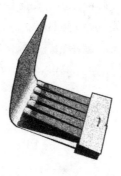

TWENTY-FOUR

I t's nine miles to the constable's office in Mudville, but it feels like more. The sheriff's office gets bigger and shinier SUVs every year, but Mayhew's car smells like hot piss and cigarettes. The AC dribbles from the vents. My hair is gummed against my cheek, clotted with soot and blood, and my shoulders are wrenched backward in their sockets. Already my fingers feel staticky and dead. One of the troopers suggested they might uncuff me for the ride over, pity on his face, but Constable Mayhew gave him a long, grim stare and said, "Not this one, Carl."

After two miles I announce that I have to pee. Mayhew ignores me. A mile later I tell him I'm going to puke and beg him, with an artfully choked voice, to slow down and open the door. He doesn't even bother to sigh.

After that I focus on scooting close enough to the door to yank on the handle, wondering how bad this is going to hurt, until he says, tiredly, "The child locks are on, Opal."

I let go of the handle. "Look, I just want to know if Jasper, if he was—" I press my forehead against the window, hard. "Do you know if they got any kids out of the motel?"

For a minute I think he's going to revert back to ignoring me, but eventually he grunts, "No."

I catch my own eyes in the rearview mirror, red-rimmed and wild, and look quickly away. The last few miles pass in silence. Bad thoughts keep trying to bubble up—like *the last thing I said to him was go to hell*—but I don't let them make it to the surface.

The Muhlenberg County Detention Center is a low sprawl of concrete jammed between a U-Pull-It junkyard and a Waffle House that doubles as a Greyhound stop. I feel like it ought to be dim and bleak inside, but it's all white tile and bright canister lights. It looks several decades newer than the high school.

There's a woman with bleached highlights sitting at a kiosk. The constable sets a plastic baggie on the counter and she takes it without looking away from her desktop.

"Is that my phone?"

Neither of them look at me. My phone buzzes against the counter.

"Excuse me, that's mine—give it to me—"

Constable Mayhew tips his dumbass hat to the receptionist and hauls me away by the elbow. My tennis shoes squeal across the floor. "Who's calling? Can you see the name? Please!"

Mayhew pulls harder and I go limp, dangling by one elbow while he swears through his mustache. "Just tell me who it is, I'm *begging* you. There's a fire and I don't know if my brother made it out."

The receptionist looks away from her computer long enough to observe my ash-streaked clothes, my scorched eyes. She glances down at my phone with the expression of a saint performing a reluctant miracle. "Somebody named Heath Cliff? Like the candy bar?"

I sag, shoulders shrieking, heart shattering. "Can you check my missed calls? Please, I just need to know—"

"Come on, Opal, time to go." Mayhew hooks two hands under my armpits.

The receptionist is scrolling, acrylic nails tapping on my screen. "Just Heath, again and again." She clucks her tongue. "He's got it *bad,* hon."

"Can you check my texts? You know how kids hate to call—"

The receptionist is flicking over to my texts and Mayhew is giving himself a hernia trying to lift me when the glass doors bang open.

It's Bev. Reeking of smoke, glaring through smeared ash like an avenging angel with a buzz cut. Charlotte trails anxiously behind her, offering a pained smile to the receptionist.

Bev stops halfway across the hall and crosses her arms. She rakes her gaze across us with scathing deliberation, and if I had room to feel another ounce of emotion, I would be terrified. That motel was her life and livelihood, her *home,* gone because I decided to punch the wrong person in the teeth. I wonder if Constable Mayhew can get me behind bars before she murders me in cold blood.

Bev asks, slowly, "Would somebody like to explain to me just what the hell is going on here?"

The constable drops me and puffs out the concavity of his chest. "Ma'am, I'm going to ask you to leave the premises. I'm investigating a crime."

"Well whoop-de-do, Constable. I'm *investigating* why you handcuffed one of *my guests* rather than handing her over to the EMTs."

I meet Charlotte's eyes behind Bev's back and manage a single, strangled word. "Jasper?"

Charlotte says, "They got the fire out, and they haven't found any— anybody. I don't think he was there."

I miss the next few sentences because I'm busy heaving my guts out on the floor. When it's over I feel hollow and brittle, like plastic that's spent too long in the sun. The receptionist lobs a roll of blue paper towels at me and I ignore it, trying to remember the trick of breathing.

By the time I peel my skull off the tile Bev is jabbing her finger in the constable's face. "Don't talk to me like that, you goddamn mall-cop cowboy—"

"Now look here, Bev, I am elected by the people of this great state—"

"You drive your mom's *Pontiac,* Joe! They don't even let you use the lights anymore!" She's inches away from him now, voice dropping to a strangled threat. "We thought she was *dead* until somebody told us you dragged her down here."

Mayhew tries very hard to look down his nose at Bev, who has several inches and at least twenty pounds on him. "An eyewitness reported this young lady acting in a suspicious manner tonight."

"Well, I'm an eyewitness telling you I never saw her this evening. She hadn't gotten back from work." Bev enunciates each syllable, like she's talking to a broken speaker at a Burger King.

"Her manager reports that she was fired several hours before the event in question, after getting violent with a customer. Given her volatile actions, I think it likely that—"

Charlotte speaks for the first time, her voice soft and deferential. "I was there, too. Opal wasn't anywhere near the motel this evening."

Constable Mayhew narrows his eyes at Charlotte. "And what were you doing at the Garden of Eden this evening?"

"I was just . . ." Charlotte looks at Bev, and Bev's face goes taut. Charlotte trails away.

Constable Mayhew hooks his thumbs around his belt loops. "Were you a paying guest?"

"No, sir."

"Were you visiting a paying guest?"

"No, sir." Charlotte's voice is fainter with each word. The frames of her glasses are a stark pink against the pallor of her skin.

"Then what were you doing there?"

Bev steps between them, her jaw so tight she can barely move her lips. "That's none of your goddamn business."

The constable, who has apparently never seen Bev fight three drunks in a motel parking lot and is under the impression that the white curl of her knuckles means he's winning, says, "I am trying to investigate a potential arson here. I think it's worth asking this lady—who was apparently at the scene of the crime, with no reason to be there—a few questions." He holds his head higher. "Ma'am, I'm going to ask you again: Why were you at the Garden of Eden this evening?"

Charlotte looks at Bev. Bev looks at Charlotte. I might be dazed and sick, stupid with relief, but even I can see them speaking to one another, talking in the silent Morse code of two people who know each other far, far better than I thought they did.

"This is not," Bev announces, to no one in particular, "how I wanted to do this."

Charlotte's face is a map of hope and doubt. She shrugs as if she doesn't care, or as if she wishes she didn't, eyes on Bev. "Nobody's making you, sweetheart." I try and fail to recall if Charlotte has ever called me sweetheart before. If she did I doubt she said it like it was a dare, or maybe a prayer.

Bev turns back to Constable Mayhew with a reckless tilt of her chin and a fuck-it grin. "She was at the motel because that's where I live."

"And why would this woman care where you live?"

"Because," Bev inhales, "she's my girlfriend. Officer Fucknut."

Constable Mayhew looks as if he's trying to diagram that sentence on an invisible chalkboard, face crumpled with concentration.

Bev turns back to Charlotte with her arms hanging rigid at her sides. "I'm sorry."

"It's alright." Charlotte sounds a little breathless.

Bev scrubs her hand over the bristle of her hair. "No, for before. For not wanting anybody to know. I'm not ashamed, it's just—it's not safe, and I'm—a little slow."

I murmur "We know" from the floor and Charlotte manages to suggest, with the merest flick of her eyelid, that she will flay me and use my hide as a tote bag if I open my mouth again.

"Anyway, I know you're still going to leave and I don't blame you, but you should know . . ." Bev rolls her eyes, apparently at herself. "I'd go with you, if you asked. And if you stayed . . . I'd buy us a fucking billboard."

Constable Mayhew appears to be rousing from his fugue state, preparing to make some sort of authoritative statement, but then Charlotte kisses Bev, hard and joyfully, right on the mouth, and he short-circuits again. The receptionist says "Awww" and starts clapping, and I wish I could join her, because Jasper is alive and Charlotte is smiling and I will get to tease Bev about this until the end times.

The glass doors open. Heels click evenly across the floor.

Elizabeth Baine holds out her hand to Constable Mayhew, who blinks down at it as if he's never seen one before. She gives him a gentle smile. "Constable Mayhew, if you will return to your office, you'll find a voice mail explaining my involvement in this investigation. Thank you for your assistance."

Bev and Charlotte watch as Mayhew scuttles into his office. Baine transfers the clear blue of her gaze to the floor, where I sit cross-legged and dazed. I no longer want to clap.

"Hello again, Opal. Could we talk privately?"

I don't know what makes me wallow to my feet and follow Elizabeth Baine down the hall. It's the officious tap of her shoes and the ironed seams of her skirt, the way she checks the watch on the inside of her wrist, as if she has allotted a specific number of minutes to deal with our collective nonsense. The only flaw is her upper lip, which is swollen and glossy, split where my fist collided with her teeth. I imagine my knuckles would still hurt if I could feel my hands.

She leads me to a room labeled CONFERENCE ROOM C and sits at the head of a long table, gesturing to the seat beside her. I stroll past it and settle at the opposite end. I do my best to slouch insolently, but my shoulders are stiffening fast.

Baine studies me politely, chin resting on her folded hands.

I want to stare her down, but I find my mouth opening, my voice whipping down the table. "Did you know? That he wasn't there?"

She considers. "Yes." The answer sounds as if it was drawn out of a hat at random.

I picture myself striding over and slamming my forehead into the bridge of her nose.

She sighs as if she knows exactly what I'm thinking. "You are so determined to think the worst of me. Hal searched the room just before the incident. We knew your brother wasn't inside."

"And what about the other rooms? The front office? Did you carefully evacuate the premises before committing arson?"

For the first time, there is the slightest hesitation before she speaks. "The event was not intended to reach that scale. Hal is a very experienced operative, but . . ." She does a small, mannered shrug. "He claims the flames spread more quickly than they should have, and that the smoke alarms failed."

I think of the mist mixing with the smoke, the shadowed shapes I saw there; there was more than one kind of Beast running loose tonight. I smile at her, a vicious twist of my lips. "Bad luck, I guess."

Baine's eyes glitter back at me. "Yes." She unsnaps a black case at her side and withdraws a raggedy yellow legal pad. She smooths the pages flat on the table. "Hal retrieved some very interesting documents from room 12, before the fire. Your work, or Jasper's?"

I close my mouth, hard.

"Listen, Opal. All we're looking for is a little help. We don't want anyone to get hurt, but there are a lot of very serious parties with an interest in the Starling property. They hired us to get results, and I don't intend to let them down. You understand, don't you?"

Arthur and all his predecessors had fought and fallen for generations rather than let the Beasts loose on the world; Elizabeth Baine would stand aside and watch with a clipboard and a smile.

"You don't know what you're messing with," I tell her, cliché-ly.

"But you do?" Quick and eager.

"Can't you just let it alone?" I can tell from her quizzical half smile that the question doesn't make sense to her. It's the same expression a Gravely might have worn if someone had asked them to stop digging when they knew there was still coal under Eden.

Baine checks her watch again. "Let me be clear about your situation. There was an act of arson committed tonight, and a reliable eyewitness with no reason to lie and a clean criminal record is willing to swear under oath that he saw you do it."

"Tell Hal thanks from me."

She ignores me. "Add arson to identity fraud, and no judge would find you a fit guardian for your brother."

Panic twists in my belly, familiar as a toothache. I want to shout *You can't do this* or *He needs me,* but I hear Charlotte's voice in my ear: *Does he?* I hear Jasper himself: *I'm not your job.* Maybe it's time to trust him a little more, to stop selling my soul for something that never belonged to me in the first place.

I swallow sour spit. "So? He's a big kid now, and his future is taken care of."

Her head tilts very slightly. "And what if his new guardians choose a different future for him?"

"What new guardians?"

Baine is tapping at her phone. "Well, his family, of course."

"*I'm* his family, you—"

Which is when the door opens, and the CEO of Gravely Power walks into the room.

The last time I saw Don Gravely he wasn't anything to me. He was a sweaty handshake and a polyester suit coat, and the only thing I noticed about him was the way he flinched away from me. I remember glaring at him, not out of any personal grudge, but just out of solidarity with Bev and her luna moths.

Now I find myself staring, trying to force his features to assemble into something or someone familiar. But there's nothing of Mom in this man, nothing of me, except maybe the eyes: gravel-gray, cold.

He pulls out a seat and sits with a harassed sigh. I don't think he's even noticed me yet. "Look, Liz"—Baine's face gives an imperceptible twitch— "you can't just order me around. I'm a busy man."

"Thank you for your patience, Mr. Gravely." She smiles at him; he doesn't seem to see the malice in it. "I was just talking to your great-niece here about her future."

For the first time since he walked into the room, Gravely faces me. His entire body recoils, his head retracting into his collar. I have the childish urge to stamp my foot at him, just to see if he'd fall out of his chair.

He produces a smile that makes me think of a stray dog licking its canines. "Delilah's girl. How are you?"

So: it's all true. This man is my family, my history, my roots, and everyone knew it but me. Hot shame floods me, the sense that the whole town must have been laughing at me as soon as I turned the corner.

I work hard to make my voice come out flat. "Been better." I rattle the handcuffs against the back of the chair.

"Ah, well." Don Gravely isn't looking at me anymore. "We always meant to reach out, of course, since Delilah finally went and did it. We—my wife and kids—we'd love to have you over sometime. You could meet the rest of the family. We could take care of you." Baine widens her eyes very slightly at him, and he adds, "And the boy, your brother. You're Gravelys, after all."

Scenes flash through my head, a montage of shaky home videos that never happened: Jasper and me eating dry chicken on a big suburban patio, sitting across the table from a set of blond cousins in name-brand clothes. My picture in the family album, right next to Mom's. A present under the Christmas tree with my name on the tag in pretty cursive: *Opal Delilah Gravely*.

So ordinary. So tempting. It's everything I've ever wanted, the list I thought I burned a long time ago: a home, a name, a family. I know there's a catch, a price—I know nothing is free for people like me—but for a minute I can't move, can't breathe, for wanting.

Baine interjects, smoothly, "After all this is wrapped up, of course."

I pry my teeth apart. "All what?"

Gravely makes a gesture suggesting there are gnats in the room. "This fuss over the Starling property. You've heard about the plant expansion? Well, it all depends on a new coalfield opening up. Picture it—real mining in Eden again, for the first time since we buried Big Jack. My surveyors tell me there's a good seam on the Starling property. We hold the mineral rights—always have, since the eighteen-somethings—but the Starlings won't budge. Liz here"—he nods at Elizabeth Baine, whose eyelid gives another twitch—"has a reputation for solving this kind of problem."

Baine looks coolly back at me, and I know if I announced that she was actually investigating a doorway to Hell she would deny it very convincingly.

"So we'd all be grateful," Gravely concludes, "real grateful, if you could help her out."

And there's the price tag. It doesn't seem like a bad trade, to be honest. I give them Starling House—I let them paw through an old mansion that isn't mine and never will be, I betray one brave, stupid boy—and in exchange, I get everything.

A home, a name, a family.

The word "family" sets another montage off in my head, except this one isn't imaginary. I see Bev, jabbing her finger in Constable Mayhew's face; Charlotte, asking me to come with her; Jasper, pretending to sleep so that I can pretend to sleep. Arthur's coat neatly folded on the couch. Arthur's hands tangled in chicory and Queen Anne's lace. Arthur's face turning up to mine while the poppies bow around us.

I tilt my head, studying Don Gravely—my great-uncle, I guess. This man who looked away while we lived on ramen noodles for eleven years, who would have kept on looking away if it weren't for his bank account and his business plans. And why not? We share a little blood, maybe a curse, but he's never stayed in town long enough to know what it's like when the mist rises. There's nothing that ties us together except a name I didn't even know I had.

It occurs to me, looking at those eyes, chips of cold limestone, that the

Starlings probably had it right. That the only name worth having is the one you choose.

Gravely is getting impatient, his jaw working, his fingers tap-tapping. I smile at him, and from the way he flinches I think it must be my real smile, mean and crooked. I lean across the table, shoulders screaming in their sockets. "Go fish, asshole."

The change comes quick: Gravely's genial good-old-boy act disappears. His hands go still, upper lip peeling away from his teeth. "God, you're just like her. Leon spoiled her rotten, gave her every little thing she wanted, and it wasn't enough." It was never enough, for Mom. She was all hunger, all want, insatiable. I've always hated her for that appetite, just a little, but now I feel a strange sympathy. It turns out I'm hungry, too.

Gravely's face is turning a blotchy mauve. "She goes and gets herself knocked up—insists on keeping it, refuses to marry the man—shames the Gravely name—" His sentences are fragmenting, cracking under the weight of a twenty-six-year-old grudge. "And then still, after all those years, after everything she did, Leon was going to give it all to *her*. She didn't work for it, she didn't deserve it—I was the one who—"

"Give what to her?" My voice is cool, not loud. There's no reason it should leave a ringing silence in its wake. Gravely shrivels again, turtle-like, and Baine looks like she's preventing herself from rolling her eyes only through years of elite training.

Gravely is breathing hard, almost panting. "Doesn't matter now. I burned the will myself, and your mama drove into the river before she knew what was coming."

"She knew." The words taste true. *You'll see,* Mom told me. She told Bev she was going to make things right, and I think she meant it. I think she was going to bend that stubborn spine of hers and claim the inheritance her daddy offered, and buy us a better future.

But dreams don't last long in Eden. The mist rose high, the wheels left the road, and by the time Constable Mayhew bought me that Happy Meal, my future was gone.

Stolen, by this stone-eyed bastard.

A surge of fury puts me on my feet. "You—"

"Enough." Baine's voice is cool, a little bored. "The past is over, and you can't prove anything, can you?"

I open my mouth, then close it. The only evidence I had was my mom's number written on a dead man's receipt, her picture in the family photo album. It's all ashes now, smoke and rumor.

"But let's talk about the future," Baine continues. "I think it's safe to assume the courts would grant Jasper's guardianship to his uncle, especially given his sister's . . . behavior." She cuts a glance at me, handcuffed and panting, reeking of smoke.

"You can't see it, but I want you to know that I'm flipping you off."

Baine is unmoved. "And I don't think Mr. Gravely would be inclined to send him off to Stonewood. After all, he's been offered a position in the family company. Why shouldn't he take it?"

"Because he has asthma, you fucking *ghoul*." Lacey's dad works at the plant, and she told me the hood of his car is covered in fine black soot by the end of each day. All it would take is a long shift, a broken inhaler, a walk back to the motel on a misty night.

Panic chokes me, turns my voice into something like a plea. "He wouldn't make it a year."

Gravely blinks rapidly. Baine lifts and drops her shoulder again in that delicate, maddening shrug.

I wet my lips and observe, conversationally, "I'll kill you."

"Difficult, once you're jailed for arson."

She's goading me, watching me with idle blue eyes while she screws with my whole life, and I'm sick of it. "Jesus, just *leave us alone*. I don't even work for Arthur anymore, thanks to you!"

Baine leans back against fake leather. "I know."

"And even if I did, even if I *begged*—" An image of Arthur interrupts me, the way I saw him last: on his knees, eyes closed, like some ancient penitent. I swallow. "He wouldn't give me the keys."

A flash of humor in her eyes. "No?"

"No." Arthur might want me, but I've seen him put his fist through a window rather than reach for what he wants. He won't falter, won't bend. I swallow again and meet Baine's eyes. "I can't help you."

"I know." She's still perfectly serene.

"So are we done?"

She gives me a small, patronizing smile. "No."

"Why not? What exactly are we doing here?"

Baine turns her wrist to check her watch again. "We're waiting."

A current of trepidation moves through me. I ignore it. "No, you're wait-ing. I'm leaving."

Before I can even edge around the table, there's a deferential tap at the door. "Missus Baine?"

"Constable Mayhew?"

"Another visitor is here." Mayhew sounds relieved to be reduced to a mere butler in this production.

Baine smiles at me as she says, "Finally. Show him in."

The metallic jangle of keys, a low voice. Then the door opens, and Arthur Starling walks into Conference Room C of the Muhlenberg County Deten-tion Center.

I've never seen Arthur outside the grounds of Starling House, and I can't say I like it much. He looks awkward and over-tall, as if his dimensions don't agree with ordinary rooms. His face is meant for slanted sunlight and old amber bulbs; beneath the overhead fluorescents it looks pale and lumpen, like an old bone pitted by the rain. His lip is freshly split and one eyebrow is misshapen, swelling fast.

His gaze spins wildly across the room until it lands on me with the quivering certainty of a compass needle, and God, he should not look at me like that where Baine and Gravely can see, and I shouldn't look back. The two of us are a pair of clumsy card players, showing our hands to the whole table.

"You goddamn *fool*," I breathe.

Arthur doesn't flinch, his eyes moving from my face to my scorched shirt to the painful angle of my shoulders. His jaw tightens. "Why," he grates, "is she handcuffed?"

Elizabeth Baine is smiling at him like he's her firstborn son, fondly indul-gent. "The keys, Constable?"

Mayhew unhooks a key ring from his belt, but hesitates. "I recommend against it, ma'am. This one committed petty theft the same day her mother drowned herself."

I bare my teeth at him. "She didn't drown herself. And maybe if you got me more than a Happy Meal I wouldn't have been picking your pocket, you cheap motherf—"

I'm interrupted by Arthur, who makes a sound remarkably like the hellcat and snatches the key from Mayhew's hand. He crosses the conference room in two enormous strides and kneels behind me. I can feel the heat of him at my back, but nothing more; my hands are swollen and nerveless, like plastic gloves blown into balloons.

There's a metallic tick and my arms fall forward, shoulders grinding in their sockets, blood pulsing in my palms. My flesh is a shiny, unpleasant pink, deepening to purple where it swelled around the cuffs.

I turn and find Arthur standing so close that my eyes are level with his throat. Jagged lines cut across his carotid, lurid pink and puckered. I wonder if he's been keeping the wound clean or letting it fester.

I swallow hard and hiss up at him, "Did you let Jasper take those notes? Because if you did, I'll slit your throat again."

"No. Crime runs in the blood, apparently." Arthur's voice is pitched low, lips barely moving. "Is he alright?"

"I think so." I fight a reckless urge to lean my forehead against his chest and burst into exhausted tears. I bite the inside of my cheek instead. "He wasn't there when it happened."

Arthur's voice goes even lower. "Are you alright?"

"Yes." He lifts a hand to the matted crust of blood and ash on my cheek, fingers hovering just above my skin. I bite my cheek harder. "No."

"It's my fault. I'm so—I tried to stop them—there were *two* this time, and one of them—"

I can't stand this. The grief of him, the guilt that hurls him into battle after battle and leaves him bloodied and bruised.

I push my cheek into his hand. "It wasn't your fault. None it ever was, okay?"

He chokes.

I take a step backward. "What are you doing here? What are you thinking? You know what these people want—"

"I'm glad you could make it, Arthur." Baine lobs her voice like a polite bomb between us.

Arthur's hand falls back to his side. His spine hardens. "Of course," he says, and his voice is the careless sneer I remember from winter. Gravely is watching him with an expression of sick satisfaction, but Arthur keeps his eyes on Baine.

"Thank you for your assistance, Opal. You're free to go." Baine dismisses me with a cordial nod, as if we're at a business conference or a job interview.

She gestures to the empty seat at her side, beaming at Arthur. "Take a seat. Let's talk."

I brace my feet, preventing Arthur from stepping around me. "He doesn't have anything to say to you."

Baine nods to Constable Mayhew without looking at him. "Escort her out, please."

He tips his stupid hat to her and comes clomping toward me, and I don't know how much hell I can raise with hands like a pair of boiled fish, but I'm prepared to find out when Arthur says, tiredly, "Opal. Go."

"Oh my God, will you *stop* telling me to leave?"

But two other uniformed men have appeared behind Mayhew, approaching me with a wariness I would find flattering if I wasn't busy glaring at Arthur. Hands close around my elbows, hauling me away from him. I swear and stomp, tennis shoes sliding off heavy boots, knuckles too swollen to make a proper fist. The last glimpse I see of Conference Room C is Arthur taking the empty seat, shoulders bowed, and Elizabeth Baine, smiling.

TWENTY-FIVE

The parking lot is dark except for the yellow rings of streetlights, thronged with moths and mayflies. There's a familiar pickup near the entrance, parked with admirable disregard for the white lines, and a Volvo not far away. Two women lean against the driver's side, shoulders barely touching. They look up when the detention center door slams behind me.

Charlotte calls my name. Bev is already moving, breaking into a run. I don't think I've ever seen Bev run for anything—I bet she didn't even run out of her office when it was on fire—but she's running now, for me.

She stops awkwardly before me, her arms half-raised. She says, gruffly, "You okay, meathead?"

I nod, more out of habit than conviction. Then I throw my arms around her and squash my face into the warm muscle where her shoulder meets the collar of her tank top. Bev says, "Oh, Jesus," with considerable disgust, but her arms fold around me, and if she notices the damp smear of snot on her shoulder, she doesn't say anything.

I think: *It's been eleven years and who-knows-how-many days since someone held me like this,* but that's a lie. I've never been held like *this,* sure and steady, for as long as I need; Mom only ever held me as long as she wanted.

It occurs to me that I've been mourning two people all these years—the mother I had, and the mother I wish I had—and that neither of them was the one who kept a roof over my head.

"Bev, I'm so sorry. It's my fault, the motel—I didn't think they would do anything like—"

She murmurs, "Hey, shut up," into my hair. I shut up.

Bev thumps my back twice when I pull away, as if I'm the hood of an unreliable car, and scrubs her eyes hard against her own shoulder.

She shepherds me to the Volvo. "C'mon, let's head over to Charlotte's, get you a shower."

"I can't."

"Hon," she says, not unkindly, "you smell like a burning tire."

"Look, I still don't know where the hell Jasper is because he won't answer his damn phone, but I've got to find him, and she's got Arthur in there—"

Bev squints. "He that big scarecrow that went running in a few minutes ago?" I nod. "What's he to you?"

"My . . ." I begin, but I can't think of an accurate noun. The possessive hangs.

Bev says, "Screw him," at the same moment that Charlotte says, "We'll wait with you."

Charlotte produces a cardigan and a sleeve of peanut butter crackers from the backseat, like a true librarian. She drapes the cardigan fussily over my shoulders and daubs the soot off my face with a T-shirt that says KIDS WHO READ, SUCCEED! on the front. I lean on the bumper, eating crackers with clumsy hands, watching the detention center door. Bev and Charlotte settle on either side of me like a pair of gargoyles or guardian angels.

After a silence, I say, "So, you two are . . ."

Charlotte says, "None of your business," at the same time that Bev says,

"Yeah, for a couple years now." I feel their eyes meeting over my head, a pair of wry smiles colliding.

"And here I thought you brought my library holds to the motel out of the purity of your spirit." I cluck my tongue. "But really you just had the hots for my landlord."

"At first I came in spite of her," Charlotte admits. "But then she started requesting her own holds, and we started talking . . ." Charlotte lowers her voice to a stage whisper. "Did you know she likes poetry? Like the really corny stuff, we're talking the *Romantics.*"

Bev flaps her hands as if sentiment is a mosquito she can shoo away. "I was just trying to impress you, I told you."

"I'm sure you were, sweetheart," Charlotte says, insincerely, and I have the disorienting experience of watching my landlord blush.

I give Bev a doubtful squint. "Are you sure, Charlotte? I mean, she eats Vienna sausages straight out of the can. Like an animal." Bev thwaps the side of my head. "I'm just saying, you could do better."

"Maybe I could," Charlotte says, speculatively. Then her eyes meet Bev's, soft and sober, and I feel abruptly as if I've walked in on them kissing. "But maybe I don't want better."

It's a good thing Bev flips me off and says, "So eat it, kid," because otherwise I might cry again.

We wait in silence after that, except for dull buzz of bugs against the light bulbs and the rustle of the cracker wrapping. There's a weird stillness in my head, a muffled tension like a pillow pressed over a screaming mouth.

A silhouette moves on the other side of the glass door, tall and narrow. I'm walking toward him before the door is fully open.

Arthur doesn't look hurt, but there's something weird about the way he's moving. His shoulders aren't hunched around his collar, and his stride is wide and easy, as if he recently put down some immensely heavy object. He meets my eyes across the parking lot and I catch the white sickle of a smile. If he's trying to reassure me, it doesn't work. A chill skates down my spine.

He stops beneath a streetlight and waits, hands tucked in his pockets, wearing the fey smile of a man who has recently pulled the pin from a grenade. The indentation in his left cheek is deeper than I've ever seen it. I scowl at it.

Arthur is unfazed. He tucks a gritty, ashen lock of hair behind my ear, casually possessive, as if he's done it a hundred times before. As if his fingers don't leave a phosphorous streak across my cheekbone, white-hot. "Nice cardigan," he says, and I restrain myself from grabbing his shoulders and shaking him very hard.

"Did she drug you? Are you alright?"

He answers with a shrug, loose-boned and easy. I am going to shake his teeth loose from his skull. "What happened in there? What are they going to do now?"

"Nothing." There's a calm certainty in his voice that makes the hairs on the backs of my hands stand up. "To you or to Jasper. Ever again."

"Arthur." I'm close enough to see the tiny flicker in his eyes when I say his name, a flash of something like physical pain. "What did you give them?"

Another smile, and I resist the impulse to set my thumb in the black curl of his dimple. "Don't worry about it."

"Don't worry about it? Don't *worry* about—"

A muffled ringtone interrupts me. I whip back to face Bev and Charlotte. "Is that my phone?"

Charlotte is already holding out a plastic baggie, lit pale blue by the glow of my screen. "We talked the receptionist around."

I run back and rip the bag open, swiping up without looking at the caller. "Where the fuck are you?"

"Wow, okay, where the fuck are *you*?" At the sound of Jasper's voice, my legs go for the second time this evening. I catch myself against the Volvo, my back sliding down hot metal, my throat clogging with tears.

"Jesus, Jasper." My voice comes out thin and wavery. "Why didn't you answer your phone?"

His sigh is a gust of wind through the speaker. "I turned off my ringer for like one hour and everybody has a heart atta—"

Then both of us are talking, trampling one another's sentences. "Listen, I'm so sorry I said—"

"Did you really burn down the motel? Because—"

"Who said that? Of *course* I didn't, God, Bev would murd—"

"Is she okay? Did she—"

"Yeah, Bev's fine. She's right here. Where are you now?"

"The library."

"Why are you—never mind." I inhale carefully, forcing my legs to take my weight. "Stay there, I'm coming to get you." I hang up before I can do anything I'll regret, like cry, or call him terrible names, or tell him how it had felt to see the smoke and know I was too late.

Bev and Charlotte both start asking questions, but before I can answer I hear a faint, metallic jangle. Arthur is facing me with his arm outstretched, a key ring dangling from his fingers. I see the faded Chevy symbol, the tiny plastic flashlight that doesn't work.

I reach for the keys, but pull up short. I keep a careful ledger in my head, a tally of debts and favors, but I no longer know what he and I owe each other. He ruined my life and then tried to repair it; I saved him and then ran from him. We'd achieved a miserable but tolerable species of balance between us, until tonight. Until he showed up at the detention center and made some terrible bargain on my behalf—I don't know what kind of deal he made, but I know a devil when I see one—and offered me his truck. Again.

I meet his eyes, looking for the catch, the price. He looks steadily back at me, asking nothing, offering everything.

I take the keys.

Charlotte touches my shoulder before I turn away. "We need to talk, after you get Jasper. I found something in the Gravely papers that I think you ought to—"

"I already know," I interrupt her, gently. "Everybody did, apparently."

Her face crimps with confusion. "I'm not sure they did, Opal. I have to take it up to my lawyer friend in Frankfort but I really think—"

But I don't have time to worry about the Historical Society. I kiss Charlotte once on the cheek, give Bev an awkward high wave that might be a salute, and head for the truck.

Arthur follows a half step behind me. I slide into the front seat and he leans into the open window. "Get him out of Eden. Tonight, if you can." The eerie giddiness has drained away from his voice, leaving it flat and low.

That sense of premonition returns, the chill settling low in my stomach. "I will."

"Good luck. He's . . ." Arthur's mouth makes a wry twist. "A lot like you."

"Yeah, a meathead."

"I would say *strong-willed*."

I tick my chin at the passenger door. "You coming?"

A short shake of his head. "I have to get back to the house." Arthur pulls a wallet from his back pocket and reaches across me to drop it in the cupholder. His hand stops on the steering wheel and grips tight. "Opal, go with him. Leave Eden." He looks up at me and his throat bobs. "Please?"

I study him for a long second. "You know, don't you?"

"Know what?"

"My last name."

A pause, and then a terse nod. "If I'd known sooner, I never would have let you inside the house. No matter how strong-willed you were."

I say, softly, "I'm glad you didn't know." It's the truth. Those months in Starling House were—God help me—the happiest of my life.

Arthur swallows. "Go, Opal. And don't come back."

I meet the black of his eyes without blinking, without even tucking my hair behind one ear. "Okay," I tell him, "I will."

And I can tell—from the desperate relief in his face, from the way his fingers unclench from the wheel and lift to touch my cheek in fleeting, awful farewell—that he believes me.

I see Jasper before he sees me. He's waiting outside the library, neck bent toward his phone, hair combed and carefully parted. He's wearing slacks and a button-up he must have borrowed from Logan, the collar stiff, the cuffs tight. I know it's my God-given duty as his sister to laugh at him, but I don't feel much like laughing. I feel a weird ache behind my eyes, as if I'm watching something infinitely precious vanish over the horizon.

I pull up too fast and leave the brights on, silhouetting Jasper against the brick like a criminal in a black-and-white TV show. He squints into the light and flips me off. The ache recedes a little.

He slides into the passenger seat with his backpack in his lap and I give him a thorough once-over, reassuring myself that he's really here and whole, unhurt. I can still taste sour black smoke in the back of my throat, still see the gaping mouth where our door used to be.

"Hey," Jasper says, gently, and I hit the gas rather than look at him.

Neither of us says anything for a while. Jasper rolls his window down and lets the wind un-comb his hair, watching the world pass with an expression of strange nostalgia. It's like he's taking mental pictures of the landscape and pasting them into a photo album, converting the present into the past. The tarps stretched over the flea market stalls, blue and frayed. The cluster of boys with flat-brimmed hats in the Dollar General parking lot. The yellow glow of the power plant at night.

I keep my eyes on the white stripe of the road when we pass the Garden of Eden, but I can see the fire truck lights flashing against the clouds like heat lightning.

Jasper swears. "How did it happen?"

My first impulse is to lie—it's not like the motel was up to code—but I need him to run when I tell him to. So I say, carefully, "I upset someone."

A tense pause, then: "Was it him?"

"Who?"

"Because if it was, if he was mad at you for leaving him, or trying to destroy the stuff I stole or whatever, I'll help you hide the body."

It takes me several seconds to unravel this, at which point I shout "*No!*" more forcefully than is necessary. "He would never, ever—none of the stories about him are true—he's"—kind and stupid and desperately driven, tormented by his own stubborn honor—"he's okay," I finish, weakly.

"I see," Jasper says, with such mildness that I feel heat creeping up my neck.

Another mile passes before I recover enough to say, "It was that Baine woman." Well, mostly. "She wanted something from me. I wouldn't give it to her."

"Jesus." I hear bafflement in his voice, and I get it. Since when have I ever stood up for anything or anyone, other than him? "Wait—was it the notes I took? Because I'm really—"

"No," I assure him.

I bet it's even true. They took the notes, but I don't really think they needed them. I think Baine set fire to the motel, framed me for it, had me sit in handcuffs while my great-uncle threatened Jasper's whole future, solely because she wanted Arthur Starling to come save me. And he did.

The image of him walking into the room, looking at me like I was something valuable, even vital, like there was nothing on his list but my name, sends another flush of heat through me.

We pass the detention center, and I can't help looking for a lanky shadow, but the lot is empty. I wonder if he got a ride from Charlotte, or if he walked. I wonder if he took the old railroad bridge, if he paused to wallow in that old, stale guilt.

I turn right just past the detention center and cut the engine. The cab is quiet except for the hum of old neon and the distant screaking of the crickets.

Jasper clears his throat. "I actually ate at Logan's, so I'm good." The light from the Waffle House windows has turned his face an eerie, electric gold.

"We're not here for waffles, bud." I rest my head briefly on the steering wheel, reminding myself that this is for the best, that I worked very long and hard for it. Then I dig my phone out of my pocket and pull up the Stonewood Academy website.

I pass the phone over to him. "I had a whole brochure thing and an acceptance letter wrapped up, for your birthday, but the fire . . ."

Jasper's face is very, very blank. "What is this."

"Your new school."

Jasper scrolls down the page, taps twice. "A private high school? A *boarding* school?"

"It's all paid for. Tuition, room, board, everything."

"How the *hell* did you—actually, don't answer that. I don't—why is my face on this website."

"I—what?" I take the phone back and flick through the images on their slideshow. There—it's the picture of Jasper leaning against the motel wall, hands in his pockets, hoodie pulled up. But they've put it in grayscale and added sans serif font over the image. *It doesn't matter where you come from—it matters where you go next.*

"Okay, that's . . ." I don't know what it is. Weird, funny, sweet, awkward? The expression on Jasper's face suggests it's none of those things, that I have screwed up on a colossal scale.

I rush forward, trying to skate over it. "The semester starts in August, which is a little ways away, but—"

"So I'm already enrolled. Like, you enrolled me."

I wet my lips. "Yes?"

"Because you thought I would be happy at"—he takes the phone back—"Stonewood Academy. Where Greatness Grows." He taps the screen. "Jesus, how did you find someplace whiter than Eden?"

"I didn't—it won't be like that—"

"This is like Charlotte shouting at the principal all over again. I know she meant well, but those next few weeks were hell."

I feel like someone who has just leapt out and shouted "Surprise!" on the wrong date, to the wrong person: defensive, embarrassed, even a little angry.

I take an unsteady breath. "Look, we can talk about all that . . . later. What matters right now is that you have to get out of here now. Like, tonight. There's something I should have told you a while ago." I take a small, bracing breath. "Our mom was Old Leon Gravely's daughter. So . . . you and me are Gravelys. Technically."

The silence that follows is so profound it presses on my eardrums. I can almost hear Jasper's neurons firing. He says, carefully, "So . . . did they pay for this? Is that what you're trying to say?"

"What? *Hell* no, those vultures don't give a damn about us!"

"Okay, then why—"

"It's the curse. Whatever you want to call it. It—they go after Gravelys, they always have—"

"Opal?" Jasper inhales carefully. "I know. I already know all this."

"You—what?"

"I've known for a while. I'm sorry I didn't tell you, but I wasn't sure you were ready to hear it."

Jasper pauses, but I can't think of anything to say. I may, in fact, never think of anything to say again.

"Okay," he says. "Okay. Well, thank you, first of all. I don't know how you paid off a private high school, but it's . . . I know you were just trying to help." He says it earnestly—too earnestly, like a parent thanking their child for a homemade Christmas gift. A sense of foreboding thickens the air.

"Second, I'm sorry, like really sorry, but"—he hands the phone back to me and wraps my limp fingers around the case—"I'm not going." He's rarely sounded more sure about anything.

"If you think you're working at the goddamn power plant you've got another think—"

"Because I'm starting at U of L this fall." Jasper pauses, giving the syllables time to arrange themselves in my head. "I got a scholarship and financial aid, and the counselor says there are loans available, so you don't have to worry about anything."

In the original script of this conversation, I'm fairly sure that was my line. I was the one showing him the door out of Eden, handing him the keys to his own future. "You're sixteen."

Jasper smiles, a little shy, a little proud. "There's no age requirements. It's all test scores and credits and stuff. Charlotte helped me with the application and the SAT"—Charlotte, my former friend, who I now see is a stone-cold traitor—"and Logan's mom helped with the state aid paperwork, and Mrs. Gutiérrez gave me a ride to the library today. I just met with my advisor. I'm already registered for classes."

The enthusiasm in his voice falters a little, turns younger. "I know I should have told you, but I wanted it to be a surprise." He fiddles with the button on his shirt cuff, sliding it in and out of the hole. "I applied for a couple jobs, first. Didn't even get a reply. I guess I wanted to wait until I had a sure thing. And I wanted to show you I could do it. That you don't have to take care of me any-more." He looks back at me, forcing me to turn abruptly away and scrub my sleeve across my cheeks. The smell of my shirt only makes my eyes burn worse.

"Opal, hey, it's okay. I'm not leaving you for good. I've got it all planned: I'll major in business, get a job straight after graduation. And then it'll be my turn to take care of you." His hand lands tentatively on my shoulder, as if he isn't sure whether I'll bite it.

I sort of want to. How dare he scheme and sneak behind my back? How dare he tell Logan before he told me? How dare he not *need* me? Instead, I say, "I didn't know you liked business."

He laughs a little, like the question is silly, like I'm naive for asking it. "Guess I'll find out."

"You like movies. Film. Art."

He lifts his shoulder. "So?"

"So, your stuff is really good. You've worked really hard on it. Why don't you—"

"I don't remember what Mom looked like. Did you know that?" He says it without inflection, like a man sliding the rug neatly out from under his op-ponent. "When I try to picture her face it goes all blurry in my head, and all I see is you." He addresses the windshield, eyes fixed on the bulbous amber lights of the diner, voice low. "Opal, you're bossy and you always think you know best and you have horrific taste in men. But you think I don't know what I owe you?"

I thought my ribs had healed up, but I must have been wrong, because there's an awful pain in my chest. My bones themselves feel wrong, chalky and friable, like old plaster.

I wait, breathing carefully around the hurt, until I can say, "You don't owe me shit, Jasper. Do you hear me?"

"Yeah, sure."

It's suddenly vital to me that he understands, that he knows there are no scales balanced between us, no debts; that I'm nothing like our great-uncle, offering kinship only on certain conditions. That I love him, and love wipes every ledger clean. "No, I'm serious. You think I took care of you because I had to, but I didn't. I could've handed you over to the foster system—maybe I should have, for your sake." Jasper starts to object, but I talk over him. "But I didn't, because I didn't *want* to. You remember you used to sleep in my bed every night?"

An adolescent pain crosses his features, as if the mention of his childhood habits has caused him injury. "Because I had nightmares," he mutters.

"No, meathead, because *I* did." I swallow. "Because *we* did, I guess."

It's true. Every night it was either the house or the river, or sometimes both: rooms full of rushing water, stairs that disappeared into rancid white foam, black water pouring through broken windows. The only way I could sleep was with Jasper's spine against mine, his breath whistling over the hum of the radiator.

Now he's the one clutching his rib cage, bent like he's in pain. I soften my voice. "I'm proud of you. For real." I'm also pissed and sad and preemptively lonely, unable to conceive of my world without him in it, but he doesn't need to know that. "You should definitely go to U of L. But please don't major in business. Major in film or art history or fucking interpretive dance. Make weird art with the nerds from your forums. Scare the shit out of me, okay?"

"Okay." He sounds uncertain.

"No, *promise* me. I wanted to give you a gift, remember?" I wave my phone at him, where the Stonewood website is still cycling through its slide-show: ivy creeping up old brick; girls with high blond ponytails; libraries with arched windows; Jasper, standing like the bleak "before" picture of a before-and-after remodel. "But it turns out it was a shitty gift. So just let me give you this, instead."

"But—"

"Look, I've had a really long day, so just shut up and pinky swear that you won't give up on your dreams for my sake, alright?" I stick out my pinky finger. Jasper looks at it with a helpless half smile on his face and a question in his eyes: *Really?* I nod once. The smile spreads, wide and young. He looks drunk on his own heady future; he looks happy.

He shakes my pinky with his.

I let go before I burst into tears, and grab Arthur's wallet from the cup-holder. There's a genuinely upsetting amount of money in it, the bills so crisp and green they must have been withdrawn directly from the bank. I unzip Jasper's backpack and shove the cash in the top pocket. "Go get yourself a Greyhound ticket to Louisville. You'll have to stay in a hotel until campus opens, but I'll get you more cash if you run out—"

"Hold up. You mean now? Like, right now?"

"It's getting worse." My voice is entirely without affect, like I'm reading from a newspaper. "Whatever's under Starling House, it's getting meaner and stronger. And Elizabeth Baine is probably only one padlock away from setting it loose. Today, when I thought you were in the motel—" I pause to swallow several times. "Yeah. Right now."

Jasper pulls the backpack into his lap, one hand already reaching for the door. "If that's true . . . shouldn't you come with me?"

I scratch at my collarbone, where sweat and smoke have caked into an itchy gray film. "Probably, yeah."

"But you're staying."

"Yeah."

"Because of him?"

"No." *Yes.*

"But you understand you don't have to, right? You and me had the same dreams, for years and years, but it doesn't mean anything unless we decide it does. You can choose."

"Yeah, I know." And I do know. I can see Jasper's choice in every eager line of his body, in the forward tilt of his shoulders, *go go go.* He was never going to stay, no matter what he dreamed in secret. And I was never going to leave, no matter what I said out loud. "I'm choosing."

I can feel Jasper wrestling with himself, trying to decide if he should handcuff our wrists together and drag me onto the bus behind him.

I shove him, not gently. "Will you just go already? You're not my *dad.*"

He rolls his eyes and holds out his pinky again. "Swear you won't die in some very stupid and gruesome way."

I shake it. "Everything will be okay," I tell him, because I love him.

I tug him toward me and kiss his forehead, like I did when he was little, and he does me the courtesy of not physically combusting from embarrassment, and then he leaves.

I watch him walk up to the counter, where a peeling Greyhound sign hangs above the register, and slide two twenties across the Formica. I watch the cashier soften by degrees, like everyone else who talks to Jasper for more than thirty seconds, until she's handing him a mug of hot chocolate I suspect is complimentary. I watch him slide into a booth and squint through the window. I don't know if he can see me past the yellow glare of the glass, but he jerks his chin toward the county road. *Go.*

I go. It's only after I've pulled back onto the county road that I catch the bronze gleam on the dash, and realize he left Arthur's stolen penny behind. For luck.

I drive with the windows down, just over the speed limit, wind whipping the tears off my cheeks. I don't think about the motel, the drifts of ash and glass, the wracked iron bones of the bed frames. I don't think about Elizabeth Baine or Don Gravely or the long line of Starlings standing between them and the abyss. I don't even know where I'm going.

Another lie; I know exactly where I'm going.

I cross the river and drive to the place where the streetlights stop and the woods turn wild, where the only light is the faint, amber glimmer of a lit window, shining to me through the trees.

TWENTY-SIX

It's very late now, but Arthur Starling isn't sleeping. He tried, briefly, but all he accomplished was ten minutes lying stiffly on the couch, conscious of every bruise pulsing in synchrony across his body, while the House howled with worry.

The mist had thickened so fast, and the Beast had come slithering out the door before he'd even gotten the sword in his hand. The fight had been desperate and ugly, ending only when he clamped his forearm around a sharp-scaled throat. His tattoos had hissed and burned, dispersing the Beast in great gouts of steam.

And then, while he stood there panting and bleeding, the second Beast had emerged, darting past him and slinking over the southern wall.

His hands had been shaking so badly it took him three tries to get the truck keys in the ignition.

But she was alive, and so was her brother.

He's too busy to sleep, anyway. There's so much to do—preparations to make, explosives to distribute, a will to write, flowers to water, foolishly, knowing there will be no one to tend them soon—and so little time.

He supposes he might have a few days left, even a week. He'd signed all of Gravely's miserable little forms, but it will take time for him to assemble all his monstrous machines at the edge of Starling land. He gave Baine three keys—while she smiled up at him with such professional satisfaction that he briefly imagined burying one of them in her eye, the way Opal brought down the Beast—but not the fourth.

The fourth he will claim for himself, as soon as the mist rises again. He has a suspicion it won't be long, based on nothing more than the weight of the air, the prickle at the base of his spine.

Arthur thinks he should probably feel mournful, but all he feels is relief so strong it resembles euphoria, as a distance runner might feel upon entering the final mile of a very long race. It began the moment his pen touched Gravely's paperwork, the peaceful sense that he was balancing an invisible scale. Very soon now, Opal will be safe.

And anyway, he likes the symmetry of it: the first Warden of Starling House vanished into Underland never to be seen again, and so will the last. The House might mourn him, but not for long. Gravely's machines will come for it soon enough and shove it into some sinkhole, where it will rot away, unmarked and unremembered, except for the faint smell of wisteria at the beginning of summer. There won't even be stories about it, after a while.

He finishes emptying the plastic bag he stole from the strip mine and dusts pink crystals from his palms. The walls shiver around him and he touches the stone gently. "I know. But I can't have anyone following me." It seems like terrible hubris to imagine that anyone would try, but he remembers the way she looked at him when he walked into that conference room—teeth bared, eyes scorching in a filthy face—and wonders if he should have stolen more explosives.

He climbs up and up, through the cellar door, past the library, back to his little room in the attic. He lights the lamp and sits in the soft light, wondering if he should sleep, knowing he won't. A stray breeze fingers through the window, rich and sweet-smelling, and flutters the drawings pinned to his wall. One of them comes loose and slips to the floor.

Arthur bends toward it and pauses, seeing that streak of cinder on the page. He laughs, harshly, and for the first time a shard of pain pierces his weird elation. "Give it up," he says. "She's not coming back, this time."

It is at precisely this moment, as if the House itself arranged it so, that he hears the distant thud of a fist on his front door.

When someone crosses onto Starling land, Arthur knows it. It's simply a part of being Warden, a melding of land and house and body that leaves none of those things entirely distinct from the other. But he hadn't felt the draft of the gates opening, the faint tick of a foreign heartbeat.

Perhaps the House hid her from him; perhaps she's been here so many times, sweating and bleeding and breathing, that the land no longer greets her as a trespasser, but as a part of itself.

Arthur stumbles twice on the stairs. He pauses before the front door, panting, feeling desperate and helpless and hungry and profoundly annoyed, the way he always does around her.

She knocks again. He is aware that he shouldn't answer it, that it will only make everything harder.

He answers it.

Opal is standing on his threshold, looking up at him with the same wary, weary expression she wore the first time he found her outside his gates. He has a maudlin impulse to memorize her: the canny silver of her eyes and the crooked front teeth, the lunar white of her skin and the startling black of her freckles, like constellations in negative. There are swollen red rings around each of her wrists, and two of the knuckles on her right hand are split.

Arthur shouldn't reach for that hand. He shouldn't turn it in his and run his thumb over the crusted ruin of her knuckles, thinking of Elizabeth Baine's busted lip and feeling a swell of strange, possessive pride. He certainly shouldn't bring the knuckles to his lips.

He hears a quick inhalation. Opal's eyes are dark, uncertain. "Are you sober?"

"Yes." He wonders if that's true. He hasn't had a drop of actual alcohol since the day Jasper broke in, but he feels weightless, unmoored from himself, and the lights have a fevered, splintered look he associates with cheap whiskey. The entire House feels alive around him, a presence that pulses beneath his bare feet.

Opal doesn't look convinced. Her eyes flick to her hand, still held in his, then back to his face. Her chin lifts. "Are you going to kick me out again?"

It's supposed to sound like a challenge, a mocking gauntlet, but there's a roughness to her voice that Arthur doesn't understand.

"I should," he says, honestly, but he doesn't let go of her hand. He reminds himself firmly that there's no room for wishes or wants in his life, that every time he's caved to his own childish desires it's come at a terrible cost. That he has what he needs, and it's enough.

It's just that, sometimes, God help him, he wants more.

A tremor moves through Opal. He follows it down her arm, up to her face. In the split second before she looks away, he sees her unmasked. He sees her terror and desire and bitter disappointment, the particular desolation of a lonely person who thought, briefly, that they might not be. Already she is steeling herself against him, like a girl bracing against the cold.

This, Arthur finds, he cannot tolerate. His life so far has been nothing but a wound on hers. She wears the scars well—she's made her life into an act of defiance, a laugh in the dark, a smile with bloodied teeth—but he refuses to add even one more.

He opens the door wide and pulls her inside.

I shouldn't have come here, but I did. I shouldn't go inside, but I do.

The house is quiet tonight, and darker than I've ever seen it. No candles or lamps sit on the sills, no lights flicker to life overhead. Even the moonlight falling through the windows seems muted and obscure, a gaze averted.

Arthur reaches around me to shut the door and a last rush of perfume slides into the hallway. The vines on the house are blooming—I saw them when I climbed the steps, lavish cascades of flowers that turn the night thick and sweet. I always thought wisteria grew best on the riverbank, but maybe Starling House makes its own rules.

Arthur doesn't step away when the door latches. We stand facing each other, unspeaking, letting everything between us—the confessions and recriminations, the lies and betrayals—slip away into the dark, until all that's left is what comes next.

It's not something I need. It's something from that second, more dangerous list, the one I thought I burned eleven years ago. It's something I want, and the knowledge makes me feel reckless and raw, a soft-bodied animal running too fast through the woods. It's not cold, but I'm shivering.

Arthur tucks my hair behind my ear for the second time tonight, but now his hand lingers against the line of my jaw. He takes a step closer and the air between us turns thin and hot.

"May I kiss you, Opal?" The question is polite, restrained; his eyes are not.

I've never been shy about sex. It's always been easy for me, a safely transactional exchange of needs, but a tremulous fragility overtakes me now. I can't speak. I manage a shallow nod.

I'm expecting it to feel like it did before: a reckless collision, a thing that could only happen at the ragged edge of his self-restraint. But this time is different. This time Arthur kisses me with an awful, excruciating tenderness, like I'm spun sugar or fine crystal, like he has all the time in the world. It feels good. It feels dangerous. I want him suddenly to be less tender, to leave me with my lips split and my heart perfectly whole.

I'm shaking worse now, breathing too hard. Arthur's chest touches mine and my entire body flinches away, as if I'm protecting some delicate instrument behind my breastbone.

Arthur pulls instantly back. "Did I hurt you?"

"No." My voice is small and wretched.

"Do you—do you want to stop?"

"No," I say, even more wretchedly.

Arthur pauses, studying me. I can't meet his eyes. He touches his thumb to my lower lip, still so gentle I want to weep. "You asked me why I paid for Jasper's tuition."

"Because you didn't want me to come back."

"I lied." He's whispering now, his breath ghosting across my skin. "I did it so you wouldn't *have* to come back. So that, if you came back, it would be because you wanted to." Then, even softer, as if the words are coming from inside my own skull, "What do you want, Opal?"

"I want—" The truth is I want him and I'm scared of wanting him and ashamed of being scared. The truth is I'm a coward and a liar and a cold bastard, just like my mother, and in the end I will let him drown to save myself. I should cut and run right now, before it's too late, before he finds out what kind of person I really am.

But I can't seem to make myself move.

I close my eyes. Maybe there's no difference between wanting and needing except in degree; maybe if you desire something badly enough, for long enough, it becomes a demand. "This," I whisper. "I want this."

Arthur's hand slides to the back of my neck and the flat of his palm steadies me, pins me gently to the earth. "It's alright." He lowers his face until I can feel the rush of his breath on my lips. "I've got you, Opal."

And I feel myself going under, sinking into the weight of his hand. My limbs go slow and heavy. I'm not shaking anymore.

I let him back me against the door. I let him touch me, his hands simultaneously rough and reverent. He lays his jaw along mine and speaks to me, and his voice is like that, too—the tone harsh, the words sweet. "It's alright," he says again, and "let me," and once, raggedly, "*fuck*, Opal."

I let him lay me down on the floor, the rug impossibly soft under the bare wings of my shoulder blades. I let him press into me so slowly I can't breathe, can't think, for wanting.

Arthur holds himself still, then, his body strung tight. "Are you sure—" he starts, but I'm suddenly, entirely sure, and tired of waiting.

"Christ on a *bicycle*," I say, and shove him over, rolling until he's beneath me, inside me, his hair a tangled black halo on the floor. His expression is stark and scraped raw, almost desperate; it's the face of a starving man before a feast, holding on to his table manners only by the very tips of his fingers.

I imagine stamping on those fingers, one by one. I smile down at him, and I know by the hitch of his breath that it's my real one: crooked and mean and just as hungry as he is.

I catch his hands—hovering, uncertain—and slide them up my thighs. I press his fingers into my hips, hard enough to hurt, hard enough that tomorrow I will see the faint blue ghosts of his thumbs and remember his hands holding me like I belong to him.

There's no more hesitating, after that, no more doubt. There's just the two of us and the thing between us, an urgent, animal hunger that swells until it swallows us both.

I let him hold me, afterward, and the geometry of our bodies feels natural, inexplicably familiar. It feels like four walls and a roof overhead, a space stolen from the rest of the world that belongs only to me. I don't let myself think the word, but it moves through me like a shout down a mine shaft: a subterranean echo that goes on and on, loud enough to make the timbers shake.

Arthur's knuckle traces a tear from the corner of my eye to my temple. He doesn't say anything.

"Can I—" I've never asked to stay the night with anyone before and I don't like it much. It feels like turning belly up, exposing my weakest flesh to him. "It's just, with the motel gone, I don't really know where to . . ."

A darkness passes over Arthur's face, and for an unbearable second I think he's going to send me away again, but then he presses his lips to the place where my collarbone meets my shoulder.

He leads me upstairs.

Arthur has spent his life preparing—for battle, for Beasts, for his own bitter end—but he wasn't prepared for this. He wasn't prepared for the flayed look in her eyes or the feel of her above him, or the way she wept when she came, like some final barricade had been breached inside her and left her without defense. He wasn't prepared for the sight of her in his bed, the way the white tops of her shoulders would extend past the edge of his quilt. He looks away, but their afterimage lingers on the backs of his eyelids, a ghostly pair of half-moons.

Opal falls asleep easily and thoroughly, as a child would. Arthur thinks it's probably a sign of physical exhaustion more than an act of trust, but he resolves to deserve it anyway. He holds himself rigidly awake, listening for the creak of a hinge, the scrape of a key in a lock. Baast keeps him company, sitting in the round window with her eyes fixed on the ground below.

Sometime in the black hours after midnight, Opal tenses. Her hands curl into fists and her lips press together, like she's trying desperately to keep something in or out. A shiver begins in her spine and extends down each of her limbs, until she's shaking against him. Arthur folds himself more tightly around her, one arm braced across her stomach, as if there's a physical cold he can keep at bay.

Opal's eyes open on a gasp. She blinks down at Arthur's arm with an expression suggesting she's never seen one before.

He loosens his hold, feeling foolish. "Nightmare?"

"Yeah." Her voice is hoarse, as if she's been screaming. "The river again."

Guilt strikes him, familiar as a fist. He remembers the sound of Opal's voice as she told him how to find the fourth key—dull and cold, everything she isn't—and it strikes him as a miracle that she ever spoke to him again. "I'm sorry," he says, thickly. "I know it doesn't matter now, it doesn't fix anything, but I'm sorry."

Opal cranes her neck around to look at him, her face stricken. "It was *you*," she says, and Arthur wonders if she's still half asleep.

"Yes. It was me. I let the Beast take your mothe—"

"No, I mean, it was you on the riverbank." Opal doesn't look half asleep. Her eyes are bright silver, full of eerie clarity. "It was you holding me."

Arthur hadn't thought she could possibly remember that. By the time he dragged her out of the river she was half-drowned and three-quarters frozen, her flesh a sickly, mottled blue, a crystalline rime of frost forming on the ends of her hair. He was cold, too, but his head hadn't gone under and his coat was thick wool, and also he was still slightly drunk.

Arthur withdraws until there's a tiny space between them on the mattress. "I called 911, but I didn't know how long they'd take, and your skin was the wrong color . . ."

Opal is propped up on her elbows now, looking at him with inexplicable urgency. "Did you find me on the shore? Or did you—was I still—" Her chest is rising and falling too fast.

Arthur isn't sure what answer she wants, so he tells the truth. "All I saw was the car. It wasn't that deep yet so I waded in. Your window was down, your seat belt was off—but you weren't swimming out. You must have been stuck on something, because I pulled and you came loose."

That night is a nauseous blur—the Beast rising from the mist, antlered and awful; his own feet slapping the frozen ground; the scream of tires; a girl's face, blue beneath the water—but he remembers the way her wrist felt in his hand, the moment something gave way and she slid up to the surface.

Opal's eyes are huge, filling fast. "I wasn't stuck. I was holding on to—" The tears refuse to fall, pooling on her eyelashes. "I always thought I let go," she whispers, and then the tears come in a dismaying flood. Arthur isn't sure exactly why she's crying or whether it's his fault, but he touches her shoulder, tentatively, and she buries her face in his chest.

He holds very still while she cries, making his breath slow and even, as if he is trying to pet Baast without being bitten. After a while, Opal says, somewhat incoherently, "I read the letter. I'm sorry."

Arthur doesn't know which letter she could mean, but he says, "That's alright," in case there's still a chance of being bitten.

"The one from your mother. I stole it. I tried to put it back, but then Jasper found the second half . . ."

Arthur was already still, but he feels himself calcifying. It simply isn't possible that he would have left either half of that letter lying carelessly among his other notes, no matter how drunk or dissolute he'd been. Which means the House had taken matters into its own metaphorical hands.

Arthur briefly imagines shoving gum in all the light sockets, or perhaps breaking all the windows on the third floor, before he remembers that he won't have time.

He clears his throat and produces a feeble "Oh."

Opal has peeled her face off his chest. "I'm sorry. I know it was wrong." She pauses. "It was beautiful, though." She pauses again, seeming to pull the next words from some hard place inside herself. "It made me so damn jealous."

"Why?"

A fresh sheen of tears turns her eyes into shards of mirror. "Because like—at least she said goodbye. At least she tried to do right by you." But it's not jealousy in her voice; it's just grief.

Arthur asks, "What was she like?"

Opal exhales. "A fucking mess. A natural disaster wearing Daisy Dukes." She smiles, and God, Arthur is going to miss that sharp twist at the corner of her mouth, that edge that never quite dulls. "I don't know. I guess she was trying, too."

They're quiet for a little while after that. Arthur lies on his back and she fits herself easily into the crook of his arm, her arm resting in the dip of his sternum. He feels it rise and fall as he breathes. He pictures the two of them as children, separated by a handful of years and a couple of miles. Both of them lonely, both of them bound to a place that didn't want them. Both of them bent beneath the weight of what their parents left behind: a baby brother, a house, a battle that never ends.

"Arthur . . . why did you stay? She said you didn't have to."

Her hair is silver in the dark. He wraps a curl around his finger. "Why didn't you hand Jasper to the state and run away?"

"Maybe I will. Run, I mean."

"No, you won't." Jasper had been right. "And neither will I."

And maybe it's this that makes them truly and terribly alike, this refusal to run, this mad urge to dig their nails into the dirt and stay. None of the other Gravelys had risked it, but Opal had.

She makes a small sound beside him, and Arthur notices that his fingers have curled into a fist, tugging her hair. Her head tilts up to his and this time she does not flinch when his lips touch hers.

This time he holds himself over her, looking into the ravenous black of her eyes. This time she slides her wrists beneath his palms and whispers: *don't let go.* He doesn't, even when she twists and cries out, even when she sets her teeth to his throat. He can feel the trembling in her, the fear of her own appetites, and wants to tell her so many things: that there's nothing to be afraid of, that he will take care of her, that he'll hold her and never, ever let go. But he was never a good liar. So he doesn't say anything except her name, at the end.

This time when she falls asleep against him, it feels like trust. This time, he follows her.

Arthur dreams, and this time he isn't sure whether they belong to him, or to the House. It's a series of small, ordinary scenes: a pair of mugs side by side in the sink; a voice humming a song he doesn't know, just around the corner; hair spilling across his pillow like poppy petals. A life that isn't lonely, a house that isn't haunted.

Arthur wakes with a sharp pain in his chest, because he knows he'll never have any of those things.

Because the mist is rising, and he's out of time.

TWENTY-SEVEN

I'm not dreaming; I'm remembering.

I remember the water, the terror, the glove box spilling into my lap, the riverbank, the mud beneath my nails, the cold. I remember the feeling of arms around me, but this time I remember more: a rib cage pressed against my back and a boy's desperate voice saying "Shit, shit, I'm sorry" over and over. The glare of headlights and the sudden chill at my back when the boy left.

Later the nurses told me it was shock, and I believed them. For eleven years I thought that memory—that moment when I was held close, cared for, kept warm against the cold—was a childish fantasy. Until I fell asleep in the familiar shape of Arthur's arms, and learned better.

A shattering *boom* wakes me up. At first I think I must have dreamed it, but I can feel the noise reverberating in my bones, ringing in my ears. The floor itself is trembling with it.

I reach for him thoughtlessly, instantly, choosing not reflect on what that might mean—but he isn't there. His half of the bed is still faintly warm, indented by the shape of his body, but Arthur is gone.

In his place there's nothing but cold silver: the Starling sword, laid carefully beside me.

I recoil from it, half falling out of bed. The hellcat hisses and I see her arched in the window, glaring down at the grounds with her ears pressed flat to her skull. I stumble over to her, trailing sheets, and for a dreamlike second I think Starling House has taken flight, and I'm looking down at the quilted cotton tops of clouds. But it's not clouds, of course; it's mist. For the second time in a single night.

My first reaction is shameful relief, because if the mist is rising then Arthur didn't run from me. He ran to do his duty as Warden, and send the Beasts back to whatever hell they come from. But why would he leave his sword behind?

I reel away from the window. My own name catches my eye, written neatly on the back of a buff-colored folder. Inside I find a stack of double-spaced documents that I can't make any sense of. The words seem to lift from the page and swim in menacing circles: *codicils, encumbrances thereon, executor, sole beneficiary.* My name recurs again and again, and so does the word *Starling.* It takes me too long to realize they exist in conjunction, a pair of disparate nouns yoked together: *I leave my residuary estate, Starling House, and all assets, to Miss Opal Starling.*

It's a will, signed and notarized, with a deed attached.

From somewhere outside of myself, the thought comes that I am not homeless any longer. Starling House—every nail and shingle, every gold mote that hangs in the afternoon light—belongs to me. I test it out, lips moving silently: *home.*

But it's not the house I'm thinking of.

It's the boy who kept me warm when I was cold, who gave me a coat and a truck. It's the man who left me a will I don't want and a sword he doesn't need anymore, because he isn't going to battle the Beasts. He's going to befriend them, and follow them down to Underland. Just like I told him.

He must have planned this long before he let me in the door, maybe even before he cut his deal with Baine and Gravely. He was never planning on sticking around. A small, mewling part of me wants to know if what happened between us mattered to him at all, if he wanted to stay or if he was just running out the clock until the mist rose—but most of me is too busy cussing him out and digging through his dresser.

It occurs to me, as I roll the overlong sleeves of his shirt up my arms, that I could run. I could take the deed and walk out the front gates. I could catch a bus to Louisville and maybe in a few months I'd see a headline about a man missing in Muhlenberg County. I could sell the land to the power company and get an apartment so new it still smells like sawdust and fresh paint. That's who I am, isn't it? A survivor, a cut-and-runner, a pragmatist.

Except if that's really who I was, I would have bought a second Greyhound ticket and left with Jasper hours ago. I would have walked right past that amber window last February and kept working at Tractor Supply. I would have let go of my mother's hand and saved myself. But I hadn't saved myself, that night; Arthur had.

And now he's gone into Underland, and it's my turn to save him.

I can feel the attention of Starling House like a weight in the air around me, a gaze facing inward. The windows rattle in their frames and the pipes howl in the walls. There's a tremor in the floor, like the house has suffered some secret wound and is holding itself upright through sheer stubbornness.

"Tell me what I have to do," I say.

The house doesn't answer, but a stray shaft of moonlight falls through the window and finds the silver edge of the sword. It flashes at me, a vicious wink, and I remember Jasper's voice, oozing disgust: *some kind of blood oath.*

The hilt is cold and heavy, already familiar. I cup the blade with my left hand, laying the edge along the first scar Starling House ever gave me. I should have known, then, what it wanted from me. I should have known I would wind up here, with the house leaning hungrily around me and my pulse beating loud in my ears, no matter how hard Arthur tried to drive me away.

I close my eyes, shout a swear word, and draw the sword across my palm.

It cuts deeper than I meant it to, falling through the strata of my skin, biting deep into the wet muscle at the base of my thumb. Blood fills my palm and spills between my fingers. It falls to the floor in a syrupy stream, pooling at my feet.

Nothing in particular seems to happen, except that I feel queasy and stupid.

Maybe my blood is tainted in some way. Maybe the house can taste the Gravely in me, every sin I inherited from my ancestors. But honestly, screw that: I don't know my name, but I've never been Opal Gravely. My mother shed her name like a skin and raised the two of us to be no one, or anyone. I have no name but the one I choose.

I clench my fist, squeezing hard. My blood lingers for another second, two, before it soaks into the wood, as if an animal lapped it away.

And I feel myself tipping over an edge and falling downward, slipping into delirium. The boundaries of my body turn thin and permeable. I am conscious of my blood following the grain of the wood, sliding between the boards, dripping from the points of unseen nails. I follow it along the joists and behind the walls, pumping through the secret arteries of the house, tracing the vascular map of pipes and wires, mouseholes and wheedling vines. I follow it down into the foundations and deeper still, into the hot wet earth. My blood becomes the dirt itself, riddled with small blind creatures, pierced by taproots and fence posts.

For a moment, or maybe a season, I am Starling House. I am an impossible architecture, a thing built from the dreams and nightmares of ten generations. There are wisteria roots wrapped around my bones and coffins buried beneath my skin. I sigh and the curtains billow. I curl my fist and the rafters moan.

I remember myself—myself-the-girl, myself-the-mere-human—in stages. My left hand comes first, because it hurts. Then my knees, bruised and aching on the floor, my shoulders, my lungs, my fragile mortal pulse. My mind comes last, disentangling itself reluctantly from the House. By the time I open my eyes, I know one thing with absolute certainty: that Arthur Starling was wrong.

He was not the last Warden of Starling House.

To Arthur Starling, running down the stone steps to Underland, it comes as a sudden, deafening silence. For twelve years his senses have extended past his own borders. He knew the taste of dew and the weight of dust on the windowsills and the shapes the starlings made in the sky. And now he knows nothing but the panicked sound of his own heartbeat in his ears.

He says, aloud, "No." And then, several times in a row, *"Damn you."* But the House has a new Warden now, and it pays him no mind. It shouldn't have been possible—there's never been a new Warden while the previous one still lived—but the House must have decided walking down into Underland was close enough to dying.

And then all it took was a little blood, a lot of guts, and the sword.

Arthur always planned to take it with him to face whatever waited for him beneath Starling House—Eleanor's last and best inheritance, finally finishing its work—but he hadn't accounted for Opal. Alone in his bed, fragile and trusting, that deadly Gravely blood beating softly in her throat.

It was hard enough to leave her; it was impossible to leave her undefended.

So Arthur had gone down through the trapdoor empty-handed. He had stood in the cellar while the mist grew teeth and claws, assembling itself. He had waited, unmoving, until there was a fully formed Beast staring down at him with eyes like ragged black bullet holes, and he had held out both his hands, palm up, weaponless. It had prowled closer, chitinous, sickening, and Arthur had knelt with his head tilted back, throat exposed.

"Please," he'd said. *Please,* to the thing he had fought his entire life, the thing that left his parents bloodied corpses in the grass.

And it had bent its terrible head and left something cold and iron in his hands.

Arthur did not hesitate. He opened the fourth lock and stepped through the door, telling himself that it was for the best. That Opal would remain safe and sleeping while he went down to Underland, and when she woke it would be to a House that was merely a house, and Beasts that were merely bad dreams. She would be grateful, probably. (He knew she would not be grateful.)

But the House had woken her too soon, and she'd taken up the sword, as he should have known she would. Anyone who would face down a Beast with keys between her knuckles would not shy from a fight.

But even if Arthur could turn back—and he made sure the door would not open again—he wouldn't. All those years of study and practice, all those ink-stained needles, had led him here, to the end of it all, and the only direction left is down.

He will leave her, with the Beasts rising and their enemies at the gates, with nothing but a rusting sword and the House he's hated for twelve years.

Arthur rests his forehead against the damp stone wall of the passage and attempts an extremely overdue apology. "It was never your fault." The inside of his mouth is coated in dust, and the words come out thick and glottal. The foundations of the House moan back at him. "You did your best for them, I always knew it." He remembers, reluctantly, the first time he walked back into the House after finding his parents' bodies. The funereal black cloths across every mirror, the mournful groans of the stairs. He'd been too furious to care, too selfish to see the grief in it.

He presses his forehead harder into the stone, until he can feel tiny indentations forming in his flesh. His voice is like the scraping of a rusted key in a rusted lock. *"Do better for her."*

Arthur Starling makes his final descent while, far above him, the monsters rise.

TWENTY-EIGHT

I can feel them, the way you'd feel flies tiptoeing across your bedsheets. There's more than one Beast this time, and they've already made it out of the House. I feel hooves that leave rot behind them, claws made of vapor and hate. I experience a disquieting urge to rush out and do battle with them, like every Warden before me, but I brush it aside. Arthur spent his whole life protecting this ugly, ungrateful town; tonight, they'll just have to wait their turn.

I leave Arthur's will on his desk and run down the stairs with the sword held awkwardly in my right hand. The lights pop to life ahead of me as if an invisible row of butlers is flipping the switches, and the House arranges itself so that I come out into the kitchen.

Something has gone badly wrong in here. The cabinets are crooked, doors swinging open, plates splintered on the counters. The floor is more slanted than usual, sloping downward, and there are cracks in the tile big enough to swallow the hellcat whole. Mist rises from the cracks like steam, gathering on the ceiling and rolling down the hall.

In the pantry I find the trapdoor thrown wide, the lock hanging ajar. I throw myself downward with a weird sense of playing out a scene I've already lived, except this time I'm the one holding the sword. I'm the one chasing after someone who's made a stupid choice and hoping against hope that I'm not too late.

The air turns hot and acrid, like the morning after the Fourth of July, when you can still taste gunpowder in the back of your throat. Dust stings my eyes, forms a sweaty gray film on my skin. I hit the last step and stumble over a pile of stone and plaster. The cellar looks like a bombed-out building from a social studies textbook: the rafters overhead are cracked, dangling at odd angles, and the walls are leaning dangerously inward. The floor is scorched black in a way that makes me remember the deep boom that woke me up.

"Arthur, you *ass.*" Imagine being so stupid, so gratuitously noble, that you try to explode your own cellar rather than risk someone helping you.

His plan only half worked. I scramble over the rubble and shove a rafter away from the door. The entire wall seems to be collapsing, falling into whatever hell lies under the House, but the door itself is still standing.

And it's still locked. If Arthur found the fourth key and went down to Underland—like he's always wanted to, like I know he did—then he must have closed it behind him.

Since the moment I woke up, the moment I reached for him and found nothing but cold silver beside me, I've been afraid. I'm pretty good at ignoring emotions it would be inconvenient to feel, so it's been nothing but a dull buzzing at the back of my head—until now. Now the noise rises, rushing through me. What if this is really it? What if Arthur is already gone, lost somewhere I can't follow? I picture myself all alone in this grand, cursed, dreaming house, just another lonely Starling doomed to spend her life discovering the terrible distance between a house and a home.

I fumble for a stone and bash it against the hinges, knowing it won't work, too angry not to try. It doesn't leave so much as a scratch. I try my own blood next, slapping my gory palm on the wood. The door remains serenely shut.

I experience an unpleasant tugging sensation, like a stranger yanking at a strand of my hair. There is a key turning in my front gate. The tumblers are grinding and the hinges are screaming, but they can't resist for long. Very soon I feel the tread of boots up the drive, and the nauseous certainty that there's someone on my land who shouldn't be.

Nobody born and raised in Eden would set foot on Starling property before dawn, especially on a night like this, when the fog is up and the moon is missing—which means I know who it is. Which means I know the precise terms of Arthur's deal. He gave Elizabeth Baine the keys to Starling House, offered her every secret his ancestors fought to protect—for me. When I find him I'm going to push him against the wall and cuss him blue, right before I kiss him bloody.

I can feel Baine advancing, others following behind her. My land recoils from their touch: the driveway twists back on itself, lengthening and dividing until there are many paths through the woods, none of which lead to the House. The trees crowd close, bending low as lovers, and the briars sharpen into green coils of barbed wire. The ironwork beasts on the front gates lick their metal lips and in the woods the real Beasts lift their heads.

A certain dark eagerness runs through me—let them find out what happens to trespassers around here, let their bones rot in my woods—but then I realize: if there are still Beasts aboveground, then there's still a way through this door. If Arthur could do it, why can't I?

I'm in the kitchen, running for the back door, when the screaming starts.

I fall twice on the way out of the house. The floor is uneven, groaning and popping beneath my feet like the deck of a sinking ship. I wonder if the whole thing is going under, if the cellar will open like a mouth and swallow it down.

A mottled white creature streaks past my ankles when I open the front door. The hellcat, disappearing into the trees. At least one of us still knows when to cut and run.

I make it down the front steps and across the lawn, following the screams. I see the Beasts only in peripheral glances: a sinuous flash of scaled flesh, a cloven hoof striking the earth, the flick of a forked tail. Ghostly white creatures that move between the trees without displacing a single leaf or snapping a single twig. They're chasing toward the front gates, pouring over the land with a sickening hunger that makes me think of those old stories about wild hunts led by the devil himself.

My feet hit the bare clay of the drive. The old sycamore is gnarled and black overhead. There are people in dark clothes coming toward me up the drive, but I'm not worried about them, because suddenly there is a Beast between us.

It emerges from the trees, trailing fog. This one is almost deer-shaped, except its spine is far too long and its antlers branch too many times, like a tree uprooted. Maybe I've gotten used to them, or maybe I've lost my mind, but it doesn't seem as awful as the first Beast I saw. There's a grace to it, an elegant horror that reminds me, disconcertingly, of Arthur's drawings.

One of the men walks ahead of the others. He can't see the Beast, but he must sense it. Some ancient, animal instinct turns his face pale and sweaty, makes his eyes dart from side to side. I want to shout a warning, but it's too late: the Beast is loping to meet him, leaving a line of dead earth behind it.

It doesn't attack. It merely moves through the man, like a cloud breaking around a hilltop. For a moment I think he's been spared. Then I hear the hollow snap of bone. The screaming starts again.

The people behind him scatter, ant-like, scurrying toward him or away, talking into radios, receiving answers in bursts of static—except one. The starlight shows me a sleek bob, the gold flash of a watch. Elizabeth Baine continues up the drive to Starling House without faltering or slowing. I can feel the weight of my keys in her hand.

She walks past the fallen man—now clutching his ankle and emitting a high, childish whimper—without looking down at him. She sees me, maybe catches the glint of my sword, and her smile stretches Cheshire-like in the dark. As if she isn't surprised or concerned. As if, even now, with her men falling around her and the land rising against her, she doesn't believe anything could truly stand between her and her desires. I wonder what it would be like, to move through the world without bothering to distinguish your wants from your needs, and a weird envy unfurls in my belly.

Baine keeps walking, keeps smiling. There's something wrong with her face. There are dark gouges clustered around her eyes and mouth, glistening, oozing a little.

Another scream splits the air, followed by a muffled shot, then silence. She doesn't look back. But even if she had, she wouldn't have seen the second Beast prowling behind her.

Hateful. Beautiful. A vulpine jaw and a sinuous body. The wrong number of legs ending in too many talons. Black, black eyes, fixed on Baine. Its body brushes through the woods, and I see leaves curling and dying, bark turning soft and wormy, pale shelves of mushrooms blooming from the trunks of trees.

A wrenching, splintering crack cuts the air. The old sycamore makes a mournful sound before it begins—gently, with great dignity—to fall.

Baine still hasn't faltered or flinched. She'll die with that damn smile still on her face.

There is a moment here I'm not proud of, where I hesitate. Where I'm the House again, watching Baine fly toward me like one of those dark-flecked birds that crash sometimes in my windows. I feel nothing but distant pity for these fragile, foolish creatures. But then I remember I'm a person, about to watch another person be crushed to death, and my legs start moving.

My shoulder hits Baine in the belly, driving the air from her lungs and throwing her to the ground in grand action-movie style. She hits the earth with a hollow thud, like a watermelon on pavement, just as the sycamore crashes around us. The trunk misses us, but the canopy slaps and claws across my hunched back, tearing cloth, scraping skin.

Silence. I take one breath, two, before uncurling from my crouch. Baine is struggling upright, her expensive hair mussed and white welts swelling across her cheeks. Up close, I can see that those black gouges are dozens of tiny, gory wounds. Her lips look like the pulpy wet pit of a peach.

"How did you—it doesn't matter, you can't s-stop me." There's something dark trickling from Baine's temple and her eyes aren't focusing quite right. She looks weak and fleshy, and I find I'm no longer afraid of her at all.

I am, however, afraid of the Beast, which is now looming above us like a cresting wave. Its eyes are fixed on me, dark and mad.

I stand, raising the sword on instinct. It takes an enormous effort to lower it, to loosen my grip and let it fall back to the soft white undersides of the sycamore leaves.

Befriend the Beasts. So simple, so unnatural. I wonder what it cost Arthur to leave his sword behind, to approach his oldest enemies without a weapon.

It's easier for me. I read Eleanor's books so often her nightmares felt like old friends. Sometimes, on the bad days, I imagined the Beasts would greet me as one of their own, another thing with teeth, and let me sleep in Underland forever.

"Please." My voice breaks on the word, going hoarse. "Please. I don't want to hurt you."

The Beast watches me. Every desperate instinct, every cell in my body is telling me to run, to reach for a weapon, to put anything at all between myself and the nightmare looking down at me.

Instead, I hold out my gory left hand, palm up, as if the Beast is just a strange dog I met behind somebody's trailer. I screw my eyes shut.

I think: *Gravely blood.* I think: *That's not my name.*

An imperceptible chill touches my skin, a faint pressure against my hand. I open my eyes to find my palm licked clean, the wound bloodless and white. The Beast runs a long silver tongue across its lips.

I might be sick. I might laugh. "I need to go down. To Underland." A part of me is standing outside myself, watching the scene as if it's one of the ghost stories I used to tell Jasper. My own image blurs in my mind, merging with little Nora Lee.

A rippling, buzzing sound rises around us, and for a wild moment I think the Beast is purring at me. But it's the hellcat, trotting out of the trees to wind herself around the Beast's forelegs. I meet the Beast's eyes and find them subtly changed. They're still the same abyssal black, but there's a gentleness to them, an aching sadness. An image comes to me, of those same eyes looking up at me from a field of flowers.

"No," I whisper, and the hellcat gives me a cool amber stare, rubbing her cheek against the mist-colored fur. It occurs to me that she's only ever been that affectionate with one living creature.

I reach for the Beast without deciding to, the same way I reached for Arthur across the empty bed. For a moment I think it's going to work. I think it's going to give me the key and lead me down—but it rears back before my hand touches it, eyes sad and fierce. Then it's gone, vanishing down the drive and taking my only way into Underland with it.

The hellcat gives me a long, accusing look before trotting after it.

Fear rises again, filling my ears, my mouth, drowning me. There was something of Arthur in that Beast—God knows how—which means he's already gone. He's deep under the earth, deeper than the longest roots of the oldest oak, just like Nora Lee.

But she wasn't the first, was she? The hare told her the way down. In another version it was Nathaniel Boone who told Eleanor Starling. The stories mirror each other too closely to be coincidental, a single history told a dozen different ways. But all of them agree: long before Starling House, long before Eleanor and her keys, there was another way into Underland.

Cold fingers grab my ankle. Baine is slumped on one elbow, blood softening the stiff collar of her shirt. "The a-aperture. Where is it?"

At least some of her goons have fallen back, but others are crashing through the trees, still heading for the House. "My people will find it eventually, of course, but if you assist us . . ." Her pupils are mismatched, wrong-sized. One of the wounds around her mouth goes all the way through to her teeth; I can see the wet white of the bone.

I kick my leg out of her grasp. "You should get out of here. Call your people and leave."

Baine attempts one of her urbane laughs, but it comes out off-key, far too high. "What, *now*? When we're so close?" For an uncomfortable second she reminds me of Mom: a woman whose wants outweighed everything else, an endless appetite. "I made it past the gates. Past those fucking birds"—I picture a dozen sharp yellow beaks driving into her flesh, again and again—"and you think I'll stop now?"

"If you go in that House, I guarantee you'll have a bad time." It sounds like a bluff, but it's nothing but the truth. I can feel the House at my back like a living thing, a guard dog with its hackles high. The explosion seems to have pushed it off some secret edge, sent the entire structure a little farther out of reality. It's less a house now than the idea of one, and a house is meant to shelter some people and keep out the rest. If Baine forces her way through the door she will meet nothing but misery.

She isn't listening to me. She's scanning the ground with her mismatched gaze, blinking too often. Her eyes catch the iron shine of a ring of keys and she dives for it, clutching it to her chest as if she thinks I might try to take it away, as if she still imagines she has anything I want.

A tortured, resentful pity moves through me. I'm suddenly tired of standing here talking to this vicious, hollow creature. "You go ahead and hold on to those," I tell her, not ungently. "I don't need them."

By the time she opens her mouth to reply with some other offer or threat or bribe, I'm already gone, running for the front gates.

I t hurts, leaving Starling land. Stepping across the property line is like tearing myself free from a briar patch, leaving blood and skin behind.

The gates swing wide for me, and I step through them, ignoring the twitching, whimpering figures tangled in metal. The iron animals frolic in my peripheral vision, their sides slick and red in the moonlight.

I feel smaller on the other side, less than I was.

Arthur's truck is waiting right where I left it, except now it's obscured by a pair of black vans and half a dozen people. I'm braced for questions and accusations, scrambling for a lie that will explain why I'm barefoot and bloody-handed—but I receive nothing but glazed stares. One of them is making violent gestures to her companion, saying, "Fire me, fucking do it. I'm not going back in." One of them is slumped on the back bumper, crying quietly into his hands.

I slide into the driver's seat and try the key twice, three times before the engine turns over. I try not to think about where I'm going, or how high the river is, or whether I can find the old mines with the mist up.

The bridge looms out of the fog like a black rib cage, the struts silhouetted by the glow of the power plant across the river. My knuckles are sharp and bloodless on the wheel. I hear the road change under the tires, going hollow and rattly, and I keep my eyes firmly on the other end of the bridge.

But the end is blocked. There are vehicles parked at bad angles across the road, shards of glass tossed like glitter over everything. A light is flashing, infusing the mist with red and blue. Through the strobe I can make out the boxy shape of an old Pontiac, and the silhouette of a cowboy hat. It looks like Constable Mayhew got his stupid lights back from the real cops, somehow.

I hit the brakes hard enough to make the rubber squeal. The cowboy hat lifts, tilting in my direction, and I know with sudden certainty that I won't make it past him. Mayhew's never needed much of an excuse to handcuff me, and now I'm covered in blood at the scene of a bad wreck, having somehow slithered off the hook for the motel fire a few hours earlier. Even someone without a personal grudge would probably have a few questions for me.

But the mines are on Mayhew's side of the river, on Gravely land. I can picture the rotten boards, the endless green hearts of the kudzu vines. Just around the bend, a short scramble down from the road.

Or up from the river.

The door handle is slick under my sweating palms. The old railroad ties are rough under my feet. A flashlight shines in my direction, blunted by the fog, followed by a shout. "Who's there? Is that you, girl?"

My legs feel very far away from my torso, and poorly connected, like the trailing limbs of a neglected puppet. They carry me to the very edge of the bridge. The mist is so thick and viscous tonight I can't even see the river, just the curl of my toes over the edge and then nothing at all. I can hear it, though: the same sweet siren's song I've heard in my head since the crash, the endless rush of the river calling me back down.

I tell myself it won't be that cold, this time of year. I tell myself I used to jump all the time, before my body knew how to be afraid, back when I thought Mom and Jasper and me were untouchable, inviolate, not lucky so much as too quick for the bad luck to catch up with us. I count slowly backward from ten, the way Mr. Cole taught me.

It doesn't work. My legs remain stiff and motionless. My heart thrashes in my throat. I can feel the shudder of Mayhew's boots coming closer, see the sickly blue shine of the flashlight on my skin.

I just can't do it. Won't. I've had too many nightmares about going under, fought too hard to stay on dry land.

Except: Arthur went down, and I know him too well to imagine he's coming back up unless I drag him behind me, a sullen Eurydice. I know the hard set of his jaw and the soft slide of his lips, I know the terrible guilt that drives him and the scars it left behind. I know he is the thing I have been chasing and craving, searching and waiting and hoping for my entire life: home.

I step into the mist and let it carry me down soft and slow. I slip into the river easily, almost gently, as if the water was waiting for me, open-armed.

TWENTY-NINE

I was never a strong swimmer, and it's been
eleven years since I was in deep water.
Bev said there used to be a public pool down
in Bowling Green, but they filled it with cement
rather than desegregate in '64, so most kids only
know enough dog paddle to keep their chins
above water.

I don't even do that much, tonight. I let the
current sweep me south, my toes dragging sometimes
against weeds and stones, my mouth full of the
metal taste of the water. My face bobs to the surface
three times before I see the stretch of riverbank beneath
the mines. I'm not sure how I recognize it in the dark,
but I do, just from the particular tilt of a willow
oak, the bend of the bank. Apparently the maps
you make in childhood never fade, but are merely
folded away until you need them again.

I flail for the shore and crawl out on hands and knees. The silt under my nails sends bile up my throat, and I waste five heaving breaths reminding myself that I'm not fifteen and there isn't a red Corvette sinking behind me. I stand, and my legs are a pair of matchsticks, jointless and fragile.

Voices fall down from the bridge above, hitting the water and echoing downriver. I hear the words *where* and *Jesus*. A beam of light tunnels through the mist, pointed at the place where my body went under the water. I can almost picture Constable Mayhew shaking his head, doleful and sanctimonious. *Just like her mother.*

Maybe he's right. My mom scrabbled and fought and hoped right up to the very end, and so will I.

I scramble up the bank, the clay slicking under my feet. I can't see the shaft entrance beneath the dark mass of undergrowth, so I thump my fist against the bank until it rings hollow. I rip at the vines like an animal digging a den, breaking long strings of kudzu, uprooting ivy in uneven bursts, until the air smells weepy and green and my palms are tacky with sap. In the red-blue flash of the light I see old wood, the rusted remnants of a sign that now reads, ominously, ANGER. The boards have gone ripe with rot, and mist slips through the gaps and trickles down to the river. I'm almost relieved to see it, because it means I was right, and there's another way down to Underland.

The wood crumbles in my hands, spilling rich earth and pill bugs down my sleeves. The air that rushes from the mine is stale and fetid, a motel room left all summer with the AC off and the windows shut. The hole I've made shows me nothing but featureless black, a darkness so complete it seems almost solid.

I kick through the last of the boards and step into the mines. I have no light, no map, no plan except to place one hand on the dewy stone wall and walk, feeling like a kid who took a dare she shouldn't have and wants badly to back down.

The floor is uncomfortably soft, my toes sinking into alluvial drifts of soil and fungus, followed by sudden hills of sharp rock, then clammy limestone. I crack my shin hard on a fallen timber and climb over it awkwardly, blindly. In some places the walls have collapsed inward, so that I have to crawl over the pile with my spine scraping the ceiling. The air is cool and foul on my face. The wall vanishes beneath my hand sometimes, when a tunnel branches off, but I never hesitate long. I choose whichever direction leads me down.

I go deeper. Deeper still. I picture weight accumulating above me: dirt and tree roots, paved parking lots, the great metal bones of Big Jack himself.

The tunnel narrows, and the timbers grow sporadic, less square. Soon the shaft is no wider than my shoulders, a rathole carved roughly into the earth. I think of the story Charlotte played for me in the library, that old woman's voice shaking with a fear that had been passed down through her family like slow poison. Under my palm—raw and stinging now, from dragging along the stone—I can feel the desperate scars of picks and drills, the scratch marks of men driven beyond themselves, into madness.

I think of the Gravelys with their grand columned house and their Sunday dinners, surrounded by an entire town that admires and resents and relies on them, that never thinks for a single minute about this place. This mine, buried beneath them like a body, like a sin tucked under a mattress. I have the sudden, ugly sense that Eden deserved every year of foul luck, every bad dream, every Beast that padded down the streets.

Ahead of me, I see light. The faintest phosphorescence, like the dying hours of a glow stick. After so long in the black I don't trust it, but it disappears when I close my eyes and returns when I open them.

The light gets brighter. The shaft gets smaller. The air clots in my throat, thick and wet, and a noise rises from the stones, a ceaseless rush. My foot lands on something smooth and hollow, which cracks like an egg. In the eerie half-light I can make out an eye socket, half a grin, a jumble of vertebrae and phalanges. They seem terribly small. From somewhere far away, high above me, comes the somewhat hysterical desire to take a picture and text it to Lacey, as proof that Willy Floyd wasn't sacrificed in a Satanic ritual.

I step over Willy's bones and turn sideways to scrape around a final bend, contorting myself through a last desperate crack, and then I'm stumbling into open space. My knees hit stone, and I throw my arms high, expecting teeth or claws, some attack by whatever lives down in this hell below the world.

But it's no hell. It's a long cavern, receding into darkness in either direction. On the opposite wall there is an arched doorway set in the wall and a set of stairs rising into the dark. The steps pull at me, strangely familiar, and I know they lead up to a locked door and a cellar full of rubble, to a house collapsing like an old soldier after a long war.

And between the stairs and me, running like a pale ribbon down the middle of the cave, is a river.

I think, distantly, that I should have guessed. I should have known by the sycamores that line the drive to Starling House, the wisteria that riddles its walls. Things that prefer creeksides and swamps, low hollows and valleys that never quite dry out. Their roots have made it all the way down here, worming through the cave ceiling to trail their white fingers in this underground river, drinking deep.

The current is fast but strangely glutinous, slurried. The water is sickly gray, like the Mud River after a big storm, when the utility company has to send out boil advisories. There's a thin layer of fog lying on the river's surface. By its pale, dreaming light I can see two shapes caught beneath the current.

Bodies. Eyes closed. Limbs drifting.

One of them is a woman, middle-aged, a little ugly, wearing a long colorless dress that strikes me as a costume, a prop from the Old Time Photo Booth down in Gatlinburg. Except I know it isn't, because I recognize her. Her mouth hard and small as an early apple, her face overlong, her sleeves stained with ink. I have her picture saved on Jasper's laptop, copied and pasted from her Wiki page.

Eleanor Starling ought to be nothing but dirt by now—maybe a few molars and metatarsals, the half-moon of a skull—but her skin is smooth and pliant under the water, as if she's simply sleeping.

The other person, of course, is Arthur Starling. It's harder to make out his features because the water runs rougher above him, as if his body is a jagged stone. It almost seems to be boiling, and beneath the torrent his tattoos look blistered, raw, as if the river doesn't like the signs he carved into his skin and wants to wash them away.

I walk into the current without deciding to. The water is precisely the same temperature as my skin, so that I can see it rising up my legs—ankles, shins, knees, thighs—but barely feel it. I reach for Arthur's collar, holding my chin just above the surface, and tug hard.

He doesn't move. It's like his pockets are filled with stones, like his hands are fisted in the riverbed, holding him fast. I try Eleanor next, because why not, because there's nothing I won't try now. I'm half expecting her flesh to tear away under my touch, like one of those mummies exposed to light after thousands of years, but she feels exactly like Arthur: soft and alive, but anchored.

I shout one, vicious "*No!*" and punch my fist into the river. The water splashes into my face, runs into my mouth. It tastes wrong. Sweet and rich and metal, like honey and blood. I swallow reflexively and the river leaves an oily trail down my throat.

A sickly drowsiness washes through me. I have an urge to lie down in the water, warm as skin, and sleep. I resist it, thinking of Dorothy and Rip Van Winkle and all the fools who fell asleep in fairy rings.

But then I think of older stories. I think of the five rivers of the underworld: oblivion, woe, wailing, fury, fire. I think of that handwritten note I found so long ago in the margins of Ovid: *a sixth river?*

The only way into the underworld is to cross a river; the only way into faerie is to fall asleep. I am not in Underland yet, but I know how to get there.

I scoop the water into my hands, a palmful of silver, and drink deep.

Sleep moves through me, tidal, inexorable. I lie back and feel my hair lift from my scalp to float around my face in a bloody halo. I close my eyes and open my mouth, and the river comes in. It fills my mouth, slips between my teeth, slides like warm syrup into my lungs.

My hand finds Arthur's. I lie down beside him on the riverbed, and sleep.

I am awake. (I am still sleeping.)

I am standing before Starling House, the sky the color of shale, the air hot and motionless. (I am still lying on the riverbed. There is silt beneath my spine and water in my throat.)

Arthur is here, too. He isn't, I know he isn't—somewhere above myself I can still feel his fingers beneath mine—but here, in Underland, he's awake.

He is standing with his back to me, a little ways up the drive. All I can see is his silhouette, but I know him by the too-long tangle of his hair and the set of his jaw, the way his heels are dug into the dirt and his shoulders are braced. He looks like a person who has chosen his direction and will not change it.

Standing between Arthur and the House, watching him with the black pits of their eyes, are the Beasts. They're more substantial down here, more real and more awful for their reality. They aren't made of mist now but of meat—I can see sinews moving beneath milky skin, knobs of bone at every joint, claws flattening the long grass. None of them are moving, but all of them are watching the man standing at their feet.

"Arthur!"

It's just like that awful night when he fought the Beast before. He wasn't moving, but a new and awful stillness falls over him. When his head turns toward me it looks unnatural, grindingly slow, like a statue looking over one shoulder. His lips move, and it might be the word *how*. It might be the first syllable of my name. I decide it doesn't matter.

I run to him, stumbling over the darkened drive. He catches me awkwardly against his chest, one-handed, because there is a sword in his other hand. Old and battered, inlaid with strange silver shapes that glow very faintly: the Starling sword, the same one I left abandoned in the world above.

Arthur pulls away, his hand gripping hard on my shoulder. "What are you doing here? How did you—I made sure—"

"Shut up. Shut *up!*" All my terror and panic and pain, everything I've felt since I reached for him in the night and found nothing but cold sheets, comes boiling to the surface. I know we're in an eerie not-quite-dream with monsters poised to strike, but I'm so angry I can feel it like a second pulse beating in my skull. I can't speak so I punch him, good and hard, right where his ribs meet.

"*Ow—*"

"You deserve it! You left me up there all alone, after we—just when I thought maybe somebody gave a shit about me—"

"I *do,* that's why I had to—"

"Leave me? With nothing but a sword and a fucking will?"

"I was trying—I didn't want—"

But I don't want him to explain or apologize, because I'm still pissed. Because if I stop being pissed for even a second, I'll start crying. "Well, I don't want it. I never did. I wanted *you,* you bastard, you goddamn *fool,* and if you didn't want me to follow you down here maybe you shouldn't have left."

He stops trying to explain and kisses me instead. It starts rough—a bruising collision of lips and teeth, the taste of blood and fury like hot metal in our mouths—but then his hand slides from my shoulder to the back of my neck, his thumb framing my jaw. His mouth softens against mine.

When he pulls away, his voice is hoarse. "I didn't want you to follow me." He rests his forehead heavy against mine and breathes the next words against my skin. "Thank God you did."

I discover that my hands are fisted in his shirt. I flatten them against the place I punched him, not quite sorry. "Where are we?" I look up at the Beasts, still motionless, still watching us like hunting birds waiting for a pair of mice to scurry out into the open.

"I don't know." Arthur's body tilts back to face the Beasts. "I thought if I found out where they came from I could end it, like stepping on a wasp nest. I thought I would find another world, not . . ." His eyes flick up to the familiar shape of Starling House looming behind the Beasts.

I follow his gaze and see something small and pale in one of the windows. A face. A girl.

She's gaunt and fragile-looking, with skin so pale it approaches translucence and shoulders so sharp they look like the folded wings of some small, dark bird. She's wearing an old-fashioned dress with a high collar, and she's watching us with no expression at all.

I find Arthur's wrist and squeeze it once. I know the second he sees the girl, because a shiver runs through his frame.

"What happens if you go toward the House?" I ask.

"They attack." Arthur's chin points at one of the Beasts, a feathered thing with too many teeth. It holds one of its legs curled into the white down of its chest. Its blood is a startling red in this colorless place.

"Ah," I say. I stare hard at the girl in the window and make a guess, lifting my voice. "Nora Lee?"

I shouted the name, but the girl doesn't flinch. I know I'm right, though— I've seen that small, angled face in the pages of *The Underland,* I've dreamed myself wearing that fusty old dress, running down and away from everything.

I glare until her face begins to blur in my vision. It merges with the face that glared down at me from the portrait in Starling House, the face I saw sleeping in the river. I already knew their stories were distorted reflections of each other, like a single girl reflected in a cracked mirror. The letters of her name dance in my head, pirouetting gracefully to new positions.

"Eleanor?" I don't yell it this time, but I don't have to. The girl cringes back from the window, and her eyes meet mine.

THIRTY

Until I said her name, Eleanor Starling's face was entirely empty, her eyes like a pair of hard black periods typed in the center of a blank page. She looked down at the gathered Beasts without dismay or surprise. I wondered if she could still feel anything at all, or if this place had reduced her to a thin illustration rather than a person.

But the sound of her true name hits her like a fist through a window. Her eyes widen. Her lips part, as if she can taste the word through the glass. She looks at me intently, almost hungrily, before turning abruptly away. She vanishes into the shadows of the House.

"Arthur, I think—" I begin, but a sound interrupts me. A high, wavering howl, like a cornered cat, or a distant coyote.

Another Beast picks it up, and another. A ripple moves through them. A hoof hits the earth. They are not impassive anymore.

I make a noise somewhere between a sob and a snort. "I thought you befriended them, or whatever."

"Apparently it didn't stick." Arthur's voice is dry but he's lifting the sword again, one elbow high, blade laid flat across his forearm. "Get to the House, Opal."

My eyes slide between the Beasts, stalking closer, and the hard knot of his face. "Because you think that's the way out of here or because you're being a jackass again?"

Half his mouth curves, joylessly. "Yes." The curve flattens. "Please, Opal. This time, just this one time, will you go when I ask you to?"

The thing is: I think he's right. I think if there's a way to destroy this place or escape it, Eleanor Starling knows it. I take a breath, short and hard. "Okay. Alright. But don't—you can't—" Swallowing is harder than it should be. "I'm not letting you kill yourself fighting these things. I don't even think that sword is *real*—"

Arthur takes a wide warning swing at one of the Beasts and it hisses, recoiling. "Real enough," he says.

"Fine! Whatever! But I'm coming back for you, and if you're dead, I'll kill you."

He smiles that small, bitter smile, so I hit him again. "I'm not joking. I'll go, if you swear to stay."

Maybe it's the way my voice splits on the last word. Maybe he just wants me to go. But he meets my eyes and nods once, so deeply it's almost a bow, or a vow.

It's not enough; it's all we get before the Beasts are on us. It's hell—lips retracting over long pearled canines, muscles coiling, talons extending—but so is Arthur Starling. The sword arcs and bites, hacks and sings, cutting so quickly through the air it leaves a silvered trail behind it. There's no beauty to his movements, no grace. He doesn't look like a dancer. He looks like a boy who wanted to grow flowers but was handed a sword instead. He looks like a man who gave up on hope a long time ago, but who keeps fighting anyway, on and on. He looks like a Warden of Starling House, gone to war.

Arthur takes two steps forward, another to the left. He slashes, fast and brutal, and wrenches the blade out of splintered bone. The Beasts draw away from him, just a little, and there it is: a way to the House.

I don't hesitate. I run, arms tucked tight to my chest, head ducked low.

My feet slap on stone. I fly up the steps of Starling House and hit the door hard. It's locked.

But surely, even in whatever upside-down sideways version of the world we're in, Starling House won't turn against me. For months now I've fed it my sweat and time, my love and blood. My name is on the deed and my hand held the sword; I am the Warden.

I press my palm to the scarred wood and say, softly, "Please." I pour all my wanting into the word, all my foolish hope.

I feel a softening of space around me, a sense of unreality, like being in a dream and realizing, suddenly, that you're dreaming. The world bends for me.

The lock clicks. The door opens. I look back once at Arthur—my brave, stupid knight, my perfect goddamn fool, still fighting, his form vanishing beneath a snarling, ravening wave of Beasts—before I slip inside Starling House.

This is a different Starling House from the one I know. The trim is yardstick-straight and the wallpaper is crisp, unmarred by light switches or outlets. Every piece of furniture is polished and every floorboard gleams. It looks fresh-built, as if the painters left an hour ago. It's beautiful, but I find myself looking for cobwebs and stains with a weird ache in my chest. The House feels like a mere house, a dead structure that hasn't yet learned how to dream.

Eleanor isn't in the hallway, but my feet know where to go. Up one set of stairs, and another, and another, into the attic room that now belongs to Arthur, but didn't always.

It looks bleak and bare in his absence. There are no pictures tacked to the wall, no warm lamps lit. There's just a narrow iron bed where Eleanor sits with her ankles crossed and her hands folded. Behind her, its body curled protectively around her, its dimensions hideously distorted to fit inside the room, is a Beast. This one has the short, curved horns of a goat, but its body is sinuous, almost catlike. It makes no move to attack me, but merely watches, vertebrae twitching.

"Hi," I say, very awkwardly, because I don't know what you're supposed to say to a girl who is also a grown woman, a fictional character who is also a person, a villain who might also be a victim.

It seems I chose poorly, because Eleanor doesn't answer. She doesn't even blink, just watches me with those hard black eyes.

"I'm Opal." I hesitate, uncertain whether the names Gravely or Starling would please her or upset her, and leave my first name unaccompanied.

Still, Eleanor watches me. I'm suddenly very tired of this haunted Gothic orphan performance, tired of waiting politely while Arthur bleeds below us. "Listen, I'm sorry to bother you, but I need you to call off your, uh, friends." I gesture uncomfortably to the Beast still curled at her back. "That man down there isn't your enemy."

"No?" Some rational part of my brain flinches away from the sound of her voice. It's too low, too precise, too knowing—an adult's voice in the mouth of a little girl. "He came to make war on my poor Beasts, did he not?"

"No. Well, maybe, yes, but he has to. Do you know what they do, up there? They *kill* people. They—my mother—" I feel it again, the weight of the river on my chest, the chill of the water in my lungs.

An odd, furtive look crosses Eleanor's features. It makes me think of Jasper when he let the hellcat into room 12 even when he knew she had fleas. It's the first time Eleanor has looked like an actual child. "It's in their nature." It's almost a pout.

I cross my arms and use the same voice I used on Jasper. "What are they, Eleanor? What is Underland? Is this—are we in another world?" I feel stupid saying the words, but I'm also standing in the ghost of a house that hasn't existed for more than a century.

Eleanor has turned away from me to smooth her hand over the gray seam of her quilt. "I used to think so."

I want to cross the room and shake her, hard, but her Beast is watching me with an eye like a dead coal. I wait her out, instead.

Eleanor strokes the ridge of its skull, almost lovingly. "I used to think the Beasts came from somewhere else—Hell, I thought at first, then Heaven, then history, then myth—but now I know better. Now I know they only ever came from me."

"What," I say, with a degree of patience I find admirable, given that I left most of my heart on the grass three floors below us. "Does that mean."

Eleanor tilts her head, her tone cooling. "If this river had a name like its sisters in the underworld, it would be Phantasos, or maybe Hypnos, and it would belong to Morpheus." I'm flipping through threadbare memories of

Edith Hamilton and *Metamorphoses,* trying and failing to understand, when Eleanor says, softy, "It is the river of dreams."

The word "dreams" strikes me like a thrown stone. It sinks into my mind easily, as if I were expecting it, leaving no ripples behind.

"What does that mean?" I ask, but I already know the answer.

"It means these waters give form to our dreams, however foul. It means the only monsters here are the ones we make." Eleanor looks at her Beast again, her small hand vanishing between the white blades of its hackles. The look in her eyes is almost tender, as a mother to a child, or as a dreamer to their favorite dream.

Repulsion rises in me, and anger. "You made them? You—*why?*"

Her head twists on the fragile stalk of her neck, uncannily quick. Her eyes are mean slivers. "You don't care." It sounds like a well-worn complaint, whetted by years of use. "No one ever did before, no one does now. None of you know the truth of it, and you prefer it that way."

The words strike an uncomfortable resonance in my skull. I swallow twice, dry-mouthed, and say, "So tell me."

"You won't listen." Her tone is still low and vicious, but there's a new emotion rising from the mean depths of her eyes. An old and desperate hunger, a want she tried and failed to bury.

I walk across the floor, which doesn't creak here, and kneel beside the bed. "Tell me, Eleanor. I'll listen."

She fights it, but the hunger wins in the end.

This is my story.

No one listened to it before, and if they listened they did not believe it, and if they believed it they did not care. I am certain you are the same, but I will tell it anyway, because it has been so long since I had anyone to tell.

My story begins with my mother's story, like everyone's does. It goes like this: Once upon a time there was a rich young woman who thought she was in love. But as soon as the marriage license was signed—or, more specifically, as soon as all her accounts were placed in her husband's name—the young man vanished. He left her lonely and laughed-at, further along than she ought to be.

I was born in the spring of 1851. She named me Eleanor, after herself, and never spoke our surname aloud.

My mother died young—a cancer, the doctors said, but I think it was bitterness—and the courts sent me to live with my only living relation. I took the train to Bowling Green and a flatboat to Eden. My father had never seen me before, so he stood on the shore while the passengers stepped off the ramp. Every time a young woman passed by he asked: *Eleanor Gravely?* It was the first time I heard my own name spoken aloud.

My father lived well off my mother's money. He and his two younger brothers—my uncles—had started their own company, Gravely Brothers Coal & Power, and now they owned a few hundred acres, a dozen men, five black songbirds imported from Europe, and a big white house on the hill. I thought at first I might make a tolerable life in that house—might spend my days sewing and reading, teaching new songs to the birds—but my uncles and my father were bad, bad men.

(You want to know more. You want every miserable, gruesome, ordinary detail. But surely you can imagine the sorts of sins that hide under the word "bad," like grubs beneath a stone. Surely the precise shape of the wounds doesn't matter as much as how much they hurt, and whose hands dealt them.)

They were bad men, and they grew worse as the war worsened and the coal ran dry. They burned through their own profits and dug deep into my mother's coffers. They drank more and slept less. They came to resent every bite of food I ate at their table, every stale crust I slipped into the birdcage, and they punished me for it.

My father was the worst of them, if only because he was the oldest, and had six more years of practice in cruelty. I took to sleeping as many hours as I could, wrapping myself in dreams of teeth and blood, blades and arsenic. I was sleeping when my uncle came to tell me my father had drowned.

I didn't do it. Half the town suspected me, and I almost wish they were right—I assure you he deserved it—but the other half of Eden blamed the miners. The mist had risen that night, and when it cleared my father was dead, and there were no more slaves in Eden.

I did not mourn my father, of course. My uncle John stood beside me at the graveside, twisting the flesh at the backs of my arms so viciously it was purple and green the following morning, but I refused to shed a single tear for him. Maybe that's when the rumors began, about that cold, strange Gravely girl. *I heard she killed him,* they whispered. *I heard she only smiled once, when the first shovel of dirt hit her father's coffin lid.*

If I had been smiling, I soon stopped. In the absence of a will I inherited my father's remaining fortune, which had belonged first to my mother, and should have belonged to me. But, as I was not yet of age, my circumstances changed very little except that my guardianship transferred from one bad man to another.

John Gravely was the second-oldest brother, and the second-meanest. I thought I might at least survive him, but slowly I became aware that he was watching me more closely than he used to. He studied me as if I were a difficult equation that needed solving. He asked me twice when my birthday was, and drummed his fingers restlessly on the table each time I answered.

That night I counted on my fingers and realized I would turn eighteen in twenty-three days. And on that date my money would be my own, and my uncles would have nothing but a few failing mines, a filthy birdcage, and a wealthy niece who no longer belonged to them. I was a songbird in a den of foxes, and they were so hungry.

I thought he might poison me, or drown me. I thought he might lock me away until I signed everything over to him and his brother, or have me shipped off to an asylum. He wouldn't even have had to bribe the physicians; I was quite unwell by then. I chewed at my own lips until they scabbed. I never brushed my hair. I no longer sang to the little black birds, but only spoke to them in hoarse, mad whispers. I slept and slept, because even nightmares were preferable to reality.

My uncle John did not poison me or lock me up. He came to a different solution, one which I berated myself for failing to anticipate. It was, after all, the same solution that occurred to my father when he met my mother. He was a poor man and a bad one, and she was a wealthy woman and a weak one; what could be easier, or more obvious?

But, at seventeen, I must still have possessed some childish, idiot faith in the rules of society. Yes, they were bad men. Yes, I had heard the weeping from the mines and seen my uncles return from the cabins late at night. But that was different, that was **allowed**. I was a young white woman of good breeding, and I still believed there were some lines they would not cross.

So when my uncle John summoned me to breakfast one morning and told me I was not to call him Uncle any longer, I didn't understand. He picked up my left hand and shoved a cheap tin ring on my second-smallest finger, and I still didn't understand. I felt heavy and strange, as if I was sleeping. I looked at my uncle Robert, the youngest and least cruel of the Gravely men, and saw the look of faint disgust on his face, and only then did I understand.

Our engagement was announced in three separate papers. My name was listed differently in each one. Eleanor Grand, Eleanor Gallows, Eleanor Gaunt. Perhaps my uncles thought it would help people convince themselves they'd heard my name wrong. *That girl was never a Gravely,* they could tell themselves. *She must have been a foundling, an orphan, some stranger we let into our midst.*

Because that's what they did, of course. They didn't march up to our big white house and drag my uncle John into the streets. They didn't damn him or castigate him or even take away his place in the first pew at church. They simply told themselves a different story, one that was easier to believe because they'd heard it before: Once there was a bad woman who ruined a good man. Once there was a witch who cursed a village. Once there was an odd, ugly girl whom everyone hated, because it was safe to hate her.

I kept waiting for someone to object, but the most I got was a pitying glance from the neighbors' maid, an awkward grimace from my uncle Robert. Everyone else drew away from me, like hands from a hot coal. They averted their eyes from evil and, in so doing, became complicit in it. I watched my uncles' sin spread over the town like night falling, and finally understood that no one was going to save me.

So, on the morning of my wedding, I took my father's birdcage into the woods behind Gravely Manor and opened the door. A rush of iridescent feathers and clever black eyes, a few piercing trills, and they were gone. I didn't know if they'd survive out in the wild, but I'd grown too fond of them to leave them alone with my uncles.

I chose two stones, smooth and heavy, and slipped them into my skirt pockets. Then I walked down to the riverside.

I would have done it, if I hadn't met the boatman. A hare, I called him later, because he had a sly, sideways manner of regarding a person. He stopped me, and then he listened to me, and then he gave me an even greater gift: he told me how my father died. He told me Hell was real, and so were its demons.

I did not walk into the river that day, after all. I went back to the big white house on the hill and let them dress me in white lace and ribbons. I let my uncle Robert walk me down the aisle of the empty church. I could not make myself say the words, but I let my new husband kiss me, his lips damp and thin.

I don't remember the rest of the day, but I remember the light changing: noon to dusk, dusk to twilight, twilight to night. My uncle John stood up from the dinner table and held out his hand, as if I would take it, as if I would follow him to his bed like a sow to slaughter.

I ran. He followed.

He followed me to his own mine, and hesitated at the edge of the dark. I heard him calling after me, cajoling, pleading, cursing, demanding, but I did not stop. I went down, and down, and down.

I found the river. I drank the smallest sip, like the boatman told me, and fell into Underland. And there were the creatures from my nightmares, animals made of teeth and claws, fury and justice. They looked at me as if they'd been waiting for me. I wept with joy, with terror, with awful love. I told them about my uncle and showed them the ring on my finger, and they ran into the darkness. When they returned, their muzzles were wet and red. I wiped them clean with the muddy hem of my wedding dress. Then I slept, at peace.

I woke up at the bottom of the river. I crawled to the shore, retching, coughing. I was too frightened to return to the mines—what if it had all been a lovely dream? what if my uncle was still alive, calling for me?—but the boatman had told me there was another way out. A natural cave that twisted up to a sinkhole on the north side of town. I didn't know till later it was on Gravely land.

It was a hard climb back to the surface. By the time I saw the sun again my palms were raw and my dress was ragged. I crawled out into the dusking light and lay in the wet grass. I saw five birds cross the sky above me. All birds are black at that hour, but I decided they were my birds. Starlings, my father had called them, purchased only because he liked the look of caged things. But they were free now, and so was I.

They say I was laughing when they found me. I don't recall. I don't recall much of the court proceedings, either. All of it felt mystical to me, a series of rituals that led to my own metamorphosis. I had been a nameless little girl, and now I was a rich widow. I had been trapped, and now I was not.

I could have gone anywhere in the world, do you know that? I could have run away from Eden and lived off my mother's stolen fortune until I forgot the sound of the river above and the taste of the river below. But I stayed. God help me, I stayed.

As my uncle's widow, I had a claim on Gravely land. I let Uncle Robert skulk off with the more valuable half—the mines and the big house—but I kept the acreage on the north side of the river. They made out the deed to my married name first, but the sight of it sickened me, so I tore it up and had them write another. *To my maiden name,* I said. *Eleanor Starling.* The name tasted clean in my mouth.

I hired an architect as soon as the deed was signed. I'd never had a home, you see. My mother and I had moved from rented room to wayhouse, dodging rumors and surviving on what little my father left us, and the white house on the hill was merely a place I couldn't leave. So I built myself everything I'd ever dreamed I would have: drawing rooms and ballrooms, libraries and parlors, hallways full of doors that only I could unlock.

It was more than a home, of course. It was a labyrinth, with the way to Underland at its heart, and high stone walls all around. I couldn't tell you whether I was more terrified that someone would find their way down there, or that something would come crawling out. All I know is that I dreamed of the Beasts every night, their teeth stained with my uncle's blood, and that I was often woken by the noises I made in my sleep. I could never tell if I'd been laughing or screaming.

I thought I would be happy there. I had a name and a home of my own, and enough money to keep both for as long as I lived. But instead I was a ghost haunting my own house. I wondered sometimes if I'd drowned that night, and just didn't know it.

It was the loneliness, I think. The townsfolk hated me and kept hating me, with an intensity that comes from shame. The only company I had was my starlings, who bred and multiplied until they rose sometimes from the sycamores in great black clouds. I used to watch them from the attic window, the flock lifting and falling, writhing like a dark ribbon in the sky, and think of my poor Beasts trapped under the earth.

I was too frightened to go back into Underland and find them, but I loved them too well to leave. So I studied them. I had the twin privileges of time and money, and I poured them all into Underland. I ordered books on history and geography, mythology and monsters, folklore and fable. I taught myself Latin and puzzled through the Cherokee syllabary. I made charms and wards, forged four keys and a sword guided only by myth and mysticism. There was nothing in my library that precisely resembled Underland or the Beasts, but I saw their shadows in every tale of demons or monsters, every story about teeth waiting in the night.

Yet their origins eluded me. Where did they come from? How could I dream them before I even knew they existed? I wouldn't understand until much later that they existed only because I dreamed them, that all my studies were merely a snake swallowing her own tail.

I began to draw in the evenings, dark, ugly sketches of a girl with dark, ugly dreams. I wrote my story down, softened a little, because I already knew no one cared for the hard facts of it. I don't remember making a decision to publish it, but I remember sliding the prints into an envelope and mailing them north. Maybe I was a little proud of my work. Maybe I wanted to see my chosen name immortalized in print, to erase my given name like a wrong mark on a chalkboard. Maybe I simply wanted people to know the truth, even if they mistook it for a children's book.

But no one wanted my story, even with its teeth pulled. The last piece of mail I received from my editor was a notice that they were turning my books back into pulp, to make room in the warehouses.

I was not surprised. My studies carried on as they always had, except I stopped drawing in the evenings.

I grew restless and strange over the years. I took to carrying the sword with me from room to room, as if I thought the Beasts might come for me at any hour of the day.

And then, one evening, one came knocking at my door. This Beast wore a suit and a wide smile, but I knew him too well to be fooled: the youngest Gravely brother, the last of my flesh and blood, come for me at last.

My uncle Robert informed me that the time had come for Gravely Brothers Coal & Power to pursue their claim to the mineral rights to my property. I'd gotten the fortune and the land, he said, but the company owned the coal.

I was not a frightened little girl anymore. I told him I would fight him tooth and nail before I let him touch my land.

And my uncle—the kindest of the Gravelys, the one who used to slip me extra crumbs for the birds, the one I had almost forgotten to fear—smiled at me. Then he told me all the things he could do to me, with nothing but a friendly drink and a firm handshake with the right person.

He could tell the sheriff he saw me murder his brothers in cold blood. He could tell the preacher I was a witch, practicing devilish magics. He could tell the judge I was mad and ought to be locked up.

They would all believe him. Can you imagine it? A world that bent to your every whim, where any story you chose to tell became the truth, simply because you said it?

I felt the floor thinning beneath my feet, the walls turning weak as damp paper. Everything I believed was mine, everything I suffered and killed for, would be taken away from me. My name, my house, my money, my safety.

No one would listen to me. No one would save me. I was damned, well and truly.

But I would take him down to Hell with me. I gave my uncle one final chance. I told him he could leave and swear never to speak of this again, or he could die like his brothers. His smile faltered, but just for a moment. It's difficult for predators to imagine teeth closing around their own throats. They don't have the right instincts.

As soon as he left I did three things in quick succession. First I drafted a small addition to *The Underland* and addressed it to my editor, in the event that a new edition was ever published. Second, I wrote a letter to the boatman. In all of Eden, he was the only one that did not deserve what came next.

Third, I dug the key from around the sycamore roots. I'd buried it years before, perhaps in an effort to avoid the awful temptation to go back to Underland. But hunger always wins, in the end.

I returned to the river deep below everything. I drank and drank and drank, so that I would sleep and never wake.

My Beasts were waiting for me. They were subtly changed, closer to the childish drawings from my book than my memory of them. I understood then that they were my own creations, born of my own desperate nightmares. I found I no longer feared them, but loved them as a mother would love her children, however monstrous.

I let them run in the world above sometimes. When I feel the mist rising off the water, when I sense a crack in the defenses of that damn house and its keepers. When I think of my father and my uncles and the sins they committed against me, and of the town that turned the other cheek instead of giving me an eye for an eye.

I thought Starling House was my home, but I was wrong. This place— where I am never alone, where no one can hurt me, where the truth is what I dream it—this is my home, and always will be.

THIRTY-ONE

Eleanor Starling tells her story, and I
listen, and when it's over I think, numbly:
That was it. That was the story I've been chasing
since I cut my hand on the gates of Starling House,
since long before that—since the first night I dreamed
of Starling House. I've found pieces of it, the details
blurred by time, transmuted by each teller, but still
legible. I can see them all now, truths and lies all lying
one atop the other. The Gravely brothers, who were
respected businessmen and enslavers and predators.
Eden, which was a good little town and a terrible
little town, full of good and terrible people. Eleanor,
who was a frightened girl and a murderer and
eventually a ghost that haunts us all still.

I thought finding this first, truest story would feel like snapping the last piece into a jigsaw. I thought I would feel satisfied, triumphant, maybe a little proud of myself. But now there's a vicious, lonely little girl sitting in front of me, her eyes hard and accusatory, and all I feel is sorry.

So I say, inadequately, "I'm sorry."

Eleanor's gaze doesn't falter. "They were, too."

"Who?"

"Everyone!" The sudden vehemence sends me a half step backward. "The neighbors' maid, the woman who brought eggs and milk every Tuesday, the preacher who married us and the judge who signed the papers. They looked at the tin ring on my finger and they were all so *sorry,* but what good did that do me?"

"You're sure they knew?" I shouldn't have asked, but some part of me is still in desperate, nauseous denial. "They knew that he was your—that you were—"

Eleanor's lip curls in an expression of chill disdain no natural child has ever worn before. "Of course they knew. My father greeted me by name on the riverboat. Half the county called me 'the Gravely girl' rather than learn my name. But when my uncle John asked them to look aside—when they weighed my life against his coal company, his generous donations to charity and his big white house on the hill—they did not hesitate."

I open my mouth, close it, and say again, "I'm sorry."

Eleanor gives me an up-and-down look, her eyes picking out each torn seam, each stain. "You grew up here, didn't you? You should know."

And I do know. I know what it is for your own people to turn their backs on you as easily as turning a page. I know all about cold shoulders and sideways looks, about being the only girl in sixth grade who didn't get a birthday invitation. I know the way people talk loud and slow to my brother, as if he might not speak English, the way they watch him in grocery stores even though everybody knows I'm the thief. Now I know about my mother, who was cast out for the ordinary sin of sex, and the far greater sin of refusing to be sorry about it.

The circle of sky I can see through the attic windows is boiling black now. In the world above, you could see the power plant from here, an unwavering light, but not here.

I press my forehead to the glass of the round window and look down. The Beasts are larger and brighter than they were before, their limbs long and thin as femurs. They seethe and twist, a writhing mass of beautiful, monstrous flesh. They're gathered around something, but I can't see it clearly, and I can't seem to remember what it is.

I picture them running loose in the world above. Perhaps chasing down the county road after Constable Mayhew. Perhaps plucking Don Gravely from his big house like the soft meat of an oyster from its shell. They would deserve it, God knows.

"You could stay here with me, you know." Eleanor's voice slinks over my shoulder like a warm hand. "A few others have found their way down here—lost children who went too deep in the mines, treasure hunters who followed strange stories—but they didn't last long."

"What do you mean?"

"Their dreams were weak, unformed things, too soft to survive in my Underland." I can hear the shrug in her voice. "But you—you're hungry, and you like the dark. You're like me."

"I'm not like you." It sounds good—a vehement denial, each word hard and certain as a gavel striking—but of course it does. I've always been a good liar.

I'd felt the truth every time I read *The Underland* as a kid, every time I traced the sharp white angles of Nora Lee's face on the page. Her eyes were drawn in uneven black ink, like a pair of holes torn in the paper, but I pretended she was looking straight out at me, smiling that sly little smile.

At night I'd dreamed of rivers and doors and houses that weren't mine, a dark and quiet place where I could sleep, safe at last, finally sated. In the morning I had wept from the certainty I could never really run away, never follow any Beast down to Underland, because who would microwave Jasper's instant oatmeal then? Who would zip his sleeping bag all the way up on cold nights, and steal him hot chocolate packets from Bev's continental breakfast?

And then there was Bev herself, and Charlotte, and the hellcat, a whole string of things that needed me, or things that I needed, each one tied tight around my wrist. Then came Starling House, grand and broken and beautiful, and then came—

Arthur.

His name rings in my ears like a church bell, high and clear. I remember, suddenly, that he's here with me in Underland, that I left him battling the Beasts. I look down at them again and this time I catch the thrust of a sword, a glimpse of dark hair. Arthur looks like a toy soldier from up here, far too small and fragile for the task, but unable to run away.

I reel away from the window, hand already reaching for the door, but it isn't there. The walls are all smooth white plaster, as if they were built that way, as if there has never been a way in or out of this room.

Two breaths, ragged, overloud. I turn slowly back to face the narrow iron bed, and the girl still sitting with her legs crossed neatly at the ankle.

"Let me go." I say it calmly, with authority, as if I'm talking to a child who has locked the bathroom door.

Eleanor's eyelids lower, heavy with scorn. "Why? So you can go save a little boy still scared of the dark?"

"Yes."

"You don't need him." A vicious flick of her fingers, as if Arthur is a toy or a treat.

"No." My voice is still calm, so calm. "But I want him." The two words have lost their distinction in my mind, merging into a single bright hunger.

Eleanor pauses to study me, with the expression of a predator looking for a limp or a scar, some old injury that never quite healed. "He'll leave you, too, you know," she says, and I can't help it: I flinch. She moves her head forward, scenting pain. "Everyone else has, haven't they? One day he'll do the same, and then you'll be all alone again."

A century swimming in her own nightmares has made her very good at this. Her voice has a prophetic weight, a certainty that sinks straight through my breastbone. Except: I wouldn't be alone, would I? Even then, I would have Jasper and Bev and Charlotte and the hellcat.

I look back at Eleanor, my head tilting like I'm playing one of those spot-the-difference games in an issue of *Highlights*. But it no longer seems difficult to tell the two of us apart. Eleanor never had a home, no matter how hard she tried to make one; I had the backseat of Mom's red Corvette, and then room 12, and then the House itself, a series of homes made out of wishful thinking and love. Eleanor was always alone; I never was.

An uncomfortable emotion moves through me, hot and prickling. It feels a little like pity, but it's hard to pity someone you see so clearly. "Eleanor. I'm not staying. And neither should you. You've been here a long, long time—"

"*No.*" Her voice is high and shrill, as if I'm waving a knife or a gun at her. "This is my home, and I will stay here until Gravely and his children and his children's children are dead, until their gravestones are too worn even to be read." The Beast is growling at her back, its jaw lengthening, its claws tearing into the floorboards; I wonder if it can smell the Gravely blood in my veins, the inheritance I never asked for. "I will scour Eden itself from the earth, every house and every name. They tried to bury me, but I will bury them all in the end."

It's a curse, the kind you neither break nor escape, the kind I never quite believed in. "No," I say. I don't sound very convincing.

"Yes," Eleanor says. "The river has been running high and fat for a long time now, did you know that? The mist rises thick now, and often."

I picture Arthur, surrounded by gravestones. Jasper, telling me the Wardens don't last as long as they used to. "Why?"

"The Beasts have told me about the black lake they built on the surface, where they keep all their corrupted water."

"The—are you talking about the ash pond?" I feel my brain twisting, worlds converging. "People say it leaks, but the power company says—"

"Of course it leaks." Eleanor's tone is almost amused. "The earth here is porous, full of caves and graves. It leaks all the way down to the river, to me, and we feast on it." And she actually licks her lips, as if the tailings from a power plant are a special treat. "And now, tonight—with the Warden gone, and the gates unlocked . . ."

She trails away, but I can see it unfolding before me: the Beasts running loose down the streets of Eden. Fires, floods, disasters and deaths out of season. An assault so terrible the town is abandoned, undone, given over to the honeysuckle and kudzu. Soon there will be nothing left but the mist, padding down empty streets on silent feet.

The room darkens around us. The windows blacken, not with night, but with the sleek obsidian bodies of birds, rushing past the panes in an endless flock. Eleanor is watching me, smiling a little.

I feel my chin jutting, my fingers curling into fists. "No," I say again, but this time I stamp my foot, like a child. The floorboards ripple beneath me. The birds wheel back from the windows.

A small shock moves across Eleanor's face, there and gone again, replaced quickly by malice. Her Beast rises, filling the room, lips peeling back over long dog's teeth. And I think: *The only monsters here are the ones we make.*

That Beast is just a little girl's dream. So are the walls around us, the windows, the sky. Well, I have dreams, too, even if I spent half my life trying to forget them. I ignored them and mistreated them, did my best to burn them, but they persisted. Even now I can feel them just beneath the surface of my skin, hungering.

It's easy, really. All I have to do is want.

I close my eyes, and when I open them again, the room is changed.

There are a pair of twin beds pressed against the walls, the covers rumpled. There's a microwave from the late eighties sitting beside a half-sized plastic coffeemaker. There are water stains on the ceiling, a map of dark brown blooms I know by heart.

We're in room 12 of the Garden of Eden, the way I remember it, the way it will be only in dreams, now.

Eleanor is standing now, glaring hard, panting. She looks wildly out of place, like a Victorian portrait come to awkward life. She curls her lip and spits, once, viciously.

I recoil, but she wasn't aiming at me. She was aiming at the thin carpet of the motel. The spit hisses where it lands. A curl of smoke rises, followed by a thin blue flame. Then fire is racing across the floor unnaturally fast, crawling up the walls, leaping from bed to bed like a mischievous child.

I think: *Not again.* I close my eyes, but I can't seem to think beyond the glow of the flames against my eyelids, the heat of my only home burning.

I fumble for the door, fall out into the twilit parking lot.

It's full of people. Some I know well and some I don't, all as familiar as the sound of the river or the shine of the streetlights. The mailman. The cook at the Mexican place. Bev and Charlotte. The girl who ratted me out to the teacher in sixth grade. Don Gravely, Mr. Cole, Constable Mayhew, Ashley Caldwell, Arthur. *Jasper.*

None of them are moving. None of them are speaking. They're watching me with damp, incurious eyes. I'm choking on smoke, coughing out words like *please* and *help.* Surely someone will call 911 or find a hose or at least reach their hand out to me and tell me it's alright, even though it isn't.

I should have known better. This is a town that turns away from anything troubling or unpleasant, anything that threatens their belief in themselves as decent, upstanding folk: off-season hunting and illegal dumping, hungry dogs and children with five-fingered bruises, even their own poisonous history. Why did I think I would be an exception?

The people in the parking lot turn their backs to me in eerie unison and walk away. Even Jasper.

I feel my attention snag. I stop coughing. Jasper might sulk or swear at me—he might steal the last pack of good ramen or ignore my texts or apply to jobs behind my back—but he would never turn his back and leave me like this.

This is just a bad dream. I have better ones. I close my eyes and reach for something else, a memory so polished and golden it's become a fantasy. When I open my eyes, the parking lot is gone.

I'm standing on the banks of the Mud River. The sun is dipping low, striking bright sparks off the water. It's dark enough that the swallows are out, and the fireflies are gleaming in the low places beneath the trees. It feels like the very end of June or the beginning of July, when you've lost track of time and it doesn't matter because you have nowhere in particular to be, when summer stretches so luxuriantly on either side of you that you begin to doubt the existence of other seasons.

Eleanor is standing beside me. Her feet are small and bare in the mud. She's not glaring at me anymore, but looking out at the river with a helpless, aggrieved kind of love, as if she would carve the love out of her chest if she knew how. She slips her hand into mine and I hold it reflexively, because it's small and cold, because it reminds me of waiting with Jasper for the bus. I rub my thumb along her knuckles.

Eleanor makes a small noise of disgust, as if she cannot believe anyone would be that stupid, before she pulls me into the river.

The water should be warm as spit this time of year, but it isn't. It's a stinging, sapping cold, the kind that cramps muscles and stops hearts. I wrench at our joined hands but Eleanor is unnaturally strong. Her fingernails dig blue crescents into my wrist, pulling me deeper, deeper, until I'm drowning again except this time I want to let go and can't. This time there's no one to pull me back to the surface and curl his body around mine.

I catch the edge of that image and hold on to it. Arthur, warm and alive. Arthur holding me while the word "home" ricochets through the cavity of my chest like a stray bullet.

I am not drowning anymore. I open my eyes and I am standing in the cozy sitting room of Starling House, the one with the squashy couch and the pastel wallpaper and the portraits of the Wardens. Except it hasn't acquired any of those things yet. The floors are shining with fresh polish and the plaster is perfectly intact. The only portrait on the wall is Eleanor herself.

"Really, Opal? Here?" The real Eleanor laughs. "This is *my* home."

I face her, sick of her mean little laugh and her cold little eyes. "No, it isn't. I mean maybe it used to be, but not anymore." Her mouth gets very small and hard in her soft child's face, like the seed in the center of a persimmon, so I keep going. "You left it behind and it became somebody else's home, over and over again, and all of them loved it just as much as you did. Probably more."

Her tiny persimmon-seed mouth moves. "No they didn't."

"They did. And you know what? It loved them back. It was just a house when you lived in it, a big dead thing full of other dead things, but it's woken up over the years. Or maybe gone to sleep, I don't know which." I think of those long ivory roots trailing in the water, drinking deep from the river of dreams. I think of the wisteria wound around every part of the House, running under the skin of it like veins. Dead things don't dream, but the House did, and so it was no longer dead. It spent a hundred and fifty years drinking the water and dreaming whatever houses dream—fires in hearths, dishes in sinks, lights in windows—and when it found itself empty it called another hungry, homeless person to itself, and did its best to keep them safe. Until it couldn't.

I always thought of it like a lighthouse, but it was more like a siren: a beautiful thing perched above certain death, a sweet and deadly voice in the night.

But I swear there will be no more portraits on the wall, no more graves to tend. I swear I will end this, here and now. I will be the last Warden of Starling House.

Eleanor is backed against a wall, her arms outstretched as if she can hold her house still, unchanging. I feel sorry for her. "The House sent me dreams before I ever saw it. It needed me, and I needed it." I remember the window shining through the trees like a lighthouse. Arthur's face on the other side of the gates, furious and alone. Motes of dust sparking in slantwise light. My blood soaking into the floorboards.

The sitting room shifts around us, becoming the room I know in the world above. The wallpaper fades and the plaster cracks. The floor polish turns dull and scratched and stains bloom on the bare wood. The narrow Victorian furniture is replaced by a sagging couch, and the walls are crowded with mismatched portraits. The atmosphere shifts, accumulating years of long sunsets and deep winter evenings, rainy afternoons and bitter mid-nights, decades of striving and hungering and fucking and letting the coffee go cold because your book just got good. Whole generations of living, lead-ing down to Arthur, and then to me.

"Starling House might have been yours in the beginning, Eleanor, but it's mine now." I say it as gently as I can, but Eleanor flinches as from a hard slap.

But she bares her small, sharp teeth at me, and says, "Take it, then. I don't care." Her eyes shine with an awful light. "You already lost everything else."

Then she runs from me, disappearing into the House, and I follow.

I don't have to hurry. I can hear Eleanor's small feet slapping the stairs, doors slamming behind her, but this is my House now. It will take me wherever I want to be, and no lock will hold against me.

I find her back in the attic room, perched back on her bed with her Beast beside her. The Beast is small and fragile now, like an underfed stray, and it watches me from beneath the safety of Eleanor's elbow.

"What did you mean?" I ask her, and I am calm, so calm.

That mad gleam still shines in her eyes, triumphal, terrible. "I mean it's over. I mean that black lake—the ash pond, you called it?—was never built the way it should have been. So many little cracks and fissures, so many places it could break, with just a little bad luck."

How many times has Bev ranted along the same lines? All anybody has to do is say "coal keeps the lights on" in her hearing and she's off, showing them pictures of Martin County on her phone. The dirt turned to gray sludge, the houses stained with arsenic and mercury, the ghostly white bellies of the fish floating for miles down the Big Sandy.

The House shakes around me. I breathe carefully. "Eleanor, listen to me. If that stuff hits the river—"

"Then they'll get what they deserve."

"*Who* will, for fuck's sake?" I'm not breathing carefully anymore. The pipes are whining in the walls, the curtains billowing. "Not Gravely Power, that's for damn sure. They'll pay a fine and reopen in two weeks."

For the first time, Eleanor looks unsure. I sit beside her on the bed, the mattress dipping beneath me. "Why did you stay in Eden, Eleanor?"

I wonder if she'll answer, or if she'll stay spiteful until the very end. But she says, "I had a right." She chews hard at her own lips. "I wasn't from here, but I wasn't from anywhere really, and after everything I thought I deserved to be from somewhere. Like my starlings—they didn't come from here and nobody liked them much, but they stayed. Why couldn't I?"

It's a familiar story, a tune I've sung to myself many times: a little girl who loves a place that doesn't love her back, a child making a home when she was never given one. I clear my throat. "They're still around, your starlings. There are thousands of them now. They bother the hell out of the whole town."

An unnatural bending occurs somewhere around Eleanor's mouth, which must be as close as she gets to a genuine smile. It unbends quickly. "And there are still Gravelys."

I clear my throat. "Yes."

Her voice goes low and bitter. "And they're still rich, still riding high on everybody else's misery."

"Yes." I hesitate, then: "My mother was a Gravely, actually." Eleanor looks straight at me for the first time since I entered the room, her body recoiling like a cornered animal. "And so were you, until you decided different. So did my mom. And so did I, I guess." My mom lied to me about a lot of stuff, but this is the only lie that was also a gift: she cut away the rot of the past and gave me a life made only of right-nows and tomorrows. She let me grow up nameless and homeless, and now I get to choose my own name and make my own home.

But Eleanor is still rooted deep in her own terrible history. She's been down here festering and hating, punishing and poisoning, and it's still not enough. Even now she's looking at me like she might sink her baby teeth into my throat. I let my voice go very low and soft. "The men who hurt you are long dead."

"So I should let their descendants go unpunished? Let them profit off their father's and grandfather's sins?"

"I mean, *no,* fuck them." I think of Don Gravely, looking at me with those dead gravel eyes. Only very belatedly does it occur to me that I, too, am one of their descendants. "I just think maybe you should leave it to the living."

Eleanor's tiny jaw goes mulish. "They don't know what I know. They've twisted the story, forgotten it on purpose. None of them know the truth—"

"That's why you wrote *The Underland,* isn't it?"

"I—" Her nostrils widen. There is a motion in her chin that might, in a real child, be called a quiver. "I wanted them to see. To know. I thought maybe if . . ." The quiver vanishes. Her eyes narrow. "How did you know the title."

I pull both legs onto the bed and turn to face her, so that we're sitting like two kids up too late at a sleepover. "Because I read your book. Everyone has. It's famous." Her eyes are very wide now, ringed in ivory. "There's a plaque in front of your house with your name on it. The name you chose."

Liquid sheens her eyes and pools on her lower lashes, refusing to fall. "But no one believed it, did they. They thought it was just a silly story. They didn't understand."

"Most people probably didn't," I agree, evenly. But I think of E. Starling's Wiki page, of the long list of related works beneath her inaccurate bio. One girl's pain transmuted into generations of beautiful, terrible, unsettling art. "But some people did. I did."

The tears are so thick now that her pupils are magnified, huge and black in her face. I slide my hand across the mattress, not quite touching her, and lower my head until I'm looking at her straight and level. "I'll tell them, Eleanor. About the Gravelys and the Starlings and you. I mean I've been sort of collecting all the stories, all the lies and half-lies people tell about Starling House—my friend Charlotte is writing a history, or she was, she'd help me—I don't know how we'd make sense of it all . . ." I picture that map of the Mississippi again, all the rivers that aren't anymore but had been once, laid together on the page. It didn't make for a very good map, but it was the whole truth. Maybe the truth is always messy that way.

I take a little breath. "But I swear I'll try. I'll tell the truth." Sometime, much later, when I'm not caught in the river of dreams talking to a dead woman, I'll think it's very funny that all my lying and scheming and cheating brought me to this: promising to tell the truth, and meaning it.

"They won't believe you." Eleanor's voice is low and biting, but her eyes are still wide and wet, full of want.

"Maybe not." I'm not even sure I believe all of it, and I'm living it. No wonder she wrote it as a children's book. "But some of them will."

"They won't care." The first tear crests and falls, tracing a shining line down her cheek.

"Maybe not. But some of them will." I ooch closer, finally catching her hand under mine. She doesn't pull away. "Wouldn't that be enough for you? Aren't you tired?"

The tears are falling fast now, diving one after the other down her face. "They *deserve* it. All of it." Her voice is thick and wet.

"Yeah, maybe." I permit myself to consider, just for a moment, the full weight of what Eden deserves. I think of the Gravely brothers keeping a little girl like a bird in a cage, committing every sin against her in the name of profit; of the men who dug the first mines, their chains rattling in the dark, and all the good God-fearing folk who looked away; of the river that runs rusty brown now and the power plant that pumps ash into the air and the big white-columned house with its cheerful, awful lawn jockey, smiling out at the town. Eleanor's rage seems to multiply in my head, until it's only a single white-hot spark in a whole constellation of sins.

My hand tightens on hers. "They deserved everything you gave them, and probably worse." I brush the lank bangs from her forehead. The skin feels chilled and clammy under my fingers. "But you deserve better, Eleanor."

She collapses into me, her head like a cold stone on my breastbone, and sobs. I run my palms up and down over the points of her spine and make small shushing noises. I pretend she's Jasper after a bad dream or a long day, wrung out from holding too much in the brittle cage of his ribs.

"It's too late," she cries. "I already—the lake was already coming out, everywhere—"

"It's alright," I say, even though it's not, even though there are tears running down my cheeks now, fast and silent. My poor, broken, sinful Eden, flooded by its own poisonous waters. There's a rightness to it, in an Old Testament kind of way, but no mercy, and no future.

I lay Eleanor down on the bed and pull the quilt up to her chin. She looks more human than she did before, more like Eleanor Starling than Nora Lee.

Her hand darts out from the covers, her fingers hard and small against my wrist. "I didn't let it go to the river. I tried—the Beasts guided it away."

I have to swallow before I can speak. "Where?"

"A hole, they said. An old grave. They said nothing was living there, anyway."

"Okay. Alright." I close my eyes and hope, as hard as I can, that she means what I think she does. "You can go to sleep now, Eleanor. It's all over."

"I don't think I know how, anymore." There are lines on either side of her mouth now, and a few streaks of early gray in her hair. Her Beast has paled to a misty translucence.

I touch the hair on her forehead again, as if she was still that small and vicious child. Then I sing to her.

It starts out being that sad old waltz about the blue moon, but I find the notes wandering, the key shifting. It turns into that Prine song that came out a couple years back, about summer's end coming faster than we wanted. I never get the words quite right, but the chorus still circles in my head, plaintive and sweet.

"Go on home," I sing, and Eleanor's eyelids hang heavy. "No, you don't have to stay alone, just go on home."

I know the precise moment she falls asleep, because the room changes around me. The windows lighten to dusky summer. The walls fill with sketches in a hundred shades of char and silver. A vase of poppies appears atop a heavy desk, the blooms red as pricked fingers. The quilt softens beneath me and the floorboards are warm against the soles of my feet.

Eleanor Starling is gone, and this room is no longer hers. It belongs to Arthur now, and Underland belongs to me.

THIRTY-TWO

Starling House sighs around me, a great easing of timber and stone, and I sigh with it. I can feel the House like a living thing again, a great body with joists for bones and copper pipes for veins. I stand, a little unsteadily, feeling older and tireder than it should be possible to feel.

Something white darts off the bed and slips around my ankles. Eleanor's Beast looks suspiciously like the hellcat now, if the hellcat had fur the color of fog and eyes like the sockets of an old skull.

"I'm not sure you should exist," I tell it, conversationally.

The Beast bites me, casually.

I don't have to climb down any stairs, which is nice, because I'm not sure I could. I simply open the attic door and I'm standing on the threshold of the House, several floors below. I rub my thumb over the doorknob in thanks and the rug ripples under my feet like a contented animal.

The Beast dodges around my legs and bounds down the front steps, tail standing straight in the air. I run after it, expecting to find Arthur staggering with exhaustion, maybe smiling in relief—

But he's still fighting. There are still Beasts seething on all sides, just as vast and terrible as before, circling like white vultures. The ground beneath their feet is crusted with frost now, as if entire seasons have passed while I was in the House.

Except Arthur doesn't look any older. He looks younger, younger than I've ever seen him in the waking world. His hair is cut almost neatly and his skin looks eerily smooth, the tattoos and scars wiped away. He's wearing his long wool coat, but his shoulders don't fill it properly yet. His face is soft, slightly rounded, unmarred by pain. He's just a boy, and he's crying.

It's then that I see the bodies around his feet. A man and woman lying side by side, their ribs broken open like milkweed pods. A line of people still wearing hard hats and uniforms, frost creeping over their faces like lace. A pair of burnt corpses. All the people taken by the Beasts over the years, every accident and unexplained fire, every sudden illness and run of bad luck, every person Arthur couldn't save.

One of them has red hair, longer than mine. Her face is turned away, but I would know my mother by the curve of her ear, the exposed nape of her neck.

There's a body lying beside my mother's, and it takes me longer to recognize myself. Or the version of myself that would have existed if Arthur hadn't pulled me out of the river that night: my flesh is blanched and swollen, my clothes are heavy with mud. River reeds straggle through my hair.

This is Arthur's Underland, then: a world where he's too late and too weak, surrounded on all sides by enemies he can't stop, doomed to fight alone, forever, for nothing. I thought the Beasts would disappear with Eleanor, but of course they didn't. They belong to us now, horrors handed down like ugly porcelain.

I shout Arthur's name, but he doesn't hear me. His gaze remains fixed on the Beasts, his face furious with grief, his sword lifting and falling, lifting and falling.

He won't stop. He won't sleep. He'll stay down here, trapped in his own nightmare for always and always.

Except I won't let him, because I need him. And I might be a liar and a thief and a cheat, but I'll walk barefoot through Hell for what I need.

I step forward, into the raging, snapping, slavering circle of Beasts, and shout his name again.

A rthur Starling wants to sleep very badly, or to wake up, to do anything except what he's doing. His body has been reduced to a system of pulleys and wires, limbs that lift and drop, sweep and cut. The sword is immensely heavy in his hand, but he can't seem to let it go.

He doesn't know why. Why should he keep fighting when everyone he's ever loved is lying on the ground around him, wide-eyed, unblinking? His mother's mouth is open and there's grave dirt caught in the seams of her teeth; his father is still holding her hand, his glasses blind with frost. Arthur tries not to look at any of the others, especially the one with hair like a lit match, but he stumbles across them sometimes. Their flesh is hard and frozen beneath his feet.

Still, the Beasts keep coming. Still, he keeps fighting.

And then, after a very long time, Arthur hears his own name. This gives him brief pause, because he hadn't thought there was anyone left in the world who knew his name, or cared enough to shout it.

His name, again. It floats through the tangle of snapping teeth and many-jointed limbs and settles over him gently, like a blanket across his shoulders. It's a voice he knows, a voice he has heard swearing and singing in every room of the House, in every good dream and half his nightmares.

The Beasts have gone strangely still around him. They withdraw slightly, watching him like a pack of wolves gathered around some thrashing thing, waiting for it to die. Arthur's skin shivers with the expectation of attack, that last killing blow that will leave him like the others.

Instead, the Beasts part. A slim gap appears between them, and a figure walks through it.

She comes slowly, easily, as if she doesn't notice the fangs and talons bristling on either side of her, as if she can't see the bodies broken like eggs on the ground before her. The light falls strangely on her, warm and golden, nothing like the bitter winter around her.

Arthur thinks dazedly of *Proserpine,* a painting they'd studied in art history. Most Persephones were wan and tragic, drawn just as Pluto dragged them down to Hell, but this one was different. She stood alone in the underworld, weighing a pomegranate in one hand, blazing through the dark like the sun itself. Maybe it was her expression, a little sad, a little fierce. Maybe it was the color of her hair: a hot, rich red, like coals, like blood, like wild poppies.

Opal walks through the Beasts and stops inches away from Arthur. "You're dead," he tells her, regretfully.

She smiles her sharp, crooked smile at him. "I'm not."

Arthur's lungs are misbehaving, filling and emptying far too quickly. He has an urge to look down at the body of the drowned girl and represses it, because if he sees her lying dead at his feet then he will fall and not rise again.

He addresses her phantom instead. "You're not real. You're a dream."

"I'm not." A faint uncertainty crosses her features. "Or maybe we both are. I don't know, everything's weird down here." Opal steps forward and takes his hand in hers. Her skin is warmer than his, which it never is, but it's real, solid. Alive. "Remember, Arthur? You came down here to save me, like a damn fool, and I followed you, like a worse one. And I'm okay, we're both okay."

Arthur does remember, abruptly and clearly: The Beast bending its head, laying a heavy key in his palm. The door to Underland creaking open, pouring mist into the cellar. Striking a match and tossing it, pulling the door shut behind him. Then the stairs, then the river, then the water burning against his skin. Opal running into his arms, Opal punching him, Opal making him promise to stay alive. He remembers nodding, because he was afraid if he spoke she would hear the lie.

But she came back, and he's still alive. He's certain he won't be for much longer. "You have to go," he says urgently. "This place is dangerous, evil—"

"It's not." That must be a lie, but as she says the words Arthur feels them becoming a little more true. The air is warmer than it was, and the Beasts are a little smaller, a little less awful. Birdsong is rising from the trees, as if dawn is coming.

Opal runs her thumb over his knuckles, warming him. "*We* make this place what it is. It's just our dreams, reflected back at us."

Arthur stands quietly for a moment, considering. Then he laughs, harshly and not entirely sanely. "You should still run, then, while you can." He pulls his hand away, and she lets him. "All my dreams are nightmares."

Opal's smile turns wry and fond. "No, they aren't." She points, inexplicably, at his feet.

Arthur doesn't want to look down. But Opal is watching him with that wry, warm expression still on her face, and he discovers there is very little he wouldn't do to keep it there. He looks down.

There are no bodies or gravestones. Where there had been nothing but frozen grass, dead and tangled, there is now a small, anxious patch of green. The jagged leaf of a dandelion is caught beneath his shoe, and even as he watches a violet lifts its bent neck above the lawn. There are flowers blooming in Underland.

"I don't—I'm not—" Arthur isn't sure what he doesn't or isn't, but Opal steps closer before he can work it out.

She reaches for his sword hand this time and unpeels his fingers from the hilt. Her touch is gentle, patient. "You spent a long time alone, fighting a war that wasn't even yours. It got given to you, and you did your best not to give it to anyone else. You did so well, you really did." Another lie, of course, but Arthur permits himself to imagine how good it would feel to believe it. "But it's over now. Eleanor's gone. The war's over. It's time to dream your own dreams."

Arthur's hands feel weightless and empty without the sword. He isn't sure how a person usually stands, what they do with their arms. "I don't know how," he says, honestly.

Opal steps even closer, so that their chests nearly touch. She goes up on tiptoe to lay her jaw along his and says, "It's alright. I've got you, Arthur."

She kneels on the grass—there's more of it now, a green wave cresting like spring over the earth—and pulls him down beside her. She sets the sword between them, scarred and ugly, and lies down beside it, curled on her side. Arthur lies down with her. Their bodies are a pair of parentheses around the silver exclamation of the sword, their faces close enough to kiss.

Arthur looks into her eyes—that dangerous gray, sharp and bright as a sickle moon—and she looks into his, and their breathing falls into an easy rhythm. She doesn't say anything, but Arthur finds she doesn't have to. He's already spinning wild stories in his head, an extravagance of dreams: Starling House in bloom, the gates thrown wide; the sword forgotten in the attic, the blade rusted and idle; the two of them like this, curled together in an endless dusk, with nothing to die for and everything to keep living for.

The grass grows high around them. Flowers bloom all out of season, tiger lilies knocking gently against cornflowers, scarlet knots of clover wrapped around bursts of tickseed. They bend gracefully in the breeze, brushing over Opal's shoulders, her hair, the hard line of her jaw. Arthur thinks there are things moving around them—Beasts, maybe, except their bodies are sleek and lovely, and they leave flowers where they step, instead of rot—but he can't seem to care.

He watches Opal's eyes drift slowly closed. He remembers how very tired he is, how long it's been since he wasn't tired.

Arthur Starling sleeps, and dreams good dreams.

EPILOGUE

This is the story of Starling House.

There are lots of stories about that house, of course. You've heard most of them. The one about the mad widow and her poor husband. The one about the miners who broke into Hell and the monsters at the center of a maze. You've even heard the one about the three bad men and the little girl who gave them their comeuppance, although nobody tells that one, not yet. (They will, I swear they will. I've broken a lot of promises, but not this one.)

This story is my favorite, because it's the only one with a happy ending.

It usually starts when somebody mentions the power plant, or the fire last summer. *Remember that night back in June,* they say. *First the motel burns, then the dam breaks.*

Somebody else might mention the wreck by the old railroad bridge, or the string of out-of-towners that wound up in the hospital with strange injuries, or the way their dogs stared into the mist with their hackles high, not quite daring to bark.

Bad luck, I guess, someone says, and everybody nods, just like always.

Except it seemed like Eden's bad luck was all used up in that single night. There was a bad spell right after, of course, and everybody worried about jobs. The ash pond flooded the power plant and took out the lights all the way to Nashville. They said you could see it from the International Space Station, a black stripe cut right out of the country.

But FEMA showed up quick enough, and power got diverted from someplace else. For a week or two the whole county was covered in government officials wearing plasticky suits, collecting groundwater samples, but when the tests came back they said it wasn't as bad as it could've been. They said most of the spill flowed downhill and settled in a low spot. *Big Jack, still hard at work,* people said.

The out-of-towners got discharged from the county hospital and climbed into their sleek cars. They drove north, their expressions haunted but strangely vacant, as if they didn't know what they were driving away from but didn't dare slow down.

The mist rose once or twice more that summer, but it didn't linger as long, and it didn't leave new patches of rot and tragedy behind it. People said it smelled sweet, like wisteria, and left flowers blooming behind it. A woman on Riverside Road said she opened her kitchen door and found a luna moth stuck to the screen. She took a picture and showed anyone who asked and several who didn't. Everyone leaned over her screen and admired it dutifully, the size of it, the pale green of the wings, like fox fire on a dark night.

Don Gravely gave a big interview to *The Courier-Journal* in July, assuring everyone that the expansion plans were still underway, that they would rebuild stronger and bigger than ever. Except in that very same issue there was an article about a lawsuit being brought against Gravely Power and a newly discovered will. That librarian woman from the eastern side of the state found it tucked in a Bible, Luke 15:32, in Leon Gravely's own handwriting. Turned out Old Leon hadn't willed the company and family fortune to his brother, after all, but to that no-good daughter of his. She was long gone, drowned on another one of those bad-luck nights, but her children were still living.

Except nobody could find them. The boy—what was his name? Jason? Jackson?—was rumored to be up in Louisville now, but his sister couldn't be found. The woman who used to run the Garden of Eden Motel went around the whole town, banging on doors and having herself a good yell at anybody that held still long enough, but nobody'd seen Opal since that night. The constable told the former owner of the Garden of Eden Motel, as kindly as he could, that girls like that never came to good ends, and the former owner of the Garden of Eden invited him to say that again, louder. The constable declined.

Some people said the motel owner even went up to the Starling place and rattled the gates, hollering, but no one answered. She kicked the groceries that were piled at the end of the drive, spraying curdled milk across the road, and left.

Nobody had picked up the groceries in weeks, and the store manager finally stopped delivering them. The rumor was that the Starling boy ran off the night of the fire and the flood, disappeared or maybe died. No one could say for sure, but it was true that there were no more lights seen flickering through the trees.

The house sat still and empty all that summer. Shingles littered the lawn, and the grass grew lavishly long, lying over itself in deep green drifts. Wildflowers straggled over the walls, wild roses and blackberries.

There was some talk about deeds and property rights. Don Gravely kept trying to bully the county surveyor out there, but the surveyor told Don he wasn't paid enough to set foot on Starling land and that Don no longer had enough money to bribe him, which was perfectly true. With the plant closed and the family accounts all tied up in court because that librarian just would *not* let the case go, Don was starting to fall behind on his accounts. The mailman reported the delivery of several bills with pink paper visible through the plastic window. People said it was only a matter of time before a Realtor hung their sign up on the front lawn of the big brand-new house.

But by early fall even regular people were starting to wonder about the Starling place. As the leaves shriveled you could make out little slices of the house through the bare branches, and what you saw didn't look good. The walls were leaning funny, slanting inward, so that it looked like the only thing keeping Starling House upright was wisteria. The county administrator began to mutter about health hazards and seizure rights. The older folks in town told him to hold his horses, that a new Starling always turned up at these times.

No one did. But one night at the end of September, right when summer finally starts showing signs of wear and the occasional dry breeze goes rattling through the woods, there was a light seen at Starling House. A high round window, shining like polished amber through the trees.

Some time after that the front door opened, and two people stepped out. They were looking up at the September sky like they'd woken from a very long sleep and weren't sure whether they were still dreaming. There was a cat twining quite shamelessly around their ankles, and they were holding hands.

Nobody else will tell you this next part, but I will.

One of the people—a tall, hunched-up man with scraggling hair and a face like a sickly vulture—looked up at the big, ruined house and said, *I'm sorry.* And then, *I know you always wanted a home.*

The other person, a girl with red hair and a mean smile, said, *Yeah, and I found one.*

The man said he was sorry again. (He says that often.)

The girl nudged him in the ribs, good and hard, but she didn't let go of his hand. She said, *I wasn't talking about the house, fool.* She was looking at the ugly man as she said it.

A tiny indentation that might have been a dimple appeared in the man's jaw. He bent to stroke the cat, which bit him.

They keep to themselves, mostly. The gates open every now and then, and certain people go in or out. A pair of middle-aged women, arms slung over one another's shoulders. A boy with glossy black curls and a backpack full of expensive cameras and fancy lenses. A whole stream of lawyers and contractors, followed by a few pickups full of lumber and stone, chalky sheets of drywall, bags of concrete.

Those two must have all the deeds and rights in order, people think. *They must have money to burn,* people say, although they aren't entirely clear on where it came from. All they know is that Starling House would not rot away after all. No one can say whether they're sorry or not.

The house is an awful thing, of course, but it's a familiar awful thing, and it's nice to have new Starlings to gossip about. *Don't understand what they do up there all day,* people say, in tones that suggest it isn't anything good. There are plenty of theories, suppositions, lewd suggestions, and wild rumors. A few of the theories (and all of the lewd suggestions) are perfectly true, but none of them are the whole truth.

Most people conclude, somewhat mysteriously, that they're writing a book. The hairdresser heard it was a romance, and the old meter man is hoping for horror. A member of the Historical Society claims it's a history of the town—that one of their very own founding members is fact-checking it, in the form of footnotes and a bibliography—but that's dismissed as typical hubris.

Whatever it is, it must be illustrated. Several people have seen the young man on the banks of the Mud River with a sketchbook propped on his overlong legs, sketching in subtle grays and stark whites, a hundred shades of velvet black. *A children's book, then,* people say, but there's only one children's book they know of that has pictures like that.

Lacey, the new manager at Tractor Supply, claims she's exchanged texts with the redheaded girl (who does look a bit like the young Gravely girl, it must be admitted, although nobody remembers Opal smiling unless she was committing a crime). Lacey says she asked what they were working on, and Opal said, a story.

what kind of story?

a true one

Lacey found this intentionally obscure, but she was a bighearted person who had always hoped for the best for Opal, so she offered her thoughts and prayers. Opal stopped responding, and eventually the gossip got old and people stopped talking so much about Starling House.

In spring the sycamores bud out and the honeysuckle goes green, so that you can't even see the house from the road anymore. Just the wrought-iron gates and the long red lick of the drive, maybe a glimpse of limestone crosshatched by honeysuckle and greenbriers.

But there are still the dreams, sometimes. You should be afraid—there are stories about this house, and you've heard all of them—but in the dream you don't hesitate.

In the dream, you're home.

BIBLIOGRAPHY

Bond, Gemma. *Witches, Devils, and Haints: Kentucky's Haunted History.* Lexington, KY: University Press of Kentucky, 2015.

Boone, Calliope. Interview by Charlotte Tucker, July 14, 2016. Interview 13A, transcript and recording, Muhlenberg County Historical Society Archives.

Hagerman, Eileen Michelle. "Water, Workers, and Wealth: How 'Old Gravely's' Coal Barge Stripped Kentucky's Green River Valley." *The Register of the Kentucky Historical Society* 115, no. 2 (2017): 183–221. http://www.jstor.org /stable/44981141.

Higgins, Lyle. Interview by Charlotte Tucker, July 04, 2018. Interview 19A, transcript and recording, Muhlenberg County Historical Society Archives.

hooks, bell. *Belonging: A Culture of Place.* New York, NY: Routledge, 2009.

Joseph, A. *Problems in Paradise: An Environmental History of Kentucky.* Chicago: The University of Chicago Press, 2002.

Murray, Robert K., and Roger W. Brucker. *Trapped!: The Story of Willy Floyd.* Lexington: University Press of Kentucky, 1999.

Olwen, T. and C. Olwen. "E. Starling: Recluse or Revenant?" April 24, 2017, in *Bluegrass Mysteries,* podcast (Season 2, Episode 1).

Rothert, Otto Arthur. *A History of Muhlenberg County: With More than 200 Illustrations and a Complete Index.* 1st ed. Louisville, Kentucky: John P. Morton, 1913.

Simmons, Bitsy. Interview by Charlotte Tucker, October 10, 2015. Interview 12B, transcript and recording, Muhlenberg County Historical Society Archives.

Starlings, The. *Starling House Record of Incidents,* from the private collection of Opal and Arthur Starling.

Winter, E. *The Beasts We Could Not Bury: Sin and the Southern Gothic.* Chapel Hill, NC: University of North Carolina Press, 2003.

ACKNOWLEDGMENTS

This is the story of *Starling House.*

It started as a dream, like most houses do. I still lived in Kentucky at the time, but I was getting ready to leave: scrolling real estate sites, boxing up old baby clothes, trying to brainwash our friends into coming with us. I'd left home before—again and again, actually—so the dream I had was a familiar one: that I found a way to stay.

Dreams don't grow into houses (or books) without the time, talent, labor, love, patience, and sheer will of dozens of people. The unfair thing is that, if they do their work well, it's mostly invisible by the time guests arrive.

I am grateful to my agent, Kate McKean, who saw the blueprints for this book and not only didn't burn them, but found the perfect place to start building. To my editor, Miriam Weinberg, who walked through during construction and wondered aloud if we really *needed* four bedrooms (we did not). To Dr. Rose Buckelew, for her inspection of an early draft, and Dr. Natalie Aviles, for connecting us. To the entire production team—Terry McGarry, Dakota Griffin, Rafal Gibek, Steven Bucsok, Lauren Hougen, and Sam Dauer—who patched all the holes and asked, politely, if I meant to put two kitchen sinks right next to each other. To Isa Caban, Sarah Reidy, and Giselle Gonzalez, the marketing and publicity divinities who are the only reason any of you are here. To the cover artist, Micaela Alcaino, and designer, Peter Lutjen, who made this place something worth seeing, and to the legendary Rovina Cai, who graciously hung her work on the walls. And extra thanks to Tessa Villanueva, editorial assistant, without whom I wouldn't even know who to thank.

I am grateful, too, for my friends, even though sometimes they asked how the book was coming—Taye and Camille, Sarah and Alli, Corrie and José—and for their beautiful babies, who never did. To the Kentucky writers who still speak to me even though I moved outside the Ale-8 delivery region:

Gwenda, Christopher, Lee, Olivia, Sam, Ashley, Z, Alex, Caroline, and Ellie. And to the bunker, which sounds like a doomsday cult but is actually a Discord server.

And I could never have written this book—or any book, really—without my family. My dad, who gave me my grandfather's toolbox when I was sixteen and took me to see Prine when I was seventeen, and my mom, who read every version of "Beauty and the Beast" with me. I know I moved away from home, but I see you both every day in the mirror.

My brothers, who never needed me half as much as I need them. Finn, who would stand bravely before the beasts, and Felix, who would befriend them.

And Nick, who is my house and hearth, my foundation and my four walls. I haven't been homesick since the day we met, my love.